The Visitor

Katherine Stansfield grew up on Bodmin Moor in Cornwall. She moved to Wales in 2002 to study at Aberystwyth University where she worked as a lecturer in Creative Writing for several years before deciding to concentrate on writing full time.

Her novel *The Visitor* was published by Parthian in 2013. It went on to win the fiction prize at the 2014 Holyer an Gof awards. *Playing House*, her debut poetry collection, was published by Seren in 2014.

The Visitor

Katherine Stansfield

PARTHIAN

Parthian
The Old Surgery
Napier Street
Cardigan
SA43 1ED
www.parthianbooks.com

First published in 2013
This edition published 2015
The Visitor © Katherine Stansfield
All Rights Reserved

ISBN 978-1-909844-08-7 hardback
ISBN 978-1-909844-09-4 paperback

The publisher acknowledges the financial support of the
Welsh Books Council

Cover design by www.theundercard.co.uk
Typesetting by Elaine Sharples
Front cover image © Jonathan Stead / Millennium Images

Printed and bound by lightningsource.com

British Library and Cataloguing in Publication Data

A cataloguing record for this book is available from the
British Library

For my parents, for introducing me
to Tom Catchamouse

When I have pictured

a calm sea, there is your boat, waiting.

Ruth Bidgood, 'Linked', *Above the Forests*

PART ONE

1936

One

'Keygrims,' Nicholas says, 'will call you by name. You'll be sleeping. This is how they sound.' He scratches his knife across his plate. It's answered by a shriek of wind down the chimney. A cold gust blows round the room. She moves closer to his chair, hunching into the wood and biting her sleeve.

She was remembering, but she was back there, too. What was remembered was true. She was with Nicholas again.

'You know what they are, don't you?' he says.

She looks at Jack who says nothing. His arms are wrapped around his knees and he's worrying a hole in his trousers. She shakes her head.

'They're drowned men,' Nicholas says. 'Come to claim the living.'

Shadows play across his face. She can't see if he's smiling. It's winter. Night comes in the afternoon and the weather is too poor to go outside. Their parents are in the house next door, Nicholas' house, praying for fish and to be watched over whilst at sea. Nicholas is trying to scare her and Jack. He doesn't believe in any of the other creatures that live in the sea. He doesn't believe her stories, or the one Jack tries to tell. Only keygrims.

'What do they look like?' she says.

'You and me, but their skin's gone, worn away by salt. And the bone underneath, it's shells. Only seaweed holds them together.'

The rain thrums on the windowpanes. Beyond the hearth the room is dark.

'Once they've called you to the beach they wait for the waves to touch you and that's it.' He claps his hands and Jack jumps. 'The keygrims take you.'

'That's a lie. There's no such thing,' Jack says, trying to sound sure. His voice wavers. The curtains sigh in the draught. 'I know about mermaids. They—'

'There is such a thing as a keygrim,' Nicholas says. He turns to the fire and knocks some of the wood with his boot. Though the wood is almost burnt black some sparks find life and for a moment there's a glow around him. His cheeks are flushed red and his eyes are bright.

'How do you know?' Jack says.

'Because I've seen one.'

*

Keygrims, she whispered, will call me by name. The little room and the wind gusting fiercely – they were real things. She had been there, with Jack and Nicholas, talking of keygrims. She was still there, somehow, though the moment was so long ago.

Pearl held one of her hands to the sun. The skin was so thin that the light seemed to shine through it. She had lived by the sea all her life. The salt was wearing her away. The bones of her hand were raised, the knuckles lumpy and tight. Like shells. The wind whipped her hair across her face. It was long and tangled, tangy with seawater. It had to be dry before she went home, and she had to catch her breath. She couldn't let Jack know she'd been swimming. He wouldn't like it.

She followed the tide line, winding with the snake-shape of broken wood and seaweed, keeping her eyes on the sea. They were old friends. They had an understanding.

The water had been cold today. Her chest was tight. She concentrated on breathing. On timing each inhalation with a breaking wave. *When they take you, you're cursed to live in the sea and see the people you love cry because you left them behind.*

She moistened her lips against the salt that had dried them. She knew she should go home, that she mustn't tire herself. She had walked by this sea and along these cliffs every day since she could walk, apart from those when she was laid up in bed. Now her body was stiffening against her. When she woke some mornings she didn't know the creases of her face. Cups shook in her grip. Her chest was often tight, as if hands were on her ribs, pressing to hear them crack.

She was walking away from Morlanow now, away from its busy streets and empty harbour, but she could still hear the building work: hammers thumping and the sudden slide of bricks falling.

The bulk of the cliff that closed off the far end of the little beach loomed over her. She'd walked further than she thought, hadn't noticed the effort it had taken until she stopped. Her legs trembled. A pale speck was crossing the water, coming in towards the harbour wall that divided her from the town's main beach, which would be crowded at this time of day. A pleasure boat most likely, rather than a fisherman. So few fishing boats went out from Morlanow now.

This beach was usually empty of visitors. It was more shingle than sand so no good for lying on. The currents were stronger than those of the main beach, pulling a swimmer out suddenly when the bottom shelved. She loved that moment of slippage, when her feet left the safety of the stones and she was weightless in the water. That was when she felt most herself. Her chest would ease and her legs and arms were those of her child self again. She could swim and swim, away from Morlanow, never once turning her head to look back.

But here she was, back on land and the sea still taunting her with its vastness. Pearl put her hands to her eyes and blocked out the harshness of the sun, letting the hiss of waves fill her ears. She thought of the water stretching across the world's surface to places she could only imagine.

The water that came to Morlanow's sands was the same that had brought pilchards to her father's nets when she was a child, when there had been keygrims and mermaids. It had taken them away too, but the fish were there somewhere. The sea was one great pull of movement, putting things down on one coast and then spiriting them to another. Nothing was ever truly lost, though she had grown tired of hoping, tired of searching for a sign that never came. She hated herself for looking, but she couldn't stop. If she stared hard enough at the dark line of the horizon she believed she could will a ship into view. It would just be a smudge at first, perhaps mistaken for a cloud's tail, then it would dip and roll into something recognisable. Each wave bringing it closer to shore would sharpen the outline, clearing to masts and sails. Then closer still and the hull would give up the shape of a man from its wooden sides; back, at last.

It was time to go. Jack would be home soon. She had to hide her wet things. She turned back towards the harbour wall. A glimpse of colour caught her eye. It was away to the left, at the foot of the sloping field that overlooked the beach. In the past, the women of Morlanow had laid their washing out on the grass to dry and for a moment the whole field was again a patchwork of aprons and nightshirts. She looked away. That was a sight she hadn't seen for a long time.

Moving closer to the bottom of the field, she saw that the colour came from delicate blue stems of viper's bugloss. Bugloss for sadness. They had been poked between two stones that formed the middle part of a small tower. It was a cairn, no more than a foot high. Each pebble bore some kind of marking; grey spider-lines, a darker split. The cairn was all but hidden by the scrubby sea-grass that clung where the drying field joined the stony beach beneath it. Who had raised the cairn? It wasn't made for show or to be noticed, tucked here. A memorial of the old kind, built to mark a loss. She walked on. It wasn't right to intrude. But the image of the cairn stayed with her even as she moved away, the tower growing taller in her mind until it was bigger than before, bigger than her, even. So much was lost that never saw such acts of remembrance. Her sister Polly had never had a stone in Morlanow, either on the beach or in the churchyard. Polly's passing hadn't had a marker of any kind. But that didn't mean the loss wasn't felt, wasn't real. Pearl carried the cairn inside her all the way along the beach. She was weighed down by its stones.

She made her way to the harbour wall and stopped to rest before ducking under its arch. She would need her strength to get through the crowds, the motor cars. The faces she didn't know. It was summer. Morlanow was strange to her. It kept changing its shape. Streets were moving, whole houses had disappeared. She was old and ill. It was 1936, and Nicholas was gone.

Two

Her hair was dry by the time Jack got home. It needed cutting, tidying. He didn't like it when it reached below her shoulders like this, said it made her look like Alice Trelawn, the woman of their childhood who gutted dogfish for pence. He never wanted to be reminded of Alice, and neither did Pearl for that matter. Pearl's hair was grey and thin, like Alice's had been, and hard to pin neatly. But at least it dried quickly on the walk back from the beach. She'd just stowed her still-damp and sandy nightdress in the back of the cupboard by the hearth when she heard the front door go. She picked up some darning and tugged at the needle left ready in the cloth.

'Hello,' he called.

She heard him get a drink of water from the pail. She took a last glance round the room to make sure everything was in the right place.

Her husband had been a broad man in his day, heavily built from years at sea hauling in nets and pots, but now he was sunk on his frame and looked as if he was wearing a body several sizes too large for him. His once blond hair had bleached to white and tufted at his ears. He was short but strong, apart from his hands. As soon as he appeared she could see they were swollen today. He pushed the door open with a fist.

'Hello,' she said.

He sat by the hearth. It had been so warm they hadn't had to light a fire in this room for months. She was his height and when she went to his side she could see his scalp had reddened after another day in the sun. She bent down and unlaced his boots. As she eased them from his feet sand sprinkled onto the floor. She felt the need to smooth it on the flags, like salt to lay the fish on. Like before.

'All right?' he said. He was staring at her.

'Hm?'

He proffered his hands. She rubbed them, easing each hot, swollen knuckle. His hands were softer now he didn't put to sea. Watching the younger men go could soothe skin if not bone.

When he could uncurl his fingers a little she went to the kitchen and lit the stove. He followed her and sat at the table, watching her set the supper things. He hadn't brought anything home from the harbour but she didn't mention it. Some days he had something from Matthew Tiddy, their neighbour's son, or their own son George if Jack would take it from him. Cradling a bit of pollock or whiting wrapped in newspaper, Jack would lay the fish delicately on the table, as if it were a baby. She knew how he needed to hold the fish in his stiffened hands. It was more than the taste. But today the table was empty. There were some cooked potatoes left from yesterday she could fry. She wasn't hungry. She put the kettle on to boil.

'That was some to do today,' he said.

'What was?'

9

'You didn't see?'

'No. I was here all day. That darning.' She looked for the potatoes.

'Well,' Jack said, 'the palace was open. There were people inside, taking measurements.'

'Really?' She saw the palace bright with silver fish, women bent over buckets of salt. A song played at the edge of her thoughts.

She couldn't find the potatoes. She was sure there were some left. She'd put them next to the fat ready to cook today. Only they weren't there. No bother. She'd cook some fresh. The kettle began to sing.

She moved around the kitchen without thinking. Her hands knew the exact distance from table to stove to the back of the chair. Her feet felt the grooves and lumps of the rough floor, rolling and lifting as if dancing across its contours.

'Are they going to open the palace again?' she asked.

'Seems so. I always said the fish would come back. It was foolish to stop.'

She filled the teapot and left it to brew. 'But there's nothing left,' she said. Turning back to the stove he caught her hand and held it. His eyes were as washed out a blue as when he was a boy.

'You'll see,' he said.

She was about to speak when there was a shout from outside. The kitchen window looked directly onto the street. A group of young men passed by, so close they could see in. Strangers. As they went by the front door on their way to the seafront there was jostling and the sound of someone being knocked into the door, then laughing as the door swung open. A gangly man sprawled onto the kitchen floor, all legs and elbows. There was cheering from the street. He struggled to his feet while she and Jack stood motionless.

The man seemed suddenly to realise where he was. He took in the stove, the table, Jack's curled hands and mouth set in a grim line.

'Sorry,' the man mumbled, and dove back onto the street. His friends cheered again. Pearl pushed the door shut and locked it, then poured the tea.

First thing in the morning Jack went to the seafront, as he did most days. He went to watch the few fishing boats that still went out and to chew over the changes in Morlanow with the rest of those who'd stopped fishing. There were more men on the front than in the boats.

She pulled her wet nightdress from the back of the cupboard and took it to the little yard behind the cottage. The white-washed walls which separated her yard from those on either side were too bright in the sun. It was late August and still hot. The air swam with it. The nightdress would dry in an hour or so. She held it to her face and breathed in the sea. It filled her chest. She gave the nightdress a good scrub in the tin pail and hung it on the line. She could hear the workmen in the next street over, their voices a low hum broken by the blows of their tools. Which turn in the road was being widened today, she wondered. They were building on the cliff top too. New houses, though they looked light enough for the wind to lift them into the sea.

'You've had a wash on early.' Eileen Pendeen was looking over the wall. Her neighbour ran a shop, the oldest in the village. When Pearl was a child, Pendeen's stocked everything Morlanow needed: rope, hooks, linen, soap, oakum, tea, sugar, cork. Now Eileen's place sold games for the beach and towels. The fishing supplies were out the back. You had to ask to see the hooks and the cork. There were many other shops like it too.

'It's only Friday,' Eileen said.

'Didn't want this to stain,' Pearl said, 'waiting until Monday.'

Eileen looked up and down the line, taking in the single piece of clothing pegged out. 'You heard about the palace?' she said.

'It's going to be opened. Jack saw them measuring yesterday.'

'It's going to be opened all right,' Eileen said. But before Pearl could say anything Eileen said, 'I'm late getting to the shop as it is. I'll call in after, have a cup of tea.'

Pearl heard Eileen's back door open then close. She stayed in the yard, letting the sun heat her face. There was no breeze. Eileen was sharp. Pearl wouldn't risk a swim today.

She decided to go to the seafront to see the palace. Its re-opening was a surprise. She hadn't let herself think about that possibility for so long. The disappointment only became worse as the years passed and it seemed less and less likely any money would be found to repair and relaunch the fleet. When the pilchards returned, the men could afford to get their boats back. There would be money for the town's women too, curing the fish with salt and stocking their larders for the winter. Eileen would have to get rid of the beach towels and games and put the cork in the front of the shop. Pearl could still taste the dark, oily flesh of a pilchard, as if she'd just eaten one, but at the same time she remembered the hunger that so often accompanied hope of their arrival, felt the physical ache of it. At least the holiday visitors came every year without fail to Eileen's shop. The fish had never been so loyal.

From her front door the palace was only two streets away but they were crowded. People packed the road from one side to the other. Pearl gave up trying to find a way through and stayed close to the houses on one side, moving with the crowd. She kept her hand out, letting it brush against stone, wood, glass to keep her balance. There was such a jostle, this time of year.

She came to the station. Morlanow was the end of the line so there was only one platform and the ticket office stood where the tracks finished. It was a single storey building but one of the smartest in the town. From Easter onwards there were tubs of flowers outside: pink and yellow lavish-looking things that stank to high heaven of sweetness. And spiky palms too. She remembered the prick of them through her thin clothes when she was a child. Jack and Nicholas liked to break off leaves and use them as swords. They were pirates. And what was she?

There was a newly pasted poster on the ticket office door. She had seen the picture before: Morlanow's seafront, painted by someone often talked about. It was no good, she couldn't remember his name. The poster showed the seafront with several new-looking fishing boats moored up. Two people stood admiring it: a fisherman and a little girl in a pretty cream dress. The rest of the seafront was empty. The sea filled most of the poster. It was beautiful: rich blue with purple to show the gentle swell. The hills that flanked it were gold and though the sun itself wasn't in the picture she could feel it in every drop of paint. It was as if heat was seeping from the paper. It looked such a wonderful place, so still and quiet, so many lovely new boats, that she found herself wishing she could go, but then she saw 'Morlanow' written underneath. She was already here.

There was a cry from the warren of streets behind her and then the sudden tumble of stones as another wall came down. She turned round but could see only people: waves and waves of sun-warmed skin. The poster didn't show this place with its strangers, cars, and building work. But Morlanow was another place again, too. It was full of fishwives and the stink of fish. It was running along the sand with Jack and Nicholas. It was swimming and keygrims and praying.

Mrs Tiddy came out of the ticket office, holding a cloth. 'Morning,' she said. Her thick, dark hair was wrapped in a scarf and she wore an old apron over her dress. She smelled of polish and scalding. 'I called by yesterday,' she said. 'You weren't in.'

'No,' Pearl said. Her neighbour smiled and waited for more. When Pearl didn't say anything Mrs Tiddy moved to the ticket office windows and began to wipe them, though they already looked clean. The frames were painted in the railway company's colours: chocolate and cream. So were the benches and the frames round the information boards. The Tregurtha Hotel up on the cliff used them too, though Pearl hadn't been any further than the hotel's stable yard. The horses all had chocolate and cream nameplates.

'Eileen said she saw you on the beach,' Mrs Tiddy said. 'Below the drying field.'

'Did she?' Pearl said. Another pause. Mrs Tiddy stopped wiping the windows, her cloth motionless on the glass. Her back was still straight as a nail though she wasn't as strong as she looked, Pearl knew. 'I don't think so,' Pearl said.

'Now then,' Mrs Tiddy said, coming over to her. 'You know you're not meant to swim.'

The bell on the ticket office wall rang. The clerk, Mr Daniels, came out onto the platform. There was the slow chuff-chuff of the engine and then smoke came into view. The three of them watched it though there was no sign yet of the train. The track curved round the coast. The train would be nearly in and yet it wouldn't be seen until the last moment when the track straightened on the approach to the station.

They stayed watching. Pearl couldn't take her eyes from the track bed. The little stones between the sleepers made her think of the cairn on the beach. Was it still there? What if someone had knocked it down, not realising how important it was? There was a sharp whistle as the train rounded the final bend.

'I'd stand back, ladies,' Mr Daniels said. 'She's going to be full.'

When Mrs Tiddy turned to ask Mr Daniels about the pony trap, taking passengers to the Tregurtha Hotel, Pearl took the opportunity to slip away.

She wanted to turn left out of the station, to get to the seafront, but was confronted by a motor car. It was trying to inch its way round the tight corner of the station entrance, its progress hampered by the streams of visitors going in the opposite direction, towards the sea. Two young girls were admiring themselves in the car's windows as it tried to pass them, the family inside all red-faced and squashed. The car wasn't going anywhere for the moment. Pearl didn't like to get so close to cars but in the summer it was unavoidable. She squeezed past the front, catching her hand on the burning metal bonnet. Someone pushed her from behind and she stumbled. The preening girls loomed over her, blocking her way. The sun was hot on her arms, her face. She didn't recognise anyone. And still more people tried to push their way round the car. Finally the girls moved. She was safe, across the road.

It hadn't always been like this.

Eileen had said she would come round. Pearl would have to be in, all neat and tidy in the kitchen under Eileen's nosy gaze. Eileen was kind, a friend, but she did fuss and Mrs Tiddy would tell her all sorts. Pearl turned in the direction of home. The palace would still be there tomorrow.

Three

'Move?' Jack said the word awkwardly, as if it were in another language. Pearl looked up from the pastry she was working and stared at her husband's back. 'But we've lived in this house since we married,' he said. 'More than forty years.'

Pascoe stood on the doorstep. A local boy – man now, she reminded herself – but not a fisherman, despite his family's long history with the sea. Pearl wasn't sure what it was that Pascoe did do, but he always had money, was always standing drinks. He thought too much of himself, wearing fancy suits but his hair all sides up. He was trying to smooth it down now, stroking his head as if it were a pet.

'It will be a bit of a change,' Pascoe said.

'I've no doubt of that,' Jack said. He stepped forward so that he blocked the doorway, bracing each side of the frame with his tightly curled hands.

'Come on now. I dare say it will be better for you in a new place,' Pascoe said. 'A nice bit of garden.' He appeared over Jack's shoulder then, looking into the kitchen. He looked so young. He inclined his head towards Pearl but was still

16

addressing Jack. Pascoe never spoke to her directly. 'And for your wife, much better to be away from all the noise down here. We're expecting another good season next year and we all need to be ready. Morlanow has a lot to offer but we don't have enough beds at present. People are having to stay down the coast at Pentreath. The visitors from Birmingham alone...'

She stopped listening. The pastry was clammy in her hands. She looked at the low ceiling, its paint stained the colour of sand, the beams which ran anything but straight. She could still see the eyes in the grain. The thought of not seeing the ceiling again suddenly struck her. She hadn't looked at it, really taken it in, in such a long time and now she wouldn't see it any more. Her chest tightened and a coughing fit came.

Jack spun round, seeming torn between coming to her side and getting his hands under Pascoe's lapels. She put out her hand to show Jack she would be all right. Her husband lurched out onto the street.

'See what you're doing to my wife?' he shouted. 'That's what moving will do, make her ill, not help her. And don't try and dance me round as if this has come out of the air, Pascoe. This is your doing!'

'Now, Mr Tremain, there's no need for any of this unpleasantness. I'm simply acting as the agent for your landlord who has asked me, on his behalf, to inform you of his decision to sell these cottages to the railway company, who will then lease to other occupants.'

'Holiday people, you mean.'

There was a pause and when Pascoe next spoke his voice had lost its local familiarity. 'The new occupants will be staying for shorter lengths of time,' Pascoe said, 'but that's unimportant. What matters is that these cottages need to be empty no later than the end of the month. You won't be left in the cold. Accommodation has been reserved for all Carew Street residents at the new development.'

Pearl managed to ease her coughs and sat down to quell the dizziness that would inevitably follow an attack. There was the sound of paper rustling.

'The particulars are all there,' Pascoe said. 'Now if you'll excuse me, I have others to notify.'

Jack called after him. 'Is it true what I heard, that the company's bought the pilchard palace too?'

But there was no response. Jack shut the door with a bang and slumped into the chair at the other end of the table.

Pearl stared at the floured rolling pin. She had the sense that she was falling and gripped the underside of the chair to remind her body she was sitting down.

'How can they ask us to move, after all this time?' Jack seemed to be asking himself the question rather than addressing her, for which she was glad. 'Well, they can't make us, I'm sure. We're not leaving.' He seemed to remember the envelope crumpled in his hand then. He drew out the single sheet of paper and read it slowly to himself.

'Where do we go?' she said.

Jack put the letter on the table and smoothed it flat, over and over. 'Out of Morlanow,' he said. 'They're moving us up the hill.'

She couldn't take it in. The ceiling beams seemed to be looking at her again. She was meant to be rolling out pastry. It was long past supper time. Something came back to her.

'That's not true about the pilchard palace, that the company's bought it? Why would they want it?'

Jack hesitated, then said, 'Matthew Tiddy told me this morning. The company's going to make it into a hotel, with Pascoe over-seeing it. Too good a place to sit unused, being on the front. Got an easy run to the beach.'

'A hotel... but they've already got one. The Tregurtha's so big.'

'Not big enough, it seems. And Matthew Tiddy said the palace is going to be a grand one. Going to charge a fortune. Thirty bedrooms, sea views, and a big room for dances where the old cellars are.'

'Dances?'

'Pascoe's going to make it just like the Tregurtha. There's to be a man playing a piano every night while people eat.'

'They'll want fish,' she said. 'And they'll pay a good price, hotel visitors.' She saw her son George's beautiful ling, straight from the hand line and steaming freshness on bone china plates.

Jack shook his head. 'They want everything, these people.'

'Why didn't you tell me about the palace?'

He drummed his crooked fingers on the table and avoided Pearl's eye. 'Because I didn't want you to fret,' he said. 'But now what we need to worry about is us.' He thumped the table. The rolling pin fell to the floor. 'What are we going to do?'

There was nothing to be done. That soon became clear. They had never owned their cottage, no one on Carew Street did, and not many in the old part of Morlanow, its fishing quarter, did either. Rent was paid to their landlord, Mr James, a distant relation of the mine-owning family who had once been so wealthy they could own whole villages. Mr James' agent collected the money from the Tregurtha Hotel fortnightly, round the back by the stables. In a way, Pearl realised, it had always felt as if the hotel owned their house.

Jack and Pearl were regular with the money. It could never be said they didn't pay their way, even though some weeks were tight. Her mother and father had done the same. The

Tregurtha had been in Morlanow ever since Pearl could remember. It was built by the railway company when the train came, years before she was born. Mrs Tiddy had worked there when the fish stopped coming in. She told the wildest stories about it. The dresses the women brought with them on their holidays – feathers and brocade, and silk so soft it felt like water, Mrs Tiddy said. She used to run her hands through them when she was doing the rooms. She had always had such nice hands. Pearl would never have been allowed to work in the rooms, even cleaning. She'd always been untucked, untidy, even when she was trying, and the Tregurtha only took on the most presentable. There had been no shortage of people needing work when the palace closed.

Eileen called round the day after the letter came. She was younger than Pearl and still sprightly in her flowery dresses. She had come to Morlanow as a visitor herself, stepping off the train many years before. She married Simon Pendeen and had lived in the village for so long that Pearl sometimes forgot she hadn't been born in Morlanow. On the days she allowed herself to think about the past she was sure Eileen had been at school with her and Mrs Tiddy. Simon had been dead a long time.

'I heard,' Eileen said, in an affronted voice, 'that Pascoe's going to smarten these up.' She gestured round the good room. 'Laying proper floors, having electric lights. Even taps inside.' She slurped her tea noisily, as if that was making her angry too. 'Why haven't we had water inside? You've been having to make do with the pump, carrying buckets yourself – ' Eileen raised her voice ' – when you shouldn't.' There was a thump from Jack in the kitchen beyond.

'I don't mind the pump,' Pearl said. 'I'd keep everything as it is, to stay.'

'It doesn't look like you'll get much choice,' Eileen said. 'I'll help you with the packing.'

Packing. The thought of boxes made it all seem so real, suddenly. Pearl was going to have to put things in boxes and take them out of the front door, into daylight for the first time in years. She would have to shut the door behind her and not come back. How could this be true? Eileen didn't seem to feel the same sense of strangeness. She was cross, of course, tapping one of her heels on the slate floor and shaking her head with little agitated movements. But that was Eileen. Never one to give in easily. Pearl admired her for that, though of course she would never say so. Eileen didn't hold any truck with such soft talk. Pearl admired her for that too. Mrs Tiddy weaselled, poking about in people's business, but Eileen asked directly. You knew where you were with Eileen. She was looking at Pearl now. What had they been talking about? Packing.

'We can share a cart, take things up to the new houses together,' Pearl said.

Eileen hesitated then put down her cup. 'I can't be all the way up there when I've got the shop to run,' she said. 'It'd take me all morning to get down to town, and you know how often I'm late opening as it is.' She looked different suddenly, a young woman with her own business and the determination not to move. Eileen's skin looked smoother and her hair darker. Pearl felt old and untidy next to her.

'Where will you go, if not up there?' Pearl said.

'David will have me,' Eileen said. 'If he wants the shop he'll have to. I told him that.' Eileen's son was desperate to stay in Morlanow, Pearl knew, and the shop – when Eileen finally decided she couldn't run it any more – would let him. If he could keep his sister Margaret out of it, that was. Pendeen's was a prize catch. Eileen would be well looked after. There would be no room for Pearl and Jack in their son George's loft, though. It was tight for him and his wife Elizabeth, only

21

meant for storing sails during the winter. Every inch of Morlanow seemed full of people without enough room these days. How many would stay in her house, when she was gone? What would they do to her kitchen?

'Don't look so downcast,' Eileen said, patting Pearl's knee. 'You'll be at the seafront as much as you are now, I've no doubt. And it might be better up there, quieter, as Pascoe says.'

Pearl nodded. 'I don't like the cars. They fill the street and press so close when I'm walking.'

'There you are then,' Eileen said. 'You'll be away from all that up the hill.'

'The lad's here, at last,' Jack called. He grumbled on about George's lateness. Pearl left him to the crates inside. She went out and saw boxes and parcels at nearly every front door on Carew Street. Some people had moved earlier that week but most, like she and Jack, had waited until the last possible day, still hoping that something would happen, that some letter with a change of heart would come. Mrs Tiddy had gone days earlier, without calling round first. She had had to give up her cleaning work at the station because the walk down to town everyday would be too much for her. Pearl would have to keep herself busy with Mrs Tiddy around all the time, and be more careful about swimming.

A horse slumbered by her gate, its ears drooping sideways. Pearl smoothed its nose, whispered into its hair. George came from round the back of the cart and kissed her cheek.

'We've got him for the day,' George said. 'Willis doesn't need him back 'til the light goes.' Her son was thin but lean rather than frail; muscular beneath his fishing smock. He smelt of salt water and tar from caulking his boat. It was another hot day and his face was slick with moisture. It was sharply angled but warm, friendly. He was eager to help, whoever needed it, whatever needed doing, and that showed in his expression somehow. He had very dark eyes and a smile which was broad and real when it came, but which could vanish quickly, making him look young, though he was getting on himself.

'Are you ready?' George said.

She shook her head against the warmth of the horse. He squeezed her shoulder then she heard him go inside. Raised voices drifted out to the street. She pressed her face deeper into the warmth of the rag and bone man's horse.

George lifted the boxes and crates onto the cart. Jack watched, his swollen, empty hands mimicking George's. Pearl slipped back into the house. She went from room to room, trying to memorise the lay of each step, the shape of each wall. The furniture had left patches of discolouration against the wallpaper and the paint, as if the pieces had seared themselves into the structure of the house. But the paper would be stripped and the paint painted over. It would be as if she had never lived there.

She heard the back of the cart lashed up. Jack told George the rope was loose. More arguing. She took a mussel shell from her pocket. In the corner of the kitchen was a cracked floorboard. Pearl pushed the shell into the gap, forcing it out of sight. She stayed crouched over the wood, breathing in the years of cooking, washing clothes, and waiting. The cairn on the beach came from the same need to leave a physical trace, a marker. It felt right to use a shell here. The sea had always been with her, even inside the house.

A hand touched her elbow.

'Come on, time to go,' Jack said.

She hadn't heard him come in. He helped her to her feet but as she wiped her face he turned away.

Eileen came to see them off. She'd packed them a cold lunch and presented it to Pearl as if she was going on a picnic, rather than moving away.

'Now don't you go getting any airs and graces once you're a grand lady on the hill,' she said. 'I don't want you thinking you're too good to come into my shop.'

Pearl grasped her hand and saw that Eileen too was trying not to cry. She couldn't say anything so pressed Eileen's hand back and nodded. George gave the horse a slap on the rump and the cart lurched forwards. Eileen waved for a moment then turned back into her cottage. Even today there was no fuss. Eileen would get on with her move. She wouldn't stand around moping. Pearl steeled herself to do the same.

She and Jack sat in the cart with their boxes and bundles while George walked at the horse's head, encouraging the animal with clicks and soft words she couldn't hear. The hill that led up to the new house was steep and they had to stop several times to let motor cars pass. Pearl sat facing the town, watching it grow smaller. The bulk of Morlanow was hidden from view until you were almost on top of it. Then whitewashed houses appeared like mushrooms, crammed into the small cleft of the cliff, vying with each other for light and air as if they were still growing. The roofs were all grey slate, all the same size. For a long time they had formed one block of colour from this distance but now there were gaps where the workmen had broken and re-made the village into a town. Everything sloped towards the harbour. The sea was too vast next to the clustering buildings; it seemed strange that the waves had never washed Morlanow away.

Finally they turned off the main road. The new houses formed a terrace which was perched on a ledge jutting from the cliff, close to the top. A lop-sided sign proclaimed the row *Wave Crest*, but the houses were so far from the seafront it

was hard to make out the waves at all. They were exposed to
the wind here, and it was cooler than it had been in the town.
It would be wild in the winter though, Pearl thought. The
winds around this coast were vicious. The visitors were long
gone by then; they never saw the storms or the fog. The
railway posters would always seem true if you came to
Morlanow only in summer.

Their house was the last on the row. It was much taller than
their Carew Street house and the outside walls had a cleanliness
that surprised her. They were made of red brick, bright in the
sunshine. The old house had been very grimy, she realised now,
the white-wash coming away to reveal the grey stone beneath.
The patches of wash that were left were grubby from the visitors
pushing through the town. Several motor cars had knocked into
the front wall in the last year, one leaving a scratch of green
paint below the window sill. But the new house seemed so
insubstantial compared to the old one which hunkered into the
earth, low next to the sea. The *Wave Crest* house looked
precarious, too new. How could it hold them, up here?

It was the same inside. Nothing felt solid, made to last.
Downstairs was a kitchen and another smaller room with a
fireplace. Nothing like the good room at home on Carew Street
but perhaps she could make it nice. Perhaps with their things
dotted around it would be all right. The stairs were very
narrow and creaked alarmingly once you were halfway up.
There was a bedroom and box room above. Both felt dark.

It only took the morning to unload Pearl and Jack's
possessions. George seemed relieved to be able to get back
down to town and leave them to the unpacking. Before he
went Pearl managed to rouse herself from the window sill,
where she had sat since they first arrived.

Seeing George to the cart she asked him, 'Your loft – will
you have to move too?'

He pushed his dark hair from his face and screwed his lips together. 'Pascoe says no, but the palace is so close. If it really does become a hotel then I can't see how me and Elizabeth can stay. Once it's finished he's bound to want the rest of the street too.'

Inside, Jack dropped a box on the floor and cursed it. George took that moment to kiss Pearl goodbye. He had moved out of the Carew Street cottage when he was young, too young, she had often felt. The rows with Jack had heated every waking moment and simmered in sleep. The distance since then had left only an uneasy peace.

She stood listening to George's footsteps retreating. She was in the drying field watching Nicholas go. Her breath caught in her throat. Then it was over. She went back inside.

'You going to help me?' Jack stood in a nest of crumpled packing paper and blankets. 'Might make you feel more at home.'

Pearl looked round the new kitchen. There wasn't much space and a draught was coming from somewhere. Near the ceiling the wallpaper was already peeling. Unpacking wouldn't help; it would only make it worse to see their things arranged in this strange place. But it would take Jack all week on his own, his hands the way they were, and he would only work himself into a storm.

She nodded and began stacking the pans on the table. Even though she had known them all her life – her mother had taken such care of the heavy-bottomed saucepans – they had changed somehow, in their journey up the hill. Pearl felt as if she had never seen them before.

Four

When she woke she knew something was wrong. There was a stillness, as if the sound had been sucked from the air. Her own chest tightened in response as she tried to remember where she was. She couldn't hear the sea. Why was she locked in the quiet? Was she in the palace's cellar?

Then she remembered. She was in the new house.

Jack was still asleep. It was barely light. She went to the window that looked down the hill to the town. The morning was already hot but there were thick clouds and a heaviness in the air. Her head was muggy. A good downpour would freshen everything, help her get on with unpacking the rest of their things.

She filled the kettle from the pail by the back door. There were taps over the sink but there was no water in them, despite the assurance from Pascoe. When she had turned them on yesterday they gave a weak gasp but that was it. Each house had a small dirt yard behind it. Beyond these ran the cliff path where a shared tap was connected to a nearby spring. That would have to do for now.

The rain came suddenly, like a wave over the roof. She could smell the bare earth now wet. There was the sound of water nearby, too near. She followed the sound to the bedroom and felt water on her arms and face. She looked up. There were drips across the ceiling. Jack's face was wet. She woke him and together they laid saucepans in an ever-changing pattern across the floor. After a while they gave up and sat in the kitchen, which seemed to be spared, waiting for the rain to stop.

'Roof's badly done,' Jack said. 'You can see it from the road. Hardly a slate on right. It's no good, no good at all.'

Pearl was thinking of the sloping doorstep of the old house and how her foot felt against its shape as she walked inside. When Jack broke off she looked up and saw that he was watching her.

'No good at all,' he said again. He massaged one hand with the other. It was a relief to have silence then. Pearl was tired and wanted only to look out of the window. The sea lay before her, too far away to see any waves but just knowing it was there brought some comfort.

The rain eased. She could hear seagulls again. Jack went outside and presently she caught the smell of tobacco. She opened all the windows to air the house but over the course of the day the damp didn't dry. When she went to bed that night the bedding was cold against her skin.

There was another downpour the following morning. She lit a fire to dry the plaster but the chimney smoked so much that the house became unbearable with the smoke and the extra warmth so she put the fire out. The sky looked clearer from midday so she decided to risk drying the sheets on the gorse bushes which encroached at the back of the yards.

The other yards were empty. Carew Street had been moved

up the hill together. Pearl's neighbours on the cliff were still the women she had known all her life, as children, as wives, on the beach and in the palace. There was only one man in the row other than Jack: Betty Thomas' husband, but he was much younger than Betty. All the others were gone, taken by the sea or serving in the reserves. On Carew Street the women always stopped to talk, which had been a bother at times. People were so nosy. But since the move from the seafront the women scuttled from their kitchens to their yards and back again, like anxious gulls fretting for their nests, and Pearl missed the talk. If only Eileen had come up the hill.

Pearl was struggling to spread her sheets across the gorse when Mrs Tiddy appeared and took hold of the other end of a sheet. Already out of breath, Pearl was forced to let her help and then do the same for Mrs Tiddy's damp linen.

'All night it was dripping from the roof,' Mrs Tiddy said, reaching for another sheet. 'And my chimney smokes…'

'And ours,' Pearl said.

'I'm worried it'll catch light. It's enough to keep a soul from sleep, fretting like this.' She pulled at the corner of a sheet to straighten it over an arm of gorse. 'Is Jack going to see Pascoe about the house?'

'I don't know,' Pearl said. Had he mentioned it? She supposed he would have done but she couldn't remember the conversation. She bent to lift another sheet.

'I wouldn't ask,' Mrs Tiddy was saying, 'only my Matthew's got work from Pascoe. I don't know when he'll come up here next.'

Pearl stopped to catch her breath. There was an ache at her temple. The weather was still so hot, despite the rain the last few days. The feeling she'd had, stuck inside the hot house earlier, hadn't left her. Nicholas was playing at the edges of her thoughts, though she tried so hard not to think about him.

He was stretching out a piece of white cloth, then a sail was being raised. The wind was pushing it full but there was no wind. It was too hot.

'Are you all right?' Mrs Tiddy said.

But Pearl was already on her way back to the house. She needed to lie down, to send him away.

When she woke it was dark. There was still a warm pressure at her temples but it was weaker now. Jack was standing by the window.

'How long have I been asleep?' she asked him.

'I don't know,' he said. 'You were in bed when I got back from the front.'

'That must have been hours ago. You've had nothing to eat,' she said, struggling to sit up. She couldn't seem to focus in the poor light.

'I'm fine,' he said. 'Mrs Tiddy called in, to see how you were. Said you were taken bad hanging out the sheets. I said you were in bed so she got me some supper.' He wouldn't meet her eye. 'My hands weren't good today. I think it must be the heat.' He looked at his curled fists but without emotion. They had been that way for a long time.

'Well I'll have to sort out the kitchen then, if she's been in there,' Pearl said. This time she was able to sit up and swing her legs out of bed. She'd be better once she started moving. It was no good getting into bed in the middle of the day. Her mother had done that and she'd been dead a few months later. Once you stopped, that was it.

'I'm going to see Pascoe tomorrow,' Jack said. 'About the house.'

'Good,' Pearl said. 'We can go back to Carew Street. I don't fancy a winter here. These draughts.'

He nodded. 'I said I'd ask Pascoe about Mrs Tiddy's place

too.' He helped Pearl to stand. 'As she's on her own.'

'She's got Matthew,' Pearl said, shaking off Jack's hand. 'What does she need you for?'

'Don't be uncharitable,' Jack said. 'We have to look after each other up here.'

Five

The next day Jack made a fuss down at the Council rooms, along with Betty Thomas' husband. The two of them spoke for all of *Wave Crest*. A motor car brought them back up the hill, with Pascoe driving and two other men in overalls in the back.

The men in overalls spent the day moving from one house to another, working their way down the row. When they came to Pearl and Jack's, the last one, they poked the soft plaster in the bedroom and a great load came off the wall. Dust drifted over the furniture, making Pearl cough. She waited in the yard while the dust settled. There would be so much cleaning to do, she was tired just thinking about it. Presently the men came out. One measured the angles of the windows while the other wrote figures in a pocketbook. She was going to offer them a cup of tea but they didn't speak to her, so she decided not to. Pascoe went down to the town again and returned with a ladder strapped to the roof of the car. One of the men climbed onto the roof of Pearl and Jack's house and measured that too, calling down his figures, at which the other man tutted. Jack watched them, smoking and peering at their numbers. He ignored Pascoe, but Pearl wanted to ask what had happened to the old house: were the taps in? They had heard nothing more about the palace becoming a hotel. She hadn't been back down to the town since the move. It was easy to forget, to pretend Morlanow was the same as when she was a child. Nicholas would call for her and they would go down to the seafront. There was a boat he wanted to show her.

As the sun began to set the men in overalls and Pascoe got back in the car and drove away.

'What did they find?' Pearl asked Jack.

'Said it would take a few days,' he said, 'to do the calculations.'

But the next day the men in overalls were back, joined by two others. They didn't come to the houses but struck away from them, heading inland. They were carrying all sorts of devices and sticks. Pearl looked out for them during the day but didn't see them pass *Wave Crest* again.

She was sitting by the window when Jack came home from the seafront.

'There's still things to be unpacked,' he said. 'You've not taken out your mother's china, or the pictures of Polly's family.'

'There's no point,' she said, smiling at him. 'We're going home soon.'

She was alone in the new house much of the day. Jack continued to go to the seafront despite the long walk back up the hill in the hot evenings. She did enough to keep the house running – a bit of washing, airing the bedding – but nothing more. They weren't staying, she was sure of it. Even though she wasn't as busy as when they were in the old house she didn't seem to have any time. She sat at the window late morning, looking down to town, and then the clock would strike and it would be mid-afternoon. She wasn't aware of slipping into melancholy but it often found her. It was having to wait to go home. She had time to think about the things she usually managed to keep pushed down in the dark. The white sail came to her again and again, and that terrible word: keygrim. It seemed to be in the clock's very tick. A swim would sort her out. But she wasn't meant to. Mrs Tiddy was watching. That was her now, sneaking in.

'Mother?' a voice called.

It was George come to see her. He kissed her cheek. He smelt of the town and she realised how much she missed it, even with the crowds and the cars.

'It's such a walk up here,' he said. 'However does Father manage it?'

'He's fitter than you think,' she said. 'Only his hands stop him doing things, and even then he'll try.'

George wouldn't let her put the kettle on. 'Water'll be fine,' he said. He took a cup from where they lay still packed in a box and went to the sink.

'Nothing there,' she said. 'Pail's by the door.'

'You've no water?' he said.

'Oh, we've plenty,' she said. She told him about the leaks, and the chimney, and the measuring men. She was tired listing it all off.

'Has Pascoe said when he'll fix it?' George said.

She shook her head, but the movement seemed to hurt. There was that warmth at her temples again.

'I'd do it myself if I wasn't going out,' he said. 'I've not caught much this week and the rent's due. I can only stop for a bit. Wanted to see how you were keeping.'

She tried not to move her head when she spoke. 'I'm not too bad.'

'It's not like you to be shut in like this. It'd do you good, Mother, getting some fresh air.'

'I don't know.'

'Just an hour, get your blood moving.'

George was right. Since the move she had felt a little off-colour, a little wisht. When he said goodbye she told him that she would try and go for a walk, for him.

The next day she wrapped her hair in a scarf, buttoned her coat, and set off. After so long indoors the air was potent; breathing felt like drinking river-fresh water, so crisp it made her head light but without the persistent ache of the last few days.

She chose to walk into town by the cliff path that ran past the back of the house. It was only a clearing in the grass, worn to dust by successive generations of feet. She didn't want to brave the road. Cars came down the winding hill so fast and there was no pavement. The cliff path was steep but she could go at her own pace, standing aside for the visitors out for a walk. They were polite, most of them thanking her for not being in the way, saying what a nice day it was, how lucky she was to live here. She didn't say anything back. She didn't want a conversation. She had one thing clear in her mind today.

The path wound down to the base of the cliff and joined the seafront where she turned away from the sea and into the stuffy maze of back streets. Each time she met a workman or a piece of scaffolding she chose another narrow alley, slipping into the passageways still to be opened up to the light. It took her a while but she managed to criss-cross the centre of town. Finally she stood outside the old house on Carew Street. Standing so close she longed to see her kitchen's cool, dark corners. If she could just get inside, she would be right again.

All these thoughts catching at her would be gone, back to the past where they belonged.

She moved towards the front door but there were several pairs of boots lying any old which way on the doorstep. Her flower pots had gone. She had expected the house to be empty. She and Jack had only just left, she was sure. There hadn't been time for others to come into her house. Her house. There was some mistake.

The front door opened and a tall, thin man wearing a smart jersey and tiny spectacles looked at her.

'Can I help you?' he asked.

Pearl looked at the ground and shook her head. The thin man stayed watching her from the doorway. She felt his eyes on her back all the way down the street.

She went to see Eileen but the shop was too busy. There were people queuing outside. That was good for Eileen, and her son David too. Another day would do for a visit.

Her chest was tight but she didn't want to wait for it to ease. She wanted to get away from Morlanow and the only place to go was back up the hill. She began to climb the cliff path. Herring gulls jeered overhead. She didn't let herself look out to sea.

There was a letter waiting for her when she got back. Perhaps this would say when they could return to Carew Street, and what that man was doing in her house. She didn't pause to get a drink of water, just ripped open the envelope, her pulse loud in her ears.

It was from Pascoe. *Wave Crest* was sliding towards the cliff edge, their house on the end worst of all. The men in overalls had found subsidence from the mine workings inside the cliff, from back when there was still tin to be prised from the rock. Miles and miles beneath the cliff the miners had gone, out below the sea. But Pascoe with his papers and plans hadn't thought about the shafts, and neither had the railway company.

In the letter Pascoe promised that the problems in the new houses would be put right, but what with the work on the palace hotel he couldn't say when exactly. It was too late to move back to Carew Street. The visitors were there. She was stuck up the hill and she wouldn't be able to keep Nicholas from her thoughts any longer.

Her hand was shaking. She let the letter drop to the floor and then felt her legs give way. She slumped against the wall, dust and sand rough on her bare calves. Here he was, pushing through, his hand reaching for hers. He whispered her name in her ear. There was heat at her temples again but this time rushing, bringing a wave of darkness, then the white sail again. All whiteness as the sail wrapped itself round her and covered her face.

PART TWO

1880 and 1936

One

It's so sunny that when she looks up from the water all she can see is white light. The sun is high overhead. It must be midday. She knows the time of day by the tide and the light rather than numbers, and she knows the season by the fishing. Everything follows a pattern and patterns must be learnt. School will end soon as pilchards are expected which means it must be summer. It is 1880 and hopes are high for another good season of fishing. The last few have been the best anyone can remember. The sea is full and their nets the same. When this year's fish come, all hands will be needed in the palace, however small they may be. Until then she spends each afternoon on the seafront or on the beach, with Jack who is twelve and Nicholas who is fourteen.

The three of them live on the same street, three houses all in a line and Pearl's house in the middle. The three fathers go out in the lifeboat when the flare goes up, and everyone goes to chapel. Each family works together in pilchard season. The men go out in the same seine team to catch them; Pearl's mother and Nicholas's mother, Annie, bulk the fish in the palace, packing the hard shining fish in salt. Jack doesn't have a mother but Pearl knows she's not supposed to talk to him about it. If she does, his very blue eyes get bluer as he cries and he bites his thick bottom lip.

The boys like to roam Morlanow and their games are much better than those of the girls she goes to school with. Pearl likes to climb things, and to pretend sometimes too. Nicholas is good at those kinds of games. She often forgets where she really is, lost in the things he can make her believe. She falls over then, or gets caught on gorse, or wipes her muddy hands down her dress without thinking. She's as untidy as a seagull.

'Can't you keep your skirts clean at least?' her mother said last night. Pearl came home dripping seawater and with dirt rubbed deep into her hems. 'That dress has got to last you. You're twelve, not a child anymore. I'm not chasing after you with a scrubbing brush only for you to go clambering with those boys.'

Even when she tries, Pearl can't seem to look as nice as her older sister Polly. Polly has lovely pale skin and long brown hair she keeps neat in plaits that never fall out. Pearl's hair is somewhere between blonde and brown but so full of knots she can't work her fingers through it for plaits. Her face is tanned. Her fingernails are bitten to the quick and permanently lined with dirt. Polly somehow keeps her hands clean and smooth, despite being old enough to salt the fish in the palace when they come in. It must be something to do with being friends with Sarah Dray.

Sarah is Polly's best friend. She has long, thick hair as black as coal. Her mouth is usually set in such a way that it seems she's sneering, or that she has a secret about you she won't tell. She's beautiful though, and never gets dirty. Polly becomes even more beautiful and clean when she works with Sarah Dray in the palace. It must be catching. Some of the artists have asked Sarah to pose for them and they offered good money too. The one from the north, Mr Michaels, wanted her on the beach with a creel of fish, looking out to sea as if waiting for something. But when Sarah's father found out he was livid and shouted at Mr Michaels on the seafront, in front of Miss Charles, the teacher from the art school. There was a sermon about it at chapel. Pearl hasn't seen much of Mr Michaels in the fishing quarter since, but Sarah has a new smugness about her, tossing her black hair even more, which makes Pearl less inclined than ever to spend time with her. She follows Nicholas and Jack comes too. Morlanow has many places for games and for hiding.

On the beach they have to dodge the stinking dogfish innards that litter the sand and the diving gulls that fight for them. When the tide begins to slink back in between the harbour wall and the cliff, the three of them retreat to the streets, or the drying field as long as it isn't washday. There's hellish fuss if the children clamber over the whites laid out in the sun. Sometimes the boys go to a place she doesn't like called Skommow Bay. She plays by herself then, or sits in the backyard talking to the chickens until she hears the boys come home.

Skommow Bay is a cold place. It's not a bay at all but a rocky shelf on the other side of Morlanow, where wrecks are left to rot. The broken ships and boats frighten Pearl so she stays away, but there's rich plunder if you scrabble around the tilting hulks and are brave enough to climb the ruined hulls. That's where the boys get scraps to make their little boats. They are making a grand one today.

'No, Jack. Like this.' Nicholas takes the knife from Jack's podgy fingers. Nicholas has long, thin fingers, what Miss Charles from the art school calls 'elegant'. Not everything about Nicholas is elegant though. He is tall, towering over her

43

and Jack. His knees seem huge in his legs. 'The keel needs be sharper or she won't turn,' Nicholas says.

Jack scowls, folds his arms and looks away. The three of them are sitting on the seafront wall, their legs dangling over the edge. There's the chop of thick knives cleaving dogfish and the prattle of Alice Trelawn on the sand below them. She's a fallen woman, Pearl's mother says, which is why she'll see to foul fish that's only good for bait.

Jack's mouth is screwed up. He looks as if he's trying not to cry and the effort is turning his face red. Nicholas grips the crude model boat between his knees and planes the bottom.

'There!' He holds up the boat and turns it round for Pearl and Jack to admire. Jack still looks grumpy. 'Let's go and launch her,' Nicholas says.

The three of them walk down the slipway to trek to the other side of the bay where the rock pools wink to them in the sun. The sand crunches under her bare feet. As they go, her mother calls down from the harbour wall where she's mending nets.

'You be sure to tuck your dress into your knickers if you're for wading.' And to Nicholas, as the oldest and in charge, 'Go steady now, you know she's not to run. Doctor said.'

The doctor's always saying, according to her mother, though Pearl doesn't remember ever having seen him. It was when she was a baby. He put his ear to her chest to hear her breath catch.

Pearl walks and looks at the sea lying asleep beyond the harbour wall. It's green today, no blue or grey, and no waves either. Calm as stone. This is a different sea to the one that throws ships onto rocks and swallows people.

Nicholas takes one of her hands. 'Day-dreaming again, limpet-legs? Come on.'

She trots along beside him. Jack, hands in his pockets, kicks a stick of driftwood along the beach. Nicholas and Pearl reach the spread of rocks at the bottom of the cliff first. He helps her climb onto the nearest one from which she is able to cross the others unaided, but she pretends she can't so that she gets to keep hold of his hand for longer. The rocks have sharply rippled surfaces that dig into the soles of her feet making her lurch about, unbalanced. Nicholas laughs and helps her steady herself. They come to a stop at the deepest pool and look in.

If Pearl stood on the bottom the water would be over her head, but it's so narrow that she wouldn't be able to stretch out her arms. The walls are the colour of the undersides of mussel shells, dotted with green furry plants that feel soft underwater but slimy out of it. Tiny crabs scuttle from the shadow she and Nicholas cast over them. The smell of seaweed is everywhere, salty and old.

Jack slopes up. Nicholas lets go of Pearl to hold the boat in both his hands, the sun gilding its edges.

'What shall we name her?' he asks as he sets the boat oh so gently on the water. There's a terrible moment when Pearl thinks it might sink. The boat quivers, tilts and dips forward.

Jack reaches out to grab it. 'The keel's too sharp.'

Nicholas slaps his hand away. 'Give her a minute. She'll right.'

And she does, settling in the water. The sail, made from a white handkerchief belonging to Nicholas, stretches out when he gets behind the boat and blows. He's like the north wind in the picture book at school; his brown curls slip over his eyes, which are as dark as the rocks. Pearl claps her hands as the little boat moves forward on waves stirred by Nicholas's breath. She knows what the boat should be called.

'Let's name her *Fair Maid*,' she says.

Nicholas purses his lips and looks up, considering the matter. 'That's only a seine boat.'

'What's wrong with that?' asks Jack.

'This is bigger; more of a mackerel driver like the east coast men sail,' Nicholas says. Jack is silent. 'How about *Storm Beater*?' Nicholas asks, his eyes wide with the certainty of his idea. 'She's one of the fastest east coast boats.'

Nicholas always decides, because he's the oldest. Jack's face reddens again and his hands curl into fists. For a moment he stands rigid apart from a shake in his arms, then he picks up a stone and hurls it into the water. The splash upsets the boat and it tips over and sinks, the handkerchief closing up like a jellyfish as it goes.

Two

The windowpane was cold against her cheek. One side of her body was full of stiffness and it took a moment for her eyes to focus. The white sail seemed to have burned them. Her boots were by the front door, splayed and pale with cliff path dust. Had she just come in? Yet here she was in the bedroom looking down at the sea and the light gone from the day. She moved to gather the boots and felt the roughness of sand between her toes. She smelled seawater in her hair.

Footsteps on the other side of the front door made her jump and she was afraid but didn't know why. The sound stopped and there were voices: Jack and Mrs Tiddy. Pearl picked up her boots and stood them together by the wall, then hurried to the kitchen. That was where she was meant to be now. It was dark. That meant supper. An ache in her head collected at her temple. She leant against the table to catch her breath.

Someone was coming in. It was Nicholas. She would lock the door, keep him out. Her breath was harder to catch. She heard herself wheezing. The door opened. But instead of the young man with narrow lips and dark eyes, tall and lean in a smart jacket, it was Jack.

'It's a fair walk from the front in this heat,' he puffed, putting a newspaper parcel on the table. Nicholas was gone. The smell of fish and sweat filled the room. Jack had been talking to Mrs Tiddy. The woman wanted something, she always did. Jack rubbed his sunburnt forehead with his arm; she noticed the freckles and white hair on his skin, the small twists of his ears. When had he become so old? His trousers had another hole at the knee: something else to mend.

She went over to undo his boots but when she bent to kneel, the ache in her head broke in to a flare of pain and she fell against the table. Jack caught her by the elbow and then lowered her into his own chair.

'What have you been up to now then, eh?' he said.

'Nothing. I... nothing.'

Jack tutted and fussed. He went to put the kettle on but burnt himself trying to light the stove.

'Leave it,' she said. 'I'll be all right.'

He looked at her hard from across the room. 'You've not been swimming, have you? You know how it makes you.'

Pearl shook her head but even as she did so she wasn't sure. She was tired, as if she'd done something vigorous. She tried to push her wet hair behind her ears, to hide it from him, but it was so tangled. Jack began to pace, still in his boots. Pearl breathed slowly to ease her chest. Jack stopped as her soft rasps came.

He waited until her breathing calmed. 'You need to be careful, Pearl. I'd not be much use if you were laid up in Pentreath, would I? Eight miles away, and me here on my own.'

She wanted to tell him he wouldn't be on his own, that he would have George, but the words wouldn't come. Jack wouldn't want to hear them, and Mrs Tiddy probably wouldn't leave him alone either.

'You'll be all right, won't you?' She nodded, and he went on, 'No need to worry the doctor then.'

She was able to undo his boots but didn't lean too closely into his legs in case he smelt the seawater. Certainty came to her then.

'I went down the hill, to see the old house.' Yes, that was it. She was tired from the walk back, as Jack had been. But her wet hair?

'Why ever did you do that?' he said. He rolled the tiredness of the day from his still broad shoulders. 'It'd only upset you.' He got up to wash his hands, a sign that it was time for supper. She stayed kneeling on the floor, not able to find the energy to stand as she thought about the man in her house. 'What's this?' Jack went over to the front door. There was the scrap of white again. The handkerchief sail had slipped inside the house. Jack was picking it up.

It was Pascoe's letter.

When she had washed the supper things they sat together in the room next to the kitchen. There was no mantle for the pictures or the clock, which was now partly hidden in a recess by the window. The wallpaper was peeling in this room too, though not as badly as in the damp bedroom, and the floor wouldn't come clean no matter how much Pearl scrubbed.

Jack read the newspaper, humphing to himself every so often, but never sharing his thoughts. There didn't seem to be anything to say. The Carew Street house was lost. She was mending, Jack was reading. It was just as before. Except it didn't feel like that. Something had shifted when they moved up the hill. Something had come loose.

The trousers Jack had been wearing when he came home

lay across her lap, showing a tear at the knee. She threaded the needle and pulled the pieces of cloth together, making a lip to stitch and it was done, mended. The trousers would do another day, though the weave was thinning round the tear. She held them up to the light. Soon they would need a patch, but Jack was used to such making do.

He had never had fine clothes. He had barely had clean ones until she married him. Not like Nicholas. She had tried to forget about him for so long but here he was, in the midst of her thoughts and it was wonderful to think of him, but at the same time awful.

He was hard to ignore, liking to cut a dash. Working on shore helped him stay tidy, once the Master took him on. When the great shoals of pilchards came in there was money for everyone, and often a bit of something extra for Nicholas, for the man who tallied the fish and counted out the shares. The clever man who had been a clever boy, reckoning the worth of a shoal while it was still being brought ashore. She saw him standing, face to the sea, watching. The desire to touch him, to cup his cheek and turn his face to hers, burned through her and she was shocked at its force after all this time. But why should the feeling disappear? She had stayed here, stayed the same. The years since she had last been able to touch him made no difference. Her body was old now, but it wasn't beyond this need. It was hers still. She clung to it fiercely.

The hidden clock chimed the hour. Jack burred a gentle snore. The trousers had slipped to the floor and as she bent to pick them up the clock's low ting swelled to a peal. She kept her head lowered. Nicholas's face came clearer. He was turning round, looking away from the sea. There was his long, sloping nose, his thin lips pressed together against the cold. The lamp burned red then went out. The clock chimed on and on.

Three

The bell is ringing from the cliff top and everyone is running. Even people that Pearl thought were too old to run, like Mr Isaac senior, the cooper. He's galloping towards the seafront, using his stick to propel him over the cobbles, his black hat a cormorant bobbing in a sea of clothes.

'Hevva!' shouts Mr Isaac senior. The fishermen rushing to get their seine boats to the water's edge shout it back at him. *Hevva*: they are here. A magic, longed-for word that lets the whole village know pilchards are in sight, and to Pearl it's veined with money.

The first shoal of this season is on its way into Morlanow's waters and the fish are early. There hasn't even been launch day yet, Pearl's favourite day of the year; even better than Christmas. But sometimes the fish are like that, not doing what they're supposed to. Time gets away from Pearl then, without the patterns she's learnt. It's easy to forget.

She's following a group of boys to the seafront to watch the boats being hastily launched. Nicholas and Jack are there, with Timothy Wills and the two Pengelley boys, James and

Stephen, all from school. They're shouting and knocking into one another. She wants to be in the crowd of their excitement but when she comes closer Timothy spins round and shoves her over. 'Go away,' he says. 'You're bad luck.' He has crooked teeth and a wide nose. In the schoolroom he flicks ink at the ceiling when the teacher isn't looking. Pearl would like to push him in the harbour.

She looks to Nicholas but he's looking out to sea, watching the boats, and hasn't noticed her. Jack is pretending to do the same, but she can see the red flush he gets when he's nervous creeping up his neck. He won't talk to her while Timothy's here. She picks herself up and sees dirt slashed across her dress.

She moves away from the boys, back down the harbour wall onto the seafront. As she passes the palace doorway she sees the Master wringing his big square hands. 'An early shoal, ill luck,' he mutters to himself. 'Ill luck to come so early.'

He's a fancy man, a duck-eater, her father says. Born in a big house on the hill near the Tregurtha Hotel. But he works with the fishermen as well as being fancy. Today the Master's wearing a scuffed black hat and a dark blue greatcoat which is buttoned against the rain that always comes with the fish. Pilchards will only come when it rains so Pearl prays for that every night before she goes to sleep.

The Master spies a knot of his women coming out onto the seafront and sets off towards them, waving his hat. Her mother is there, and Polly, and her father's sister Lilly. They see the Master and look as if they might run away, like in a game of chase at school, but it's too late.

'Inside!' he shouts, flapping at them. 'Get inside, my dears, and close your eyes. Here, take my hand, Annie,' he says to Nicholas's mother, catching her wrist and holding on tight. 'I'll guide you.' The other women hold hands and are led to the palace by the Master, their eyes tight shut, making a snake of aprons. 'No more looking,' the Master says. 'You might've cursed us further if you looked at that catch. Fish'll be straight back out to sea.'

Pearl tries to duck behind a hogshead but is too late. A hand grabs her skirts and she's hauled along by the Master. 'You too,' he says.

In they trip beneath the overhanging roof that rings the palace and then across the uncovered centre of the courtyard. There's a cellar at the far end, beyond the rinsing troughs. The Master drives the women down the uneven, slippery steps and locks the trapdoor.

Darkness; except for a few shafts of light that fall through the holes in the trapdoor. The cellar reeks of fish and each mouthful of air tastes like a Saturday catch eaten on a Monday. The walls and floor are wet and the darkness weighs down. It's airless and awful and Pearl needs to get out. Struggling to find the steps leading up to the trapdoor, her feet slip and she falls into cold, dirty water, and begins to cry. Someone takes her hand – she knows by the long plaits that tickle her face that it's Polly, and as her sister whispers to her, the dark loses its deeper shades and the bad air seems to sink away.

'How many fish will Father catch?' asks Polly.

'I don't know.' Pearl sniffs.

'He's going to get a fair few, I should think. Enough to buy you a present.'

'Really?' Pearl says.

'You could have a dress. What colour would you like?'

'I'd like a bathing suit, with red and white stripes. I saw Miss Charles wear one when she went in the sea and Mr Michaels looked at her and he said—'

A cough disrupts them. Pearl recognises it as her mother's

and knows that lusting after bathing suits is wicked, and Miss Charles the art teacher is wicked too, somehow. Polly must realise it as well because she doesn't say anything else, only holds Pearl's hand.

As her eyes adjust to the darkness, Pearl picks out shapes squatting on the puddled floor or leaning against the uneven walls. One apart is Alice Trelawn, her face turned away from the faint light coming through the trapdoor's chinks. No one will work near her in the palace either. Nicholas's mother, Annie, begins a prayer, which the rest of the women join in with, Alice's voice the loudest.

After a while they run out of steam and silence returns. Pearl squats between her mother and Polly and the afternoon creaks on. Her knees grow stiff and her stomach grumbles its hunger.

'Why can't we go out and watch the fish coming in?' she asks. 'I want to see Father shoot the net.'

Her mother eases her fingers through the tangles of Pearl's hair. 'You know we must do as the Master says, however foolish it seems.' The shapes against the walls titter.

Pearl jerks her head away. 'It's not fair. The boys don't have to come down here.'

Somehow in the dark she can hear her mother's smile. 'They say ill luck can be skirted,' she says. 'If shutting us in here gets the fish in then that's what must be done.'

What must be done. The Master is in charge of the harbour, agent for the three Mr Tillotsons who own the mines near Pentreath. They own many seine boats and nets too, and this palace, the biggest in Morlanow. Pearl's never seen the Mr Tillotson brothers. They are a little like God the Father, believed in but not there to look at.

She can't tell how long she's been in the cellar when there is suddenly light and fresh air and the enormous grin of the Master beaming down.

'It's a good one, my girls!' he says. 'It'll be a long night ahead.'

Pearl stumbles up the steps and into the daylight, the women behind pushing her forwards in their hurry to get out. In a flap of aprons and skirts they run shrieking to their stations in the palace. Already, piles of pilchards wait to be bulked: laid into their salted beds before they lose their freshness. Pearl's eyes water with the glare. As they clear, a shape stoops towards her. It's Nicholas, his dark hair lit by the sun and his face glowing with the warmth of his smile.

'Not crying, limpet-legs?'

Pearl shakes her head, wrinkles her nose and blinks hard to dry out his still blurred form.

'I'd guess there's at least fifty hogsheads-worth been enclosed in *Fair Maid*'s net,' he says, 'so nothing to cry about today.'

All around them people hurry, running backwards and forwards, shouting but laughing too. They are smudged to Pearl. Nicholas is the only clear sight.

Her mother calls to her from the spot she has chosen near the rinsing troughs. Reluctantly Pearl leaves Nicholas and joins her, and Polly who's on her hands and knees, spreading salt across the floor. It's Pearl's job to go to and fro between them and the stone tubs of salt that stand near the doorway of the palace. Her mother and Polly mustn't run short of salt, but Pearl mustn't make her chest tight carrying it to them either. As she lugs back her first bucket of the gleaming white grains, she sees Nicholas on the other side of the courtyard, carrying two buckets at a time to where his mother is bent over. Jack is just behind him, struggling to match Nicholas's load, having to drag one bucket forward at a time. He has no mother to keep stocked with salt so he goes wherever he's needed, answering to shouts and waves across the courtyard.

When he's not quick enough getting to Sarah Dray she hurls a pilchard at him and it glances off his cheek. Pearl's mother sighs and shakes her head but everyone else laughs, and Aunt Lilly aims another fish at Jack, making him run to her with his salt bucket.

More and more pilchards are brought inside the palace. As fast as the women can pack them in salt a fresh load arrives. The sea-pebbled floor is soon covered in a scummy soup of brine and scales. Pearl's feet and hems are soaked through even though she tries to avoid the channels that collect the liquid. The farmers will want it to make their crops taller with the goodness of the fish.

The fish themselves are much prettier than their slops, coin-bright. Today's is a good tuck, an unexpected gift, and her mother is up to her arms in the glittering fish, the scales sticking to her skin. The women will work until there are no more, but still pairs of men bring the gurries, gripping the slippery handles front and back, pilchards piled in the trough between them.

Pearl can never believe that the walls of pilchards will grow so high. Her mother and Polly are working opposite old Mrs Pendeen, who is so old her skin is more wrinkles than smooth bits and her hair is whiter than the salt. Her daughter-in-law is called young Mrs Pendeen so people know the difference. Old Mrs Pendeen usually has to be helped to her feet when she's finished in the palace, but her hands are still quick at bulking the fish. She's worked in the palace since Pearl's mother was a child. For a few hours old Mrs Pendeen is there, spreading her salt and talking to Pearl's mother about a Sunday school treat which will happen soon. There's baking to do and old Mrs Pendeen wants Pearl's mother to make hevva cake to celebrate the catch: criss-crossed on top, like a net, but with raisins inside, not pilchards. The layers of fish build up around them. They begin small, a layer of fish laid out on the salted floor in a neat path, one fish deep and three feet wide. Then more layers are built on top, with the outermost layer all fish heads and no tails, so that the palace is full of eyes. Fish and salt. Fish and salt. Pearl goes back and forth between her mother and the salt tubs, winding in and out of the growing walls built by other pairs of women. Her mother and old Mrs Pendeen keep talking but now there's a wall of fish between them so they can't see each other. Their conversation has changed. They're talking about Alice. Even though they don't say her name, Pearl knows it's her.

'Drinking again,' old Mrs Pendeen says.

'I could smell it on her in the cellar,' Pearl's mother says. 'May the Lord lead her back to the one true path.'

Old Mrs Pendeen snorts and packs a handful of salt more firmly than before.

Alice is working in a little patch of her own, as usual. She even has to fetch her own salt. Pearl would like to get some for her but somehow she knows, without it ever being said, that that isn't allowed. Alice must do for herself for the same reason she guts the dogfish. She's not pretty like Sarah Dray, or Aunt Lilly with her small waist and pink cheeks. Alice is short and has a limp from being ill as a child. She can't help that, like Pearl can't help her bad chest, but Alice has no family in Morlanow to care for her. She's not from the village, though no one knows where she came from and why she left there to live in Morlanow. She had a daughter but she died and the preacher wouldn't let her be buried behind chapel with the other graves. Pearl doesn't know where she went. Maybe Alice raised a cairn somewhere. There has to be some kind of stone when you die.

As Alice stoops to and from her bucket of salt Pearl sees the thinness of her arms and the lines of dirt that cross her skin.

Alice stops and looks up, seeing Pearl watching her. Pearl knows she shouldn't be staring. She runs back to her mother and Polly, lumping along her bucket.

At dusk the Master hands round bread and cheese, and everyone in the palace rests for a brief while. The lamps are lit and the fish shine in the flicker. They blink at Pearl. In the lull, she goes outside to clean her lungs of the foul air. She can feel the telltale tightening in her chest, and this is what her mother has told her to do when she's taken bad.

Lamps are lit to mark the way from the palace to the boats and silhouettes dance in and out of the glow. Only the palace women and the children go inside its open ring. She hears her father's voice, and that of Mr Tremain and Mr Polance, Jack and Nicholas's fathers. The seine men have come ashore, the early catch safely in. A crowd has gathered to watch the fish being unloaded. There are artists in their paint-covered clothes, their trousers that stop at their knees, and she recognises Mr Michaels. He is with three other men, some of whom are making sketches, as she has seen them do often all over the village. Miss Charles is talking with the Master, arranging for some fish for the art school, but for drawing rather than eating. The preacher, Mr Taylor, is watching the coming and going of the fish and the men, smiling and nodding his head. There will be a thanksgiving service soon, she knows, once all the fish have been put to bed in the palace. Mr Taylor looks like a fish himself, his face wide and flat as a ray. It looks like his stretched glasses will pop off his nose at any moment.

There are also the few local people who don't work for the Tillotsons, and strangers too – men with pocketbooks and pencils stand near the doorway. The Master goes to talk with them, all smiles now that the catch is his. He speaks to the strangers. Pearl is too far away to hear what is said but the strangers keep nodding and writing things in their pocketbooks. One man, who carries a walking stick even though he is young and doesn't have a limp like Alice, leaves the others and peers into the palace. Instantly Aunt Lilly is in front of him, blocking the way.

'A penny gazey-money, sir? A penny for us fair maids if you want to come in.'

The man looks Lilly up and down, tucking away his pocketbook inside his coat. 'My dear,' he says, 'I have no intention of paying you anything to see inside this filthy place. Kindly move aside.'

Aunt Lilly calls behind her. 'This gentleman's not paid, ladies.' Then she smiles and does as he asks. The man takes a last gulp of clean air and steps forward. A pilchard slaps him square across the jaw. The man with the stick splutters and swears, while his friends roar with laughter. More fish follow before the man has time to retreat. Aunt Lilly sways back inside the palace to hoots and cheers from the women.

There's the sound of them getting to their feet, the rest over. From inside comes a sad song, soft and low, about a boy in a seine boat who is lost.

The corn was in the shock,
And the fish were on the rock,
When the boats went out from Sennen with the pilchard seine;
But the morning broke so fair,
And not a boat was there,
And the lad I loved was with them and he came not back again.

All the women know it and sing to ease the work. Pearl looks for Nicholas in the clumps of people still gathered outside the palace's thick granite walls but she can't see him.

Inside her mother is back on the floor, fixed rigid apart from her hands which dip and dip into the salt. She is cast in a net of gold from the lamp behind her, her face a shadow. Voices float through the ripe air, weaving dark and light across the cobbled floor. They catch the silver and ring off the granite, floating up to the stars through the open roof.

Four

'What on earth's kept you?' Eileen said. 'I was beginning to think you were glad to be rid of me when you moved up the hill.' Eileen steered Pearl to a chair by the shop's counter, which was covered in tins.

'It hasn't been that long, surely,' Pearl said. She sat down and was grateful for the chance to catch her breath. 'We had to unpack, and then there was all that business with Pascoe and the house.'

'I've not see you for weeks,' Eileen said. 'A month, actually.' Pearl was about to protest but Eileen was already bustling about as she usually did, not waiting for a response. 'You sit there. I've got to put these out though why anybody would want to eat them is beyond me. Then we'll have a chat.'

Pearl looked at the tins. Pilchards. The beautiful silver fish squashed into a tiny little box and sealed up. And they'd come from so far away. Africa, it said on the label. The palace was empty. There were no walls of fish. Her mother was dead. And yet the past seemed so real when she remembered, when she let herself remember.

It was cool in the shop and quite pleasant to sit behind the counter and watch the people in the street as they made their way down to the beach. As a little girl she had wanted to work in Pendeen's, to arrange all the hooks and corks, to feel the softness of the cloth piled in bolts to the ceiling. Eileen's shop sold games for the beach and things to put in a picnic hamper. Her grandson pushed an ice cream cart along the seafront in the afternoons. The shop was busy today and several customers interrupted Eileen putting out the tins. A woman came in asking for a guidebook and she and Eileen disappeared to the back of the shop.

Near the door there was a rack of picture postcards. Some were views of Morlanow from the cliff path near the new house and there was a lovely one of the Tregurtha Hotel. Pearl couldn't see any postcards of the fishing boats and certainly none of the palace which was a very ordinary building to look at from the outside – inside was a different world: women, silver, and salt.

A brightly coloured postcard caught her eye. It was printed by the railway company. She recognised the brown and cream. Pearl got up to look at it. 'Morlanow' was written in big, curling letters across the top and underneath, in smaller writing, was 'timeless Cornwall'. The main space of the picture was taken up with a map of the county, with Morlanow and Pentreath marked very clearly, so that their names seemed to fill all the land, and, now that she looked properly, there weren't any more names marked on. The rest of Cornwall was empty. But there were other things on the map. King Arthur was at the top, near the border, clutching a sword and looking stern, and in the sea just off Morlanow there was a mermaid. She had long blonde hair and a silly little smile, perching on a rock and admiring herself in a mirror. A grizzled-looking fisherman beamed at Pearl from one corner of the postcard, his bearded face fat and red. By his side was a full bussa jar of pilchards.

'You can have that one if you like,' Eileen said, coming up behind her.

Pearl shook her head. 'No, thanks.' She moved closer to the doorway and looked out onto the street, her face quickly hot in the sun. She closed her eyes to let that blinding white light come again. She would give in. 'Do you miss the old days, Eileen?' she said.

'What do you mean?'

Pearl heard the rustling of Eileen's skirt and the tins clinking together, but she didn't open her eyes. 'The fishing,' Pearl said. 'When the pilchards came.'

'That was before my time.'

'Was it? It doesn't seem that long ago.'

A hand on her arm, the smell of dust and newness that fought through the shop. 'Come and sit down,' Eileen said, brusque as ever. 'I've made us some lunch.'

They sat behind the counter and shared some smoked fish and bread. Pearl tried to seem keen but she wasn't hungry. In the street the holiday visitors continued to stream past.

'By the time I got here there weren't any pilchards,' Eileen said. 'They'd gone.'

'You've not eaten a fresh one then?'

Eileen shook her head, her mouth full. She swallowed and then said, 'This is good though, this mackerel. And I like the ling your George catches.'

'It's not the same. The taste of them, they were so rich. And the sight of them coming into the bay was like nothing else. All that colour beneath the water, rippling and racing towards us. There was always the worry they'd get away. Nicholas used to...'

Eileen was waiting for her to finish but Pearl couldn't. That was the first time she'd said his name aloud in such a long time that it was like one of Aunt Lilly's charms: Pearl's lips were stitched together by it.

'It wasn't all good though, was it, when the fish were here?' Eileen said. She straightened some boxes on the shelf nearest the counter. 'I heard from my Simon how little food there was, that last summer. And it's harder now than it was then. Your George is out in all weathers fishing and barely gets by.'

Pearl bristled. 'He does all right.'

'Now don't pretend,' Eileen said. 'I know you worry about him. If he'd just take visitors out in his boat like my David does he'd make far more, and he wouldn't be going out to lay his lines at night and in weather he shouldn't risk.'

'He won't stop fishing,' Pearl said. And part of her was glad, even though she knew Eileen meant well, and that she was right, Pearl did worry about George when the weather was bad. But he was a fisherman. That was what he did. There had always been fishermen in Morlanow.

Eileen made a show of straightening a box that was already straight. 'That man you mentioned, Nicholas. I've heard his name before, but not from you.' There was a sly look in her eye, a devilishness that reminded Pearl of Mrs Tiddy.

'Have you?' Pearl said. 'I thought everyone wanted to forget it.' Her breath was thickening and she knew she had to stop it or she'd never get back up the hill. 'Do you believe in keygrims, Eileen?'

Eileen snorted. 'That nonsense? No I don't. You're just trying to stop me asking about things you don't want me to. I know you.' She waggled a finger at Pearl, pretending to tell her off. 'You like your secrets, Pearl, and I'll let you keep them. None of my business and all so long ago it hardly matters now.'

'No,' Pearl said, 'it doesn't matter.'

Eileen opened her till and poked the coins around, checking the change. Each little compartment was so full of coins that Eileen could barely close the till again. 'It's all the railway company anyway, isn't it?' she said.

'What is?'

'Keygrims,' Eileen said, 'and mermaids and all that talk. Though why anyone would want to come on holiday to find a keygrim is beyond me. Isn't the beach enough? And it frightens the children. My Simon was just as bad as the railway company. He'd tell my David and Margaret all sorts of things and they had terrible dreams. Margaret used to wake up screaming there was something in the room with her.'

'That's how they come for you,' Pearl said. 'And then they call you by your name.' But Eileen wasn't listening. A family had come into the shop and she was nodding and smiling as they asked about ice creams.

There were people on the beach below the drying field today, sunning themselves on bright towels, so Pearl went right to the end. Cliff falls had left huge rocks on the beach which offered some privacy. The water came in close. She could take off her dress and get into the sea in an instant.

As she hunkered down behind a rock she saw another cairn. At first it looked like one of the rough heaps of pebbles the sea sometimes left, but then she saw it was a careful pile, just as the last had been. There were flowers poked through this one too. It was in a different place than before, much closer to the cliff, but it was the same.

The cold was such that she gasped but kept on ploughing through the waves. It both soothed and shocked her skin and she realised she'd been sunburnt on her way down to Eileen's. She pushed off the stony bottom and kicked her legs, finding more strength the more she kicked. The years fell away when she swam, as if the effort of each stroke took her further back in time. Perhaps if she swam for long enough she could find the young girl watching Nicholas launch a model boat with a white handkerchief sail, find the fish salted in the palace and her mother singing them to sleep. But there was always Jack to worry about. She never got far enough.

She turned back to look at the shore, bobbing in the water. Jack rarely came to this beach. The retired fishermen liked to cluster by the lifeboat house, all still wearing their jerseys, watched by the holiday visitors. The nets were empty though. The fishermen had nothing to show the visitors. George would be out, far beyond the harbour, on his own on the swell.

She liked to let herself drop every now and then, the water surging round her ears and slopping over her head. She licked the salt from her lips. She couldn't touch the bottom. There were miles and miles of water below her now, she liked to pretend. All that space, dark and cold. And on the sea floor were the wrecks, and with wrecks came the Bucca. Pearl could tell Eileen's Margaret a few more things to scare her.

Five

After supper the lamp is lit. Polly washes the plates in the bucket Pearl has filled from the pump. Polly's plaits keep falling in the water. When she tosses them over her shoulders her shadow on the wall jerks like a fish on a hook.

Her father sits by the hearth and tells them about his day. He has a big beard, which is mostly brown but has red patches, and his face is deeply lined though he's not very old. He smells of tobacco and the sea. His voice is soft – he never shouts. Her mother is the one for shouting. Her father is best at telling stories. On nights he's not at sea she gets one before bedtime prayers. Tonight's story is one she's heard many times before.

'When we're out in deeper water, past the harbour wall,' her father says, 'we know the Bucca's likely to be about. He's a spirit so he's tricky to catch sight of, but if the wind's blowing the right way and you listen very hard, you can hear him coming, crashing around on the seabed beneath you.'

He slaps his hands across his knees to make the noise of the Bucca's lolloping then stops all of a sudden and leans

'The Bucca's not real,' Nicholas says. 'Your father's spinning you a tale, Pearl.'

'My father doesn't tell tales!' she says.

'He does, because there's no such thing as Buccas, or mermaids.' He sees she's growing angry and softens his voice. 'Come on, limpet-legs. They're only stories.'

They watch Alice heaping the bloodied bits of fish into a basket. She looks up, but not at them on the harbour wall. Someone, a man, is walking towards her across the sand. It's Mr Michaels, the artist from the north. He speaks to Alice, though Pearl can't hear what he's saying. Alice nods and then Mr Michaels points towards a building on the seafront. It used to be a loft for keeping nets dry in the winter but now it's loaned as a studio. Miss Charles from the art school uses it for her pupils. Alice wipes her hands on her apron and leans against a rock to rest her bad leg. She's nodding again. Mr Michaels leaves her then and Alice goes back to chopping fish.

'Are we going to Skommow Bay?' Jack asks.

When Pearl goes home for dinner Jack comes with her. Her mother has set a place for him at the table, as she often does. Jack's father is out at sea today, as her own father is, and Nicholas's, but Jack has no mother at home to make his dinner. Pearl's mother does all the cooking in their house, helped by Polly. There are often potatoes and turnips, and eggs from the chickens that live in the yard. Before they eat they say a prayer for full nets and to keep the men safe at sea. Today they have mackerel left from the morning's catch.

Her mother and Polly have been out selling the fish. When her father has unloaded the catch and most has been given to the Master to sell on the seafront, her mother and Polly pack as much as they can carry of what remains into their willow cowals. These baskets sit high on their backs, with shiny leather straps that go on top of their hats to keep each cowal steady. Her mother and Polly sometimes have to walk miles to sell the mackerel; to Govenek, the next village down the cliff path, and the hamlets on its other side, even to Pentreath if no one buys closer to home. On those days each of them returns home with a red band across their forehead, like an angry halo. Today they must have sold well in Morlanow because they're back for dinner. Mackerel sometimes shy away from her father's nets and there is nothing to put in the cowals. The earthenware bussas of pilchards then have to stand many a meal in Pearl's house and in most of Morlanow's. These fish keep everyone fed through the winter and are so important they have two names: Pearl has heard pilchards called 'fair maids'. Other fish are neither boys nor girls, but pilchards are special, and more beautiful. That's why her father's seine boat has the same name.

There are no salted pilchards left from last year's season but the fish from the early catch are nearly ready to be woken from their salted sleep and Pearl's mouth waters at the thought.

After they've eaten Pearl and Jack go to the yard behind her house. Jack's house has the same yard but he doesn't have any chickens. He hangs back while Pearl reaches into the warm straw for eggs.

'You can get them too,' she says. He shakes his head. A chicken comes close to his feet to peck the ground. He gives a shriek and presses himself against the wall.

'They won't hurt you,' she says. 'Watch.' She picks up one of the wriggling, fluttery bodies and puts her arm around its side so that the chicken doesn't mind being held. She loves to feel its heart beating against her own chest. If she had two hearts she might be stronger and allowed to swim more often. After a moment watching to make sure nothing terrible happens, Jack inches forwards and cautiously reaches out a hand. His fingertips graze the chicken's soft, creamy-red feathers. He manages a small smile.

'Jack!' a man's voice shouts, startling the chicken so it squawks and flaps free of Pearl's arms. Its wings are in her face and she cries out, trying to protect herself, unable to see. She's aware of Jack near her, similarly frightened, and when the voice shouts his name again she realises it's not the chicken that scares him. It's his father.

Mr Tremain is looking over the shared wall into her yard. His face is as lined as her father's but it looks like anger on Mr Tremain, while her father just looks tired. Jack's father is dark-haired and with huge furry eyebrows that are frowning now as he looks at the pair of them. 'Get in here,' he says, 'that's woman's work.'

Jack backs away from the chickens and hurries into Pearl's house, without even saying goodbye. Mr Tremain goes inside his house and presently shouts drift into the yard where the chickens are scratching about, calm now. Pearl feels something tickling her cheek near the corner of her mouth. She puts her finger to it and finds blood. The chicken must have scratched her. Before she realises what she's doing she's got blood on her dress. Her mother will shout but it's Jack she's really thinking about. He has no mother to wash his clothes, or to soothe his father's temper.

Six

Jack woke her with a cup of tea and then sat close to her on the bed. He looked like he was trying to say something so she waited, sipping the tea which was too weak but at least he'd tried. There was that dull ache at her temple again. Had she been dreaming? Her face was cut. The chicken squawking. Jack's father shouting. She put her hand to her cheek but it was dry. Nothing.

'You promised that you wouldn't go swimming,' Jack said. His voice was low and he said each word with cold precision. She put the tea on the side table by the bed.

'I haven't. Whatever Mrs Tiddy's been saying—'

His curled hands tightened. 'What's this then?' He gestured to the floor. There was one of her nightdresses, wet and sandy.

'That's from before. I've not been in a long time, weeks. I don't know when.'

'It's still wet, look!' He grabbed the nightdress in a bunched hand and pushed it into her face. The sudden stench of old seawater made her gag and then cough. He didn't wait for her breath to ease like he usually did but shouted over her, 'For God's sake!'

'Don't shout at me,' she managed to say. 'You're just like your father.'

That silenced him. Jack went to the window. Its lean was worse. There was a gap between the sill and the wall at the bottom, and a squeak of fresh air pressed through.

She'd have to placate him somehow or he'd stay at home, keep watching her. He probably had it cooked up with Mrs Tiddy. They were thick as thieves, always had been. 'I didn't go far out anyway,' she said, 'just paddled below the drying field. A wave soaked me.' As she said it, it seemed to come true in her head. It sounded true. Perhaps that was what had happened.

He turned round to face her and he was a child again, afraid of the chickens.

'Come here,' she said and held out her arm. He came and sat down on the bed. His eyes were wet.

'I'm not like him,' he said. 'I'm not.'

'Shh. Don't fret. I bet Mother has left us something for dinner. You can come and eat in my house. He won't shout while Mother's there.'

He pulled away and looked at her as if she was a stranger. But he was the stranger. An old man with hardly any hair and a mouth hanging open in confusion was sitting on her bed. And yet there was something familiar about him too, someone she knew was hiding inside him. The man was getting up and she saw his poor hands were swollen and clenched. He was a fisherman, and then she knew him. Of course she knew him.

'You're not yourself today,' he said.

She laughed. 'Neither are you,' she said. 'Who are we then?' It was a game. But where was Nicholas to join in? She wasn't to mention him. That she knew for certain. Perhaps that was part of the game too. Yes, she'd been playing that game for a long time and she was really good at it. She kept his name safe inside her mouth, felt it on her tongue hot and bad.

'You're not well, Pearl. Can't you see that? You mustn't swim.'

She threw the bedclothes off and struggled to stand. Her head hurt and there was the bright light again, swinging round to dazzle her. Jack was trying to get hold of her, to manhandle her back into bed, but she struggled free. 'Stop telling me what to do! I won't have it any more. I won't!'

'Pearl...'

'You let go of me, Jack Tremain. I'm not yours. Not ever.' She stumbled to the wardrobe and leant her forehead against its good dark wood. She heard Jack mumbling. She turned her face towards him. He was on his knees by the bed, his hands clasped together. His lips were moving but she couldn't hear the prayer. She was far away from him. She was with Nicholas again.

Seven

Pearl's no good at telling the time from the clock's twitching face. She knows when to be home for dinner by the growl in her stomach. She knows when a new week's beginning because Sunday is a day like no other, for sitting quietly and praying, and is followed by washday. For the rest of the week hours nip past her, hiding their seams.

Today Pearl knows that a month must have passed since the early shoal was bulked into walls because the pilchards are ready to be woken up. Their bodies have sipped up as much salt as they can hold so that they won't rot on their long journey across the sea, or before they are eaten here in Morlanow and the rest of Cornwall.

Her mother and Polly go to the palace as soon as it's light, and Pearl joins them once she's fed the chickens and retrieved the eggs from the straw. The palace is nearly as crowded as the day the shoal came in, although there's less hurry today. The hands that bedded the fish with salt now break them out of their quiet rest and sling them in troughs of seawater at the back of the palace. Scales tumble and cover the floor with shining scraps of silver.

Pearl helps carry the clean fish from the troughs to the hogsheads, which are big barrels made just for pilchards. The thick lids are forced down by pressing stones, great boulders taken from the seabed. Today her mother and Polly are working with Aunt Lilly and old Mrs Pendeen to pack the fish. The barrels are the same height as Pearl; you have to have long arms to reach inside them. Everything about Aunt Lilly is tall and slim. When she leans into a hogshead to place fish at the bottom she lifts one leg for balance but she doesn't fall over. She looks graceful, like the herons Pearl has sometimes seen inland, by the river which flows into the sea at Morlanow.

Old Mrs Pendeen is grumbling as she leans over a hogshead, arranging the fish. She definitely doesn't look graceful, swathed in shawls and skirts and aprons, all browns and greys. She looks more like a heap of fishing nets.

'The fish'll spoil at this rate,' she says. 'Why aren't they here?'

'Who?' Pearl's mother asks.

'The children,' old Mrs Pendeen says, giving a fish a hearty thump as it joins the others in the hogshead. 'There's a good few missing. And Alice Trelawn.' Old Mrs Pendeen sniffs. 'Thinks she's too good for honest hard work, when that's what'll bring her back to the Lord.'

Pearl looks around the palace. Old Mrs Pendeen is right. Sarah Dray is missing, and some of the boys too. And Alice.

'Where's Sarah?' her mother asks Polly. But Polly only goes red and doesn't say anything, shaking her head and keeping her eyes fixed on the fish.

Five hogsheads are now filled but they haven't got their lids on yet. Pearl wants to see what the fish inside look like. Her mother and the others move on to the next row of barrels; there are so many more to be filled, and so many fish to be locked inside. Pearl hooks her hands over the top of the barrel's sides and tries to haul herself up, her feet scrabbling against the wood. She can't quite see, though the smell of the fish is thick. Then there are hands under her arms and a chest pressing against her back, lifting her up.

'Here you are, limpet-legs.'

She beams at the fish, picturing Nicholas' face behind her. He smells of cooking: indoor smells, house smells, and his body feels warm against hers. He holds her over the barrel. Her boots knock his shins but he doesn't mind. The pilchards have been packed in circles and the last layer is a star of fish with a centre of tails. The silver is so bright it hurts her eyes. She reaches to lay her hand in the light.

'Get out of it!' shouts young Mrs Pendeen, rushing towards them. Nicholas lowers Pearl to the cobbled floor. She stays close to him. Young Mrs Pendeen is very stern and her arms are thick with muscle from working the press. 'That lot's going to Rome,' she says, 'and the buyer's always looking for a reason to get a better price. You two breaking the scales would be reason enough.'

Pearl and Nicholas back away. She can see he's as ruffled by the telling off as she is. In silence they pick their way through the maze of hogsheads that has replaced the walls of fish. There are oily puddles all around them. At the coopers Mr Isaac senior fashions the barrels with leaky staves on purpose. When the stones are pressed on the lids they force the oil from the fish. It runs into a gutter beneath and collects in the pit.

Nicholas goes over and peers in. She won't go near it. It's deep, set into the floor and full of the thick, foul oil. A square monster which might drink children. She takes a deep breath, grabs Nicholas' hand, and pulls him away, back towards her mother and old Mrs Pendeen.

'Stop pouting, Pearl,' old Mrs Pendeen calls. 'Be thankful

for the Lord's bounty. Lamps of London are lit with that oil.'
Her mother smiles and nods. Polly is looking towards the open
entrance of the palace, not listening.

The thick oil is like the Papists' holy water and most of it
leaves Morlanow just as the pilchards do. Pearl can't imagine
what London is like, or where it might lie. It hangs in her
mind as a grey space, empty but for thousands and thousands
of street lamps sizzling fish oil into the cold night air. The
railway line connects the two places, the great city and its
source of light, but London seems as far away as where the
Papists are, and it takes a ship to get fish to them. She has a
sense of the place the Papists live though. The railway
company pastes pictures at the station. They're brightly
coloured and nice to look at. Nicholas is good at reading. He's
helped her follow the letters underneath the pictures so she
knows that some of the pictures say that Cornwall is the same
as Italy, where the Papists live. That makes it easy to imagine.

Nicholas lets go of her hand and moves to the entrance.
Timothy Wills is standing just outside, gesturing to Nicholas,
asking him to hurry, his eyes flicking between the palace and
the street. His crooked teeth stand out in his nervous smile.
Nicholas looks to where his mother is rinsing fish, her back
to him. He grins and goes over to Timothy. They leave, and
Pearl knows that there's a secret. Something inside her that's
wicked burns to know it, to be with Nicholas and not to be
left out. Polly has seen the boys go too and stands twisting
her filthy apron in her hands. Her mother is walking to the
rinsing troughs, old Mrs Pendeen leaning on her arm. Pearl
runs to catch Nicholas.

The sunlight stuns her for a moment but when she can see
again she spots Nicholas and Timothy further down the
seafront. She goes after them. Polly grabs her hand, pulling
her up short.

'What?' Pearl says. 'Do you know where they're going?'

Polly hesitates, bites her lip. 'Don't go with them,' she says. 'They're going to see a bad thing. We mustn't look.'

Now Pearl wants to know even more. She slips free of Polly's hand and runs to catch Nicholas. She begins to cough but she doesn't care. She has to see what it is. The boys disappear down an alley that cuts from the seafront to the street behind. She follows, her boots slipping on the cobbles. When she reaches the street she sees them on the right, halfway down. They're at the back of the old net loft used by Miss Charles. There's a rickety set of wooden steps to the top floor. Nicholas and Timothy reach the platform that runs the length of the outside wall, joining Jack and James Pengelley. And Sarah Dray, Pearl sees with a stab of jealousy. Why has Pearl been left out of the secret? That's not fair. She's nice to Jack all the time, even when he's being sulky. She told him the story about the Bucca and he didn't tell her about whatever it is that's happening in the net loft, though Sarah Dray is here. Pearl will just have to look for herself, that's all. Keeping secrets is wicked.

Everyone's taking turns to peer in the small window next to the door, trying not to make a sound. Everyone except Jack. He hangs back, closer to the steps. He doesn't meet her eye but curls his hands into fists. She climbs the steps then pushes her way towards the window. James and Timothy move to let her through, too caught up in hushed sniggering. Sarah has her face close to the glass and her hands on each temple to block out the light. Nicholas is doing the same. There's a scrap of sailcloth hanging across the window inside the loft but it has half fallen down and has tears in so if she angles her face she can see into the room.

At first it's difficult to see anything and she wonders what all the fuss is about. There's only white that might be sailcloth. Then she sees that the white is in squares and arranged tidily. Canvases, empty ones. Next to her, Sarah gasps and draws back from the window. Her mouth hangs open and her dark eyes are wide. She puts her hand over her mouth and goes to the other end of the platform, by Jack. Pearl moves to where Sarah was looking, where the sailcloth has fallen. The only sound is gently breaking waves on the other side of the loft.

She can see someone's back, a brown jacket. The figure turns round: it's Mr Michaels. She ducks. When she dares to look again he's only picked up some paint; he didn't see her. He moves forward, towards something, but she can't see what as he's blocking her view. Then he disappears beyond the window and she sees Alice sitting on a chair without a stitch on.

Alice is very still, almost as if she doesn't know Mr Michaels is there. Her thin hair is combed out and sits on her shoulders very prettily, somehow looking more reddish than it usually does. Her cheeks have lost their sallowness and have a flush instead. There's a stove in the corner of the room. Pearl thinks how kind Mr Michaels is to keep Alice warm and then remembers that it's sinful. Alice doesn't have any clothes on and he's looking right at her, all over her. He stands before a big canvas and adds paint to the image of Alice already there, putting shadows across her chest and shoulders. Pearl looks at the real Alice and sees that there *are* shadows there, because she's so thin, but she's not thin all over. Her stomach is very round. She's having a baby.

There's a flash of green movement on the other side of the loft. Pearl angles her head to see better and the green turns out to be Miss Charles' dress. She's standing by her own canvas, painting Alice too, so there are three Alices in the loft. No, more than that. Beyond Miss Charles, at the far end of the loft, are many other pictures of Alice. Alice standing, Alice holding a dogfish, Alice in a tin bath. All these Alices look at Pearl in a way the real Alice doesn't: right in the eye.

'I'm going to tell,' Sarah Dray whispers. Her mouth is set firm but her hands are trembling a little.

Nicholas looks away from the glass for the first time. 'No,' he says. 'You mustn't.'

Jack takes a step forward, as if protecting Sarah from Nicholas' words. 'I'm going to tell, too. It's wicked.'

Timothy and James give great whoops and jump down the steps as if some signal's been given that it's all right to make noise now, that the spell is broken. Jack and Sarah follow them and all four run in the direction of the palace. Pearl wants to stop them but she can't move her feet.

It's only Nicholas and Pearl left on the platform. 'Come on, they'll have heard us,' he says. They go down the steps and into the alley that leads to the seafront. It smells of fish and muck, like the archway under the harbour wall but not as bad. As she thinks this she realises that's where she wants to be. She wants to hide, to get away from the sail loft and the sharp taste in her mouth when she thinks of Alice, and of Sarah Dray going off to tell. She starts walking and Nicholas follows her. They go down the slipway and onto the sand. Under the arch neither of them says anything. They're both waiting. Presently they hear the shouts and the many running feet.

Eight

It was Sunday. She knew where she was. Sunday gave a fixed point in the week with its own rules. She would get straight after today, be more on top of things. She wouldn't let herself get upset again. It did no good. She'd let all this lie a long time ago. Thinking about it, going back – it made her ill. Jack had said so and maybe he was right. She didn't feel herself.

After a sparse breakfast she cleared the table and joined Jack in the room next to the kitchen. He sat opposite her with the Bible open on the table. It was a family copy, passed down through his father's side, the only thing Jack possessed from him. It was bound in black leather, which had split several times across the front. Inside was pasted a tangled list of names and dates. The Tremain record of grief. His father's death was unrecorded.

Usually Jack read aloud but since the other night he'd been sullen with her, though she'd tried her best to be soft with him. The day stretched ahead, long and dull. She couldn't even get on with darning. Any kind of occupation, except preparing the most basic meals, wasn't allowed. He was punishing her today by making her idleness silent. At least George was coming for his supper.

Sundays had been difficult since she and Jack were married. Though she had resented chapel it had made the empty time easier to bear. The morning and evening services framed the slow hours and Jack was better out of the house. Now there was nowhere to go.

Not long after George had left home the chapel was found to need a new roof. She remembered the dampness of the back room from when she was a child, attending Sunday school, and how the clamminess gradually worked its way through the whole building. When she had prayed – a long time ago now – the words always came with that smell: old, fusty, wet. Once the rain had poured through the ceiling in the middle of a service the problem could be ignored no longer. But there hadn't been the money for a new roof. The congregation was too small. So many people had left Morlanow. Those who remained had lost the zealousness that made the building ring with prayer when she was a child. After what happened, the event that even now she shied away from remembering, getting up to get a drink of water rather than think about it, the fire of faith cooled then went out. The chapel was sold to a man from London and only a little fuss was made. In a way it was a relief. Any sense of guilt was gone. The roof was mended but the benches were taken out, new lights went in, and now paintings hung on the walls. You could go in and look, buy something if you had what they were asking. Some of Mr Michaels' pictures appeared from time to time, though never any of Alice. His paintings of the sea were worth a great deal, she'd heard, but she never went to see them.

Jack's hand slipped on the page. He'd fallen into a fretful doze. Pearl went to the window. She breathed on the glass and traced waves in the condensation.

The clock struck three, making her jump. Her hand was on the window, her hip full of ache. She must have been standing there a good while. She left Jack where he was, still sleeping, and went upstairs to get the second best tablecloth from the linen drawer in the box room. She wanted everything ready when George arrived.

Her son had married late, though he was a fine-looking lad. His wife Elizabeth was a Govenek girl who had come down the cliff path one day, looking for work, and had found George at the bottom, sorting his fishing gear, as if he was waiting for her. She had a wan look to her and kept indoors whenever there was hint of a chill. There wasn't enough flesh on her, that was why. She was taller than George and had a kind of childish lankiness to her. She dipped her head when she spoke, like some kind of wading bird, and wore long, baggy dresses Pearl couldn't abide. There were no children yet, but Pearl was still hopeful. Elizabeth was a few years younger than George. On Sundays the couple went to their separate families for supper, if Elizabeth could manage the walk to Govenek. If she was taken bad, George would stay with her at home.

When George did come to supper, both he and Jack made an effort, gripping their knives and forks, and passing the salt and butter a little too quickly. Some meals went well and George would even stay after the table had been cleared. Other times there would be a row and a slammed door before the food was finished.

She took the cloth down to the kitchen and left it on the chair, ready to spread once all the food was prepared. When she opened the drawer to get the boning knife for the fish George would bring, the knife wasn't there. She roused Jack in the other room.

'Have you had the boning knife for something?' she said.

He stretched himself awake. The Bible slipped to the floor. 'No. Why?'

'I can't find it and I'll need it for the fish. You must have had it,' she said.

'Why must I?'

'You know.' The reason had slipped from her but there it was, just slightly tucked away. 'For making the little boat,' she said.

Jack paused as he reached for the fallen book, his head tilted on one side. 'Little boat?' he said. 'What are you on about? The knife must be there, probably right in front of you.' He got to his feet, rolled his shoulders and said, 'I'm going to have a lie down before supper.'

When he had gone, Pearl went to the window again. The sea was just audible, at the very edge of her hearing, and as she listened for it Nicholas was there before her, unbidden and unwanted.

A cry came from above and then Jack's feet were thumping down the stairs. He flew into the front room, clutching the boning knife.

'It was in the bed! And I found *this*—' he thrust the kettle, which was in his other hand, at her face, 'in the wardrobe.'

'Why on earth did you put them there?' she asked him.

Jack stared at her. 'You think I put a knife in the bed? I'm not the one who's been sitting staring out of the window since we got up here, paying no heed to anyone.'

'It wasn't me, Jack!'

'Well, if I didn't do it and neither did you, who did?' He threw the knife and the kettle on to the chair. 'I need to get some air.'

The potatoes were ready to be put on to boil. Pearl furiously pared some green beans to go in another pot. Why would she have taken the knife and the kettle upstairs and hidden them like that? It was ridiculous.

The beans rubbed their coarseness against her palms. She knew she had to slow herself down and be careful with the vegetables, wanting to get them just how George liked. Had to make sure he got a plate that wasn't chipped, as well. Anything to keep him coming to visit now they were away from town, though the mood Jack was in it would hardly be a relaxed evening.

George was born at high tide beneath a full moon, and cried from his first breath as if he knew he had come into the world having already lost something. Pearl gave him enough love to do for her and Jack, who couldn't bear the noise and the steaming piles of washing that soon filled the house on Carew Street, but it was no good. The tears had dried and smiles had come, but George could do no right for Jack.

Jack looked after George though, in his fashion. There was food on the table and Jack taught him to fish as soon as he could hold a line, and later got him a skiff so that he could scull out to deeper water for a bigger catch. Jack lent him his passion too, his comfort on the waves and feeling for the tides. But they often clashed, whether it was to do with the state of a hull or the chance of rain.

Pearl laid the tablecloth and smoothed a ruck. In the first days of their marriage she'd tried her best with Jack. She managed to hold back her tears until he'd put to sea for the day and she could conjure a smile when people in the street asked how she was finding married life. When the baby that followed George passed on, she knew the marriage was only a means of tying her and Jack together. The child didn't see out his first week, and somehow she had known he wouldn't. He came from disappointment and his body was thin with it.

Jack didn't speak of the child after he was buried and George was too young to remember. The lost baby slipped back into the dim gloom he had emerged from, and Pearl was relieved that no more came.

From then on she learned to live with Jack rather than love him. She held him when his sleep was dark with dreams. She folded and put away his clothes. She saw that love couldn't be worked at, but living could. Living aged well, adapting over time, but love left a sting.

George brought a large ling wrapped in newspaper. He sat in the kitchen while Pearl boned the fish. She had readied so many she felt as if half the contents of the sea had passed through her hands. She laid this body down on the scarred wooden board with the tail towards her. It was a large fish and would do for all three of them. One fillet for George and another shared between her and Jack.

George stretched his long legs. 'Keeping all right then, Mother?'

Just the two of them. Sometimes she wondered what life would have been like if she had kept to that, but there was no use wishing.

'Can't complain,' she said. 'How's Elizabeth?'

'She's well. Going to stay with her sister tonight so I'm seeing Matthew later.'

'Oh yes?'

'He's low about that girl he'd taken up with. You know, I told you – the one who's been painting him. Well, she's going home as her lessons at the art school are done.'

Pearl ran the knife behind the ling's head and felt the resistance from the backbone as she sliced through. You had to do it firmly or blood would run everywhere. A clean chop was needed.

'Matthew's always getting attached to those maids and he knows they won't stay,' she said.

'I know but he won't learn. Can't resist a woman who asks to paint him.'

He was a rascally one, Matthew Tiddy. All that switching about and everyone knowing. She wondered what Mrs Tiddy thought of it. Things were that different now. The knife slid the length of the backbone, paring the cool damp body between her hands. Gently steamed, the flesh would fall away from the fork.

'He's worried about his mother,' George said.

'Hm?'

'Have you seen much of her since you got up here?' he said.

'Oh, around and about, you know. She keeps herself to herself and that's fine by me. Mind out while I get the plates. There isn't room to move in here.'

George brought his legs up and straightened on the chair, losing his easy grace in an instant. He was suddenly all angles and seriousness.

'But you've known each other such a long time,' he said.

'It doesn't matter how long I've known that woman,' Pearl said. 'She won't keep her nose out of other people's business and that brings trouble.'

George rubbed a grimy finger against his nose and sighed. 'I don't understand what it is she's done that's so upset you. But then if you won't tell me about the past, how can I?' He slumped in the chair, his dark hair falling across his forehead. 'I been meaning to ask you,' he said. 'Eileen told me—'

'Can you get me that little knife there?'

If you shut a hogshead tight it would make it to Rome without a single fish chipped or bruised. If you sealed the past the same way, nailed down the lid and set a brand, you could save yourself from bruises.

George cleared his throat. 'I spoke to Eileen in the shop and she said you'd mentioned someone. Mother, watch the pan!'

There was steam everywhere and searing heat on her hand. The potatoes were lost in an angry mess of water.

George swung her away from the stove. 'Did you catch yourself?'

'Only a splash,' she said, trying not show how much it hurt.

'Here, get it in the pail. I'll go and get some more water to soak it.' George was cursing Pascoe's failure to get running water as he went out the back door.

By the time George came back Jack had returned from his walk. Pearl did her best to save the potatoes. George's unasked question circled through the steam.

Nine

She knows she can't ask questions about Alice. Her mother yanks the comb through her hair and then forces it into plaits. Because it's Sunday her hair has to try and behave, just as she has to try and not get dirty. That's easier today than on other days. There's no chance to play with Nicholas and Jack on a Sunday. Indoor days keep muck away. Though the back room of chapel smells of wet coats, it's scrubbed so often by Nicholas' mother Annie that there's no dirt hiding, waiting to grime Pearl before she realises.

She's thinking about Alice though. Pearl can feel a question inside her mouth. It has spindly legs and is trying to slip between her lips and get into the room. There would be trouble then. To stop it she hums a tune to herself and concentrates on tying her laces. Polly whirls into the bedroom where Pearl and her mother are. She grabs her good dress from the back of the chair where her mother has laid it ready. Her father shouts from downstairs. They're late for the morning service.

Out onto the street and Pearl has to run to keep up. It's a dry, roasting sort of day with no wind. Soon she's short of breath and rasping. Her eyes water and there's a hot sickness at the back of her throat.

'You go on,' her mother tells her father and Polly. 'We'll catch up.'

Her mother rubs her chest hard, which helps but hurts at the same time. They're by the steps to the net loft Miss Charles uses. Pearl doesn't want to go near them but she hasn't got her breath back to say. Her mother sits her on the bottom step and Pearl leans her head against the rail.

Her mother tuts. 'Just look at your boots,' she says. 'You've not been out of the house five minutes.' The laces have untied themselves and trailed in something muddy. While her mother tuts some more and fusses with them, Pearl looks up at the landing. The door to the net loft is half hanging off the frame, the wood next to the lock splintered. Where has Mr Michaels gone, and Miss Charles?

'Better now?' her mother says. Pearl's not sure if she means the laces or her chest but she nods anyway. She doesn't want to stay here any longer. Her mother takes her hand and together they walk down the street towards chapel. At the end they turn right, away from the sea, and go up a steep hill. The chapel looks down over the village, its windows eager eyes to watch them all. Pearl's mother carries her, to rest her chest, though she's too big for that really. Pearl feels like a giant, her head and shoulders far above her mother's. Her mother puts her down at the doorway and Pearl has a clear view of the sea. But there's something wrong. The sea is dotted with boats. That can't be right. It's Sunday, isn't it? She's standing outside chapel. Unless this is a dream and she's actually still in bed, still to have her hair combed. But then she realises it isn't a dream because her mother is looking too and has tightened her hand on Pearl's shoulder, so much it almost hurts and you don't feel that in a dream.

She's going to ask who's fishing on a Sunday but when she sees how pale her mother has gone and the look in her eyes Pearl realises that isn't a good question to ask either. Her mother remembers chapel then and they go in, though she seems distant, distracted. She even forgets that Pearl has to go to the Sunday school room first rather than the main room, leading her into the grown up service instead.

Mr Taylor the preacher leans his wide face low over the wood, sweeping his gaze across the whole village. Alice is in the front pew, pinned between old Mrs Pendeen and Mr Taylor's wife who is very fat and will only wear brown dresses. She reminds Pearl of a boat. Alice looks so small between them, her shoulders hunched and her head lowered.

On Sundays Mr Taylor's words are bright with fire. Often he preaches against entertaining superstitious fantasies, like leaving a bit of the catch when the boats are unloaded for the Bucca to eat when no one's looking. Then the fishermen lower their heads, letting Mr Taylor's sternness fall on them, but on Monday evening when the boats return from the day's fishing several morsels of mackerel will be tucked under a stone on the harbour steps, to keep the shoals close to Morlanow. But today Mr Taylor is talking about a different kind of sin.

'In the Book of Hosea doesn't the Lord tell us what befalls the tribe who bear children out of wedlock? Doesn't he tell us that the crop will fail, that the fields will be barren? That sin will strike the earth and cause hunger?' People murmur back to Mr Taylor. He takes a moment to gather breath and to shove his glasses up his nose though they slip right down again. Her mother pushes her into the nearest pew. Its wood is cool against the backs of her legs. She can't see where her father and Polly are; Polly's old enough now not to go to Sunday school. Mr Tremain and Mr Polance are in the pew in front. The Master doesn't come to chapel. He goes to the church that the Mr Tillotsons go to, back inland.

'We will all suffer for the sins of one,' Mr Taylor says. 'For turning a blind eye to that which breaks the Lord's covenant.' At this the murmur is louder, proper words agreeing with Mr Taylor, saying aye, aye. He points at Alice and looks just like the picture of God in the book Nicholas' mother has in Sunday school, when God strikes down something bad Pearl has forgotten: eyes wide and staring, head leant back and cross-looking. 'This!' says Mr Taylor, 'is the sin that will corrupt us all. Have we not our own fields, is not the sea a pasture plentiful with the Lord's bounty? We must hold steadfast against sin. We must hold firm in our devotion to the Lord.'

'Amen,' says everyone, very loud now, some people shouting. Her mother's eyes are closed and her hands are clasped together so tight her fingers are white. Pearl can't see Alice but she imagines she will have shrunk down to the size of a cat, or something even smaller, to escape Mr Taylor's gaze and everyone else telling her how bad she is.

'And we will know who met this woman in sin, whose seed has defiled the Lord without His blessing of marriage. We will bring them together in God's love and see that they are properly joined.'

'Amen,' everyone says again, but quieter now. Heads are turned, just enough to see other people without showing they're looking.

'We see the power of such sin already, don't we?' Mr Taylor says. 'Govenek's men have turned their back on the Lord to fish on his day of rest, on the holy Sabbath. Wickedness has come to our waters, my brothers and sisters, as well as in our midst in God's house.'

So that's who is fishing today. Men from the east coast

come sometimes to unload in the harbour on Sundays if the weather's bad. But that's different because they come from far away. Govenek is only a little way down the cliff path, Morlanow's neighbour really. Pearl knows she's meant to love thy neighbour but she can't if they're back-sliders. Bad things will happen to them. Inland from Morlanow, far back from the cliffs, beyond even the mines belonging to the absent Mr Tillotsons, is a circle of tall stones. Except they're not really stones. The tilted blocks of granite are girls turned to rock for dancing on a Sunday. Pearl remembers these poor, foolish girls in her prayers, feeling the wind whistle through her bones as she does so.

There are some hymns then, sung much louder than normal, with everyone trying very hard to be louder than the person next to them. Loudest of all is Mr Taylor's wife whose voice is shrill and rushes the words before they're meant to be sung. Pearl's glad she's all the way at the front but feels sorry for Alice who will have to hear Mrs Taylor close up.

Nicholas' mother brings in the Sunday school then. The children troop between the pews to a space saved near the front. Her mother seems to have forgotten Pearl isn't with the others. She enjoys the astonished looks from the children who see she doesn't have to sit with them, that she's with the grown-ups instead. Sarah Dray looks really cross which is best of all. Then the service is over. It's time to go home for an early dinner before the afternoon service. She hopes it's pilchards for dinner. Sundays are better when pilchards lie between visits to chapel.

Ten

She hears the scrape of something heavy dragged across floorboards and the creak as it catches on a nail. The net is vast, a rusty weave that spills and spreads across the floor like blood. A rough hand reaches down and frees it from the snag then gathers it to hold better. There's laughing and a flash of metal in the hand – a needle darting in and out of the net faster than breath. A song begins and the women lift their voices to the beams.

The corn was in the shock,
And the fish were on the rock,
When the boats went out from Sennen with the pilchard seine,

A bell rings. The singing grows fainter. The net lies forgotten on the floor.

Pearl was hooked back to the yard by the distant peal of the town clock striking midday. Her hands were bound up with the second best cloth in the pail. But where her thoughts had been, she couldn't be sure – the door had closed again and the net was gone. A sea mist was seeping inside her, hiding some things, but making others loom with an unearthly clarity. She shook her head to dispel it and the solid edges of the house righted themselves. There was the back door, the glass in the window.

And the cloth in her hands? There was a stain. That was why she was washing it. George, getting up from the table a little too quickly, had knocked the butter dish. That was yesterday, Sunday. It was Monday morning now, though she felt as if a week had passed since the three of them sat down to a supper of ling.

Here was the proof though. She held the cloth up to the sun to better see the grease. It didn't seem to be shifting. She wrung the cloth as dry as she could then hung it on some gorse. It was hot again. No clouds, the air dry and crisp. She tipped the greasy water away and went to the tap for some fresh. The water took a while to come through, the pipe shuddering with effort. She would only half fill it. It was far too heavy full. Finally water sputtered out. She cupped her hands and brought them to her lips. It was good, earthy. She splashed her face then doused herself with more, tipping it over her head so drops teemed from her face, her hair. She needed a swim.

The front of her dress was soaked and her knees muddy where the water had softened the ground she knelt on. She eased herself to her feet and carried the bucket inside, then went to the front of the house where she could see the sea. It was crowded with boats. A good day for trips round the bay, she'd imagine. Eileen's David would be making a fortune. And George? He'd be out too, but only hoping for something on the end of a line. The beach below the seafront was full too: she could see the specks of brightly coloured towels and umbrellas from here. Another glorious day for the visitors. Morlanow packed tight as a hogshead.

It would soon change though. The visitors would leave until the season rolled around again next year, with only the hardiest artists staying on to face the winter's storms. The train would call less often and the station buildings would be closed half the week. Whoever the railway company had taken on to replace Mrs Tiddy as the cleaner would be laid off until Easter. The brass bell that announced the train's arrival would tarnish. The chocolate and cream paint on the doors and window frames would be allowed to flake from the wood. The flower tubs would hold dry stalks, then just earth, then dust. The posters would peel from their boards and become rubbish blowing across the tracks. She would do her shopping and not see another soul from one street to the next. Most of the cottages near the seafront would be empty, cobwebs forming on the insides of the windows and no one to brush them away. Her own house on Carew Street could be one of them: no one there and still she'd be locked out. The sea would remember its strength and build into tumbling walls, foaming slate-grey and bruised against Morlanow.

Busy for a while yet though and she had shopping to get in. George had asked if she wanted anything but with the weather so fine he would be fishing all hours and would have had to send it up the hill with Elizabeth. Pearl didn't want to trouble her, given her frailness. Plus it was hard to find things to say to the girl that didn't sound as if Pearl was criticising her in some way. Everything she said to Elizabeth seemed to come out wrong. It was no good asking Jack to do the shopping. He said it was woman's work. He never got the right things anyway. She would have to go down to town, brave the crowds, and the scenes that kept playing in her head. Nicholas was in the town. He was waiting for her.

*

The work on the fishing quarter meant that several streets were closed. Looking over the wooden barrier erected close to Eileen's shop she saw a group of men bringing down a wall. She recognised most of them as local boys, some from Govenek. The figure nearest her wore a red shirt, the back of which was dark with sweat, but the front was white with stone dust. He turned round and looked at her. His face was powdered too, shell-white. He was walking towards her. 'Mrs Tremain,' he said. Her stomach lurched. She tried to back away but there were people behind her. A young woman banged into Pearl's side with a shopping bag and her breath was knocked out of her. The keygrim was looming over her. It would drag her to the sea. It had hold of her arm. 'Mrs Tremain?'

The shell slipped. A face appeared. Dark brown eyes she recognised. That crooked nose. The beard. It was Matthew Tiddy. She realised she'd been holding her breath and took a few big lungfuls of air before murmuring a hello. He stayed by her side, asked how she was keeping. He was a good lad, she had to give Mrs Tiddy that.

'We're hard at it today,' Matthew said. 'This wall was supposed to be down by last week.'

'I can see,' she said. 'Hot work, I should think. Why aren't you setting your pots? Weather like this, lobsters will be good.'

Matthew shrugged. Another man by the wall, cleaner-looking, in charge she guessed, signalled to Matthew to come back to work.

'Wages are better,' Matthew said. 'Railway company's given Pascoe good money for the labour, to get the streets widened before work starts on the palace. If we can find enough men.'

She nodded, then said, 'You'd best get back.' He smiled and turned away, dusting the granite's powder from his hands. She watched for a minute or two more, then turned down an alleyway to get round the closed street. When she came out scaffolding leaned over and forced her into the middle of the crowds. She was carried along by their motion but couldn't remember where she was headed.

She slowed her pace and looked about her, coming to a halt in front of a gift shop. Hadn't this once been part of the coopers? She was certain she remembered hogsheads lined up here, by the door, waiting to be taken to the palace two streets away, but she couldn't get the map of the village clear in her head. Town, she corrected herself. It was changing, shifting its streets, closing off its alleys, but Pearl breathed deeply and could smell sawdust.

In the window of the gift shop a flotilla of model boats was riding a blue piece of cloth serving for the sea. They were crudely made. Even from the street Pearl could see the black paint didn't properly cover all the wood. A small sign was propped in front: *Morlanow seine boats*. That was pushing it. The toys' hulls were the right colour for seine boats but they had masts and the red sails of luggers.

Two boys came to the window, knocking Pearl out of the way to get close to the glass, pointing at the boats. She moved on. There was warmth at her temples again. Not a headache exactly, more like she was frowning and couldn't release the tension. It was the heat, the lack of air in the streets, the hammering from the building work.

As she neared the seafront dozens of gulls wheeled over the sea. They were disturbed by the clamour in town, she imagined, unable to get to the visitors that fed them or the chimney pots where some roosted. They were seen as a menace now, diving for the food in your hand and leaving their mess on the smart new benches. There was talk of thinning their numbers. Her father had told her that seagulls should never be driven away because they held the souls of lost sailors, letting them fly back across the world to their loved ones. They were much more pleasant than keygrims, even if they did snatch a bit here and there.

Pearl forced herself not to look at the birds and to keep walking, her head down. She came onto the seafront. Even now, after all this time, the space still appeared unexpectedly after the close confines of the streets. At the corner she saw Eileen's David touting for customers to take pleasure trips up the coast. He was short with sandy hair usually in need of a cut. He had on some smart trousers, new-looking, and some shiny boots too.

Below her, the bay's sand lay in ridges. Boats lounged, asleep in the midday sun with their tarpaulins pulled up like bedding. Behind them, the sea glimmered and the lighthouse stood tall beyond the far cliff, the sunlight catching the glass so the lamp appeared lit. At the other end of the seafront, scaffolding was climbing the walls of the only remaining pilchard palace. It was the first time she had seen it since Pascoe's scheme was announced.

In the best years, before the fish disappeared, there had been four palaces in Morlanow filled with fish and hurrying, tired women all through the summer and into autumn. The other three had been demolished or converted to flats many years since. The last remaining, owned by the Tillotsons and managed by the Master, was the largest, but even this had been empty for such a long time. Was that reason enough to make it a hotel? It was true, no pilchards had been netted in Morlanow's waters for years and many of the fishing families gave over their net lofts to the artists to use as studios even before the fish disappeared. When the artists began to thin, just as the fish had done, the holiday visitors took their place. Pearl could never blame those who turned over the lofts. The money from the rent was more than they would ever earn by fishing, and it was regular – there were no years when people came close to starving. Every family could count up their plots in the graveyard. By renting out the lofts the men were safe, and was it so wrong to be curled in bed while the wind raked up the waves?

Eileen had said that as the hotel was built, water pipes would be laid on to the whole town, and that the gas board was to connect all the houses still without a supply. And the hotel would bring work too. Just as when chapel was sold, there weren't many who would raise a fuss about the palace, though Jack thought it was a step too far. That wasn't a surprise though. He'd caused such trouble in the past when change had come. Nicholas would have understood. He looked ahead. He made you believe him; believe in all sorts of things.

Pearl walked to the palace and stopped opposite its thick walls. The strong shape appeared to be sagging under the tarpaulin. Scaffold poles pinched the sides like ticks on a dog. She wiped her eyes and could almost hear Nicholas telling her to pull herself together. It was only a building, after all. But it was more than that. It was everything that had happened inside its walls.

She leant against the seafront railings. The warmth at her temples grew hotter. There was burning across her forehead now. The sunlight was too bright. She closed her eyes against the sight of the palace and felt the heat travel to the back of her head, a lake of pain, able to slip and spread. The bustling sounds of the street faded away, replaced by snatches of song seeping up from the sand behind her.

The corn is in the shock,
And the fish are on the rock,
And the golden sun is gleaming on the Islands of the West;
I hear the huer's cry,
And I see the dappled sky,
And my heart is dead with sorrow for the lad I love the best.

It was her mother's voice. With her eyes closed Pearl could
see her sore, red hands deep in nets, running them over her
fingers to find the tears. It was a map, and a place to drown.
Pearl's hands itched to draw the net over her own fingers, like
a cat's cradle, the hemp rough as a cat's tongue. She would
drag the sprawling weight across her arm so that it streaked
a burn. The sting, hot and bright, would be comforting. It
would coil her forearm and she imagined the twisted length
around her, pulling her down.

She tried to open her eyes. After a moment when she felt the
lids flutter without admitting any light she found she could see.
Nothing had changed, nothing had moved. There was no song,
only the chatter of the visitors and the noise of the workmen.
She turned round to see the beach. There were plenty of people
but her mother wasn't there. She quickly scanned the sand,
trying to make her out in the crowds. She had been there, she
was there. Pearl caught her breath. Her mother was dead. The
loss was almost as great in that moment of remembering as the
day her mother had died, at home in her bed, her thin hands
clutching the bedding, asking again for Polly who had been gone
years before that. Why were these things coming back to her in
this way? What cruelty made the dead breathe and come singing
for her on the seafront?

People continued walking along the road that separated her
from the palace, clutching bags of shopping, ice creams, one

or two with sketchbooks. Her hands were clamped onto the railings and as she tried to let go she felt that her chest was fired with bubbles and a coughing fit came. She managed the few steps back along the seafront to the slipway and went down onto the sand, then through the arch in the harbour wall, picking a path across heaps of fly-flecked seaweed and rubbish, onto the clean sand beyond. The drying field sloped up on her left. Skommow Bay and its wrecks were on the field's other side. With each pace away from the palace Pearl felt stronger.

The beach stretched on, the cliff at the far end standing sentry as if to say *no way out, no way past*. Pearl picked up the tide line she so habitually followed, a path that led nowhere.

Her mother was dead. That she knew for certain. She'd watched her go into the ground and her father too, once his body had been washed up. Polly, she'd heard in a letter, had been hit by a motor car while seeing the children to school, eight years after leaving Morlanow. She knew that each of them was gone and safely laid to rest. The curse was not knowing, thinking someone might come back. Nicholas could be a king with a court of women. He could be at sea on his own ship, standing proud at the tiller. He could be lying beneath the soil of No Man's Land. Despite the sun Pearl shivered but let that idea come. It hurt, but it was a way of getting on, of balancing out the other daydreams. It had been easier when she believed in a heaven for him to go to.

She wound her way with the tide line's trail of debris, all the wreckage the sea scattered along the beach. From the wall of her eye she spied another little tower of stones in the grass escaping from the drying field onto the sand. It was a different cairn, closer to the harbour wall than the first she had seen, and taller than the second by the cliffs. Blue stems of bugloss were poked in this one too. The sea would always claim the living, whether calling them to the cold, dark floor or to other places, far away. It rarely brought anyone home.

Eleven

Jack lent back in his chair. He was wearing an old smock of her father's, worn to protect him from the sun when he spent days at sea, waiting for the pilchards to arrive. He'd be going out again soon, now the tide was turning, and she would lie awake and think of him there, bobbing in his boat, his hands itching to cast the net round that silver struggle. He was already imagining holding it, his hands curled, not wanting to let go.

She was rubbing his clenched hands the way her mother had rubbed her chest. It wasn't so much the action that eased pain, the movement of your hands, but the care you held in them. She was finding it hard to concentrate. The care was missing from her fingertips.

'Here now, stop,' he said. 'It won't be any use. The heat's too much.'

He could feel her lack of care. He knew. She should busy herself with something. There was a net to check. The tide was turning. Her father was getting ready to go. Why was he looking at her like that?

'You must be tired,' he said.

'Why must I?' He was going to tell her she couldn't go swimming and she wanted to go so badly. Nicholas was waiting for her by the harbour wall.

'You were down in town,' he said. 'I saw you, by the palace.'

He'd been watching her. Perhaps he'd seen her mother too. Perhaps he knew where she went. Pearl didn't like to ask though. Questions got her into trouble. The asking and the being asked. She'd been silent for so long.

'They can't get the lorry down to the front,' he said, trying to uncurl his hands again. 'Pascoe was blowing his top first thing this morning when he realised. Fool that he is. You'd think he'd know the width of the streets. He's been here all his life.'

Jack's voice swung in and out of quietness, an echo of an echo, thinning as Pearl tried to concentrate. The sight of the palace, wrapped in tarpaulin bandages, sat unshakeable in her thoughts. In its doorway was a shadow she didn't want to see.

'Did you see it?' Jack's words turned the shadow to dust and the palace crumbled with it. The light had faded though the kitchen still swam with the day's warmth. There was a plate of food in front of her. A piece of potato was speared on her fork but the rest was untouched.

'Did I see what?' she said. He was trying to trick her.

'Did you see the lorry, stuck on the corner by Eileen's place?'

She shook her head and was clearer then. 'I didn't hang about,' she said. 'Had shopping to get in.'

She went to bed early but couldn't sleep. It was still so warm and September nearly over too. The month had run its course quickly. Time wasn't behaving as it should. Days were ducking past her, shying from their usual order so that as she looked back over the last week there were holes. Clocks didn't seem to be truthful. She decided to keep to the moon instead. She got out of bed and went to the window. The moon was still new, showing the barest sliver of white.

Swimming would ease all this slipperiness, she was sure. The sea taking each limb and smoothing her out. The sea would send Nicholas away. But swimming was forbidden and gossip still found its way to those it shouldn't. Mrs Tiddy, for one, would let Jack know if Pearl swam. *I'm only thinking of you. It's for your own good.* She had thought of going at night but knew that was foolish. Bickering currents dogged the coast and in the dark it wouldn't be easy to get back to shore and escape them. She had to make do as best she could.

The next morning, when Jack had gone, Pearl took out all the sheets and spread them on the kitchen floor where there was most space, making a sea of cotton to swim in. She lay down on the sheets and when she closed her eyes and let each muscle go slack they felt as if they held the memory of water. Then sense came to her.

There was something to be got at, some re-arranging of things she couldn't quite see. The song she kept hearing, the people returning – all of it at the root of her. It was in her blood.

Aunt Lilly had been known as a pellar, a woman of foresight. She knew the weather before it came and could charm a cow back from sickness. No one crossed her, not even old Mrs Pendeen and her sharp tongue. There were stories that Lilly's mother, Pearl's grandmother, had helped a mermaid back into the sea when she became stranded by the tide. Payment was a coral comb and the power of sight for the women of that family. It didn't always come into the flesh of the bearer, but it was carried all the same. Perhaps now her blood was charged with it. Perhaps she was ready to see the truth.

She rolled onto her front, stretched her arms above her head and flexed her fingers. The linen bunched and gave under her strokes. A warm sea. September, full of waiting. There were many ways to see a place and to read its secrets.

Twelve

She struggles with the buttons on her dress. Her mother has said not to pull or they'll come away, so Pearl asks Nicholas to help. Sarah Dray and Polly are sitting on the harbour wall. They always used to swim with the boys like she does, getting down to their drawers and jumping through the waves. But they won't this summer. It's to do with being older, like how Polly's body looks more like her mother's now than Pearl's, all rounded out. As Nicholas undoes her buttons he stands very close to her and sticks the tip of his tongue between his lips, concentrating. His dark brown hair is long and smells of salt water. He has a small cut on his forehead that's not scabbed yet. There's a bead of blood bright in the sun. She wants to put her finger to it, and to push his hair out of his eyes.

Jack's shy about undressing. He stands with his back to them, taking his time with his shirt. He looks longingly at the wooden beach huts that have appeared at the other end of the sand, separate from where Morlanow's children bathe. The artists go in, one at a time, and come out showing flesh as white as the underside of a ray.

As soon as the last button slips from his fingers, Nicholas dashes over to the harbour wall. Pearl hears the splash as he jumps into the sea. Polly and Sarah cheer. She doesn't wait for Jack. He will prefer it if she leaves him to get undressed and slip into the water unseen.

Most of Morlanow's boats are away at the fishing grounds, the weather being so good. Any left at home are bobbing a little way off shore where the water deepens, their familiar shapes marking a line that the children are not to swim past. This is the only stretch of the sea that's allowed for swimming as the currents here aren't angry. Pearl has had to promise her mother that she won't ever swim on her own and that she won't swim past the boats. The sea is only waiting for the chance to keep her for itself.

She lowers herself onto the warmed sand below the seafront. She doesn't like to jump into the sea from the harbour wall like Nicholas does. That way the moment of getting into the water is over too quickly. The sand burns her feet so she runs to the water and plunges in, her legs working to keep her moving forward until she is far enough out to kick off the bottom and swim. The sea cloaks Pearl in its shivery silk, making her arms goosey with the cold and her own delight. It knows the shape of her body, the way her shoulders curve, the pits at the backs of her knees, and it slips itself around her, holding her firm. They have a way of being together which no one else understands. Not even Nicholas. The waves are her friends and her terrors. They love her but they might carry her down to their depths, far below, where nets can't reach. She knows the sea isn't to be trusted, even when the waves are as low and beautiful as they are today.

Pearl dips her head. The water pours from her face, leaving its taste on her lips. She pushes through, savouring the softness tugging her. Her chest is better when she swims.

Her mother doesn't believe her, says it can't be so and that swimming is a treat, not medicine. There are never enough days when it's thought warm enough for Pearl to swim. In the summer, she wakes every morning still full of dreams of the sea, her legs fired from imaginary strokes, hoping she'll be allowed to swim again. Today is one of these longed for days.

Nicholas is jumping from the harbour wall and showing off. His body steals the sunshine as it cuts through the air, sleek and wet with light. Pearl treads water halfway along the length of the wall, watching. He swims for the ladder as soon as he has landed, climbing back onto the wall to jump again. Jack's almost white mop of hair moves slowly through the water. He prefers to be safe in a boat above the waves rather than caught up in them.

Another splash. The water rises around Pearl, lifting her higher. Nicholas bobs up and flicks back his head, scattering drops that glint like torn fish scales on the palace floor. He grins at her then turns and goes to the ladder again. He stops to talk to Polly and Sarah Dray. Sarah laughs and tosses her hair. Pearl can see she's pouting even from this distance. Nicholas doesn't care about Sarah, he cares only for the sea, and runs and jumps again. He's a good swimmer. His arms arc high and cut through the water as if it's sea mist, but he doesn't love swimming as Pearl does. He's good at it, much better than Jack, but he doesn't need it. She wonders if there's anything Nicholas needs.

In bed that night, Pearl goes to sleep with her nose jammed into the warm crook of her elbow, savouring the smell of the sea. She dreams she's swimming. There's a swish of movement far ahead and she knows it's the pilchard shoal, silver tails beating in time with her heart.

Her mother insists on a bath in the morning, even though it isn't Sunday. It takes Pearl a few moments to remember what's special about today, her thoughts still swept along by the shoal of sleep. Then she knows: launch day.

The precious trace of the sea, locked inside Pearl's skin, is scrubbed away. She's tucked, unwillingly, into her chapel dress; the dark blue one with puffed sleeves and a thick, white pinafore over the top. A brush is dragged through her tangles and Polly braids Pearl's hair so tightly that the front of her head aches.

They walk down to the seafront but as soon as her mother and Polly turn to talk to Nicholas' mother, Pearl slopes off to Nicholas and Jack, who stand at the edge of the seafront. The Temperance band is perched over on the harbour wall, tooting their hymns. The seafront is crowded with people. All of Morlanow has come to watch the launch of the seine boats. The artists are there too. Mr Michaels is near the palace, talking to Miss Charles and some of the men Pearl remembers seeing the night the early shoal came in. Mr Michaels looks nervously about him. When a group of fishermen walk past, Mr Michaels presses himself into the palace wall and studies his hands. The fishermen look at him, mutter to themselves, but Miss Charles blocks their way, meeting their gaze with her chin raised and her hands on her hips. Her hair is as red as some of the brightest seaweed washed up on the beach below the drying field. Pearl's heard her mother say that's what makes Miss Charles bad-tempered at times, taken to flying into rages. Pearl's only ever seen the nice side of her, the kindness she shows her pupils. She gave Pearl a barley drop just last week.

There are other fishermen come to watch, east coast men with their strange accents and differently knitted jerseys. And fishermen from Govenek too. No one from Morlanow speaks to them.

The Master is walking through the crowds, his Beatrice on his arm in a fine red dress which stands out amongst the dark colours the local women wear. Nicholas looks smart as well, wearing good trousers and a shirt. Jack has a jacket on, though it's small for him: the sleeves don't come far enough down his arms. There's dirt on his collar and his hair isn't brushed.

The tide is halfway out and the sea is behaving itself, as if it knows what will take place on its back today. Luggers are pulled up onto the sand, their stark masts making a forest through the sky. Everyone mills round these boats, making them seem bigger than usual, but they're forgotten giants. No one has come to see them. The few local fishermen who aren't seine men stand on the seafront and smoke, watching the children. The band takes a break between songs and some people have ices. There's a sudden cheer from the other side of the road.

The first seine boat is on its way down to the beach. Six men carry the broad, black boat, the seine net spilling its webby legs over the sides. The band quickly hands over their ices to the crowd and the hymns begin again.

Forth in thy name, O Lord, I go,
My daily labour to pursue,
Thee, only thee, resolved to know,
In all I think, or speak, or do.

A cluster of children flock to the boat's side and escort it down to the water's edge, clapping their hands and skipping and jumping and cheering.

From all directions, from alleys and yards, seine boats are appearing. They've been tucked up safe, kept from any hint of water that would make their timbers swell, or mice that might chew through their nets. The boats have been waiting to get back to the sea, and now the village has come to welcome them. Here is her father's boat. He's carrying her with Nicholas and Jack's fathers too. When she reaches the edge of the water the men set her down. Pearl's father turns, straightens his back with a groan, then picks Pearl up and puts her in the boat.

The boat smells of grease and rope and most of all fish but she doesn't mind. Jack tries to climb in by himself but his father gives him a rough push over the side. Then with a *one two three* the men shove the boat out deep enough that she'll float. Nicholas stays on the sand to help them, rather than climbing in to the boat, his feet skidding as he pushes against the weight. Once in the water, Pearl can feel the boat's nervousness. She tilts, unsteady, having to find her way again. Pearl feels like that when she hasn't swum for a time.

The boat rights. She slides her keel into the water and sits comfortably, like a hen on a nest. Nicholas climbs in. Pearl spots her mother and Polly on the front and stands up to wave, making the boat rock again. Jack and Nicholas are fighting over the oars. Her father holds up a hand.

'Whoa, whoa. Not heading out just yet, boys. Give us a chance to see if she's fit.'

The men have waded out with the boat, just a few feet, to check if any water is slipping through her caulked skin, if she has aged too much in her sleep. They run their hands over her, her father talking to her in a soft voice.

'There now,' he says. 'You're all right, aren't you? Yes.' He pats her. 'You're fit to go.' He turns to the front and makes a yes sign to the Master who nods and goes back to talking to his scarlet Beatrice.

More and more boats have come to the sea, each one with children climbing and falling and splashing into, over and under them. Some are jumping from the boats to swim, paddling alongside and clambering back in again. Her mother has said yes to two days swimming in a row, only because it's a special day. But for the moment Pearl's happy just to watch the other children. The season has begun and the sun is warm on her arms. Jack and Nicholas are pretending to row, spotting imaginary shoals, and her father is smiling down at Pearl, saying yes, yes, you're a good girl.

Thirteen

There was nothing to be learnt in the house at *Wave Crest*. It was too new, too far away from the sea to show her what it was that was happening. The shift she could feel, the sense of Morlanow's past slipping free of the mooring rope that had held it firm for so long, was better seen outside. She needed to be away from the new house's damp and flaking plaster, the smoking stove. Its shrouding gloom.

She waited until Mrs Tiddy had finished hanging her washing in the yard and had gone inside. Easing the front door closed behind her as softly as she could, Pearl made her way towards the cliff path. It was no good though. She heard a door open. Mrs Tiddy had been waiting.

'Morning,' Mrs Tiddy called.

Pearl hesitated, wanting to pretend she hadn't heard but that would only cause trouble. Mrs Tiddy would be filling Jack's ear with nonsense, make him shout at her and stay at home, stop her from getting out and close to the sea. She turned round.

'Morning,' she said.

'Another fine day, isn't it?' Mrs Tiddy said. 'Going to see Eileen, are you?' Pearl nodded without thinking. 'Give her my love. And could you get me something? Just some flour. My Matthew's coming for his supper and I want to have some pasties made. Here.' Mrs Tiddy fished in her housecoat pocket and brought out a coin.

Pearl didn't know what to say. She hadn't planned on going into town. The errand would keep Mrs Tiddy from nosing about but now Pearl felt uncertain about the day, her earlier resolve gone. That was Mrs Tiddy's way, upsetting things. Pearl snatched the coin and spun round, striking out for the cliff path. Mrs Tiddy's distantly called goodbye only made her walk faster.

The cliff path led to the abandoned huer's hut where the men had watched for the arrival of pilchards. Here the path split: right, down to Morlanow and the seafront, or left, a mile or so along to Govenek. The neighbouring village was visible from this spot, as was its deep square harbour that appeared huge at low tide, like the remains of some ancient ruined castle. Except it wasn't ancient, not by any stretch.

Govenek was still a village, still small and without a railway station. The buildings were as ugly and industrial as they had been when she was a child, corrugated iron and brick. There was no wide, snaking seafront to stroll along and admire the sea. There were no carts selling ice creams and no shop windows with made-up boats. No visitors went to Govenek. But the narrow bay did contain one treasure: the large fishing fleet was dotted across the water. Pearl looked away.

Beyond the huer's hut stretched flat grazing land where a group of sheep pulled at the grass and bleated their contentment. Pearl looked at the horizon, as she had never been able to stop doing. As she turned from the water she saw a dance of white.

Gorse was clumped near the low walls of the hut and between two bushes she saw a small animal run, quick as a blink. Pearl kept her eyes fixed on the spot, willing the shape to show itself again. She clasped her hands together and thought of all the charms Aunt Lilly had used to bring things into view. But it was such a long time since she had heard anyone say them out loud that she couldn't make the sounds that swept through her head into the right words.

As she mumbled and sang all that she could remember of the old charms, the creature came into sight. Pearl stood as still as the huer's hut, making herself part of the cliff, and watched the animal hop forward. The white hare sat, tilted its long face. She couldn't breathe for shock. As rare as true love or gold cut from Cornish ground, a white hare was a message. A teller of storms and a vessel for lost love.

Fourteen

They can't sit on the harbour wall today. There are too many boats unloading. Not pilchards, not yet, but the weather has held so fine that there are plenty of other fish being caught: mackerel, ling, even rays. The east coast men are there, lots of them, come to get their share. It's not just the hustle and bustle that makes the three of them falter in the street by the harbour wall, deciding where to play, but the ill feeling caught up in it. The sideways glances and the short tempers. Even her father is cross as he winds his nets to store in the bottom of his boat, not speaking to either Mr Tremain or Mr Polance, who themselves are frowning and shoving their gear about.

'Let's go to the drying field,' Nicholas says. He starts walking that way without waiting to see if she and Jack follow, but they do, of course. As they pass the open entrance to the palace she hears an uneven trilling coming from inside. Alice is there, in the shade of one of the storage sheds, gutting the dogfish. Her stomach stands out from her dress so you can see the baby even when she has clothes on. She's not allowed to work on the beach, looking like this. Jack grabs Pearl's wrist and hauls her after Nicholas.

On the beach on the other side of the harbour wall they come across Mr Michaels. He's set up his easel to face the sea and is mixing paint in bright whorls on his palette. Jack marches past him, heading straight up the slope to get to the drying field. Pearl stops to look at the canvas. There's only a blue wash on it so far but it's very lovely to look at. Mr Michaels hangs back from them, standing awkwardly on a shelf of pebbles, his hands still now. He looks a little afraid. She thinks he's going to say something but then he decides not to and just looks at them instead.

'Have you got any barley drops?' she asks him.

'Have I got any what? Oh, sweets.' He looks relieved. 'No, no I haven't. Sorry.' He starts mixing his paint again, glancing round at them every so often. She and Nicholas follow Jack up the slope.

Jack seems to have brought the ill feeling with him to the drying field. He tears up the grass and throws it into the slight breeze. Nicholas has carried some pebbles from the beach. He examines the markings on each one – he only picks striking stones – then arranges them in little towers. Every so often he glances down to Skommow Bay on the field's other side, where the broken boats lie, and she's worried he'll go down there, with Jack, leaving her on her own, or, even worse, leaving her alone *with* Jack who's teasey and sharp today.

A story will help. As long as it's not about keygrims. 'Tell us the story about mermaids,' she says to Jack. 'You're always going to and then you never do.'

He uses both hands to tear up a big patch of grass, the soil coming up with it and scattering across his legs. 'I hate mermaids,' he says. 'They eat their babies.'

'No they don't,' she says, feeling suddenly sick. The picture of a mermaid eating her baby is lodged in her head. She can't shake it away. 'They can't do.'

'They love the taste of each other more than they do fish,' Jack says. Nicholas doesn't say anything but smiles as he arranges his stones. 'It's because they're wicked and sinful and go to Hell,' Jack says. He gets up and runs down the hill to Skommow Bay. Nicholas shrugs and follows him. His last tower of stones slides into a heap. They know she doesn't want to go but they don't care. She watches them disappear between two upturned hulls then turns back towards home. Jack can't be right. Aunt Lilly will know.

Pearl finds Aunt Lilly outside her house, hanging rays to dry in the sun. The smell makes Pearl's eyes water and her nose hurt. She tells Lilly what Jack said. Aunt Lilly bends to her knees and looks Pearl straight in the eye. Aunt Lilly sees what others can't.

'Well, my dear, I'm afraid that what young Mr Tremain told you is true, but he's wrong to be scaring you. The people of the sea only eat their young if they've nothing else to hand and the women of that kind, they always have something ready, just like your mother does for your father.'

This doesn't help Pearl at all – would her father eat her if her mother didn't have the fish cooked by supper time? She wants to go home, climb the stairs without anyone noticing, and roll up in bed as small as she can make herself.

The front door's wide open, as it usually is when the weather's hot like this. She doesn't want to see anyone, not least her father. In her head she sees him with a long, scaly tail and teeth made from kitchen knives. But there he is, at the kitchen table, his head in his hands. Pearl waits outside the door. He's meant to be at sea. She saw him getting his gear ready. Is he hungry? Is he here to eat her?

She hears her mother's voice from behind the open door.

'He'll have to marry her,' her mother says. 'You'll have to see to it that he does.'

'He's set firm he won't,' her father says.

'I don't care what he says, he's going to marry Alice and that's the end of it.' Her mother comes into view then, pacing the kitchen and throwing her hands above her head. 'He's leading us all to sin.'

Her father sighs. 'He's been shifty for weeks now. Cut himself with a hook this morning he was so absent-minded. Blood everywhere. When I went to help him he gave me a terrible row and then came clean. He asked her to leave, offered her money – more than he has – but she wouldn't go. Said she'd told Mr Taylor who it was, that she wants to marry Peter.'

Pearl gasps. Peter is Jack's father. Her parents look up and see her. There'll be trouble now for eavesdropping, but instead of shouting her mother only looks sad, tired. She sits down at the table.

'Come here, you sneaking little thing,' her father says, but in a kind voice. 'Jack's going to have a new mother. Isn't that nice for him, eh?'

Alice is Jack's mother? Mr Tremain who lives just next door is the sinner Mr Taylor talked about in chapel? The sick feeling that started on the drying field gets worse and she's cold and shivery too. Alice is going to have a baby that will be Jack's brother or sister but she might eat it, or Mr Tremain more likely because he's always angry and there's never any food in Jack's house. She runs past her parents, up the stairs to her and Polly's room, and buries herself under the blanket. She stays very still for a long time, hoping it will all turn out to be a dream. But she doesn't wake up.

Reaching under the rope mattress on her side of the bed, Pearl's hand searches for the soft parcel of comfort she keeps hidden there. Her fingers close on a pad of fabric just bigger than her palm and she pulls it out. It's a scuffed and blackened calico hare with mismatching bead eyes. She has to keep it hidden because not only would Nicholas tease her but Jack would be sad, and her father might be angry.

Depending on how you come across them, they can bode well or ill, but hares shouldn't be named directly as that's a sure way to curse the day. If they must be mentioned, they're given different names to ward off the ill luck they can bring. Cat of the wood. Dew beater. Stag of the cabbages.

Jack's mother – his real mother that nobody talks about – sewed animals from old clothes and gave them as presents. Pearl remembers her in pieces; a delicate pair of hands with long fingers, always sewing; clean aprons; and hair as yellow as the good sand near the drying field. Pearl can't remember her name as it's been so long, so she has given the pieces of woman a name that sounds like the memory of what she was called. Clara. Clara Tremain who came to Morlanow from Yarmouth and was always sad with a faraway sort of look.

Pearl was given the toy hare for Christmas. Everyone had just returned from the evening service at chapel and her mother had invited the Tremains and the Polances inside for a slice of heavy cake. Polly was given a green cat with a white ribbon tail, and Jack was already clutching a sky-blue horse with wool for its mane. Pearl has forgotten which animal Nicholas got. Then Clara came over to Pearl by the hearth and pressed the hare into her hand with a smile. Then there were shouts as her father, who had been watching, realised what it was. Pearl remembers seeing the fear rush up his face and stain it deep red.

'Are you trying to send us all to the bottom of the sea?' he shouted, snatching the hare from Pearl's grasp, the air forced out of his lungs with *huffs*.

Clara's lower lip twitched as her beautiful hands fussed at her hair. 'I'm sorry. I didn't mean any harm.'

Mr Tremain coughed. 'Get your coat on, Jack.'

Clara tried to put her hand on her father's arm. 'It's only a bit of cloth,' she said, 'a little hare—' As soon as the terrible word escaped her mouth, her father threw the toy into the remains of the fire.

He turned his back on Clara, staring down at the fire. Her mother looked to Clara as if she wanted to speak, and then looked away. Pearl didn't know what to do so she stayed very still, trying to disappear into the shadows by the side of the hearth.

There was silence from everyone and Clara ran from the room, followed by Mr Tremain and then Jack trailing meekly behind. When they had left Mr Polance cleared his throat.

'She's a funny maid, that Clara. What was Peter thinking, bringing her back with him? I don't know what those east coast fishermen get up to but their women aren't like ours. Right old time the east coast men must have.' He was halted by a look from his wife. 'Well, we'd best be off then.'

Mr and Mrs Polance went to the front door, followed by her mother and father to show them out. Just as he was about to follow the grown-ups out of the room, Nicholas spun round and stuck his hands behind his head, waggling them as if they were long ears. Pearl ran to Polly and buried her face in her sister's skirts so she couldn't see.

With the Polances gone, everyone in Pearl's house went to bed, without a word about the hare or Clara. For some time, shouts came through the wall that was shared with the Tremains. When she was sure her own family were asleep, Pearl crept downstairs and found the hare at the side of the grate. It was scorched and smelt of cinders but Pearl wiped it as clean as she could and sneaked it back up to bed.

Not long after, Clara wasn't next door anymore. When Pearl asked Jack about her he clutched his blue horse to his mouth and went very strange, pulling at his hair, harder and harder, trying to tug clumps out of his reddening scalp. His cries brought her mother to the yard at the back of the house where Pearl and Jack were sitting amongst the chickens. Her mother took Jack in her arms and cooed and shushed him, then told Pearl to go and play indoors while she took Jack home. When she came back they had a grown-up conversation and her mother said Clara had gone away and wouldn't be back and that Pearl was not to ever mention her again, to anyone, or she would be in proper trouble.

In bed, hidden under the coverlet with her calico hare, Pearl thinks of Jack who will have a new mother, of Alice, and that stops her thinking of the mermen eating their babies.

There are times when she is up on the cliff path by herself that she becomes aware of another living creature nearby, and if she stays very still, a brown hare will come into sight. Everyone knows that hares can hold souls, like seagulls do for sailors, and Pearl wonders if perhaps that's where Clara is, her long fingers filling the delicate paws. Hares are houses for witches too, giving them fast legs to sprint away from those they have ill-wished. Maybe Clara was a witch, maybe that's why she left.

White hares carry more magic, it's said, though Pearl has never seen one. At night she whispers to the calico hare, asking her to bring a white hare out of the gorse.

Fifteen

The summer stretches on. She has no sense of how many weeks have passed since the seine boats were launched. There's been no rain and the seafront feels thick with dust and sand. Everything needs a good wash. And the rain will bring the pilchards.

The fish at the sale lose their freshness quickly in this heat, their fins drooping and their eyes clouding. Today's sale is well under way as she passes with Nicholas. Each morning fish are laid out on the slipway, their heads up and their tails down. The Master's in charge even though pilchards aren't sold this way. He's in charge of nearly everything. His big boots step clear of the fish beneath him as he paces the slipway, shaking hands and ordering men about with one finger.

'Stevens, we need more ice. Get Jenner to bring three buckets from the store. Where's the ling from *Two Brothers*? A hundredweight, get that down. Good morning, fine day for it. Yes, a good catch. Have you seen the sole? Beautiful.' He waggles his hands above his head while his assistant scribbles in a pocketbook.

No matter the season, the smell of fish is thick. It's ripe today. Pearl only becomes aware of the stench when she returns after leaving Morlanow and that doesn't happen often. When she goes inland and returns by the cliff path she becomes aware of the ripeness of fish. It's strange, she never notices the smell leaving her nose when she goes away from Morlanow but coming home it is suddenly there, all through her mouth and her throat and her ears. She has to swallow and swallow to get used to it again. Her father says it's to do with the way Morlanow huddles against the cliff; the bad air is trapped.

Miss Charles strides past Pearl and Nicholas who are dawdling, not sure where they're headed as long as it's not home. She picks her way through groups of fishermen and buyers, holding her folded parasol high above her head to guide the students who hurry to keep up.

'The best light in the entire country,' she calls, waving at the sea with her other hand. 'Morlanow is, as I'm sure you've all noticed, almost surrounded by the sea. The bays on either side of the village reflect the sun magnificently, making it quite picturesque.'

Pearl stops in her tracks and stares hard at the village as she hears this. Is the rest of the world duller than Morlanow? True, she has seen the newly arrived artists climb down from the train and straight away they pinch their noses. They're all green at first but the smell must be worth putting up with for them to stay so long, painting the sea. Mr Michaels has been here for years. And new visitors often lurch as if they have been drinking, this brilliant light and the smell of the fish pressing in on them. They linger in the palace's open doorway. When the pilchard oil catches the sun it looks like a river of slow gold seeping towards their boots.

It's afternoon, long after the fish wrapped in newspapers have been taken from the slipway. Jack, Pearl and Nicholas sit on the headland by the huer's hut. The men keeping watch for the pilchards, including Nicholas's grandfather, Mr Jenner, are talking half-heartedly while they keep their gaze locked on the water.

From here the sea runs on and on. On clear days Pearl can see the rest of Cornwall curving away into haziness, swooping in bays and inlets and caves with no end in sight. Sometimes she thinks she might see things that aren't to be held in the eye, the way Aunt Lilly can see. It's as if Pearl can dive beneath the surface, from her place on the cliff, and make out the Bucca picking over the wrecks hidden at the bottom of the sea and mermaids making their supper. She doesn't let herself see keygrims. All this is a different sort of seeing; seeing that is knowing first and making the picture second.

At the other end of the sky a cloud is fluffing into shape, trailing grey in its wake. There is all the sea between Morlanow and the cloud, and Pearl wonders who's beneath it now, feeling the air dampen.

Jack turns from looking out to sea. 'One day, I'm going to be in charge of the fish sale.'

'Where?' Nicholas doesn't shift his gaze from the distant cloud.

'Here of course,' Jack says.

'Don't you want to go somewhere else? Don't you get sick of here, sometimes?' Nicholas asks.

'That's a wicked thing to say.'

'I want to cross the sea in a ship that can take me to the end of the world,' Nicholas says, addressing the cloud.

'What will be at the end of the world?' Pearl asks, but Nicholas doesn't reply. Perhaps he doesn't hear her, or he doesn't know the answer.

Pearl isn't even sure what's truly at the end of the railway line. She knows Morlanow like she knows her prayers, like she knows the pattern of lines on her father's face. Down the cliff path, over the hill beyond Govenek, is a wild land to her, and she has no real need to leave her home. But Nicholas wants to leave and the thought of him going uncurls like a rock pool flower in her stomach, stabbing her insides with its spines. Perhaps he's just saying it to show off or to make Jack cross.

Before an argument can start, Nicholas stands up to watch a boat rounding the lighthouse. Just a bobbing spot but becoming plainer with each wave it clears. Jack moves closer to the cliff edge to get a better look.

'That's the coal boat from Cardiff,' Jack says.

Nicholas put his hands on hips. 'No it isn't. It's not big enough. Look, only one mast.'

Jack peers harder. 'Is it a crabber? Are the Frenchies back?'

'No, I think she's the Genoa boat,' Nicholas says, and points as another, smaller smudge rolls into sight, dipping and rising clearer and clearer over the waves. 'An east coaster. Must be bad weather coming in.'

Nicholas can recognise all Morlanow's fleet and most other kinds of boat. Usually Jack joins in trying to guess them but now he's silent. His parents met in a fried fish shop in Lowestoft when his father's boat was sheltering from a storm.

Another shape has rounded the lighthouse. Nicholas puts his hands on his knees and leans forward, eyes narrowing on the boat.

'It's Father's,' he says.

Jack's father will have been out in this boat too. Will there have been talk of Alice? The wedding will be soon. Pearl's not sure when, she only knows she isn't allowed to go. Neither is Nicholas. She wonders if Jack's looking forward to having a mother again. He's staring hard at the sea and she doesn't want to ask him in case it makes him cross. When Alice is there he won't have his dinner in Pearl's house because Alice will remember about him and make him his own meal. Pearl realises she'll miss seeing him at her kitchen table. Perhaps she'll be able to have her dinner at Jack's house. She's never been inside. Her mother says it's a disgrace, so untidy and unwashed. Pearl will see Alice more, though she's not seen her much recently. Will her mother be nicer to Alice when she's married? Alice will have a baby then and women usually help one another with babies. Aunt Lilly is the one who goes for births. Alice shouldn't be alone when the baby comes.

Without a backward glance, Nicholas careers down the cliff path to reach the seafront as the boat comes in, dust rising from his heels. The men have been out overnight to drift for mackerel and now they will gently but quickly lift the tabby-skinned fish from the nets, though they're too late for today's sale. The mackerel will have to wait until tomorrow to be laid on the slipway and by that time they will have begun to spoil and their price will be lower. As the boat comes closer still, Pearl hears the gulls that have followed it into harbour circling overhead, hoping for a chance to pick off a fish.

Pearl and Jack walk down the cliff path and along the seafront to where the boat has come in. She feels Jack's reluctance grow with each step closer and she takes his hand. There's the barest hint of a smile before he lowers his head again.

Nicholas is with the two men, helping to unload their gear. Mr Polance has his arm around Nicholas's shoulder and his mouth close to his son's ear. Nicholas laughs and then they jog up the slipway together, carrying a basket of mackerel between them. Jack hovers on the seafront.

Mr Tremain sees him and inclines his head. 'Give me a hand, boy.'

Jack goes down onto the beach and his father thrusts him an armful of nets. Pearl stays on the seafront. She has a mussel shell in the pocket of her dress. She turns it over and over in her fingers, the ribbed underside a kind of charm against the worry she has for Jack. He can't hold the tumbling mess of the nets and as he tries to walk they slip from him, his foot gets caught and he trips.

'Watch it!' his father shouts.

She wants to go and help him but is rooted to the seafront. Mr Tremain would shout at her and Jack wouldn't want to be helped by a girl, not in front of his father. Jack picks himself up, untangles his foot and gathers the nets into his arms again. He struggles up the slipway with the nets trailing behind him even though he keeps tugging and pulling them back into his arms.

Jack's father catches him up and roughly takes the nets from him. 'Give me those. Useless,' Mr Tremain says.

His elbow knocks the side of Jack's head as he yanks the nets from his grasp. Standing awkwardly on the slipway Jack loses his balance and drops to the ground where he crouches and doesn't get up.

Mr Polance is standing above on the seafront and watches all this happen. Jack totters, trying to stand. He shakes his head as if to throw off a fly. Mr Polance's mouth is fixed in a thin line and his forehead is tightly wrinkled. He calls down to Mr Tremain on the slipway, folding the net.

'Peter, why don't you come in for bite to eat when we've sorted this lot? Annie will have something made, I'm bound. Been a long night.' He says this in a flat voice.

Mr Tremain stops folding the net. He doesn't answer straight away.

'All right,' he says eventually. He climbs up onto the seafront and the two men take the nets between them. Both fishermen have deep shadows under their eyes and weariness seeps from their bodies. Mr Tremain still has his back to Jack as the nets are wound and folded. Mr Polance gives a tiny, secret nod to Nicholas who goes down to Jack as his father steers Mr Tremain towards their street. The two men don't look back.

Nicholas helps Jack to get to his feet and for a moment the two of them stand together, before Jack pulls away and straightens up. His face is pale and he has sand in his hair. Nicholas looks up at Pearl and gives her a smile.

'I feel like climbing,' Nicholas says. 'What do you say, Pearl?'

He means a trip to Skommow Bay. She nods even as her stomach lurches at the thought of the smashed frames. Nicholas's smile widens. He's smiling for Pearl because he knows she's afraid. She's doing a good thing for Jack who loves Skommow Bay, but to see Nicholas smile like that she would do anything.

It isn't far from the slipway. They could go through the streets so that they skirt the steep hill of the drying field, then over the low wall, but that never seems like a proper way to get to Skommow Bay. It is more of an adventure to scale the drying field and roll down its other side, getting to the shelf by going through the sagging cabin of the big wreck that sits at the bottom of the hill.

So that's what they do. Once there, the boys go to choose a boat with Pearl trailing along behind. It always seems darker here and the air's colder, making her feel as if they're miles from home. She hates it, but she knows it's a useful place all the same.

When Morlanow's own little boats are beyond going to sea the men bring them here. Some bigger ships have ended up at Skommow Bay too, having been wrecked off this part of the coast. The largest ships, most often foreign and from far away, don't come here; they're left to break up where they beach. The sea can have them, once anything valuable has been taken safely home.

If a fisherman needs planks to mend a hull, or a new mast, or a wedge to plug a leak, the wrecks on Skommow Bay are waiting, left for anyone to use. The ruins pile up against each other at strange angles. It's odd to see boats like this, upside down or splayed over another's hull. Everything is back to front. The wood is covered with barnacles and splintered fingers point to the sky. The boats lie on a narrow shelf of black rock that's pitted with dank pools. No matter how warm the sun is, this water is freezing.

Jack leads the way across the wrecks. The three of them duck the twisted spars and crawl through holes rent by the waves. Pearl's dress is soon damp and dirtied. Her mother will be livid. Jack's clothes were mucky even before they arrived and he has dirt behind his ears as well. It's taking him a long time to choose a boat and she shivers. The afternoon's slipping towards evening and now dusk's creeping around them. The far off cloud seen from the cliff top has stretched further across the sky, promising rain. A breeze whistles through the wrecks. It sounds like a person. She clamps her hands over her ears in case she hears her name called.

Finally, Jack makes for the front end of a lugger whose broad bottom has been ripped in half, leaving only the bow. It's pitched almost vertically against a rock and will be a good place to watch for imaginary enemy crews. Jack immediately launches himself at the boat, scrabbling up the side. Below him, looking up, Pearl sees how worn his boots are. He manages to climb the remains of the boat to reach what might have once been a seat, where he perches and surveys his sea of hulks.

133

Pearl's boots skid and slide as she tries to gain a foothold but the wood is slippery to climb and she has to grip with both hands. She catches her palm on a barnacle and its jagged edge breaks the skin. As she stops climbing to look at the blood appearing, she puts her foot in a pool of cold green water which floods her boot and makes her stiffen. Nicholas hasn't tried to climb up yet.

'Come on!' Jack says. 'Why aren't you climbing?' He's smiling now, the nets and his father and Alice forgotten.

Nicholas glances behind him at the army of broken boats. They seem to Pearl to have grown taller since they arrived.

'It's getting late, Jack,' Nicholas calls up. 'Must be nearly supper time, and I think it's going to rain.'

Pearl's relieved. Home to her warm house, her mother asking her what she's been doing, how she got so dirty, and her father laughing. She squeezes her hand into a fist to try and stop it stinging. Jack picks up a pretend oar and rows himself deeper into the wooden waves.

'Time to go,' Nicholas says.

Jack scrambles higher up the lugger. 'Not yet. We've only just got here.'

'If we stay too long we won't see our way back,' Nicholas says.

This horror hits Pearl like a slap. She imagines Nicholas falling onto one of the treacherous-looking spars and clamps her lips together in case the thought should come out and be made true.

'I don't care,' Jack says, his voice beginning to whine. 'I'll stay here all night. I'm not going home.'

'Jack, don't be foolish. You can't stay here.'

'I can,' Jack says. 'Go home, go on the pair of you. Leave me alone.'

'You've got to come,' Nicholas says.

'You can't make me. I won't.' Jack lets go of his imaginary oar and curls himself over the lugger's bow. Pearl thinks she can hear him sobbing. There's a drop of water on her arm, then another, and another. The cloud has finally caught up with them and its rain is sudden and hard.

'I can't just leave you here,' Nicholas says, not with his usual confidence. 'But you're stopping us all getting out. We'll get soaked.' Water drips from his hair.

Pearl uncurls her hand to show him the cut from the barnacle. He tilts it out of his shadow and winces when he sees the angry flesh, then closes her hand up again and says to her quietly, 'It'll be all right.' Then to Jack, 'Pearl's hurt herself. Come on.' At this Jack's sobbing becomes louder.

Nicholas's voice hardens. 'You're being a baby. A big baby. Perhaps I *should* leave you here.' Jack stays hunched over the bow, unmoving. 'No wonder your mother—' Nicholas stops himself but it's too late. He's said the one thing they're not meant to talk about. Jack's sobs become a scream, a terrible wailing that gets inside Pearl.

The rain drives into her face as she looks up at Jack who wails on and on. He'll be sick, Pearl thinks. He'll make himself sick and he has no mother to look after him yet because Alice has to hide. Nicholas is standing stock still as if he has decided to play a game of sleeping lions but not told anyone, then suddenly he jumps and makes a lunge at the lugger and, with his height, manages to swipe at Jack who's torn from the bow. Jack falls into the puddle Pearl stood in and his screaming stops, momentarily, with the shock of the water, before starting afresh, louder and shriller.

Nicholas pulls him to his feet. 'I'm sorry,' he says, forcing Jack's arms to his side and holding them fast so Jack can't move. 'I'm sorry. I didn't mean it. But we have to go home.'

Jack's screams batter Pearl. She's too shaken to cry though

the feeling of wanting to makes her chest tremble the way it shouldn't, a fluttering as if a gull is trapped beneath her ribs. Her breath comes short and loud.

Nicholas' face crumples with worry as he hears her rasping. 'It's all right, it's all right.'

She doesn't know if he's saying it to her or to himself. The pain in her hand is hot and tight, throbbing as fast as her chest. There's rain all through her clothes and her mother will be so cross.

Jack's screams shudder to sobs. The noise that ripped Pearl's insides stops gushing from his mouth but still her chest heaves. The shattered forms of the boats are stirring into life and leaning over her.

Nicholas gathers Pearl into his arms. He begins to run but the haunted boats are running alongside to keep up. Water splashes all around. He drags Jack with him, through the ruined boats in the direction of the low wall next to the road. Wood splinters as they crash forward; they slosh through rock pools and puddles; and Jack's sobbing climbs with every step closer to home.

They reach Jack's house first and Nicholas bangs on the front door. He turns to go, leaving Jack on the doorstep but having to prise Jack's hand from his.

'No, no! Don't make me go in,' Jack pleads. 'I'm sorry, I'm sorry, Nicholas. It's my fault, Pearl… Father will…' His voice breaks off into wails again.

Pearl has one last glimpse of Jack before her own door opens and she's rushed inside; Jack stands in a pool of light cast by the lamp his father holds. He squirms in its glow, twisting his wet shirt in his hands.

Sixteen

She gasped, certain of her chest's desperate need for air, of its frightened closing. But there was no constriction, no panic. She breathed in and out easily. The sensation was gone. A dim memory of something known, but too far away to feel.

Skommow Bay faded, the ruined boats replaced by the holiday visitors around her. Chatter, laughter. Seagulls swooping for stolen chips. She was outside Eileen's shop. That was something, at least.

David Pendeen was at the counter. He was arguing with a striking-looking woman in a tight, printed dress. A visitor. They had such front.

'Don't you give me that,' the woman said, elbowing David out of the way of the till. 'It was three shillings, not two.'

'For God's sake!' David said, but he didn't try to stop her.

The woman wrenched the till drawer open. Pearl was astounded. What was this stranger doing in Eileen's till? Why wasn't David stopping her?

'Now see here,' Pearl said, reaching round the counter to lay a hand on the woman's arm. The woman's skin felt soft, warm, but her arm was tensed holding the till. Pearl could feel the anger in the muscle. 'This is Eileen Pendeen's shop,' Pearl said. 'You get out of there.'

The woman frowned at Pearl. Pearl felt the woman's arm relax.

It was Margaret, Pearl realised. Eileen's daughter. She felt the blood rush into her cheeks. Her palm, still against Margaret's arm, began to sweat. She jerked her hand away. Margaret looked confused. She turned to David who shook his head very slightly. Pearl couldn't think what to say. How could she have forgotten Margaret? She'd watched the child for Eileen. Given her dinner when the shop was busy, before David was even born. Margaret had a terrible sweet tooth. Pearl could remember that. A sweet tooth but hated liquorice.

Fortunately Eileen appeared then. She'd been clearing space at the back of the shop, she said, to stock picnic hampers.

Eileen ushered Pearl into the little office behind the counter. Before Eileen could follow Pearl in to sit down, Margaret caught her, drew her back into the shop. Pearl's heart was pounding. She felt jittery, embarrassed. Margaret was whispering then Eileen said loudly, 'Get on! She's fine. And don't think I didn't hear you and your brother fighting. I'm not dead yet. This is still my shop.' And with that Eileen whirled into the office and slammed the door shut behind her. 'I ask you,' she said to Pearl, 'your George doesn't give you any of this, does he? Fine lad he is.'

'Eileen, I didn't know—'

'Don't you worry,' Eileen said. 'Margaret's never here long enough for you to see her these days. Comes in when she likes, giving David a row when he's the one helping out. She's got the kiddies, I know, but still. We managed, didn't we?'

Pearl nodded, grateful. She smoothed down her housecoat. Something hard caught her fingers. She rummaged in the pocket and pulled out a coin. Margaret had been talking about shillings. Was this hers?

'Oh, *I* see,' Eileen said, smiling. 'Just come for your shopping, not to see me. Well that's charming.' She really was very pretty, and of course Pearl could see now, Margaret looked just like her. How had she not known her? 'What is it today then?' Eileen said. 'Got a list? I'll ask David to fetch things for you. Save you getting up for a bit.'

Pearl couldn't remember. Had they butter at home? There was butter on the tablecloth. The stain wouldn't come out. Soap then, for washing. She told Eileen, but as she said the word she wasn't sure. But nothing else came. It must be soap.

'No, no list,' she said to Eileen. 'Never needed them.'

It took her a long time to walk back up the hill. She fell asleep in the kitchen, having only sat down to take her boots off. She was woken by the sound of the front door opening and then being gently closed. It could only be George. Jack didn't shut a door like that. There was a cup of clouded tea in front of her. She put her hand to the cup. Stone cold. It must have been there for days. George was leaning in the doorway.

Looking into his eyes she felt that he was adrift at sea somewhere, rocking on the swell and waiting for a breeze to carry him to where he was meant to be. Not that he was unhappy, as far as she knew. He had friends and as a child had played the same games that she, Jack and Nicholas had played. He had swum in the sea and sailed model boats. He was a good fisherman and a good husband to poor Elizabeth.

George shifted his weight and Pearl felt a smile creeping to the corners of her mouth. When he was born, she had found herself smiling all the time. When he woke in the night and cried out, she went to him smiling. Just knowing he was there to be loved, that she could go and look at him, drink in every detail, was enough. George was the line between what was lost and what was kept.

'You're getting a bit ahead of yourself if you've come for Sunday supper,' she said.

George bent and kissed her cheek then took the other chair. She wasn't sure what the time was, whether or not he should have been at sea. There was a fair bit of wind today but not enough to stop him going out.

'Is Elizabeth well?' Pearl said. He nodded. 'So what's the matter then?' she said. He raised his eyebrows at her in mock annoyance. 'Not that it isn't lovely to see you,' she said quickly.

George ran a hand through his hair. 'I was passing.'

'You were passing? On your way to Govenek, were you?'

He smiled and said, 'Can't a boy see his mother now, got to be a reason?'

But there was, she knew, and she would have to watch her tongue. George was looking round the kitchen, frowning at the water stains on the walls.

'It's not right that you're living like this,' he said. 'A wonder you've not been ill. I don't mind, you know, having a look at the roof. Father'd have to let me first of course.'

'Don't get on that,' she said.

'I'm only saying. I hate to see you all the way up here. You sure you're all right? You're looking pale.'

George rubbed his arms and went to the window. Pearl saw with surprise that it was wide open, the curtains flapping.

'Here, let me shut this,' George said. 'Weather's a bit more seasonal today – aren't you cold?'

'Can't be doing with the stuffiness of this place,' she told him. 'I've got to have some fresh air in.'

Yes, she remembered; she had wanted to hear the sea better so she had opened the window and then she had made a cup of tea because her father would be back soon; he had just gone to check over the seine nets. She was waiting for him but had got lost somehow. Nicholas had found her and brought her home. He was here now to speak to her, it was important. Look how he frowned at her. She reached to smooth his brow.

George caught her hand. George.

Pearl moved to tidy her hair, then stood up. 'You'll have a cup of tea?' she said. 'And I've saffron buns, you'll have one?' She busied herself with the cup and plate, feeling his eyes on her back, following her movements. Her hand shook. She dropped the plate.

In a moment he was by her side, steering her back into a chair.

'You are ill, aren't you? I thought you weren't right on Sunday. Father not looking after you? Should've known.'

'I'm fine, really. Bit tired, that's all. Didn't sleep well last night. Worrying about you.' She gave him a smile and he looked away. Pearl put her hand on his arm. 'Why don't you make a fresh pot of tea. Mine's gone cold anyway.'

George got up and filled the kettle, set it on the stove then rinsed the cups. He was such a beautiful boy, those dark eyes, his face freckled by the sun. He went to sea so many days each year. Pearl was grateful for the Sunday fishing rule only because it meant George could come for supper, when poor Elizabeth was well. It wasn't an easy life though, always hard to make the fishing pay and now the gear was costing so much. People seemed to want to eat fish that came from tins, those that Eileen sold, rather than fresh out of the sea. If George's nets were mauled by hake or ripped by storm tides, there was no one to help. Everyone was looking out for themselves and couldn't afford to be kind, but George was working hard and getting by on his own.

He was enough to mend her. She didn't need to keep walking the tideline waiting for a ship that would never come. He was here now and that was what mattered, especially as the season was approaching. It was nearly time for the pilchards and Nicholas would come to meet her at the palace when the fish were in their walls, and they would walk up the cliff path, her arm tucked into his, and she would tell him the silly things the palace girls had been on about that day, who was stepping out with who or the famous artist who had arrived that evening on the train.

The kettle began to whistle. The cliff path faded even as Pearl tried to hold onto the image and the feeling of the arm in hers. George reached for a cloth to lift the kettle from the stove. She must be cautious with him here. He wanted something from her and she mustn't let it out.

He poured the water into the pot then left it to brew, sitting back down and fiddling with the corner of the cloth, a worn thing stained with years. He cleared his throat and she braced herself for what might come.

'Pascoe's started on the palace,' he said.

'I saw. Went down to have a look.'

'Did you? When?'

Pearl opened her mouth but she couldn't find the words. When did she go to the palace? She remembered looking at the tarpaulin and then her mother's voice, singing. It was so far away.

George was carrying on. 'Pascoe's short of help though. Got men in from Govenek as he can't find enough labour here to get it down in time, before winter.'

Pearl dug her nails into the back of her hand and the pain loosened her tongue, fixed her thoughts. 'You'll not sign up for a few days?' she said. 'Might be good pay, if Pascoe's short. I saw Matthew was working for him.'

'Get on,' George said. 'I may not have filled any seine nets—'

'There wasn't anything to fill them with,' Pearl said quietly. 'But I know it isn't right.'

'Causing a row won't keep the palace standing and it won't help you. Never does. Same with the east coast boats.' She had let it out. He would get her now. Her breath began to shorten and a shadow played in the corner of the room.

'Won't be like that,' George said. 'There's not many that care about the palace, and the trouble with the east coast men was a long time ago. I know you don't like to talk about it but...'

He had his hands round the lid she had so carefully sealed. He was going to force it off.

'Since... since Pascoe said he was going to make the palace a hotel, I've heard... Well, there's been more talk, about the east coast men, and what happened. And then Eileen said the other day that she'd heard you mention someone.'

Pearl had known it was a risk, that it was only a matter of time. A chance remark, that was all it would take. Even Eileen was talking about her.

'His name keeps coming up.' George paused and looked at Pearl. 'You know who I mean, don't you?'

Was it time to let it out now? He had had such a time growing up, with Jack the way he was. George deserved at least some truth.

'He was my friend,' she said, avoiding George's eye.

'Tell me, please.'

'There's nothing else to tell. He left. You know that, don't you?' Her voice was hard in her own ears. 'He left here without a goodbye. No note, nothing. He left, that's all you need to know.'

George dropped his shoulders and stared at the table. Pearl

wanted to gather him into her arms and coo him better like she did when he was a baby, to love him enough that he didn't need to know. She didn't want him to spend his life as she had spent hers, waiting.

She patted her son's hand. 'I should think that tea's about ready now.'

Seventeen

When had it last rained?

Pearl stepped over an exposed gorse root that lay in her way, the loose earth scattering. The air was thick and charged. The weather needed to break. She needed it to break. This hot spell, this late in the year, it wasn't right. Morlanow needed its storms. Being jammed in an exposed knot of the coast left the village open to squalls that seemed sharp enough to break windows, but that was the cost of living by what had once been the site of riches.

Storms were part of Morlanow's history. They made certain years stand out among their fellows, giving shape to the mass of the past. They were the reason for its name. Morlanow was 'high tide' in Cornish, not that many realised. From the first settlers on, the community saw odd tidal patterns: surges that drove water into the streets and sudden drags when the water dropped far below everyday levels. Morlanow was fashioned by the water patterns that put it together.

A proper storm would help clear her head, get rid of this fug that had settled since the move; and after all, she had read the white hare as a sign that a rage would come over the water. Pilchards followed the wake of a gale. She stopped walking to look out across the sea, remembering the shape the pilchard shoal made just below the surface of the water. It looked like a burnt-red cloud with ragged edges as it pulled into the bay, as if seaweed had sprung to life and was racing across the bed.

Nicholas was with her then, at her side, his thin fingers looped in hers. She walked him away. Keep walking, keep on the path and you won't stray. The Lord is my shepherd. *The lad I loved was with them and he came not back again.* Her mother would tell her to sharpen her wits, to shake off this nonsense.

The path was uneven. Pearl's boots were powdered with pale dust. She knew where to duck and where to bend her frame round a prickly outcrop of bare gorse. Some stretches of the path ran at the edge of the cliff and there was only good grace between the walker and the sea.

She reached Keeper's Point, a spinning drop to where the rocks snagged and sucked at the passing current, about a mile from Morlanow. Even on a calm day the sea was anxious here. A little further along was Witch Cove, so called for the great numbers of witch sole that were once caught there, but had disappeared even before Pearl's time. The cove couldn't be seen from the cliff path and it was a good place to swim and be hidden from the rest of the world. She hadn't been down there for years.

She looked to the horizon line. It made her burn with anger at her own folly for still searching for Nicholas there, but the past was bottled in the cleft Morlanow filled and it continued to reverberate through the soil and the waves, no matter what she did. Nicholas was everywhere and nowhere. He was hers, but he had gone.

They had walked here together and she was still in his footsteps. No matter who trod over them, Nicholas's tracks were there. No one could remove what had been. The way back was always open.

She coughed. The sound made her aware that everything else – the sea, the gulls, the breeze through the gorse – had grown silent. Slowly, the tune of the cliff top came back to her ears. Things seemed as they should be, though there was the warmth at her temples again.

She was halfway back to the house, Keeper's Point several hundred yards behind her. Another cairn stood on the path. This time there were no blue bugloss flowers poked between the stones. Instead there was a crooked stem of knapweed, its purple thistle head pointing directly towards her. Aunt Lilly used knapweed's tricks because it knew of future lovers and who a girl would take. It was crafty though, old knapweed. You had to read it sideways to learn its truth. It could tell of a husband to be, or a boy who loved you in secret. It might mean someone you loved but who didn't care for you, or a boy to watch out for – a surprise suitor.

Who was raising these cairns, Pearl wondered, and why mark this one with knapweed? Bugloss, with its tie to sadness, was right, but knapweed with a cairn – Pearl's chest contracted and she was pulled up short as she struggled to find her next breath. The cairn and knapweed together meant a lost lover, a soul returned.

She fought for breath and clutched the gorse beside her. The pain from its thorns brought her back to herself and gradually freed her chest from its constrictions.

She'd walked this way earlier, going towards Keeper's Point. There had been nothing here then. There could have been another walker behind her, coming from the direction of the houses at *Wave Crest*, but she hadn't heard anyone. Someone could have come up the path from Morlanow, or even from Witch Cove, but knapweed didn't grow by the sea; it liked deeper earth. Pearl thought she had seen some growing in the drying field but couldn't be sure when she tried to picture it there. She stepped round the cairn, careful not to knock any of the piled stones. Pearl moved to the edge of the cliff. Her eyes sought the horizon. It was an illness, this need to look. Nicholas could come back, he might. The signs were there. She couldn't ignore them.

The sun emerged from behind scraps of cloud and as its light reclaimed its grip on the sea, a stain appeared. Red and purple and for a moment, silver. Then it was gone. A wave broke. The sea was itself again. But she'd seen it, as she'd seen the white hare and the knapweed cairn. She knew what was coming now.

Eighteen

The seine boats have been waiting to put to sea for weeks, pulled up on the sand near the rock pools. Their crews stay close by, listening for the huer's trumpet call and the ringing of the bell. Pilchards are creatures of habit, like all living things, though one of their habits is to break their pattern and keep Morlanow waiting all year. When they do come, they never come close enough to Morlanow's shores to be caught in the seine nets until September, though Pearl knows that further up the coast of Cornwall they are caught a month or so earlier. Then there are only a couple of months when the fish keep coming to the shallows, before they leave to light other waters.

The first Sunday of September has been and gone, but no pilchards have been sighted off Morlanow yet.

There's talk of the early catch, when the Master locked the women in the cellar to keep his luck safe. The fish broke all customs to come into the bay for that single day in July, before disappearing. As days pass with no call from the huer's hut the early shoal becomes more and more of a bad omen for the rest of the season.

There's a hum in the village when the pilchards are expected. The seine men, including her father, Mr Polance and Mr Tremain, are strung tight as withy frames, desperate for the cry to be given and the torture of waiting to be over. Jack keeps away from home and eats supper at Pearl's house, sometimes falling asleep and spending the night. Life is turned topsy-turvy when the wait goes on. It will be worth it in the end, Pearl thinks. But still the pilchards don't come.

The weather doesn't break. The sky is cloudless, day after day, and the sea is still. It's a lake of layered colour; the pale grey of the shallows runs to slate to blue to green then dark purple where the seabed drops away. Everyone yearns for clouds, for the stirring of a breeze and the smell of rain. The pilchards follow bad weather, darting along on storm swells and chasing the winds.

Mr Taylor says special prayers at chapel, frowning at the fidgeting hands and the tapping boots. On Sunday the nervousness is worse. The fish can't tell what day it is but if they choose the Sabbath to flood Morlanow with their wealth then no one will be able to bring them in. Even pilchards are not allowed to change the rules on Sunday. The seine men will simply have to stand on the seafront and watch the Govenek men take their fish. Pearl prays every night for the pilchards to come as long as they don't choose a Sunday.

Days of sun tick on. People are listless, unable to rouse themselves much beyond hoping and watching the sea. Nets are checked and checked again. Bussa jars are scrubbed. On a morning the same as many others that have come before it, hot and empty and charged with frustration, Nicholas and Jack have a fight. It's been coming for weeks. She could feel it whenever it was just the three of them. When Polly and Sarah Dray are around, or Timothy and the Pengelley boys,

Jack and Nicholas have space between them, other voices to listen to. But when it's only Pearl there's no such peace.

They're in the shade of the sheds that circle the palace's open centre. Dusty hogsheads line the walls, tubs of salt stand ready, but there's no one else there. All eyes are on the sea. She has no stories to tell today. She doesn't want to hear about mermaids eating their babies, or Nicholas' only story, that of keygrims. In the shadows of the sheds it's easy to see boney shapes slipping between the barrels, to hear a name spoken in sour breath.

Nicholas is poking about in the nets and gurries but listlessly, with no purpose other than having something to do.

'There are rats in there,' she says. Did she hear one, its screech?

'I can fight rats,' he says, pulling a small knife from amongst the fishing gear that's used to cut flotsam from the nets. 'I can fight anything, even Jack Tremain.' He wields it, pretending to slay the armies of rats that she now imagines teeming from the dark corners. Crashing about, he slashes and cuts, lunges and half dances across the palace's floor. She's laughing but then Nicholas knocks into Jack where he stands by one of the great stone pillars, pulling at a splinter on a hogshead.

'Oi!' Jack shouts, pushing Nicholas onto the floor. Nicholas lands awkwardly on his wrist and winces. The knife clatters away from him. 'Can't you leave me alone?' Jack says. He kicks Nicholas, still on the floor.

Nicholas scowls at Jack, his forehead pulled into a deep crease. There's a pulse of anger about him then he throws himself at Jack, shoving him onto the floor. They wrestle but it's like how the girls fight, grabbing one another's hair and pushing each other's faces, until Jack gets hold of Nicholas' arm and wrenches it behind his back. Nicholas' eyes water, he cries out. She's never seen them fight like this. They row and Jack is often grumpy, like when he sank the little boat with the handkerchief sail, but actually hurting one another is something else. She can't look away and she can't speak either. She knows she should tell them to stop but she can't. Instead she drags one of the nets from the corner, braving herself against the rats and the keygrims, and throws it over Jack. He's confused and lets go of Nicholas' arm. Nicholas quickly rolls out from under the net and stumbles to his feet. Jack tries to get up but gets more tangled, binding himself. Nicholas laughs, which makes Pearl laugh too, and makes Jack fight the net even more, becoming even more caught. He stops moving. Their laughter dries up and they hear Jack crying. Through the thick weave of the net she can just about see that his hands are over his face and he's shaking.

Nicholas is on his hands and knees then, trying to free Jack. Pearl goes to help but the net is too big and heavy and Jack seems too deeply buried. She's sorry she threw it now and more sorry that she laughed. Finally Jack is able to shrug the last of the net from his shoulders and to stand. He wipes his sniffing nose with the back of his hand. His eyes are red and swollen.

'It's today, isn't it?' Nicholas asks him.

Jack nods. 'They'll be married by now. He's so angry but it's his fault. He drove my mother away and now he's a sinner. He'll go to hell. I want him to. It's his fault the fish haven't come.'

'Don't be foolish,' Nicholas says, though in a kind voice. 'It's no one's fault. It's how things are sometimes.'

'It is his fault. And hers. She's a whore!'

Nicholas puts his hand on Jack's shoulder but Jack shakes it off. Still sniffing and wiping his eyes, he leaves the palace. He'll go to Skommow Bay, Pearl thinks. He won't want

Timothy or the Pengelley boys to see him crying and everyone on the seafront will be talking about the wedding, about his father's sinfulness with Alice. About blame.

She and Nicholas go out onto the seafront. Jack's already gone. There's a wall of dark-clothed bodies looking out to sea. At least the chapel service will have been quiet. Nicholas climbs the cliff path to wait with his grandfather, Mr Jenner, at the huer's hut on the cliff. Watching for fish runs down his line. His grandfather is determined Nicholas is to be one of the men and see the shoal first as it enters the bay. Pearl goes and sits beneath the harbour wall. *Hevva*, she whispers to herself, willing the word from the air. But still the fish don't come.

*

The days roll on. Hope makes every cloud a sign, every wave becomes a clue. If all fish are eaten from their tails to their heads, luck is given to those in the boats and more fish will flood into the bay, which must then be eaten in the same manner. If the pressing stones are heard rolling in the cellars without the touch of human hands, it means that they're eager to weigh down the lids of packed hogsheads and the fish must be on their way. Aunt Lilly's knowledge is sought each morning; her gift as a pellar is to see beyond the horizon. But each morning she shakes her head, and still there are no fish.

Fishermen wait on the seafront, huddled over pipes and plans. Their talk is only of other seasons, of great catches or empty palaces. The lean year the hake ate right through William Pendeen's seine net, just as it was about to be brought to the surface, bursting with pilchards. The fishermen turn their backs on home, on families, as they gaze on the calm water, willing Mr Jenner's trumpet to sound from the cliff.

153

When big ships put into harbour to load their cargo onto the train or to pick up new crews and supplies, the men on board are asked if they have seen any shoals. If there has been a sighting, charts are spread on the seafront. The older fishermen, those who have spent their lives waiting for the pilchards to grace Morlanow, chew on their pipes and suck in their cheeks. Their thick fingers, darkened by the sun and years caulking boats, trace paths through the sea, along Cornwall's ragged coast, predicting the shoal's next route and when the fish might come to her father's net. But these can only ever be guesses, and the days roll on.

Waiting, waiting. Nets dry in the sun. Bussa jars gather dust. There are whispers that the early catch was a false dawn and now Morlanow is cursed for the whole season – no pilchards will come. There will be nothing to eat this winter.

Her dreams flicker with fish. They're always in the sea, never drowning in the nets or laid out in salt. She swims with them, as quick and lithe as a fish herself. The pilchard shoal moves as one body, called a 'she' by the fishermen. Pearl pictures the darting shimmer as having long silver hair made of all the light in the sea.

In her dreams, the shoal slips by Pearl, close to her face so she feels the tickle of scales on her skin. But the shoal gets away and the widening gap between them makes her cry. She falters then, in the water, losing her ability to move like the shoal. As she begins to sink there's a violent shift in the water; a blurred shape surrounded by bubbles crashes into the sea. Someone has jumped off the harbour wall. Pearl feels an arm around her, holding her up. She knows it's Nicholas without having to look.

When she hears the bell she thinks she must still be asleep. But then she becomes aware of movement. Polly's weight creaks off the bed. Feet run past the window, the magical word pounded in their tread. *Hevva. Hevva. Hevva.*

Her mother's lighting the lamp. 'Come along, my sweet, or you'll miss them.'

And it's real - the fish have finally come. For a moment Pearl can't breathe. Her mother rubs her chest until it softens and Pearl can scrabble for her boots in the lamp's weak light. Its oil, pressed from the bodies of last season's catches, sizzles and burns its smell into the room. The fish are here, in the house. The shoal from her dream is swimming round the ceiling, sputtering in and out of the shadows cast there by the lamp. Pearl knew they would come. If you hope hard enough, what you truly wish for will appear.

'Where's Father?' she asks.

'He heard the wind get up once you'd gone to bed. Mr Polance came for him. They've been at sea four hours now, waiting for the fish to come in close enough.' Her mother ties Pearl's laces for her, Pearl's fingers too jittery.

When her mother opens the front door onto the street, the rain blows into the house. In between gusts of wind, the trumpet sounds. The weather has broken and the pilchards have followed on its heels. Despite the wet, the whole village seems to be pouring past the house on its way to the seafront. Pearl, her mother, and Polly join the crowd and are swept along in the damp crush of hastily grabbed boots and coats; everyone's faces have blurred together in the tide of bodies. Her mother holds tight to Pearl's hand but her feet are trodden on and she takes a knock to the shin, flinching into her mother's warm shape beside her.

They go to the seafront to wait for the boats to come in. Dawn's not far off; through the rain clouds at the horizon a thin seam of lighter blue is easing itself over the dark bulk of the sea. The rain sluices the cobbles down to the seafront, but

Pearl isn't cold. Her whole body crackles with heat, radiating from her insides and filling her skin so she wonders her mother's hand doesn't burn.

Pearl leaves her mother and Polly at the front; she won't be needed yet and no one will miss her in the excitement. Passing the entrance to the palace she ducks past the Master in his usual hand-wringing state. No hiding in the cellar today for her.

At the end of the seafront a column of flickering lamps light the path up to the huer's hut. Pearl joins the line of people winding that way. The sound of the trumpet grows louder with each step. The bell's still pealing, though there can't be many left in bed to rouse. Pearl looks up from the path as shadows graze overhead; gulls are streaming across the cliff to attack the shoal, their cries chiming against the bell's clear sound. As she turns her head she loses her footing and puts out her hands to steady herself, the soft mud of the churned path meeting her grip.

The huer's hut is hidden by the mass of people surrounding it. Some are artists, standing beneath umbrellas. Morlanow's people brave the rain, smiling as it soaks them. A little way off, three other huers are dancing. They're directing different crews, employed by other palace owners. On the water below, groups of boats will move in on the shoal, trying to enclose as many fish as possible. Pearl only has eyes for her father's boat. She moves close to the cliff edge so that she can watch Mr Jenner, the huer in the Master's pay, who will direct her father and his crew from up here. Nicholas is standing by his grandfather, carefully holding the green-and-white tin trumpet.

The crowd here's quieter than the people at the seafront. It's a difficult job being huer. Her father says he would rather be in the boat than have the burden of directing the seines.

So many bussa jars depend on Mr Jenner to be filled. He's bent over from years of waiting, his whole frame leaning forward to see the fish appear in the water. Pearl can feel the tension in him, how tight his muscles are against his bones, and how his eyes burn for the longed-for sight of the fish.

Mr Jenner grasps two little moons, the bushes, gorse balled and tied to a stick to make a handle, pale muslin stretched taut around the shape. Mr Jenner wields the bushes to direct her father and the other men in the boats. All his different movements are a code that the seine men know, watching Mr Jenner from the boats while the tricksy fish play their games about them. Mr Jenner has the best view from up here on the cliff. He knows how the fish will turn when they get into the bay.

All of a sudden Mr Jenner drops the bushes and grabs the trumpet from Nicholas. He calls down to the boats far below, the trumpet making his voice boom and bounce off the cliff face.

'Steady, boys. Steady. Not yet. Damn and blast, Tremain – get round!'

He shoves the trumpet back at Nicholas, picks up the muslin bushes again and runs to the huer's hut. He climbs the ladder leaning against it, nimble despite his crooked back, and gets onto the roof where the men will be able to see him better. Once more he waves signals with the muslin bushes.

Already night is nearly over. The sky is a soft green where it lips the sea. Pearl moves forward, a few paces from where Nicholas stands. He turns to see her. He looks older, as if Mr Jenner's age and worry for the fish have seeped in to his flesh in the days he has spent up on the cliff, watching the sea. The rain has flattened his hair to his head and his mouth is fixed in a hard line. He grabs Pearl's hand and whispers to her, trying not to disturb Mr Jenner's concentration.

'Think how far they've come just to swim into a trap. All that way in the water and they'll be sent out again, next time above it, dead in a hogshead.'

Nicholas's breath mists as it leaves his mouth and his grip on her hand is icy and a little too tight. She can see the boats quite clearly now. Her father's seine boat, *Fair Maid*, pulls ahead. A few yards over lies the shoal itself.

She can't think of the shoal as being made of food, as scales circled under a stone while oil's forced out, not yet. While still in the water the shoal shapes itself into a woman, swimming and slicing through the sea. Nothing should be able to hold this strange woman, let alone a seine net cast upon her by tired and cold fishermen.

The Master's team of men are working ahead of the other crews. Following Mr Jenner's waved instructions and swearing – her mother wouldn't approve of the bad words – her father's boat and two others make a triangle at one end of the shoal. Pearl knows the men will be praying together as they do so, but quietly, as the fish don't like noise. The oldest Pengelley boy, Stephen, and Mr Polance take the great seine net in their arms. They are in *Fair Maid* and her father's in charge of the oars. Lead weights are tied to one end of the net. Pearl runs her eyes the length of it to the corks at the other. Mr Jenner swings the muslin bush that is in his right hand, the sign for those on shore to take the long warp rope, attached to the seine net, to the nearest capstan. The warp will draw the net to the surface and hold it steady once the fish are caught.

But the warp won't be pulled just yet. Mr Jenner is readying himself for the most important moment of the entire catch. He bends his knees and leans even closer to the roof of the hut, his hands spread wide as if he's holding an enormous fish that no one else can see. Slowly, he raises both bushes above his head. Pearl's chest tightens as the low murmur of voices around her falls to silence. The drip drip drip of rain on the hut roof is as loud as thunderclaps. Still holding Pearl's hand, Nicholas puts the tin trumpet to his lips; Pearl knows it's an honour to give the call. Nicholas will be closer to being thought a man than a boy. He looks up at his grandfather, waiting for the signal. His shoulders are slumped, as if he doesn't want his part in capturing the fish. Perhaps he's just cold.

In the boats below, the fishermen are stock still, locked in their positions until they are given the sign to shoot the net. The tumble of the gulls just above their heads seems wilder against their stillness. Pearl's hands begin to tremble. She's suddenly aware of the rain slipping down her back. A shiver runs the length of her. She can barely watch the boats but she can't look away either. And then at last the moment comes.

Mr Jenner brings both white bushes down at once then swings them backwards, round and round.

Nicholas shouts through the trumpet for the men to shoot the net. 'Cowl rooz!'

The statues of fishermen in her father's boat wake up and are a blur. Mr Polance and Stephen drop the leaded end of the seine net into the water. Opposite them, Mr Tremain in one of the other smaller boats does the same but with a shorter net. Both these boats move cautiously around the shoal so that their nets come together in a circle. The last boat waits at the point where the nets haven't reached yet. The boy in it beats his oars on the surface of the water; the thrashing frightens the poor shoal woman so that she doesn't try to escape while the nets are joined.

From the cliff, the shoal looks to be split into circles by the different crews, bobbing corks marking out the shapes. The fish inside them are not silver but purple, almost red where they are crammed together just below the surface. On the shore there are men straining at the capstan's beams to draw the seine net closer, out of reach of the tide which might lift the net from the seabed and let the fish escape. The crowd on the cliff has relaxed, together letting out an enormous sigh of relief. The tricky part of the catch is over, but no one will know how many fish have been enclosed until low tide. Even now, there could be fewer than is hoped; even now there's the sour taste of fear in Pearl's mouth. The shoal is a mysterious woman, able to twist herself around the nets and slip out where you couldn't see a gap.

People begin to move back down the cliff path. Mr Jenner crumples onto the roof in a heap. Nicholas is still holding Pearl's hand but the iciness has left his grip, and slow warmth slips from his fingers into hers. She looks at their hands joined together, then up at his face. He has lost the wildness that scared her earlier; he's calmer, softer, though still there's a trace of a stranger lingering there.

'What's wrong? Cold?' he says.

Pearl realises she has been frowning up at him. 'A little,' she says.

'Let's go down. They'll be tucking soon.'

Even though nothing more can be seen of the fish until low tide, no one can bear to leave the seafront. Morning has fully opened its arms around the bay and with its light the clouds untangle their dark knots and disappear, taking the rain with them. The sun, which has been hiding its head while the seine nets were shot, now hangs full and strong. Morlanow begins to steam, the damp burning up in the air.

She finds her mother by the slipway, standing with her father and Mr Polance. Her father's hands are clamped round a tin mug of tea. Shadows hollow his eyes and there's a blue tint to his lips and skin. He's shivering without noticing, it seems to Pearl, because he's laughing with Mr Polance at the same time.

'It's a good haul, I reckon,' her father says. 'They were packed deep. Like that season – what was it? 1872?'

Mr Polance whistles. 'If it's as many as that we'll be blessed,' he says.

'Just as long as they pulled the net in quick enough,' her father says. 'She was starting to lift. I hope to goodness they got her fast in time.'

Mr Polance sees Pearl approaching on her own. 'Hello, my sweet,' he says to her. 'Been watching from the cliff? Your father did a fine job today.'

Her father pats Mr Polance on the back and then lays his cold, wet hand on Pearl's head. Her mother fusses.

'Look at the state of you!' she says. 'Did you crawl up the cliff path?' Pearl notices the mud slashed across her wet pinafore. 'You'll have a chill in no time, my girl,' her mother says. 'I should get you into dry clothes.'

'I don't want to miss the tuck. Please,' Pearl begs. 'The sun's out now. I'll dry. And I'm sorry for the mud.'

Her father strokes Pearl's hair. 'You're made of sturdier stuff aren't you, Pearl? Tough as a seine boat.'

Pearl puffs her chest out.

'Have you seen my boy?' Mr Polance asks her. Pearl nods and points back along the seafront where Nicholas is walking through the crowd towards them, slowed by those who want to shake his hand.

Mr Polance waves. 'Heard you give the call,' he shouts. 'Brave job, my boy.' When Nicholas reaches them his father grips him round his back and smiles into his son's cheek. 'Your grandfather was pleased, no doubt. Where's the old salt?'

Jack is lingering behind her mother, unnoticed by anyone

else. Pearl realises she hasn't thought of him all morning, not once. He's paler than usual and looks soaked through, as if he has jumped in the sea rather than stood in the rain. He watches Nicholas and Mr Polance.

The Master appears from the direction of the palace, buttoned up in a greatcoat and looking completely dry. Her father and Mr Polance straighten up, her father brushing the wet hair from his face.

'Tuck nets need to be made ready,' the Master says. Her father and Mr Polance put down their mugs of tea and go onto the sand where *Fair Maid* is pulled up. There's no fierceness in the Master's voice but he has a way of making people jump to attention. Mr Tremain hasn't left his boat but sits in it where it's been pulled up on the beach, looking out to sea, Jack forgotten again.

'I'd best be getting to the palace then,' her mother says, giving Pearl a quick kiss and leaving the children with the Master.

There's silence then as the Master looks over the children. They know and don't know this burly, squinting figure. He was touched by the measles a long time ago. The touch got into his eyes and left them weak, likely to water. His face is stern mostly, but it often looks as if he's crying.

'I'm told you gave the call to drop the net, Nicholas,' he says.

Nicholas is struck dumb at being addressed by the Master. It's all he can do to nod. The Master bestows a smile on him and ever so gently so as you would miss it if you blinked, touches Nicholas on the shoulder.

'Thank you,' he says. Then, almost as an afterthought, 'You'll go far, my lad.'

None of the children can say anything. Pearl looks up at Nicholas. He seems embarrassed by the Master's words.

Jack makes a loud huffing noise and kicks his foot against the ground. 'I saw you,' he says to Nicholas. 'All you did was shout two words through the trumpet. Anyone could do that.'

'You didn't get to do it though, did you, Jack? No one asked you to give the call.'

Jack pouts and kicks the ground again. 'It's not fair.'

'Stop your whining,' Nicholas tells him. 'I'm going to watch the tuck. Pearl?' Without waiting for an answer, Nicholas takes her hand, and they are walking away from Jack, down the slipway onto the beach, and she doesn't look back.

Pearl doesn't see Jack for the rest of the day. She knows he's nearby, probably close enough to watch the tuck, but he keeps out of sight. Several times Pearl turns round sharply thinking she'll catch him, but he isn't there.

When the tide drops, her father and his crew get back into their boats again and row out to the circle of cork that marks their trapped fish. Fishermen who aren't seine men stand by their own little boats, ready to take out any passengers able to pay for a better view. The seine men don't mind too much, as long as those watching don't get in the way. The water soon teems with boats and the visitors leaning from them. Some of the women have changed their umbrellas for parasols now the sun is crowning the sky with its heat. The parasols look like enormous birds with their wings outstretched, drifting along the water. Pearl saw a painting of a swan once, when the artists opened up their studios on Show Day. This is what the parasols look like; white swans bent from bone frames, their cotton skins pure against the dirty feathers of the gulls.

Her mother and the other cellar maids are already inside the palace, laying the salt on the floor. Pearl should be there too but she wants to see the fish come in.

Fair Maid has cleared the corks and now sits in the middle of the circle marked by the net. Her father and Mr Polance take the small tuck net between them and gently lower it into the water. There's a long pause when nothing seems to happen but they must be casting the net underneath what she hopes is a burden of fish. The greedy hake will be waiting, circling the protective wall of the seine net and ready to charge the pilchards if they are given an inch. Pearl hears the seine men's chant, the *one two three*, and they begin to heave the smaller tuck net to the surface. The air in her chest rattles against her ribs. The water inside the circle of corks changes its skin, wobbling like a mug of tea on a knocked table. Waves grow on the wobble, rocking up foam. The water ripples violently but only inside the circle of corks. Overhead, the gulls strike up a more piercing shriek and dive for the fish they know are close. Pearl finds herself leaning into Nicholas, wanting to avoid the consuming disappointment of not enough pilchards in the net.

The water boils, spluttering itself to the colour of rust. Still the men heave on the net. Clusters of silver spot the reddish mess of water, tumbling clearer and clearer, until the silver smoothes into tails. The shoal appears as a single body for one moment more, caught a few inches below the surface. Then, with one last haul of the net, the shoal woman is broken into a million fish, thrashing and fighting each other in their desperate attempts to escape. Once Pearl thinks of the shoal as separate fish they are as good as buried in salt. That beautiful woman is gone.

The seine men let out whoops of joy as they secure the tuck net. Pearl's breathing eases and she realises her hands are buried inside Nicholas's coat pocket. She has been pulling at him each time the men heave up the net, as if he's a prize catch she can't let slip away.

'Leave off, limpet-legs,' he says, 'you'll tear it.'

She stows her hands behind her back, embarrassed. Dipper boats are heading out to empty the tuck net of its spluttering contents. Her father and the others take baskets from inside the seine boat and skim them across the glimmering quiver that is the pilchards. They begin to sing as they dip and lift each basket in unison, in time with the hymn Pearl knows so well.

The waves of the sea Hath lift up their voice,
Sore troubled that we In Jesus rejoice;
The floods they are roaring, But Jesus is here;
While we are adoring, He always is near.

When they lift the full baskets clear, it looks as if they've each captured a wealth of stars, but the men must be quick. As soon as the fish are taken from the water, a clock inside them begins to tick out their freshness. Their scales droop light, their bodies go limp. So the baskets are tipped straight into the waiting dipper boats. The seine men plunge the baskets into the fish, again and again, filling the dipper boats until they're low in the water. Those rowing the laden dipper boats back to shore sit up to their waists in pilchards, like many-tailed mermen.

It will be all right, it will be all right, Pearl murmurs. The shoal has provided for Morlanow and the Papists. Thousands of hogsheads will journey from her home to far away shores. This first catch is only the beginning; a great season has unrolled its glory today. The dippers are coming into shore. Men stand ready with gurries to carry the fish to the women waiting in the palace. Pearl turns to Nicholas to tell him that it will be all right, but he has gone.

PART THREE

1936 and 1889

One

He was coming back.

She curled herself around the memory of the cairn and knapweed flowers on the cliff path, the promise they gave. But she was afraid too. It had been such a long time.

Jack sighed in his sleep and pulled at the bedding. She let him take it, leaving herself draped in the thin sheet of moonlight that cut through the curtains. The moon was waxing, almost a quarter full. The glow was reassuring. It gave the room and its contents solid, recognisable edges. All was given up to the searching fingers of the beams. Nothing could hide here.

From beyond the window came the sound of something metal crashing to the ground. Mrs Tiddy's cat flirting with the toms and knocking things about, she thought. In the quiet that followed she could hear the sea. There was never silence in Morlanow. The day's work on the palace seemed to hang in the air, as if a chisel had only that moment ceased its ring.

The curtain twitched. The moonlight trembled across her bare legs then resettled. Neither she nor Jack liked complete darkness. When they were children, the fires under the cooking slabs in their separate yet matching houses were never allowed to go out. The safe smoulders hovered just beyond their eyelids, to be ready for stirring back into flames in the morning, and to keep keygrims at bay.

Pearl shivered and pulled the bedding back over herself, easing it from Jack's tight grip. The thought of keygrims made her skin goosey even though it was another mild night. Her mind slipped and shimmied on the outskirts of sleep, fixing a name like a brand on all her thoughts: Nicholas. In the palace. On the drying field. Leaping from the harbour wall.

The sea turned over more loudly. She could hear the slap of water on rock, like wet boots stomping home, even though the new house was far from the shore. All those years living by the sea, so close she felt it tapping on the windowpanes. Perhaps its sound had crept inside her head and taken root, repeating itself endlessly so that now when she thought she heard it, it was only the echo of waves long broken.

He would be old now. Older than her and Jack. A laugh slipped from Pearl's lips before she had a chance to catch it. She clamped a hand over her mouth. Jack shifted in his sleep but didn't wake. The thought of Nicholas at their age was ridiculous. If she tried to think of him with grey hair and skin as lined as Jack's, he appeared in her mind's eye as wearing fancy dress, as if the added years were pieces of a costume. He would throw them all off in an instant; the moment he smiled at her he would be the young man she knew best. Nicholas was preserved like that, playing out the same actions and uttering the same lines that he had all that time ago. Unlike Jack, he hadn't had the chance to age in front of her eyes, but in her memory Nicholas's repertoire was finite. Or rather, it had been, because since the move to *Wave Crest* she was remembering more, seeing him play new parts.

But the images surfacing in her mind weren't made up for actors on a stage. They must have happened or they wouldn't find their way inside her thoughts. She hadn't allowed herself to open the box they had been locked in until now, that was all. After what had happened, hiding her memories away was the only thing she could do. And now, somehow, the key had been turned, and things were escaping. Fighting in the palace. A trip to Skommow Bay. Swimming on a hot day. She had felt the burning sand on the soles of her feet. She had felt that heat. These feelings weren't imaginary, and nor were they deceitful. It was wickedness to deceive, although there were times life forced such acts on good people.

She pictured herself swimming. That would help her sleep, help her get rid of all this. She was in the sea off the beach below the drying field, underwater but not short of breath. She didn't have to breathe because her weak chest was better. The sea filled her veins, her lungs. Streams of light shone in the murky water, twisting into the shape of fish. The mesh of tails flapped in front of her eyes. She couldn't see where one body ended and another began. The room, even with the clarity of the moon, was fading, though not disappearing completely. It was as if someone was showing her a dulled photograph of a scene she knew well, then shaking it slightly from side to side. In the haze she was sure her mother was about to wake her to say that the fish had come, that she must get up. In a moment her boots would be set out in front of her and the lamp would be lit. There was its warmth, stealing up the side of her face, its light in her eyes.

Pearl felt her back lift from the bed sheet with the sway of the tide. Her shoulders rolled and she raised her arms so that her body was pulled further into the depths. She was aware of banks of darkness on the surface of the water above her,

seine boats about to drop the great net. Then the mass of it
was in the water, closing around her.

Nicholas came in at the window.

There was a draught as the sash was raised, although he
lifted it without a sound. He brought the smell of seawater
into the room. It was very cold suddenly though there was no
breeze. She waited, her pulse loud in her ears. A floorboard
creaked. Jack twitched in his sleep, reaching out as if he had
dropped something. Pearl shifted away from him. She couldn't
bear the thought of his hand finding her body at that moment.
Another creak.

Her head began to ache and the pain moved across her
skull. There was the sense of pressure on the room, of many
hands pushing the ceiling from above. Cold forced shivers
from every inch of her. Was Nicholas returning to her as an
old man, shrunken and grey but still flesh, or as a keygrim,
skinless and sour from years beneath the sea? Pearl kept her
eyes closed. She couldn't bear to know, not yet.

He would sense her anger. Even though she had willed this
moment to come, part of her rose up against him. *How dare
you. How dare you make me feel this way.* He never thought
of her, of how he shook everything inside her so that she felt
as if all the fish hooks in Morlanow had tugged her in
different directions. And there was George. The child had
suffered too, was still suffering. Her son's eyes across the
kitchen table, pleading with her to tell him of this man.

Her rage was greater now than it had been in years. It was
heavy as a pressing stone, dragging her to the bottom of the
sea where the weight of all the water of the world, all the
water he had sailed away on, would fix her still.

She was already there. Her body stiffened and arched
against the mattress. Her hands became claws and her tongue

pooled uselessly at the side of her mouth. Her head held a furnace that roared in the silence of the room.

Longing to catch a glimpse she tried to look round the room but was unable to move her head. The moonlight still shone. She thought she could just make out a furring of black in the corner. There was no furniture there, just a patch of floor between the small table next to Jack's side of the bed and the window frame. A trick of the light perhaps, or maybe Jack had piled his discarded clothes in that space. But then the clump of shadow moved.

Two

She woke thick-headed and sore, as if she'd spent the night at sea, battered by waves. A muscle in her leg twitched against the mattress. The bedroom grew into solid aspects of itself. She felt the thinness of the room. The weight of expectation Nicholas had brought was gone. He had come to her only to leave. Her tears came fast and unchecked, pouring from her jaw line on to the pillow.

Rolling onto her side she was relieved to see that only Jack's shape was still pressed in to the sheet. She held her breath and listened to the house's melodies. Beneath its usual creaks and ticks there was silence. Jack must have already left for the seafront. Pearl lay there a moment, the bed cover and sheets twisted around her like nets piled in a loft. Heavy sobs beat against her ribs but she swallowed and swallowed until the tears stopped and her breath eased. If only it were as easy to rid herself of this old hurt.

If she didn't move, Nicholas might come back. There might be some part of him left. He might be hiding, having waited for Jack to go. She waited. There was nothing. The sense of him had gone.

It was late. Through the drawn curtains she could tell the sun was halfway up the sky. She felt trapped in the bed, bound up in the sheets and twisted at an awkward angle. She struggled from them and stood up, her bare feet tingling on the floorboards. Everything looked as it should. The room was the same. Pearl moved, her head aching, to the window. Her nightdress billowed around her as if trying to hold her back. She opened the curtains and stood in the square of light. This was where the creak had started from. This was where Nicholas had come in. She ran a hand over the boards then put her finger to her lips. Seawater.

He had come last night then. Here was proof. She had held faith and had been rewarded, though even without the seawater some long-hidden core of her knew for certain. Nicholas had felt so close and to feel something so strongly – it had to be real.

Her chest swelled then constricted. What if Jack found out? She put on her housecoat over her nightdress and went downstairs. In the hall hung the one mirror she and Jack owned. It was in an awkward place, too near the front door. It had come from her parents, and before that from Mammow, her father's mother. The gazes of so many women sharing her blood had fallen on this glass. Some days, Pearl found them looking back at her. Jack never looked at himself. Even shaving he went without the mirror and would shy away from it as he left the house.

Pearl hovered in the hallway, uncertain why she had come downstairs. Nicholas swam through her thoughts, sending them to ripples. Everything was blurring. The mirror drew her closer, promising to show her what was true and firm.

When Pearl stared in the cracked and spotted glass, the face that peered back was her mother's, but it was her mother had she lived longer. A broad forehead creased and wrinkled as if she was constantly thinking of difficult things. Frowns that hadn't been smoothed away but had been joined by others. Eyes the colour of stewed tea, almost lost in the shadows and yellowing darts beneath them. The lids were rimmed red and the skin around the sockets was puffy from crying. A small nose, a sharp little mouth; never a rosebud. She fussed with her hair. Long white strands, fluffy at the crown like a young gull's feathers, the rest as thick as horsehair. Pearl turned and turned about, watching this woman who was not her mother and yet not herself either.

Since the move there had been days when Pearl knew this old woman and felt the weight of her age in her own joints. But mostly the woman was a stranger and Pearl herself was lickety-spit, a lightning swimmer ready to dive away from this crotchety, tear-marked face looking back at her. Nicholas might not recognise her but she would always know him.

Three

Her screaming wakes her. The dream again. In it she's walking on the beach below the drying field, her feet cut and bleeding. She doesn't know where she's been or why she's there until she hears it. Her name, whispered in her ear. She can't stop walking towards the water's edge. There's something rising from the waves, something covered in weed and muck. It's reaching out to her. Its hand is a broken shell. She screams.

It's hard to be certain she's awake. The line between sleep and wakefulness isn't an honest one in the dream. Her throat is hoarse. Her back's slick with sweat and sticking to the all tossed about sheet. It could still be with her, that thing in the water. Though she knows what it is. Of course she knows.

The minutes pass. There's no voice calling her name. It's gone.

The house is empty. Her parents and Polly are at chapel. Pearl had a bad chest in the night, bad enough even to miss the service, but not so bad her mother would stay at home with her. She'll be praying for Pearl.

The cup on the floor by her bed is smashed, the wood

around it damp. Her throat is dry as bone. She gets up to find a drink and her legs sway. She makes it to the top of the stairs then has to rest. Her chest is still bad though many people said she'd grow out of it. Old Mrs Pendeen was adamant it wouldn't trouble Pearl past sixteen yet here she is, twenty-one and worse than ever. Old Mrs Pendeen seems annoyed by this, as if Pearl hasn't tried hard enough to prove her right.

The house's only mirror hangs at the top of the stairs. Pearl looks a sight, but that's her usual self: still untidy and untucked, unable to shake off the little girl who became grubby as soon as she stepped outside. Her body has broken from that shell though and stretched itself thin, finding few curves to grace her. Today her face is flushed from coughing, the dream and the previous day's work. Her hands have become those of her mother's, sore and roughly musical when rubbed together, the skin split from days in the palace.

Pearl knows now that she's not beautiful. She has some sense of the way men look at women and can tell if a person is sweet on another. It doesn't trouble her – after all, nothing can be done – though she wonders if perhaps she might be thought pretty, if a person would take the time to look at her, to see past the redness of her eyes and the shadows in her face.

She stirs herself and sets off down the stairs, one at a time and with another rest halfway. Nicholas will call for her soon. She needs to be ready, her hair brushed and her cleanest skirt on, the only one that's not for best and that's not been worn to the palace. Not that he'll notice of course. Thankfully the water pail is close to the last stair. The water makes her gag at first. It tastes wrong. Of blood. Then she realises the blood is her own, caught up in her spit from the coughing. She sits on the bottom stair, her knees hunched into her stupid weak chest. Dust circles through the musty air. The dream comes back but she closes her eyes and shakes it away with thoughts of the coming day. She needs to be gone before her parents and Polly come home. She'll leave a note. Fresh air's the best thing after a coughing fit. Old Mrs Pendeen always says so. No one needs to know Pearl will have company on her walk and if they're seen and there's gossip then she can just say Nicholas was keeping an eye on her, offering her an arm. She needs looking after, doesn't she? And they're friends, that's all. Women mutter to her mother that it's not right the way Pearl still prefers to be with the boys, not seemly now that they're men. There's a shadow beneath the front door. He's here.

The streets are all but empty. She waits for him to take her arm, even coughs a little to suggest she might need it. He frowns, concerned, and takes her hand instead. But it's not just concern that makes him do it, and it's not like when he used to help her clamber over to the rock pools, when they launched model boats. It's different now. Surely he feels it? There's a something else between them, something that keeps her awake at night, makes her tongue-tied in front of him.

It's glorious to be out in the day like this, holding hands and all the gossips stuck inside chapel. The only people they see on their way to the beach are artists and they've been turning a blind eye since they first began stepping off the train. Miss Charles is long gone from Morlanow but there are more studios than when she ran the art school. There'll be more paintbrushes in lofts than nets, her father used to say when Pearl was a child. He would smile. It was a joke then, unlikely. But now it's true.

'You know what's good for a bad chest?' Pearl says.

'Someone else's?' Nicholas says, putting his hand to his own.

179

She blushes and is instantly cross with herself. Why can't she be as tart with the boys as Sarah Dray is, as Polly is, without this childishness coming on?

'Swimming,' she says.

He shakes his head but is grinning. She knows he'll let her. He'll be itching to get in the water too and when they're deep enough so their feet don't reach the bottom her blushes will go. They always do. When they're bobbing together they knock elbows. One of them will graze the other's shin with their foot. They've stopped mumbling apologies in recent weeks. They will be closer than they are on land because both of them are different in the water.

It's a warm day, the first real sign of summer after cloud and cool breezes for weeks. He turns his back when she takes off her dress though he doesn't need to as she's wearing her nightdress underneath. He keeps his trousers on but takes off his shirt. She has perfected the art of looking at his chest without making it obvious, because that would be something new, unacknowledged. That would make the gossips right. His collar bone catches her eyes today, the line of it. She wants to run a finger across it to feel the bone beneath, the smoothness of his skin. She busies herself folding her dress and placing it on a rock.

They don't rush into the sea but savour the transition from dry to wet, letting the waves splash water up their legs then their chests. His presence by her side is strong. His body is close to her. It's all she can see. He seems to block out the cliffs, the horizon.

'Better already,' she says.

'You look it,' he says. 'Let's swim out.'

He strikes ahead of her and she watches his brown hair moving away. It's grown long, to his collar, but she likes it. His skin is nearly as pale as hers. He works on land, in the

Master's office, moving numbers from one tidy column into another. He's clever, this grown up boy Nicholas has become. Still thin and wiry, still with a lean face. His eyes are dark pools.

'Hang on,' she calls. 'Wait for me, Nicholas.'

He turns and waves, twenty feet or so away. Her chest still isn't right. She can't swim as strongly as usual. She can taste blood again. Nicholas bobs where he is, letting her catch up. Her nightdress blooms around her like a sail. She reaches him and he touches her arm, very gently. She wants to grab him, hold him tightly in the water. Would he let her? He is all she wants but he's hard to fathom. He might only think of her as she thinks of Jack, as a friend. But she would never do this with Jack, never get down to her nightdress and be close with him in the water. Close enough to press herself against him. But this doubt makes her keep her hands at her sides, beating time with the waves, her pulse. Morlanow has doubts too. The women mutter about Pearl but everyone mutters about Nicholas. She has a good reason not to be in chapel today. Nicholas doesn't.

'It's nearly dinner time,' she says. 'We should go back.'

He's disappointed. Even in the water she can see his shoulders slump. But he doesn't argue. Talk in Morlanow is a dangerous thing.

They reach their street through alleyways in the fisherman's quarter rather than the open space of the seafront. In the alleys you can disappear. At the back wall of the yard behind Pearl's house they say good bye. Nicholas gives her a leg-up to get over the wall. When his hand touches her leg she blushes and again she has a desire to hold him, fiercely and without blushing. She should have done so in the sea, or said something in the alleys on the way home. This closeness is almost too much to bear. She lingers on the wall, sitting astride the bricks, looking down at the squawking chickens in her yard and daring herself to tell him about this feeling that keeps threatening to overwhelm her. She hears singing. Alice is in the yard next door. There's no sign of little Samuel. Pearl's foot knocks a loose chunk of brick. Alice looks up. Her singing stops.

'Be quick,' she says to Pearl. 'They're on their way back.'

Nicholas climbs over his own wall, elegant as ever, and nips indoors. Next time, she promises herself.

'Thanks,' Pearl says to Alice but the Tremain yard is empty. The singing is faint inside the house. Pearl half slides, half falls into her yard. She scrapes her leg on the rough brick and feels it bleeding but she can't stop to look. She has to have her nightdress hidden before everyone gets back. She has to hide this thing that's started, to keep it safe and for herself.

Four

The front door banged. She was in the kitchen, leaning her forehead against the wall. Jack was back. The day had stolen past her again. How long had she stood there? Still in her nightdress, the housecoat wrongly buttoned over it. She had been looking in the mirror, hadn't she? But crumbs of sand clung to her bare feet.

Jack hung his coat on the back of the door and put a papered parcel of fish on the table. He ran his eyes over Pearl. 'What are you doing?' he said.

The light was fading. She was supposed to be in bed. Her chest was bad. There was something she was meant to be hiding. Jack was watching her.

'I've been that busy today,' Pearl said. 'I was just taking a breath.'

Jack didn't move but continued looking at her. She smoothed her nightdress. It was clammy against her skin.

'That busy you couldn't get yourself dressed? What *have* you been doing?'

Pearl jammed her hands on her hips. 'What have I been

doing? I ask you! Washing every scrap of cloth in the house and wearing my hands out with soap. Is that enough for you or would you rather be looking after yourself these days, Mr Tremain?' That got him. 'Then I went down to the shop and felt that worn after the walk back up here that I got into bed for an hour or so.'

'Calm down. I hear you.' He sat at the table, taking in her sandy feet. 'You've not been swimming, have you?'

'I wouldn't have the time,' she told him.

Jack looked as if he was going to press the matter but instead sat quietly, waiting for her to come and take off his boots. 'You were laid thick as a lintel this morning,' he said. 'Didn't stir a beat when I left.'

She didn't move. Let him wait to have his boots off.

'I was awake half the night,' she said. 'Cat misbehaving outside.' She tried to sound relaxed though her breath was rushing quicker. 'You didn't hear anything?'

'Nothing,' he said. 'What's for supper?'

Pearl heated some fat in a pan and buttered bread, all the time aware of Jack's eyes on her. Perhaps he was lying and had been awake last night when Nicholas came to her. A fresh thought struck her – perhaps Jack had made Nicholas leave, had banished him from the room. He was crafty, little Jack Tremain, and good at hiding. Always last to be found in games of hide and seek, able to hunt out secret hollows and tuck his limbs away. Even when he was brought into the daylight and a new game was begun, Pearl had the feeling that he hadn't been found so much as given himself up, tired of waiting.

'What's that?' he said. 'You're mumbling, Pearl.'

She was chewing words into her cheek.

'Have you eaten today?' Jack said. 'You've no colour in you.'

She couldn't remember. The bulk of the day was a cliff drop. That she couldn't think what she had done with it brought a shake to her hands. She turned and managed to smile. 'Course I have,' she said. 'Go and wash. I'll put the fish on.'

But he was staring at her. Why wouldn't he look away?

Jack got to his feet. 'You have been swimming!' he shouted. 'I can see it on you. Look at yourself – jumping all over the place. For goodness sake, Pearl.' Then he lowered his head. 'I can't do for myself, you know that.' His twisted fingers groped uselessly for one another. 'You'll have to take better care of yourself, and, and...get rid of this funny business. Mrs Tiddy told me—'

'I heard my mother, on the seafront.' The words flew from Pearl's mouth before she had time to think.

He was struck dumb for a moment then said, 'What are you talking about?' He looked at her in exasperation, spreading his hands wide. 'It's this nonsense you've got to stop. People will talk and then...'

Pearl slumped into a chair. He came to stand over her.

'You'll be holed up in some hospital place,' he said. 'You see?'

She nodded. Jack patted her shoulder and left the room. She sat very still. The butter on the bread was a lurid streak of grease. A fly nosed the fat in the pan. It wouldn't do to let her guard down around Jack. He would play a long game, waiting for Pearl to give something away. It was the way he moved around her. It was obvious in that still moment in the kitchen. She wondered that she hadn't seen it before.

She stood and opened the front door. She could barely hear the sea but just the sight of its rich doily heads made Pearl more certain. Nicholas had come to her. He'd gone but he hadn't gone far and he would be back. The white hare and the knapweed cairn said so. Waiting was in her bones. Each season the pilchards played with Morlanow, making everyone linger at the seafront for weeks or months, some years never coming at all. Pearl had waited for Nicholas this long, she could wait a while yet. But she would have to be cautious. She couldn't trust Jack one inch.

Five

She's stuck indoors again. The dream came for her last night and with it a fit of coughing, her chest shut tight and hot. She's not in bed today though, not taken as bad as that, but still unable to go to the palace. The women are making ready for another catch of pilchards. They are back to waiting, Morlanow's most constant state. Nicholas might come calling. He said he would try and slip away from the Master's hut. Only to see how she's faring, of course. Nothing more than that. They'll stay inside today, keep away from prying eyes, sitting by the hearth. Just to talk, to hear the news from the seafront. But perhaps when he's told her all about the orders and the prices she'll be able tell him how she feels, and maybe he'll put his arms around her and hold her, not just graze her hand in a way that could be accidental. She wants him to say he wants her too. She needs him to say it.

There's a knock at the door and she's on her feet quicker than she should be with her chest as bad as it is. But it's Gerald Hoskin on the doorstep, Polly's young man. Gerald smiles but it's clear he's as disappointed as Pearl. When Pearl realised she wasn't beautiful it was partly because she saw that Polly had become a looker. Her sister has grown more rosy-faced and tidy as Sarah Dray's got stouter, which is something at least. Before Polly was ensnared by Gerald, men stared openly in the street and left posies of primroses at the back door, hoping her father wouldn't catch them in the act. But now Gerald is the only man who brings Polly flowers from the cliff path.

He's not a tall man, and not broad for a fisherman either, but his hands are strong. He has a big family in Govenek where he's from – six brothers and two sisters – and they all look like him. Blond with creased up eyes. He reads very well and when he's brave enough to try he can make people laugh too. But he doesn't have a boat of his own and no crews are hiring.

'Morning,' Gerald says, his cheeks colouring as they do when anyone but Polly speaks to him. 'Is she here?'

'She's at the palace,' Pearl says. 'She'll be home for her dinner, I think. You can stay and wait if you want.'

'I don't want to trouble you. I'll go and wait for her outside the palace. I don't mind.'

Pearl smiles and nods, picturing the catcalls from the women when they see him mooning about in the doorway. But he's kind and good and Polly is lucky to have someone like Gerald who so clearly loves her.

'You sure?' Pearl says. 'I can make you some tea.'

'No, it's fine. Plenty on the seafront to keep me entertained. That many east coast men using the harbour today. More of them than Morlanow men, I should think.'

Pearl doesn't say anything to that. Everyone's got something to say about the east coast men. There's no use adding to the bad feeling.

'If it wasn't for their Sunday practices I wouldn't mind

them,' Gerald says, lost in his own thoughts. 'Seem a good sort and they've got some smart gear to fish with. Getting big catches. But then who am I to talk, eh? Govenek men been sinners longer than the east coasters, and at least Sabbath-breakers have boats.'

'Gerald...'

He scuffs his boot on the ground, keeping his eyes fixed on it when he says, 'I don't know why your Polly holds out any hope for me, Pearl. Your father'll see sense soon enough and I'll be sent back up the cliff path home.'

'He likes you,' Pearl says. 'You're a fisherman.'

'Without a boat,' Gerald says. 'Not much of one.'

'Things will get better,' she says. 'Someone will take you on as a hand at least, then you'll be able to work towards your own boat.'

Gerald looks up and smiles but sadly. 'Not here,' he says. 'There's nothing for us here.'

She doesn't know what to say and Gerald looks uncomfortable. There's an awkward pause before he turns abruptly and goes off in the direction of the palace. Such melancholy isn't like him but there's plenty of that around the harbour wall. Melancholy and whispering. She's about to shut the door on it all when she hears a shout from next door, on the Tremain side of the house. It's the usual row. Mr Tremain is shouting at Alice which is soon followed by the cries of the child, Samuel. Jack will be safely out at sea at least. The weather's good. For east coast men and Morlanow men. But not for poor Gerald.

She can't settle to anything, waiting for Nicholas who doesn't come. He must be too busy in the Master's hut which is hot and filled with ledgers. Or maybe he didn't want to see her. Maybe he has other girls to sit with by the hearth. That thought is so terrible she gets up and, eager to busy herself, decides to clean the cooking slab. She rubs hard at its black iron surface.

Her mother and Polly come back at midday. Polly tears off her oily apron, hurls it in the corner of the room then bursts into tears. Their mother throws up her hands and says to Pearl, 'I don't know what to say to her. If it's Gerald she wants then she'll just have to wait for him.' And then to Polly, 'You can't have a home of your own without a wage.' At this Polly only cries harder.

'I'm tired of waiting,' Polly says, her pretty face red and swollen with crying. She won't look at Pearl or her mother, just stares at the hearth with leaden eyes. 'I'm tired of sharing a bed with Pearl, tired of making Father's supper, tired of all this.' She puts her hands over her eyes and cries again.

Their mother ignores her, getting out the plates. 'We've all had to wait,' she says, but to herself in a low voice. 'Gerald's got to get a boat. No good crying about it.'

They eat their meal in silence. The clock on the mantle ticks out their lives. Polly looks murderously towards it, as if she'd like to throw it through the window.

Six

When Sunday rolls round again Pearl has no excuse to miss chapel. After a few days resting at home – and some secret swims first thing in the morning – her chest is better. Not mended, but better than it has been in a while. Keeping from chapel will do her more harm than good, her mother says.

Gerald is waiting for them outside the house. Polly gives him her arm. He chides her for looking so miserable but in a kind way, so that she manages a smile for the first time in days. Her mother takes her father's arm and, as usual, Pearl walks alone behind them all. She thinks about slipping away, ducking into an alley and making for the beach below the drying field, or Witch Cove round the bay. Her feet slow down, her body keen to escape now the thought's there. Would anyone notice? But there's a hand at her elbow.

'How are you?' Jack says.

Her arm stiffens but she tries not to let him see. He keeps as much distance between their bodies as is comfortable whilst still making contact. He smells of the sea but his shirt is clean and his boots wiped. Alice is managing to look after Jack a little, much as he'll let her.

'Better than I was,' Pearl says. 'You're not walking in with your father?'

'No,' Jack says. Then there's silence and Pearl is grateful for the run of alleys that appear before the main street up the hill to chapel, where they have to walk in single file. When they emerge into daylight she falls into step alongside Polly and Gerald, pretending she doesn't notice that they stop talking mid-sentence. Polly is crying again but wipes her eyes and takes Pearl's arm so that they walk as a three. Jack has drifted away.

Pearl doesn't see him once the service begins. Her family sits together mid-way down. Jack usually sits on his own. His father sits right at the back. Jack won't pray next to him. When Samuel was first brought to chapel he screamed the moment he was inside the doors, kicking his legs and thrashing his arms, as if the little boy could feel what everyone was thinking. He's quiet as a lamb at all other times, so much so that people have said the boy's slow, and they all know why, of course. Alice keeps him at home on Sundays and the commonly spoken view is that it's to spare everyone the disturbance. Mr and Mrs Polance sit in the row in front of Pearl, joined by old Mrs Pendeen who'll sit anywhere she fancies, wherever her gossipy tongue takes her. Mrs Polance has given up the Sunday School classes. There aren't enough children to make it worthwhile sending them to the back room that smells of wet coats.

In the fidgety moments before the service begins people settle themselves on the hard wooden benches, easing their trousers over their knees, spreading their skirts to prevent creases. Pearl's mother leans forwards and speaks to Mrs Polance.

'Annie, where is he?'

Mrs Polance shakes her head but won't turn round. Mr Polance sits in silence, his hands gripping the hymnal. Old

Mrs Pendeen leans backwards, her chapel hat a squashed brown cake.

'Another soul lost,' old Mrs Pendeen says to Pearl's mother. 'He's on the path to sin, you mark my words. Better to cast out the devil than have him taint your home.'

Mrs Polance lowers her head. Fortunately Mr Taylor's wide face appears at that moment in the pulpit. Pearl couldn't have held her tongue much longer. What do any of them know about Nicholas?

The service begins with a hymn. Mrs Taylor plays the organ though it's so old there are more squeaks of lost air than actual notes. It's impossible not to notice that there are fewer voices now to drown out the organ in song. Then come prayers then the sermon. Another denouncement of Sabbath breakers. The east coast and Govenek men are dealt a more painful fate each week as Mr Taylor works himself into a storm. As the preacher's words ebb and flow Pearl drifts away, letting the tide take her out to sea, an arm around her waist, soft lips at her ear.

That night it's Polly who wakes Pearl, not the dream. They still share a bed though it's not big enough for them now. Polly complains that Pearl takes up too much space and gets angry when Pearl fights in her sleep, when the dream makes her walk into the sea.

At first Pearl pretends she's still asleep, ignoring the sobs half muffled by the pillow. What can she say to make Polly feel better? At least she has someone. But the sobs get louder, becoming full body cries that Pearl can feel thrumming through the shared mattress. She'll have to say something or she'll never be able to get back to sleep.

She puts her hand on her sister's shoulder and gently rolls her towards her. Pearl has only the old words for Polly. She knows they won't be any use when Polly's waiting for her life to begin properly, in a home of her own, with a man she loves, but those words are better than nothing.

'Come on now,' Pearl says. 'It'll be all right. Gerald will find some work soon. Maybe the Master will have a berth for him. I'm sure Nicholas will ask for you. He's good like that.'

Polly shakes her head. 'It's too late,' she manages to mumble.

'No, it isn't. The Master's bound to need new hands once the next shoal of pilchards arrives.'

But Polly only shakes her head more vigorously and throws a damp, screwed up piece of paper at Pearl before sobbing into the pillow again. The paper's torn from the newspaper. They don't take one in their house as neither of her parents can read and she and Polly are slow, halting readers. She recognises it though, the local edition. Nicholas can often be found reading it. She lights a candle and smoothes out the scrap on the blanket. It takes her a moment to work out what it says. The long, difficult word 'Australia' takes up most of the space and then underneath there are dates and ports listed. Then she realises what the paper is, what it means. Her body runs cold and she feels as if she'll be sick. Polly has stopped crying. The candle's flame flickers in a draft from the window. Pearl has the sudden desire to put the flame to the advertisement, to make it disappear.

'Do you want to leave?' Pearl says.

'I want to be with Gerald,' Polly says, finally wiping her eyes. Her voice is cold. 'He says it's the only way.'

To leave Morlanow. To get far away from wagging tongues, from chapel, from waiting. The temptation is there inside Pearl, thick and full as if it's been growing for years and she's only just realised.

'Then you should go,' Pearl says. She gives Polly the newspaper scrap and blows out the candle.

Seven

The following day is Monday and washday. Still no shoal has come so Pearl's task is to see to the house's clothes and bedding while her mother spends another day sorting salt and empty hogsheads and Polly absent-mindedly checks nets for holes. There's been no mention of Australia and Pearl has decided it's wiser to keep quiet until a decision has been made.

It's a day's work to scrub and rinse, to wring and press. She longs to escape the confines of the yard, its dusty stone and pock-marked weeds. All she can think of is getting to the sea's edge at the end of the day and feeling the breeze on her face. Not that she will get there at this rate. She's not as good at organising her time as Polly and her mother. Early evening has arrived and the washing is still damp. Given the hot sun today Pearl should have spread the clothes on the drying field like the rest of the women. But time got away from her again and what was going to be a hasty swim devoured most of the morning.

From the other side of the wall between Pearl's yard and that of the Polances' next door there is the scrape of boots against brick. In her yard the dozing chickens scatter in indignation and Nicholas's face appears over the top of the wall. She's struck afresh at how he has grown into a striking young man, still bearing that smile that cuts her to the quick, but still cradling his boyishness too. She can't look at him. She pretends to sort through the washing at her feet.

'You're not still washing, limpet-legs?' he says.

She pauses with her hands caught in a sheet. Why must he call her that? She's not a child any more. He can't want her as she wants him. It's clear from the way he speaks to her. She's annoyed, and disappointed. 'Finished work for the day, have you?' she says. 'All right for some.'

'I've been hard at it,' he says. 'Muddle with the amount needed for the last shipment. A palace maid too busy working her tongue instead of her wits, no doubt.'

Pearl looks at him then, can't help herself. He's smiling and she's smiling too and maybe he feels as she does. Maybe. She scoops a handful of water from the tub at her feet and throws it at him. He ducks and then laughs when the water falls short of the wall anyway.

He still has a cheek to him but she doesn't mind it, has never minded. He's clever with it. The Master, now all but blind, needs Nicholas working on his accounts. He's given him a scratchy-nibbed pen and pages of thick, cream paper that Pearl longs to stroke. Nicholas spends his days filling columns with weights of fish, prices of fish, buyers for fish, yet he doesn't go out to catch any himself. It's good, steady work to have, unlike fishing, and the wages are welcome at home. All the girls in Morlanow should be trying to win him.

'When will you be done?' Nicholas says. 'I've got to help with nets but I'm thinking of disappearing for a bit.'

Pearl wrings out a sheet then flaps it loose of the twist. 'I can't,' she says. 'I'm meant to get the supper but I'm behind as it is. Father's been at sea all day. He'll be hungry.' Though what she will find for him is another matter.

The sun is dropping behind Nicholas, turning the sky orange fired red in swathes. Gulls fleck their dark shapes against this rich display; an enormous painting, Pearl thinks, with Nicholas's head and shoulders as the centrepiece.

'Well, come out after you've eaten,' Nicholas says. 'They can't expect you to sit in with them after scrubbing all day. Just for a while.'

Her insides are as tightly wound as the sheets. She wants to go with him, of course she does. 'I can't. I'm sorry.' She picks up a pair of trousers. There's nothing she can do to change things, however much she wants to.

A door bangs in the Tremain house on the other side. Jack's white-blond head of hair precedes his washed out eyes and broad face over the top of the wall. His skin is burnt from his day at sea and freckles have spread across the bridge of his nose.

Jack nods across the yard. 'Evening,' he says.

Nicholas nods back and Jack shifts on whatever it is he's standing on. Pearl hangs the sheet on the line. She can feel both of them looking down on her in the yard below.

Finally Nicholas clears his throat. 'Good day was it, Jack?'

'Not bad,' Jack says, fiddling with a weed poking through the brickwork. 'Got ling off the lines, tiddlers though. Men of *The Dancer* saw a pilchard shoal past Keeper's Point so I'm hoping for the call tomorrow.'

'I heard that, at the sale this morning, though there was a load of hot air too.' Nicholas shakes his head. 'All that fuss. You'd think the east coast boys of *Good Girl* had set fire to chapel rather than bring in a few fish yesterday.'

Pearl's hands freeze on the washing line. She can feel Jack bristling even with the wall between them.

Jack takes his time before speaking, still toying with the weed poking from the wall. 'I can't hold with that way of thinking, Nicholas. You know it's wrong of them, going out on a Sunday, and even worse to land their fish here.'

'But Jack, it's not as if it's against the law. People have got to eat. East coasters as well as us. Govenek made the change years ago and we've been left behind. We need to try new things, go for other fish. Waiting for the pilchards each year is just foolish. The Master– '

'You'd do better to watch your tongue,' Jack says. 'There's ill feeling towards the *Good Girl* crew and the meeting will– '

'What meeting?' Pearl asks him.

'In the Council rooms,' Jack says. 'All fishermen are going. All those that go to sea.' He says these last words carefully, looking over at Nicholas who tosses his head back and looks at the sky.

'I've spoken to as many people as I can. There's been word the east coast drifters are breaking up pilchard shoals. I know your father's still out, Pearl. When he gets back, you'll tell him? Eight o'clock. Important he's there. Council are dithering about what to do.' He and Nicholas lock gazes. 'Some are forgetting themselves,' Jack says.

'There's no reasoning...' Nicholas sighs. 'Pearl – I'll see you later.' He drops back into his yard.

She shakes out an apron and hangs it on the line. 'He doesn't mean it.'

'It's no good trying to wish it away,' Jack says. 'Nicholas has strayed. I don't want to see him take you with him. I want...' He pulls the weed out of the brick and hurls it to the floor.

She's glad he doesn't finish the sentence but him standing over her without speaking is unnerving. 'How's Samuel?' she says. Anything to stop his brooding. But asking about Samuel is a mistake. Jack's face clouds.

'We have to keep to God's law,' he says. 'It's the Lord that keeps us strong in the face of sin. Samuel needs our prayers as much as anyone. Don't let Nicholas tell you otherwise.'

'Jack, please. I was only asking if Samuel was well.'

'Tell your father,' Jack says. 'Eight o'clock.' He disappears from view. She hears the door slam as he goes inside, followed by the usual shouting from the house. She rummages in the washing basket. Still two shirts and a sheet to fit on the line and no room left. How does her mother do it? The back door in the Tremain house opens and closes, this time more gently. Alice begins to sing and after a few lines Samuel's thin little voice joins in. Pearl feels her mood lift. The washing will dry eventually, somehow, even if it means her mother chiding her when she has to sort it out. Upturning an old pail, Pearl stands to look over the wall.

Alice is sitting on a battered cane chair, Samuel on her lap. They are playing some sort of game where Alice makes different shapes with her hands and Samuel has to tap them at certain shapes, before they change. He chirps and giggles when he misses his tap. Alice has her face buried in his soft blond hair. She's a different woman to the one dragged from the net loft. Her limp is still bad but she has a stick now, and her clothes are clean, cleaner than Pearl's in fact. She pins her hair and has lost the thinness in her face that made her look so ill in the weak light of the palace. She never smells of drink, though Mr Tremain is known to. Alice looks up then, as if hearing Pearl's mind turning over these changes, and smiles.

Pearl is cleaning the plates when her father comes home from the meeting. The supper was small and she's listless, tired. Her mother sits by the cold hearth, darning endless piles of clothes. Some are more seams than fabric. Polly is lying down upstairs, the advertisement hidden under the mattress.

'They won't listen, the men from Yarmouth,' her father says, slamming the door shut. 'They're determined to break faith with us.' He rattles the poker in the empty grate, seeming to enjoy the noise. 'People will buy from them once they've come ashore with their Sabbath fish,' he says, 'low prices they're asking, and that makes our Saturday fish hardly worth catching to sell on Mondays. And the east coast men are only here because landing's so poor at Govenek and we have the train.' He lifts his eyes to the ceiling, as if making sure God is listening to him as well.

Her mother's hands lie idle on her darning, her forehead puckered. 'But they'll not be allowed to carry on, surely?' she says. 'I know they've been at this trick for years, on and off, but not like this, so openly, and so many. They'll be stopped. We'll have to stop them now.'

'Of course we will,' her father says. 'Everything put to the Council tonight was reported from our own men, heard in Yarmouth when they put in during that week of strong wind last month. Council are going to sort it out, so says that lummock in charge, Trevisco, though I don't trust those men any more than I trust the east coasters. Council seem more interested in the train than boats these days. Railway men are coming again next week.'

Pearl moves the cloth slowly over the same plate she has held for some time. The water in the pail has gone cold and a layer of grease clouds its surface. It isn't right for her to speak now, to question her father, even if she felt she could unlock her lips. Nicholas's words from the yard sit heavily on her.

Her father drops the poker and leans back in his chair. 'There were some hotheads there tonight,' he says, 'trying to stir things up. Think we should nip this in the bud now, before these crews get a grip here and turn our men like those of Govenek.'

'It grieves my heart to see Govenek lost. That it should come to this,' her mother says.

Her father humphs in agreement. 'I didn't like the way some were talking, but if the Council don't want to take a lead.'

'Who was stirring?' asks her mother.

'Mostly youngsters,' her father says. 'The Pengelley brothers. That lad Timothy Wills. Some I didn't recognise. And Jack-next-door. He was the worst of them.'

Her mother tuts to herself. 'Alice does a poor job of keeping him in check but it's not her place, is it? Samuel is enough for a woman of her capabilities. And as for that father of his...' Her mother stops before she says something uncharitable. 'You should speak to Jack,' Pearl's mother says to her. 'Make sure he doesn't do anything foolish. He's been out of sorts for a long while. Not right since Peter and Alice...'

Her father gets up and stretches his back. It's almost time for him to go to sea again. 'Yes Pearl, you should speak to him. He'd listen to you.' Both her parents look at her but she concentrates on the plates. 'The last thing we want is any trouble,' her father says, reaching for his oilskin. 'Jack caught me on the way home. Told me about a snake in our midst, one of our own taking up with the east coast men and sabotaging the pilchard catch.'

Pearl drops the plate into the pail with a splash. Her mother eyes an empty pail near the hearth.

'Kettle's dry,' she says to Pearl. 'There's just enough light left if you go for water now.'

Pearl nods and picks up the empty pail, glad to be able to leave the room. Pulling the front door almost closed behind her she puts her ear to the crack.

'I don't know when Nicholas got so certain of himself,' she hears her mother say. 'Such an upstart these days.' The noise of feet across the floor; her mother always paces when she's cross. 'Look at his father, desperate for his boy to go to sea, to fish like the rest of his family. He's got a good home, not like poor Jack. Nicholas's grandfather is the best huer this village has ever had. I saw Sarah Dray this morning and she told me she'd seen Annie Polance scritching. Bad enough Nicholas sides with the back-sliders but to harm everything this village has, I can't credit it. Sarah says his father's ready to send him on his way.'

And then her father's voice. 'Nicholas has been taken off the lifeboat too. When the next flare goes up he'll not be going out. Men don't trust him anymore. Too unpredictable to risk in bad weather.'

The thud of her mother's feet nears the front door. Pearl picks up the pail and quickly moves away.

At the pump she turns over these words. It isn't the actions of the east coast crews that worry her so much – it's against the way of things in Morlanow which means somehow it will be stopped, some solution found – it's more that Nicholas should be talked of like this, and to be taken off the lifeboat as well. Others have bound his opinions to his ability to save a life, as if supporting the east coast fishermen is as good as turning his back on a drowning man.

Her fingers toy with the pump handle. Nicholas isn't afraid to speak up when he can't fit parts of life together. It's his cleverness, his way of seeing things. He seeks points of roughness and tries to smooth them out. Not everyone can see his goodness though, his desire to aid a trouble rather than worsen it. Some people, like Jack and Sarah Dray, don't want to see it. But Pearl understands him like no one else and as she works the pump handle, sluicing fresh water into the tarnished old pail, she trusts that others will learn to see his goodness too. She'll make them see.

Eight

Now she knew. Gossip was still nipping at her heels. Mrs Tiddy had been watching and telling tales to Jack, and at it again only this morning – was it this morning? No, the morning was a long time ago. She had just turned round and heard them talking, surely. They were still outside, weren't they?

Mrs Tiddy must have waited for Jack, got up early. Perhaps she had been outside the front door all night, hanging on for her chance to pounce. Pearl heard them talking, the window just ajar.

'It's not that I'm prying,' Mrs Tiddy said. 'We're all worried.'

Pearl heard Jack's foot scrape along the bare dirt, then his cough, awkward and full of his need to get away. 'Pearl has been a bit wisht these last few weeks,' he said. 'Nothing serious mind. Just the move and then bit of a chill that won't leave her go.'

'Dearie me.'

'It's laid her low and you know how her chest is,' Jack said.

'She won't slow down. Always liked her walks, hasn't she? But I've told her, she's to stay inside and rest.'

There was a pause and Pearl thought Mrs Tiddy had gone indoors but then her voice came again. 'If you're not managing, you've only to say. Eileen and I would be glad to— '

Jack cut her short. 'We're fine, Sarah.' Then, softening slightly, 'thank you. You're very kind, but really – there's nothing wrong.'

'But Eileen saw her out in just her nightdress and no shoes, only yesterday. She was hauling stones about. Jack— '

'I said we're fine.'

Pearl heard Jack's boots marching off down the hill and imagined her neighbour shaking her head, no doubt annoyed at Jack's apparent loyalty. Pearl turned away from the window and sat down cross-legged. She began to trace waves in the dust settled on the bare boards, like salt spread on the palace's cobbles. Up and down. Up and down. *And the lad I loved was with them and he came not back again.*

Her going needed to be a secret but Jack seemed always one step ahead. He hadn't decided to stay in the house during the day yet, to watch her, but she didn't doubt he was talking to people about her while he was at the seafront. He was checking on her movements, which was almost as bad as having him under her feet. Great stretches of each day were slipping past her.

The house was closing in, the ceilings lowering as water pooled from the leaking roof and the walls inching towards the centre of each room while she slept. Every day *Wave Crest* became heavier with dust. Pearl found herself constantly in corners pulling the skin off her fingers, her nails blackened with dirt. She needed to be closer to the sea and she wanted to see the palace but not when there were still so many visitors crowding the seafront. She would have to go at night.

It wasn't love that first led Pearl to brew the sleeping tea for Jack, it was pity that she would feel towards any animal in pain. His nights were disturbed by dreams he wouldn't speak of – his time in the reserves she supposed – and he was fretful after any run-ins with George. Most Sunday evenings in their old house on Carew Street she would make a pot for him, occasionally taking a cup herself.

To begin with, Jack wouldn't accept the tea willingly, doubtful of a concoction that smacked of Aunt Lilly, even though he had been born into a world that relied on her abilities. To convince him, Pearl said her tea would ease the swollen joints of his hands and that was what it did, amongst other things. Three nips of wild thyme, the purple petals finely torn, four saffron hairs – if they could be spared, dear as it was – and a bud of yellow gorse flowers, all brewed with rainwater. The tea carried the scent of the cliff path and the freshness found after a storm. These days Jack even asked for it himself, not needing her careful prompting, saying that the heat in his hands was soothed, as she had promised. Tonight though, Pearl was brewing the tea for her own ends, and those of Nicholas.

Jack drained his cup and lay down in bed without a word to Pearl. Since she had told him about hearing her mother on the seafront he had been quiet with her. It was as if he was afraid of what else Pearl might say. She waited an hour, just to be sure. When his breath stammered from his open mouth, regular and deep, Pearl crept from the room.

The night was warm. Still this strange weather, days holding a constant heat, so dry and still. Perfect for the remaining visitors, who would tell their friends that the claims of the railway posters were right. Eileen's shop would be busy. Pascoe's new hotel would be full. But where was autumn?

The only noises were those of the sea and a door banging shut as she made her way down the winding road. She didn't trust herself to manage the cliff path by night and chose the road to reach the village proper; she continued to refer to it as that rather than a town even though she wasn't sure where the boundaries were anymore. Perhaps there were no lines to shape Morlanow and it simply kept unfolding, reaching further with every day that passed.

Between *Wave Crest* and the old part of Morlanow many houses had grown. Roads had risen from the scrubby ground with new lanes sliding among them. Pearl was a little unsure of her way through these by dark – the unfamiliar walls seemingly changing their stance, shifting about – but knew that if she just kept going downhill, she must eventually reach the seafront.

Once in Carnglaze Lane the pilchards began to appear. The fish were carved into the granite walls and end posts of old Morlanow. They were set above lintels and tucked almost out of sight below gables. They were by place names and alongside guttering. In the past, building work had been haphazard, not like Pascoe's well-ordered angles now. Doorways hung in the middle of houses, sometimes with steps to connect them to the ground, sometimes without. Rooms had been built on wherever space allowed, making many secret, shaded alleys.

As Pearl stole through the unbalanced streets with their strange corners and pockets of darkness sounds of the trade stirred around her. She heard the jangle of a bit between a horse's teeth and the pull of a saw making hogsheads. Voices called out the price of mackerel and a bell began to peal. The smell of fish, warm and ripe, rose from the ground.

Pearl turned down an alley that ran between two shops. She was hurrying now, her slippered feet sliding on the cobbles as she neared her destination. Just round one more curve, down one more side street. She was close to the seafront. There was the pop of firecrackers as the sea was hauled over pebbles. Her breath came too fast and she began to cough. What would Jack think when he saw her pallor the next morning? She would have to slow down but air was harder to find and now she was so close she couldn't stop.

And there it was. Pearl stood still in the middle of the street. The scaffolding poles caught the light and gleamed eerily before her. Stone was piled at their feet, mallets and chisels lying alongside. Hiding the destruction was the layered dress of tarpaulin. Even from here Pearl could see how much of the palace had already gone. The shape of it, intimately known by so many generations of women who had been stowed within its bows, bulking and breaking out pilchards beyond number, was changed.

The scaffolding was set back from the road. The outer front wall must have been taken down. A rope was tied around the site, cordoning off the whole area. Pearl walked over and ducked beneath it. In front of her the tarpaulin hung like a pair of curtains. Her fingers found a gap. As she slipped between the layers, the sheeting caught her bare arms and for the first time that night Pearl felt cold.

It took her a moment to find her bearings. With the front wall gone she had stepped straight into the open air courtyard. The moon seemed to hang directly overhead, as if it had aligned itself with the ever wide eye of the palace's centre. Pearl took another step forward. Circling the central space were the various storage rooms with lofts overhead. The roof that had covered these, sloping inwards towards the courtyard, had also gone, but the thick granite pillars that had supported it remained: precious authentic relics that would be used to flank the hotel's grand entrance. But what else could be done with such a place?

Pearl walked to the middle of the open space, unwilling to enter the dim recesses of the storage cells. Rats and mice had always lived there. Without all the cats once kept to catch them she didn't like to think how many might have settled in. The pebbled floor sloped to the pit in the middle. She peered in. It was dry as driftwood with cobwebs clinging to the sides. No fish to fill these depths with oil.

She turned back to face the entrance, remembering the way the sun had pushed through the arch, flooding the messy scene inside with light strong enough to make you wince. Each scale burned its silver and each drop of oil winked. There had been days of rain too, drops the size of pennies firing off the iron roof. And nights.

Pearl closed her eyes and willed the memory on, wanting it to swallow her and return to her all that she had lost. But it was being taken away, this precious place, and with it the traces of her and Nicholas together. The bright light grew, throbbing white heat through the palace. What would happen when the fish returned? Pearl wouldn't be able to build them into salted walls alone.

'I'll help you.'

She heard Nicholas in her head, closer than her own thoughts. A charge raced through her. The light blazed and slipped behind her eyes. Her temples burned.

'Pearl, let me help you.'

Nine

'Pearl, let me help you.'

As she leaves the palace Nicholas springs forward and takes the bussa jar from her, easily carrying the half-weight of salted pilchards that makes up her pay. His fingers graze hers. Free of the weight she rolls her shoulders, glad to be rid of the jar but reluctant to admit it. A fine mizzle threads the air, cooling her face and working its dampness into her stained clothes. He's been waiting for her.

They pick their way past carts and piles of crab pots and heaps of nets, stepping round puddles and knots of fishermen and fishwives. A gang of children run past, flicking up muck in their wake. And all the time she's thinking that he was waiting for her.

They walk in the direction of their street, neither wanting to hurry despite the light rain. A month has passed since the meeting about Sunday fishing and the seafront has become an uneasy place. Men she recognises from chapel stop work and whisper in twos, which soon become threes and then more. All those from other ports, including Govenek, don't talk with the Morlanow men as they once did. But in the cramped bustle of the seafront and harbour wall there isn't room for separate camps and fishermen are forced to pass each other close by.

In amongst those who go to sea are other strange men. One crosses their path now and Pearl has to look away. The man's face is too thin, making his eyes look huge and sunken as they desperately try to make contact with a generous soul, not that there are many in Morlanow who can spare anything. The tattered trousers the man wears are filthy and the smell rising from him turns her stomach. He moves away from them, heading towards the Master's hut.

'He won't find help there,' Nicholas says. 'Master can barely keep on who he's got now.'

There have been many of these poor thin men since news came that the Tillotsons have closed a mine. Another two are said to be failing. There's little left in the ground already opened to the light and there's no money to sink new shafts. Fresh advertisements for cheap passage to Australia, America and Southern Africa are pasted weekly on the seafront. They promise much.

Pearl keeps her voice low, aware now of the weight of some words. 'Got nothing better to do than hang around here?' she says to Nicholas. Let him say that he was waiting, that she was worth waiting for.

'Oh I was just passing, on my way to court some young lovely, when I saw my dear friend Pearl struggling.' He gives a mock shrug and raises his eyes, his voice loud, unabashed.

She hides her disappointment and punches him playfully on the arm, then realises there's pilchard oil covering her skirt and apron and that her hair has half fallen down and is clinging to her face with sweat and rain.

'I must look a state,' she says.

'No more than usual.'

It's true. The season is in full swing and six days out of the past seven Pearl has worked in the palace, alongside her mother, Aunt Lilly and the other women. This is Pearl's first season as a palace maid proper and it's different from being there as a child. There doesn't seem to be quite the same pace to the work. The walls of fish look lower. Pearl tells herself that this is simply because she's older. But she can't escape the knowledge that the shoals have come less often. She knows too that she's lucky to be taken on at all, but when a shoal does appear not a fish must be lost due to lack of hands. It's hard work, long days and often nights, cold floors, and the air fouled by the pilchards constantly brought by the gurry men. There can be no complaining though: catches mean wages and food.

The last three years have been poor and many bussa jars have been empty. As much good pilchard stock as came in was sold to pay wages and to repair the seine boats, though there are far fewer now that go out. Each spring following a bad pilchard season there are more who believe the promises of the advertisements, leaving home to try their luck across the sea. Their faces are soon replaced though. Visitors step off the train into Morlanow's famous sunlight and not many of them come to paint.

Today wouldn't make a good picture anyway. There's no sun. Thick cloud lies over the village. It's late morning and the catch has finally been bulked. Gazes are once more fixed on the sea, waiting for the next shoal to come. She knows it's wrong but Pearl hopes there's a little while before they come again. She needs to sleep.

'I've not seen you all week,' Nicholas says. 'Fish more of a draw than I am?'

Pearl laughs. 'They're wonderful company. Give no cheek, no teasing.'

They round the corner onto their street. Nicholas stops and shifts the awkward jar in his arms. 'Come out later. I've got something to show you.'

Pearl sighs, the week's work heavy in her arms, her back. She has barely slept since the shoal was caught; sent home for a few hours each morning when the sun rose and a woman came to replace her, having taken rest herself. All Pearl wants to do is fill the tin bath with scalding water and steam herself clean of the palace, then go to bed for days. But that will mean fetching water from the pump and boiling pans on the stove. That will take effort she hasn't got. Perhaps she will just sleep where she falls, coated with scales and oil, but too drained to smell herself. Nicholas is waiting for her to speak. His eyes are full of eagerness and he's smiling that smile that makes Pearl forget everything other than him.

'All right,' she says. 'Just let me get washed.'

They walk on until they reach her doorstep. Nicholas sets the bussa jar down. That he won't bring it inside for her is unspoken. Nothing has been said to Pearl directly – after all, her father and Mr Polance are still in the same seine crew – but there has been a shift in how Nicholas's name is greeted: her father's dry cough and her mother's clattering of plates. Pearl can't imagine how his parents have reacted to him speaking up for the east coast men.

As Nicholas is turning away the front door of the Tremain house opens. Jack bowls out.

'Bleeding useless, why don't you clean this place up, you little– ' his father's voice calls after him before Jack slams the door.

Pearl can hear Samuel crying. Jack doesn't stop to talk. There are deep pits under his eyes and his clothes flap around him only half pulled on. He nods to Pearl but makes a point of ignoring Nicholas before stomping in the direction of the seafront.

'What was that about?' she asks Nicholas.

He continues watching Jack's retreating back. When he speaks his voice is low. 'The blasted Sunday fishing. This damn backwardness will lead to ruin.'

'Nicholas! Mind your language, please.'

'Sorry. But they won't see sense. I heard it all again this morning, this jaw-ache about the east coast men landing here. No one'll listen to reason. Jack was there, unloading. We, well... we had a bit of a run in, you might say.'

Pearl feels her body sink lower, tiredness and dread weighing her down. 'My father says Jack's planning his own course to deal with the east coast men,' she says.

'That'll do no good, not in the long run.' Nicholas's lips are set in a grim line. Then he brightens, throwing the worry aside. 'Come to the bottom of the cliff path,' he says. 'I'll meet you at nine.'

Pearl nods then lifts the bussa jar over the threshold. As she closes the door he winks at her. Her heart soars.

By the time she goes out again the earlier mizzle has dried but left thick mist hanging on the seafront. The gas lamps flicker and spark, their flames managing only a paltry glow. Most of the seafront is shrouded in gloom. Gradually, she becomes aware of a small light moving ahead of her down the seafront. She quickens her pace to catch up with Nicholas on his way to the bottom of the cliff path, but as she gets nearer she sees that the person carrying the lamp is shorter and has fair hair. Pearl stops. It's Jack.

The light keeps moving. He hasn't heard her. She lets him widen the gap between them. She has no wish to speak to him though she's curious where he's going. The mist has probably stopped him putting to sea to set his lines but why then isn't he tucked up inside, enjoying a rare rest? Even as she asks herself this she knows why. Jack is trapped like Polly is trapped. He has nowhere to go either but his home doesn't have the welcome of Polly's. Alice and Samuel have one another. Jack only has his father, which is worse than being alone.

Pearl walks on again, keeping Jack in sight without getting too close. He reaches the end of the seafront and stops. She hopes he hasn't run into Nicholas. Jack seems to be waiting for something. She drops down onto the sand below the seafront. With all the bad feeling about Sunday fishing Pearl's instinct is to keep out of it, to stay hidden from view, though she's not sure why. It isn't a crime to walk along the seafront of an evening. But still, she's meeting Nicholas, alone and after dark, and there's a need for caution, of keeping an unsteady boat on an even keel.

Jack's light is joined by another two weaving out of the mist. Pearl strains forward to make out who they are: the Pengelley brothers, Stephen and James. The three men have a brief conversation though they speak too low for Pearl to hear, before they climb the cliff path. She follows at a safe distance, her feet quietly crunching along the wet sand. When she reaches the point where she and Nicholas are to meet she stops again and looks round, but there's no sign of him. She looks up at the moving lights and then to the cliff top. A lamp burns in the huer's hut.

Pearl jumps at the sound of feet on sand behind her. Nicholas stands grinning. 'What are you hiding down here for, limpet-legs?' he says.

'Shh!' Pearl points to the lights. 'It's Jack, with the Pengelley boys. I think they're going to the hut.'

His smile disappears. 'More nonsense about Sunday fishing. Let them scheme and pray for our souls. There's men on to them. I heard from the Master. They're going to put a stop to whatever Jack's planning.'

Pearl feels a load she wasn't aware she was carrying lift from her shoulders. The problem with the east coasters will die away. Things will go back to how they were. Nicholas will be welcome at home again. She brightens her tone. 'Well, I've come out in this mist. What did you want to show me?'

He gestures for her to follow him down the sand, towards the towering bulk of the cliff. Jack and the Pengelleys are far enough up the cliff path now that they won't hear them. Pearl peers into the deeper darkness of the cliff's recesses but can't see anything. Nicholas walks forward and appears to take hold of a layer of black and pull it aside. A little red boat sits on the sand, her oars neatly laid inside and a sail lying in her bows. Nicholas throws aside the tarpaulin that had melted so well into the cliff.

'What do you think?' he says proudly.

'Is she yours?'

'She is. Bought her myself. Not got a name yet but I thought you could help me with that. I've no talent for such things.'

Pearl runs a hand across the boat's newly painted side. 'She's lovely, but why did you want a boat? You could go out in your father's. And anyway I thought you had no truck with fishing.'

Nicholas climbs inside and sits on the plank seat, facing the sea. 'I don't. Fancied seeing a bit more of the world.'

Pearl laughs. 'In this little thing? You'd not get much further than Govenek. And why is she over here instead of by the harbour wall?'

He fiddles with the oars. 'I wasn't sure she'd be all right there, the ways things are. All this talk.'

Pearl climbs in alongside him. They sit close to touching on the narrow seat. Nicholas suddenly seems weary. His boyishness has left him, his cheerful eagerness too.

'Don't you ever wish you could just sail away from here, leave all this behind?' he asks without looking at her.

Pearl thinks of the advertisements pasted on the seafront, of Polly's crumpled piece of paper. 'I do wish it,' she says. 'Sometimes. But then I think of what it would mean to leave. Of saying goodbye. I don't know how I could do it.'

'We could go anywhere,' Nicholas says.

Pearl's stomach flips at that: 'we'. She can't speak, though she knows that this is the time to do so. But she doesn't need to. Nicholas takes her hand and holds it in his lap. He looks at it, frowning, like he's not seen it before and it's some marvel. She doesn't move, hopes he can't feel the tremble running through her body. She doesn't want to ruin this, or, if this is the closest she will get to knowing that he wants her, to rush the moment to its ending. If this is all she has then it has to last and last. It has to sustain her through the emptiness of the nights to come when even the hope that he loves her is gone. Nicholas runs a finger over her knuckle, backwards and forwards. Still she doesn't move. He leans forwards and rubs his cheek against her hand in a way that reminds her of an animal. His lips graze her skin. He presses them, hard, against the bones of her hand. He breathes in the smell of her. She lets her other hand rest, gently, on his head. His hair is soft, feathery. They remain still, then he says, speaking into her hand so that she feels the vibrations of his words pulse through her, 'Where shall we go?'

Ten

The door handle was cool in her palm. Pearl swept her fingers over the shape which was at once familiar and strange, half recognising the spots of discolouration that came from the salted air eating through the metal. She knew she had to put her mind to this handle. There was something she had to hurry to do but she couldn't catch on what that was. All she wanted was to lie back in a little red boat with her eyes closed, not having to think about anything other than the sea beneath her and Nicholas beside her.

She came back to herself with a shudder. It was the front door handle of the new house. She was outside *Wave Crest* and the treacherous light of dawn was baring everything.

Nicholas put his hand to Pearl's cheek to wipe her tears but the hand was too small and the knuckles too raised in the fragile skin. The warm pressure at her temples came again. The hand was her own. Nicholas was gone.

She pawed the tangled hair from her eyes. Jack would be awake soon. Getting indoors and back to bed, that was the important thing. She had to keep ahead of him, and ahead of the stalking widows who were ill-wishing her days so that parts of them vanished.

Pearl opened the door and crept into the hall. As she climbed the stairs each one seemed desperate to give her away. She slipped into the bedroom. Jack lay on his back with his arms flung above his head, the bedclothes bunched at his feet. Pulling the bedding back over him, she saw that his face was ashen, beads of sweat peppering his forehead. His lips were clamped together, white at their edges, and he was breathing heavily through his nose.

'Jack,' she said.

He opened his eyes and gave a low cry but without seeming to see Pearl. His gaze hovered over her shoulder at the window, a tremor coming into his hands as he tried to pull the blanket over his face. Pearl turned to look at what he was staring at but saw nothing except the partly drawn curtains and the suggestion of light between them.

Jack jumped suddenly. 'No, no!' he shouted. 'You can't... I won't let...'

Pearl laid her hand on Jack's arm to calm him but he flinched at her touch as if he had been burnt.

'Get back,' he cried. 'No, get away.... No, no...'

Nicholas could have come to the house again, looking for her and finding only Jack. Would Nicholas be angry with her, for marrying Jack? Pearl paced the room but couldn't feel the weight of Nicholas's presence that had come before. There were no creaking floorboards, no furring shadows to give his spirit shape. Everything felt ordinary. It was only a room just before dawn, holding two people and some furniture.

Jack whimpered, closed his eyes, and grew still beneath the blanket. Nicholas wasn't there. Jack was only dreaming and there was nothing Pearl could do to soothe him. She couldn't soothe herself.

She felt she had only just closed her eyes when Jack banged the front door shut behind him. Her head ached and it took some time for her eyes to focus. A swim would help but there was no way to risk it with the widows keeping watch, so, as usual, she would have to recreate the sensation as best she could.

The light in the bedroom was poor, giving the impression of an overcast sky. Perhaps autumn's rain had finally arrived to finish off this lingering summer. The damp patch on the ceiling appeared to have spread but it had been so dry; the house's water stains could only be from the sea working its wet breath inside the walls, slipping between the beams and their nails. At this rate the ceiling would be more rot than plaster and when it fell, she and Jack would disappear under its crumbly blanket. When the storm came as the white hare predicted, and with it all the rain that had been missing from Morlanow recently, the weak little house would fold in on itself like cardboard.

She needed to get out of bed and near some proper water. These mouldering traces weren't enough. Pearl opened the curtains. There was dirt on the floor at the end of the bed. It was on her side and shaped like the marks of a heel and toes. Bending down, she saw that as well as mud sand lay on the floor, and something else, something small and shiny that she couldn't quite see. She licked her finger and put it to the dot of silver, then brought her finger close to her face.

Her breath died in her throat and she fell against the bed. The room was fading, its edges disappearing. The white light was galloping in towards her. She was going to drop into it and never get out, but she had to know for sure. She made herself concentrate, pulling the room back towards her again, because she had to think clearly about what this scrap of silver was. She blinked and stared hard at it. It was as bright as if it had just fallen from the flesh: a torn pilchard scale.

Pearl had seen millions in her lifetime but none were as precious as this. She knew what should be done with it for the time being, until the shoal returned. Pearl licked her finger again, swallowing the scale to keep it safe.

She was in no doubt now that Nicholas must have been in the house again. There was the physical mark of his boot – she couldn't be imagining such a thing, it was right there in front of her. And he had left her the token of the scale so that she would keep faith with him.

Pearl got up from the floor and went downstairs to get a cloth. Jack wouldn't have seen the mark on the floor as he dressed and it wouldn't do for him to find it when he got home that evening. He was looking for a way to catch her out. Pearl wiped away the trace of Nicholas, thinking of the scale held inside her, and felt a gleam of light coursing through her blood.

Singing to herself and every stick of furniture, she filled a pail from the outside tap, and staggered back with it. When had such an everyday task become as difficult as when she was a child? Inside, she leaned against the door, waiting for her chest to ease, swallowing the coughs that rose in her throat. Then she hunted for the largest bowl she owned and eventually found it underneath the table, which wasn't its usual place at all.

She filled the bowl and carried it into the room next to the kitchen which got more light at this time of day. She took off her boots then sat down and plunged her bare feet into the bowl of water. The delicious chill wove up her legs, giving her body a hint of paddling in the shallows. Pearl wiggled her toes, sending fresh waves of pleasure over her feet to convince her body she was in the sea. It wasn't as good as getting into the tin bath, where she would be completely covered with her eyes open underneath, but this would have to do.

Pearl rolled the balls of her feet backwards and forwards so that the cold snapped at her ankles. Water slopped onto the floorboards but she didn't care. She closed her eyes and saw the bowl's contents flipping and growing, waves rising and pouring into the room, as if there was some invisible source pumping the salt water into the house from the shimmering hole of the bowl, now a foot or so beneath the surface. As the water level began to rise, the tension returned to her temples and Pearl was aware of a change in the good room's settled air. It was the same she had felt the night that Nicholas had first come back to her: a force pushing on the walls.

She was good at detecting the presence of others. It was some part of Aunt Lilly's pellar gift making itself known in Pearl, perhaps. She had been the best at finding Jack when he crouched amongst the hogsheads during hide and seek, though she didn't give him away every time. She had the same feeling now, that she wasn't alone, but she wasn't frightened. Nicholas had been a gentle soul and he had loved her once, she was sure.

The sea had come into the house through the bowl of water and now its tide grew darker, swallowing the daylight. The water ran across the floor and lapped at the bed, then dipped and pushed on again, coming up to the window ledge. Her boots bobbed past, looking like leather wrecks about to founder. On and on the water flowed, filling the whole room with darkness so that Pearl was lifted off her chair. She floated towards the ceiling, and as it came close to her face, she rolled over and dived down to the shadows of the seabed where the floorboards had been.

A horn was sounding its call, plaintive and low. A ship was coming. Nicholas was coming to get her. She lifted her arms to hail it and her elbow brushed something hard. It was the arm of the chair. She was in the room by the kitchen, her feet resting on the sodden floor and the bowl overturned nearby. How long had she been gone?

The horn sounded again and was joined by another. Pearl padded to the window and saw a stationary line of motor cars packed nose to tail, evidently trying to descend the road into Morlanow.

She drew the curtain to hide the sight of the cars, though their horns and ticking engines followed her into the kitchen. She lit the stove and put the kettle on. Her fingers were jittery and she wanted to be calmer before Jack arrived back. A cup of tea would help. She sat down and waited for the kettle's whistle.

The cars had started with the train, strange as it seemed now. It was the train that opened the village up to the world. Wedged deep into the cliff as Morlanow was, the engineers had to blast a tunnel through the rock to get the engine there and then another to get it out again. There were trains for people and trains for fish, hogsheads of pilchards and crates of mackerel riding first class to London. Sometimes there were trains for paintings and sometimes the fish were packed in alongside them, if a big enough catch came in, and there were rows at the station when word came back from London that fish oil had seeped into the canvases.

But then the pilchards didn't come back and the mackerel dropped off too. The artists brought money, by way of rent and buying supplies, but they were usually hard pressed. So many of Morlanow's own people went away, never to be seen again. Those left behind stood in the streets with their hands spread, as if to say: what do we do? It wasn't their fault.

The kettle was shrieking its readiness. As she lifted the cup of tea to her lips she saw the next sign. Just as when she saw the hare and the knapweed cairn, she didn't know she was looking for something until it came, but there it was. A stalk floated on the whitened surface of her tea: a visitor was coming to her door.

Eleven

As Pearl nears her front door she hears crying. At first she thinks that it's Samuel in the Tremain house next door but then she realises it's a woman. She's never seen Alice cry, not even when they dragged her, naked, from the net loft Miss Charles was using as a studio. No, the crying is coming from Pearl's house.

Inside, the first thing she sees is her mother curled into a shaking ball on the floor beside the hearth. A moan pours from her open mouth. Her strong mother who is tough as boot leather, bearing no fuss, no hysterics. Something must have happened to her father. Pearl grips the door frame as her legs buckle. She can't speak but looks round wildly. Is he here? Have they brought him home? Polly is standing at the other end of the room, looking at their mother on the floor but not going to her, just standing staring. Then Pearl sees Gerald behind her, his arm around Polly's shoulders. They are leaving then.

Pearl manages to stand and goes to hold her mother's heaving shoulders, kneeling on the floor. Her mother looks at her but is unable to speak. Pearl smoothes her hair and whispers soft sounds, as her mother does for Pearl when her chest is bad. Pearl looks to Polly and Gerald and gives them the best smile she can, weak and poor as it is, because this isn't their fault. They are going to be together. They are going to start their lives.

Eventually they manage to get their mother into a chair and persuade her to have a drink of water. She doesn't say anything as the details come, just sits rigid as if dead and propped in the chair. Gerald has borrowed the money for the passage from his brothers. Once he's got work he'll send it back in dribs and drabs but it will work out because people are making fortunes in Australia. It's impossible not to succeed. Not like in Morlanow where it's harder and harder just to make ends meet. They have no choice but to go. Gerald says this over and over again. No choice. Polly has no choice if she wants to keep Gerald, Pearl thinks, but she doesn't say that. It's hot in Australia and there's open country for miles, Gerald says. When Pearl asks him about the fishing there he just smiles and says he might be a farmer, or a carpenter, or a mine worker. Anything's possible in Australia.

Their mother stirs into life. 'When do you sail?' she says.

There's a long pause before Gerald says, 'next week'. And Pearl is close to shaking and crying on the floor herself. So soon. How will she say goodbye? The door opens and her father is home, standing in his sea boots and knowing straight away that something terrible has happened. Pearl doesn't want to be around when they tell him, to risk her mother falling apart again, or even worse seeing her father cry. She slips out, pulling the door closed behind her. The news will be known soon enough but there should be some privacy for the shock first.

She gets to the pump in the street and stops. There's nowhere she wants to go. No purpose to her actions anymore.

Polly is leaving. Polly will never come back. There will only be letters now. She will never see her sister again and it's all the fault of the fishing. No boat for Gerald, no pilchards for him to catch. And yet the east coasters with their smart gear heave full nets from the sea. Even on Sundays they find more fish. She can't understand how the sea can be so mean, so wilful. Where is the Lord when His people need His love?

There's a movement beneath the gable at the end of her row. Jack squats next to her but doesn't say anything, for which she's grateful. She couldn't bear any spiritual talk now.

'Polly's leaving,' she says and begins to cry as the words are out, making it true. 'Australia. With Gerald.'

'I'm sorry,' Jack says. 'You're not going too though, are you?'

She looks up and sees the concern on his sunburnt freckly face. He's a good soul, despite his rages and his stubborn chapel rules. She shakes her head. 'I've no money for the fare.'

'But you would go, if you had it?' he says.

'Yes. No. I don't know,' she says. 'How could I leave mother and father now? And this is my home. Morlanow is...' She can't finish the sentence. What is Morlanow? Home, yet full of gossip and distrust and not enough food. Her father risking his life every time he puts to sea and her mother praying for his safe return, never sure until the front door opens that he's alive. Is that what the future holds for Pearl?

'I wouldn't want you to go,' Jack says. 'I'd... I'd miss you, seeing you around the place.' He gets up and stretches his legs. Looking down at her he says, 'you belong here, Pearl.'

She's angry at that. She belongs where she damn well pleases to belong. Who is he to tell her otherwise? But he's walking away, striking off into the evening, certain of his rightness. And she has no words to tell him.

When the day comes there are no more tears. They've cried themselves out, their bodies dry as rays hanging in the sun, and the brief wedding the day before has raised spirits a little. Many people come to the station to see Polly and Gerald off. They will take the train to London, packed amongst the barrels of fish and crates of lobsters, to board *The Great Britain*, the ship that will take them to Australia. Aunt Lilly supports her mother, bracing her shoulders, whilst Mr Polance stands with her father. Mr Taylor comes to say a prayer for safe passage and old Mrs Pendeen is there just for the spectacle.

Gerald's family come over from Govenek with their friends and neighbours but even in this shared moment of loss the communities are separate. Those from Govenek stand apart, divided from the Morlanow party by a heap of luggage being loaded onto the train, even though fish from both villages are being packed together inside the carriages.

Sarah Dray hugs Polly for a long time, each promising to write each week, promising never to forget her best friend. The world is full of promises these days. It's Pearl's turn next to say goodbye but the words she lines up in her head don't say enough about how much she doesn't want Polly to go, about how she wants to go herself. So she says nothing and the short embrace in the chaos of the other passengers saying goodbye and boarding the train is too brief. It looks as if she doesn't care when really she cares too much.

Others push past her to say their own goodbyes. Pearl is forced to stand with Sarah Dray, pressed against the cases. Sarah gives Pearl a pitying look. 'Try and be happy for them,' she says to Pearl. 'They're starting a new life. You'll be settling down yourself soon, I shouldn't wonder.'

'What are you talking about?' Pearl says.

'Come on now, don't be coy.' Sarah is her usual smug self,

all pretence of care gone. 'Your parents have great hopes to have you settled now Polly's gone. A house of your own.'

Pearl's blushes come in force but she's confused. Sarah loves to know everyone else's business. It's not the time for this now anyway. The guard is walking through the crowd, telling the passengers it's time to board. All too quickly Polly and Gerald are inside the carriage, leaning out of the window, waving, waving, and the train's whistle screams and the smoke begins to pour from the engine. They're going too quickly. It must take longer than this. There needs to be more of a leave-taking when the loss is so great. Pearl begins to cough and in spite of herself she's forced to lean on Sarah's proffered arm. The train is jolting away, disappearing in a cloud of smoke. It's over. It's done. She's left behind.

Twelve

'Come on now,' Jack said, helping her to stand. She stumbled. Her boots were on the wrong feet. However had she managed that? Her head hurt. Her whole body hurt. It was because Polly had gone. The train pulling out of the station had bruised her. Jack's hands under her arms made it worse.

'You're hurting me!' she said, but he only held on tighter.

'Come on, Pearl. Up you get.'

Coughing. She couldn't breathe. Her skirts were all wet. He was trying to drown her. No. She was sitting on a dirty floor.

'There now,' he said, setting her skirts straight and tutting at their dampness. Her boots were on the wrong feet. She kicked them off. He sat opposite her at the kitchen table. He put his head in his hands for a moment, took a loud breath, then looked at her. He had such a glum face. Would stare until people felt they had to look away. But Polly. He would know.

'Have there been any letters?' she said.

'Letters?' Jack said. 'No, no letters.'

'Tomorrow maybe. She said she'd write to Sarah every week. She should write to me too.'

'Eileen asked after you when I was on the front yesterday,' he said. 'Said she hadn't seen you for a while.' He looked expectantly at Pearl.

'Who?' she said.

'Eileen. In the shop.'

'It's Polly that's meant to write.'

He was being difficult. He wouldn't listen. She'd have to find someone else to ask. She stood up. Even Sarah Dray would do. Anything to know how Polly was. To know if leaving had been worth it. She needed to put her boots on.

'Polly's dead, Pearl,' he said. He came and stood next to her. She let him put a balled hand on her shoulder. 'She died a long time ago.'

'No!'

'You know she's dead. There was a letter then. That's how we heard. Remember?'

'A letter?' she said. He nodded. 'Has a letter come? She said she'd write.'

'No. A letter hasn't come. There was a letter to say that she'd been—' He licked his lips. 'To say what had happened. To Polly.'

Pearl pulled on her boots. She was going out. He wouldn't talk sense. But her boots wouldn't go on right. There was something wrong with them. Her feet couldn't slip inside. They were the wrong shape. Or the boots were wrong. Quickly, quickly or she would forget what she was looking for. She had to get away from Jack and this dirty old house. She had to get back to the other place, where she knew where she was. That's where it made sense. In the truthfulness of the light that came when she wasn't ready. But she was ready now. She shut her eyes and willed its blaze. She was ready to leave.

Thirteen

Everything in the palace stands ready but the season is poor. There's no pretending otherwise. The fourth in a run to be thin with fish. Day after day the sun shines and all is quiet at the huer's hut. The wait between catches is long, weeks at a time, and the amount each seine net lifts to the surface varies wildly. Even the most bruised fish are deemed fit for bulking, though the merchants acting for the Papists have returned some hogsheads, claiming the pilchards are no good.

While the wait goes on, Pearl's evenings are mostly free of work, once supper is over. There's nothing to do but pray. At any moment the cry from the huer might come. She just has to stay within hearing distance.

She and Nicholas go down to the hidden notch of Witch Cove and sit on the shelf of pebbles, watching the green waves curl and release.

'What do you wish for most in the world?' he asks.

'You'll laugh at me,' she says, already blushing.

Nicholas puts both hands over his heart. 'I won't. Promise.'

She follows the path of a wave as it lifts from the surface of the sea, tracks diagonally and breaks on the stones. She thinks of telling him what she longs for most, what she goes to sleep wishing for, but her nerve fails her.

'A bathing suit,' she says. A guffaw explodes from Nicholas. She turns away from him and crosses her arms. 'See! I knew you'd laugh.'

'I'm sorry, I am. It's just that a *bathing suit*.... What's wrong with swimming in just your drawers? Only visitors wear bathing suits.'

'I've always wanted one, a proper one, with stripes. I remember Polly said once that I could and then, I don't know, it never came.'

He stops laughing at the mention of Polly. 'A bathing suit's a fine thing to wish for,' he says, 'and you made me laugh, limpet-legs, which there's not been cause to do lately.' He gently knocks his shoulder against hers then picks up a stone and hurls it towards the water's edge.

Witch Cove is a precious place shared between them, tucked behind a swell in the cliff. For Pearl the shelf of sharp stones is worth sitting on for the secrecy it gives and for the view of Cornwall flying away into a haze, torn cliffs laid with soft fields, white cottages clustering at their edge, the pointed fingers of the engine houses that mark the mines, stark and strange amongst them. Pearl's own land, though she has seen little of it.

'What do you wish for?' she says.

'I wish you'd come out in my boat.' He puts his hand down on the pebbles, just touching hers. 'I've named her. The boat, I mean. You were taking too long.'

'It's a hard decision to make,' she says. 'Let's hear it then.'

'*Oyster Girl*,' he says, and her blushes are terrible.

She knows oysters, of course, though no one near

Morlanow dredges for them. Near Falmouth, on the estuary there, many are scooped out, and some weeks of the year oysters come in to Morlanow's harbour on foreign boats to be unloaded onto the train and whisked away. Like mussels you steam open the shell and eat the quivering toughness living there. But there's something else about them that she remembers. She can't meet his eye.

'Why that?' she murmurs.

'Because... Because of what's inside. You know.' He twists his hands together. 'If you don't like it, just say. It's foolish, I'll think of something else.'

He's looking at her, waiting for her to say if she likes the boat's name, but she wants to push him now he has opened this crack into his thoughts.

'When did you decide this?' she says.

'When I was in the library at Pentreath, I read—'

'Pentreath?' The town is miles inland, where the Tillotson mines grew and took over the country. Further than Govenek, which is the furthest from Morlanow that Pearl has ever been. 'I didn't know you'd been there,' she says. 'When did you go?'

He shrugs. 'Few times lately, on the train. You were in the palace. The Master lets me finish early sometimes, if the accounts are in order. I do some errands for him while I'm there, to pay for the ticket. But that doesn't matter. What do you think of the name?'

'I like it, I suppose. It's more grown up than "limpet-legs". But why did you go to the library?'

'There are things I wanted to know, and they have maps, huge great maps that show places other than Cornwall.'

He throws more stones at the hissing trough of the sea. Pearl is torn two ways, with joy that Nicholas wants to name his boat after her, in a secret sort of way, and fear that he has been keeping things from her. And maps – why must he be so caught up with other places?

Pebbles clatter down the shelf as Nicholas gets to his feet. 'So you'll come out with me then, now she's got a name?'

The question is harder to answer than he thinks. It's not just 'yes' or 'no' and a matter of going or not going. It's a decision beyond that. It's what it would mean to go, to leave the safety of land and to be with him on the shifting slipperiness of the sea. To be unsteady. Now that there is this understanding between them, now that he has spoken of leaving, can she keep her balance on the water with Nicholas? She's not certain of her own anchor any more. She is not the person everyone thinks she is. Her thoughts are those of a sinner. But here he is in front of her and she knows what she's going to say. The sea is a block of green behind him, a perfect canvas on which to lay his dark curls and the outline of his clean, pressed shirt, his unworked hands and angular wrists. *Oyster Girl* waits on the beach and the waves wait to carry Pearl out beyond Morlanow's troubles.

'Yes,' she says. 'I'll come out with you.'

The setting sun fires a last blast of brilliance. Nicholas smiles at her. Pearl is already far at sea.

They meet the next evening at the bottom of the cliff path where the boat has been left. The beach and the seafront are empty but for a few strangers, late visitors, taking the air, unconcerned with what she and Nicholas might be doing on this beautiful evening. The unseen huers will be at their posts for a little longer, blinking away illusions of pilchards caused by the fading light, the children are in bed, and most of Morlanow's own people are packed into chapel where another meeting is taking place. No one will expect Nicholas to attend and Pearl told her mother only a half lie, that on such a warm evening chapel would be too stuffy for her chest.

Pearl has tried her best to look decent. It's easier to stay clean when there are no pilchards arriving. Her skirt is spotless, the hems repaired that morning before anyone was up. She has brushed her hair and pinned it back, using stolen drops of her mother's precious rose water to smooth the wayward strands. Pinching her cheeks has given her a bit of colour and she chewed parsley to rid her breath of the bussa pilchards eaten for supper. She barely heard her mother say that it was the last full bussa jar in the house.

Nicholas calls from behind. 'Ready?'

The red boat still sits in the shadow of the cliff. Nicholas has painted *Oyster Girl* on her side in his neat, straight hand. Pearl can only smile at him, her voice lost. They lift a side of the boat each and carry her down to the water. The boat is more awkward than heavy. Pearl can feel the greater strength in her arms from working in the palace. Nicholas appears to be struggling. As he strains against the boat's side she sees the cords of his neck and the leanness of his frame.

They reach the water and drop the boat into the shallows. A strand of hair has escaped from her pin and Pearl tucks it back behind her ear. Nicholas is looking at her.

Pearl pulls off her boots and tosses them into the boat. 'Come on. We'll lose the light at this rate.'

Together they push the boat off the sand, splashing into water almost up to their knees until she is afloat, then scramble over the sides and collapse in a heap of laughter. As the boat begins to drift they both reach for an oar as there's no wind for a sail.

'Give that here,' Nicholas says. 'I'm rowing.'

'But you're out of breath. Let me help.'

He smiles and shakes his head. 'No. It's my boat and you're a passenger, as well as a girl. I'm in charge, though you can have the tiller.'

Pearl pretends to hesitate then hands him the other oar. Nicholas settles himself in the centre of the boat and begins to row. She isn't certain how to use a tiller but Nicholas doesn't row at any great speed. She has time to work out its action before he asks her to steer them more to the right, heading along the coast towards Witch Cove, out of sight of the village. They round the cliff head where the huers' hut stands far above them. The only sound is that of the oars dipping into the sea. The waves have all but vanished. Pearl can feel Nicholas's gaze on her. He clears his throat and her pulse thrums at the thought of what he might say.

'Do you agree with the rest of them – your father, Jack, all the others – that Sunday fishing is wrong?'

This is what he wants to talk about now that they are alone? She tries not to let her disappointment show, taking her hand off the tiller and letting her fingers feel the cool slip of the sea. 'Of course it is,' she says. 'To fish on the Lord's Day, to make money. How can you think otherwise?'

He leans forward. 'They're bigger, the east coast boats, and they have more men in the crew. If they didn't go out seven days a week they couldn't afford to go at all.'

'Well if they want to use our harbour they should have smaller boats, like we do.' This is tedious. It's like talking to Jack. She didn't put rose water on for this.

'And they catch anything, everything,' he says. 'They've got more room on board for the gear.'

'So? If they come here they should do as we do,' she says. 'It's only right.'

He laughs. 'What about when our boats leave here for herring? Do you think Irish ports are pleased to see Cornish boats in their waters?'

'It's not… it's not the same. The east coast men are wicked, Nicholas. Why do we have to talk about this?'

235

The trip in the boat, the beautiful evening together – everything is spoilt.

'I've spoken to the east coast men, Pearl, when no one else will. They have wives, children.'

'Don't try and talk me round.'

'There's no legal ban on fishing on a Sunday here,' he says. 'What the Council have ruled in the past – it's just a by-law. The east coast men need to fish then. We should do as they do. You know pilchard catches are down again.'

He has changed tack to wrong-foot her. For a moment she is thrown, then says, 'What have pilchards got to do with this? East coast men fish for mackerel here, not pilchards. Numbers could pick up yet. The season's not finished, and you know how tricksy the fish can be, suddenly coming in when you thought they were gone.'

Nicholas shakes his head. 'They're leaving.'

Something cold drops inside her. She can't find a response in her rising breath.

Nicholas carries on. 'It's not just in Morlanow. All along this coast there are fewer pilchards and that's not the fault of the east coast men. It's because we've taken so many.'

'No, no you're wrong. There've always been pilchards here.'

'But there won't be for much longer. It's not just a bad season, Pearl. It's the end. Morlanow should be moving forward, forgetting pilchards.' He rows faster and faster. 'And the east coast men are the answer, not the problem. There's no sense stopping fishing for Sundays when there's so little coming in the rest of the week. East coast men and their boat owners, and Govenek's men too for that matter, they've all realised that and they're taking the advantage while we sit twiddling our thumbs. If we go out on Sundays we could pay for better gear and catch more fish, other fish, like they do. We've relied on pilchards too long.'

'You think you know it all,' she snaps. His arms go slack as he stops rowing. 'Is this why you asked me to come out with you tonight?' she says. 'To convince me so I'll talk to my father, to Jack?'

And then all at once Nicholas has his lips against hers.

Pearl freezes. Nicholas is kissing her. How did this happen? Is she kissing him back? But she doesn't know how to. Perhaps she is doing it now, just by staying still. His hand slides up the inside of her leg. She feels his fingers catch on her drawers. She jerks away.

They stare at one another, only inches apart; Nicholas still half in Pearl's arms. She sees flecks of amber in his eyes and beads of water on his long lashes.

'Pearl...'

He is a stranger, and Pearl is a stranger to herself. It isn't quite dark and the huers might still be outside their hut. What if someone has seen them? Pearl would give anything not to be like Alice, good for gutting dogfish but never forgiven her sins. Nicholas has to want Pearl properly, in chapel, in front of everyone. But even as she thinks this she sees her father's downcast face, feels her mother's scornful words. Pearl has risked too much in the boat. She has given in to sin.

Pearl tries to move away, to get closer to her end of the boat, never taking her eyes from Nicholas's.

'I'm sorry,' he says. 'I didn't mean to.... Please—'

Her foot skids against an oar and with a cry she falls down in the belly of the boat. Nicholas is immediately above her. 'Are you all right? Did you hurt yourself?' He leans over her, his hands on the planks either side of her shoulders. He's going to kiss her again and she wants him to and she is going to go to Hell and it's her own fault.

Somehow the right words come to her wicked lips. 'No,' she says. 'It's wrong. Take me back.'

Her breath is coming in whimpers and he still isn't moving, his tall shape filling the mauve sky above. She scrambles to the tiller and huddles against it. Nicholas takes up the oars and begins to row again. It's all Pearl can do to concentrate on steering them back to Morlanow's shore and they come close to the cliff more than once, Nicholas seeming as distracted as she is.

Finally she feels the thud of land against the bottom of the boat. In silence they climb out and pull her back up the beach. Everything has changed since they left the shore. Pearl is closer to Alice than to herself. Nicholas's hand between her legs has made that happen, but she let him touch her there. She wanted him to.

As soon as the boat is well above the tide line Pearl turns and hurries up to the seafront, to get home before anyone sees her, certain there must be some mark on her to show what's happened.

'Pearl!' he calls. 'Wait!'

She turns to see him standing on the beach. His arms are wide open, imploring her to come back, but she doesn't trust herself to take a step closer to that embrace. What she has felt for so long is out now and she's frightened by its power, and that Nicholas feels it too. She runs home, avoiding any light that falls close to her path.

She doesn't sleep that night and stays in bed when her mother calls her in the morning. It feels so cold without Polly's body next to hers. Inevitably, feet are soon heard coming up the stairs. Her mother doesn't knock before coming in; knocking is only to alert those who keep secrets, and there are no secrets in a good and honest household. It's bad enough that Pearl closes the door to her room at all.

Her mother comes straight over to the bed and sits down.

'What's keeping you in bed?' When Pearl says nothing her mother puts a hand to her forehead and to Pearl it's full of chill. 'You're that pale,' her mother says. 'Your chest?'

Pearl doesn't lie but she doesn't tell the truth either, only coughing and rolling onto her side. 'I need to rest,' she whispers.

Her mother smoothes Pearl's hair from her face. 'It's strange, isn't it, without her here.' They both look round the room, taking in the gaps where Polly's few possessions used to be: her hand mirror, her boots. 'They must be nearly there now,' her mother says. 'I'm sure there'll be a letter soon.'

And what good is a letter, Pearl thinks, but she nods. Anything to make her mother worry less.

'Sleep then, my sweet,' her mother says. 'It's hard on us all.'

Waves crash on Witch Cove and their spray, sent far into the sky, spins a fog. Pearl is trapped inside this cocoon of damp air, lost and alone, but walking. She hears her name. A bony hand catches her wrist and drags her into the fog.

'Pearl?' It's her mother's hand on hers, her mother's face peering down at her. 'You were dreaming, my sweet. Only dreaming.'

She's darning when Pearl comes downstairs and sinks into a chair by the hearth.

'What were you doing last night, before we got home, to leave you looking as wisht as this?' her mother says. She'll have the truth even if it's dragged out. Pearl's lips are moving, unable to stop themselves.

'I...'

The sound of the door saves her. Her father is back from a day waiting by the seine boats. Before saying a word, he takes her mother in his arms and kisses her. Pearl is struck with fascination and can't take her eyes from their tenderness. Unbidden, she can feel the press of remembered lips against hers and as she puts her fingers to her mouth the room begins to swirl.

Her father stares down at her hunched in the chair. Her stomach is a fist of nerves and she curls over herself to ease it.

'Bit wisht, aren't you, my love?' her mother says. She puts a hand to Pearl's cheek. 'Still warm.' And then goes to her father by the table, thinking Pearl won't hear, and says, 'Swimming, do you think?'

Her father sits with her by the hearth. It's only when he's still and quiet like this that Pearl can see how he has aged. The weeks since Polly left have been hard on them all, wearing him out further. His once full head of hair has thinned and lost its hue, greying at his temples. His face, always scored with lines, is further marked by years in the sun, waiting for the pilchards. He has taken to cutting his beard much closer to his skin, which makes his face smaller, gaunt almost. Is this what Nicholas will become, if he stays in Morlanow for a lifetime? There is a spark in him now, as there was in her father once, and she doesn't want it put out.

'What happened at the meeting last night?' she says.

Her father yawns. 'The Council finally agreed that something has to be done and there were some strong words. To hear Jack-next-door speak against the east coast men like he did, fishermen like himself even though they do forsake the Sabbath, well.' Her father turns round to her mother. 'He was like a different boy, wasn't he?'

Her mother is peeling turnip for a pie. 'He was,' she says. 'But he's not a child anymore, none of them are.' And she looks over at Pearl briefly, the knife motionless, before resuming peeling. 'They'll take their own course, for better or worse.'

'So what will they do, the Council?' Pearl says.

'They restated the by-law against fishing on the Sabbath in Morlanow's waters and landing Sunday catches at our harbour. Council vote was unanimous.'

No wonder Jack isn't satisfied. 'Will it be any use?' Pearl says.

'It should be!' her mother says.

'And there's to be a petition sent to the Fishermen's Committee in Yarmouth,' her father says. 'It's to ask their members to respect the faith of those whose waters they're in, and their pockets too. Prices this month have been lowest I can remember. Oldest of the Tillotsons told the Master he's not to repair anything that needs serious work doing once this season's over. There's not enough of a profit to pay for it.'

'How many boats will go then?' her mother asks.

'Well, there's at least three seine nets cut to pieces, that I can think of, which means three more crews without wages.'

'But if people here are suffering, shouldn't they go out on Sundays too? That way there'd be more money to repair the boats.' The words leave Pearl's tongue before she can haul them back. They are Nicholas's words. He has worked his way inside her.

Her mother drops her knife. 'I know where you're getting these notions. Keep away from that boy, Pearl. He's no good.'

Pearl bows her head. 'I'm sorry.'

'The Sabbath has and always will be kept in Morlanow,' her father says, his voice close to a shout. 'It is the Lord's Day and He will provide for His people.'

Her mother comes to stand behind her father's chair, resting her hand on his shoulder. 'You must pray, Pearl,' she says. 'Pray for fish and for the east coast men to see the error of their ways.'

Her father packs his pipe, knocking it against the wall to

settle the baccy. From her mother's hands comes the chop chop chop of turnip for the pie. The clock ticks their lives away, louder with each second lost. Snaking into Pearl's thoughts comes the dismal certainty, clearer and sadder than anything she has ever thought before, that the pilchards are leaving. By kissing her, and touching her, as he did, Nicholas has handed Pearl a pair of spectacles. She can see Morlanow the way that he sees it and he's right. So now she has to see him. There's nothing else that can be done. He is where the future lies. He is her future. He has offered her a way out.

Fourteen

She wishes that on the night Nicholas kissed her they had both been drowned. Inside her a ceaseless wave drags her stomach over rocks. A morning with her mother, collecting cockles and mussels, comes and goes. She falls into the water many times and her mother gives up trying to hold a conversation. After three hours Pearl has barely half a pail of shells and supper will be lean again.

She wants to help find food, to ease the worry that leaves her mother sleepless, and to banish the soreness of hunger. But she can't set her mind to anything since that night in the boat. Her thoughts have become sinful. She will be turned to stone like the dancing girls who broke the Sabbath.

As if they belong to someone else, her feet carry her from the house, through back alleys and concealed passages. Only the sea greets Pearl's arrival at the front. Sunlight glances off its back. A breeze has risen from the heat and rakes the water into short-lived peaks that cut and cross one another on their way into land. Low banks of cloud scatter wandering shapes on the tilting surface. The morning's fish sale is coming to its close and there isn't much stock left on the slipway; not that there would have been much to start with, just what the east coast crews brought in. Morlanow's fishermen only have eyes for a red-purple stain rushing to shore.

Pearl's glad for the people milling about and for the faces she doesn't recognise; the artists with their canvases; the holiday visitors ambling past, taking in the sea air. The Master's wooden hut is smaller than those used by the visitors to change on the beach. When Nicholas is inside working, his head and shoulders are visible through the little window. Peering from the other side of the street, half-concealed behind a cart loaded with empty hogsheads, Pearl sees him. He doesn't lift his gaze from his pages. Is he thinking of her?

A hand cups her waist. ''Scuse me, 'darlin'...' A fisherman Pearl doesn't know steps round her from the alleyway behind. Stubble darkens his face and he reeks of stale tobacco. He grins, revealing half a set of blackened teeth. With his hand still on her waist he leans down at Pearl as if challenging her to resist.

'Leave go of me!' She wrenches herself free and stumbles across the street, opposite the harbour wall.

Nicholas is bound to be short with her for having left him on the sand after their trip in the boat, and for keeping away since. She's hasn't formed the words to let him know she's sorry, that he's right. She isn't sure she will ever have them.

Nicholas stands in the open doorway of the Master's office. 'Pearl? What's the matter?' He comes and takes hold of her hand and she realises it is because there's a tremor in it, throughout her body.

If she leaves now, all will be lost. The unspoken words will choke her. 'I need to tell you something,' she stutters.

'Now? I'm working, limpet-legs.' He can't be angry if he calls her that. She grips his hand. 'What is it?' he says.

'In the boat, when you… when we… '

But all that she has been practising in her head is lost in shouts coming from the far end of the harbour wall, followed by a crash of splintering wood. Nicholas pulls her to where a crowd is knotting.

A stack of hogsheads has been knocked over and in the midst of a broken barrel the stranger with the missing teeth is trying to get to his feet. Standing over him is Jack with a red stain on his cheek. Stephen and James Pengelley hang back behind him.

Jack is trying to catch his breath but the rage in his throat all but chokes him. 'Think you can do whatever you please, you people.'

Pearl tries to stop Nicholas but he steps forward, only feet from Jack. The other man wipes his hand across his face, smearing blood that drips from his nose. 'You should be more careful,' the stranger says to Jack. 'Nets were left in our path.'

Pearl recognises the broadness of his speech and her stomach sinks. East coasters. Jack leans down and grabs the man by his jersey. 'You ripped through my nets deliberately,' Jack says. Nicholas opens his mouth to speak but Jack raises his hand to stop him. 'Keep out of this, Polance. You've no place to interfere.'

The Pengelleys push close to Nicholas. Stephen, the taller of the two, gives his shoulder a shove. 'We all know where your loyalties lie,' Stephen hisses.

Nicholas stands his ground. His voice doesn't waver. 'This is the Master's business and I'm the Master's eyes. What I see, he sees. What's the matter with your nets?'

Jack spits on the floor. 'I went to haul them in this morning, my drift nets, and they were rent through. Look.'

Tattered clumps of net lie dumped on the ground. All the hours spent breeding them, the women crouched in bad light, the ends of their fingers growing hard from the heavy, blunted needles. Destroyed in an instant.

The stranger staggers to his feet and spreads his hands wide. 'It was an accident. Sorry for your loss but it weren't our fault.'

Jack puts his face close to the other man's so that their noses are all but touching. 'It's wicked enough that you defile the Sabbath,' Jack says, 'but that you should stop decent men going out the rest of the week—'

Nicholas slips his thin frame between the two bristling men and pushes them apart. 'Jack, there's no way to prove it wasn't an accident. Nets get caught all the time, you know they do.'

The east coast man swaggers back to his crew who wait where their boat's tied up. He calls to Jack over his shoulder. 'Ain't our fault you lot don't like hard work. And you should listen to your friend, mate.'

'No friend of mine,' Jack says quietly, looking Nicholas in the eye. 'How can you side with them? What about us?' The two men stand and stare at one another then Jack remembers the blow to his cheek and puts his hand to the pain, before turning and marching away. The Pengelley boys are at his side but not before Stephen has jammed his elbow into Nicholas's ribs. Pearl goes to him, catching a flurry of skirts at the corner of her eye. Sarah Dray has broken from the blurred wall of those watching and is following Jack from the seafront. The rest of the crowd wanders back to work, whispering.

Nicholas steadies himself on a hogshead, one hand holding his side. His head is down. 'Jack's a fool,' he says. 'Anything could have torn through those nets. The hake.'

Pearl grabs his chin and pulls his gaze to meet her own. 'You shouldn't get involved.'

'And what would have happened if I'd let them get at one

another? You saw the Pengelleys itching to join in and the rest of the men from that east coast boat. There would have been a brawl.'

'Yes, and with you at the centre. I don't want to see you get hurt. I couldn't bear it.' She doesn't need to say any of the words she's been rehearsing. In the slight inclination of his head, in the colour that has returned to his face, she sees that he understands. 'What shall we do?' she whispers.

He squeezes her hand. His skin against hers sends fire to her toes. The sea is loud all around her.

'There's a packet expected,' Nicholas says. 'She'll take us.'

A rising voice breaks into Pearl's ears.

'Nicholas? Where are you?'

Nicholas turns away from her, letting go of her hand. The voice calls again. The Master is feeling his way down from the step of the office hut, his arms outstretched. Nicholas jogs over and takes his elbow.

'I'm sorry, I shouldn't have left you,' Nicholas says close to the Master's ear. 'There was a scuffle. Some nets have been damaged.'

'Nets?' says the Master. 'There's more than nets to worry about, my boy.'

The Master's wits remain but the once tall grace has gone. His sight and his Beatrice are lost and now he is hunched, as if he has spent his life at sea rather than only directing other men to go. It's a blessing he can't see the scarcely covered palace floors.

The Master, steered by Nicholas, goes back inside the office. Nicholas turns to give Pearl a low wave, all but lost in his sleeve, before he follows. It's enough.

The harbour is cooler without him. The wind has picked up and catches her hair. The east coast boat is still moored by the wall, her crew looking as if they are about to make sail.

To get back onto the seafront Pearl has no choice but to go past them.

She breathes deeply to steady her quickening chest, holds her head up, and strides forward. She will founder if there are high spirits on their part. She keeps walking, trying not to break into a run as she nears the group of foreign men. Only a few paces away. One foot in front of the other, her boots beat on the uneven stone. She is next to the men. She is moving clear of them. Eyes lift from ropes and nets and glance across her. But that's all. No cat-calls, no obstacles in her path. They seem no more ready for a fight than her father's crew. They are just as weather-beaten, just as grimed. Even the man with missing teeth looks older now, tired and with hollowed cheeks.

She should have been at the palace by now, though given the lack of work there no one will upbraid her. The remaining palace maids are hunting chores from corners, waiting for a shoal. The last pilchards caught are still straining under the load of the pressing stones, but these have only one or two more days before they are released.

Pearl steps into the palace courtyard. Old Mrs Pendeen waves her over. There's no chance for Pearl to slip past unnoticed. No doubt the elderly woman will want to put in her two pennys' worth about the east coast men and Jack's nets. If Pearl's rude then old Mrs Pendeen will only tell her mother and that'll cause more trouble. Pearl resigns herself to hearing again how Nicholas has turned his back on Morlanow.

Old Mrs Pendeen is sitting on an upturned crate, her knotted fingers running across a net, searching for tears. They don't stop as Pearl approaches and she wonders how many times this net has been worked by old Mrs Pendeen this morning.

'Your mother was here,' old Mrs Pendeen says, her jaw

working even when she isn't talking, the bare gums reaching for one another. 'Says you're to go straight home for your dinner. Straight home.'

Pearl helps her gather the net in her arms, surprised. 'But it's not dinner time yet.'

'It's getting there and she wants you early. Special day,' she says with a sly look. 'Straight home, child. It's about time you did as you were told.'

When Pearl goes back out onto the street the growing wind claws at her skirt. Fishermen hurry to tie their pots together. The wind chases Pearl to her front door and slams it shut behind her. Inside, her mother whirls about the kitchen. The warmth of pasties fills the already stuffy lower floor – when was there last meat for pasties? There's a cloth on the table.

'Where have you been?' her mother flaps. 'Look at your apron. Go right up and change into your Sunday dress and tidy that hair. Go on, quickly.'

'Why? What's the matter?'

'Your father'll be back any minute. Get up the stairs.' Her mother shoos her with the back of her hand and rushes to set knives and forks. Four pairs.

Perhaps Polly's come back. Pearl's heart leaps at the thought but then falls. It's a foolish notion. Polly's gone. It's best not to think of her.

There's a hum of voices below. Her father has come in with another man. Plates are set. Pearl pulls on her best white dress, now bagging over the protrusion of her hip bones. She eases a comb through her tangled hair. With each stroke she whispers, *Nicholas, Nicholas, Nicholas*. She is still standing with him on the seafront. She is beside him at his desk. She is the breath in his throat. Could her parents have changed their mind about him? Could he be coming to dinner?

'Pearl!' her mother calls up.

She's waiting at the bottom of the stairs, a tight smile pinned to her face. Pearl rushes down, ready to see Nicholas at her father's side, forgiven, but stops on the last step. Rising from the table, wearing his own Sunday best, is Jack.

Fifteen

A visitor. The tea stalk in her cup proved it. Nicholas would come to Pearl again. It was a question of waiting. Even now, though, it might be too late. To come back to her as this fleeting flicker of himself was torturous. Why come back if only to leave again?

The cold hit her face and surrounded her, soaking her clothes. She struggled to cry out but her mouth was filled with a choking sourness that made her gag. Pearl managed to lift her face from the smother and saw that it came from a puddle of dank water in which she was lying. She had fallen, but where? Her knee was throbbing and as she turned her head awkwardly to look down the length of her prostrate body she saw the dark seep of blood through her skirt.

A shriek and a sudden flurry of wings above. From where she lay Pearl couldn't see where the birds were but for a moment was certain they were just above her, about to tangle their beaks in her hair. She covered her head and lay still, turning her face so that the water didn't go into her mouth or nose, and waited until the sound was gone.

The puddle dragged her down but without the peace water usually gave her. This was dirty, not the clean, fresh tang of the sea or even the icy gurgle from the shared tap. Pearl breathed deeply to force air back into her lungs. Then she knew where she was. The wet reek of generations of rot was too familiar though she had avoided it since the day she thought she might die here, Nicholas having to carry her home, Jack screaming all the while.

She hadn't meant to come to Skommow Bay – would never mean to. There was a rattle in her chest when she breathed in. Her hands were covered in dirt and scratches. She hadn't felt any pain until she looked at them. Pearl laughed. To have Nicholas back was what she had always wanted and look what it was doing to her. A wretched old crow who was just as much of a mess as Alice had ever been, but the funny thing was – and here Pearl laughed again, hearing the rasp as if it came from someone else's mouth – there wasn't any dogfish left for her to gut. Even that had been taken away.

She reached for a twisted spar that loomed over her so she could haul herself to her feet. The softness of the wood made her recoil. This was a place of death. That the palace should disappear yet this part of Morlanow still remain made no sense. But then, even Pascoe wouldn't be able to make Skommow Bay an attractive proposition for the visitors, despite his honeyed tongue and the railway company's money.

The quickest way out was to go straight along Skommow Bay to the road, rather than trying to climb back up the hill to the drying field. It would be dark soon. The thought of a night amongst the wrecks made her start walking.

She was somewhere on the right hand side of the bay, not far from the next cliff that marked its end, standing on a raised ledge of rock. Below was a large splintered hull. Pearl tried to stay on the higher ground; she didn't want to get lost in the maze of shattered pieces, but every so often a bigger obstacle stood in her path and she was forced to climb into the pit below. It was slow going. Her arms ached from climbing back onto the plinth again. Flies clustered and her skin was soon itching from bites.

All the heat of the day seemed to be here, swelling from the shattered frames in waves. Pearl's throat scratched with thirst and a headache ticked itself through her skull, becoming sharper with each step forward. She had to keep going.

This was more than likely the path that Nicholas had taken that day when he carried her home, though she hadn't been in a state to see. It had been his cruel words to Jack that had made her lose control of her breathing. The memory of her chest's pain pressed faintly at her now, though it was only that: a memory.

Pearl stopped to judge her bearings and rest her knee. She was back on the raised rock. There was the curious sense of someone stopping behind her. Not a noise as such, more of a change in the layering of air. She turned round but there was no one to be seen. An animal maybe, hidden from view. There were still cats around Morlanow, even without many nets to protect from mice. Pearl waited, but there was nothing.

She had perhaps two hundred yards until she reached the road into town; its surface gleamed like water in the sun. The way here was even more jumbled with wood and she was so tired, so thirsty. She wasn't sure how she would get through the last bulk of ruins but get through she must. There was no chance she was going to get trapped.

She limped on, her head throbbing and making her vision dance. If only she had a drink. The waves of heat broke and remade themselves around her.

There it was again – a shift behind her. Pearl turned round and this time the feeling that someone was there didn't stop, but moved towards her, the heat waves twisting and turning until they meshed to form the outline of a person she knew so well.

Nicholas came on, featureless but clear in shape; passing straight over the obstacles Pearl had struggled to climb. Closer and closer, until he was only a few feet away. Would he stop and let her hold him? No, he was still moving, he was going to pass right by her.

'Wait, Nicholas! Please wait.'

She held out her arms, imploring him as he had implored her that night after they had gone out in the boat, but the shimmering shape didn't stop. As it passed there was a burst of scent: salt and gorse and pilchard oil all mixed together. Skommow Bay and all the years since Nicholas had left her disappeared; her chest was mended and a glowing sense of peace swept through her. But as soon as the feeling came it vanished and when the rich smell drifted away, just as the shape did, it was replaced by something else. A stronger, darker smell that filled her mouth and nose until she thought she would be sick: blood.

Pearl spun round to see where Nicholas had gone, convinced that once again he had left. But no, there he was, or rather there his outline was, still moving forward at the same steady pace. He was showing her a way out. Pearl scrambled after him, once more having to drop down from the shelf and losing sight of him as the shattered wood rose above her.

'Stop! Wait for me, Nicholas!'

Those were Jack's words on that dreadful day here and all he got at home was a thrashing. She blundered on, tearing her skin on the spars. Her blouse sleeve snagged on a splinter and she had to stop and wrench herself free. Back up onto the shelf and she could see the glimmering Nicholas, now much further ahead but still showing her the way. Pearl hurried desperately to catch him, certain that if she could just put a hand to that slippery form he wouldn't leave her again.

Ducking beneath a half-snapped mast Pearl stumbled out onto the stretch of stones next to the road. Nicholas was nowhere to be seen. He had led her out but nothing more. Pearl dropped where she stood, ignoring the pain from her knee, and howled at the sky.

'Come back. Please come back.' Her voice cracked in her dry throat. 'Let it be over.'

Eventually the pain in her knee forced her to stand, shakily, with her pulse loud in her ears. She joined the road and began the walk back into Morlanow. At the bend where the road curved round to become the seafront, Pearl saw, through the haziness of tears and thirst, a familiar looking pile of pebbles.

It was on the old village boundary where a marker stone had stood before Morlanow expanded to become a town. There were no flowers poked into this cairn but otherwise it was identical to the others.

She heard the boom of something foreign. A force from behind knocked her to the ground. Her breath caught as the road's hardness jammed into her ribs. Pearl tried to refill her lungs and found in a panic that she couldn't. A shadow stooped over her. Nicholas had come to help her again. She reached a hand to him, trying to talk but finding she could only wheeze. He put an arm around her back and pulled her to her feet but Nicholas had a different face, crossed with a scowl and dislike.

'What on earth were you doing in the road like that? Bloody danger this corner is. You shouldn't have been in the road.'

'Clive! Don't shout at her.' Another face, concerned but with a drawn on mouth and thick ink on her lashes. There was the smell of cheap scent and drink. 'Are you quite all right, dear?' A gloved hand on Pearl's arm.

'It's not my fault, dammit,' the man said.

'Clive!' the woman said again. Then to Pearl, 'Here, sit down.'

The two of them lowered Pearl onto the passenger seat of the motor car. She had never trusted these machines. Now trapped in one she recoiled against the cool leather that squeaked against her calves. There were all sorts of levers and dials. She curled herself up so as not to touch anything.

She struggled against the two strangers. 'I need to go home,' she said. 'Let me out.'

'Shh, shh,' the woman fretted. 'We just want to see if you're hurt. Oh my goodness, there's blood – Clive, look.'

He held a cigarette to a shaking lighter. 'It wasn't my fault.'

Nicholas would sort Pearl out. She just had to get away from these people and their awful vehicle.

'It wasn't you,' she told them. 'I fell, before.' Relief passed across the man's face. 'I live near here.'

They looked at one another, the woman plucking at her sleeve.

'Well then...' the man said.

'We can't just leave her here, Clive.'

The scowling man was about to object when Pearl saw the painted woman give him a stern look, which cut him short.

'For God's sake,' he said under his breath.

The woman held Pearl against the seat and then shut the car door. She got in the back and the man started the engine. The woman leaned forward and hissed in his ear. 'I said you were driving too fast. Didn't I say? I knew this would happen.'

Pearl clamped her eyes shut as the roar began. The sickly scent was close to her again.

'Where do you live, dear? We'll take you home.'

Where was Polly? She would answer for Pearl when she didn't feel like speaking, or if the question was difficult, but there had been no word from Polly for such a long time.

'Dear?'

Pearl knew she had to think – it was the only way she would get out of this rattling thing – but it was such a hard question.

'Behind the seafront.' Yes, that sounded right. 'Carew Street.'

Finally the car stopped its jerking movement though the engine rumbled on. Pearl opened her eyes. There was a scrabbling near her, on the outside of the car. The woman had come round to open the door to help Pearl out, but Pearl's fingers were clutched so tightly to the inside handle that the man, who was still in the driver's seat, had to lean over and prise them off.

The woman took her arm and Pearl stepped onto the ground, relieved to feels its firmness.

'There we are then,' the woman said. 'You're sure you're not hurt? Oh I am sorry.' The man beeped the horn, making Pearl jump. The woman spun round. 'Yes, I'm coming!' Then she turned back to Pearl, tumbling her words. 'You'll be fine, won't you? Yes, it was just a little knock and you really were in the road but he shouldn't have been going so fast, and I am sorry, but you'll be fine.'

She was still talking as she got back in the car, more to herself than to Pearl, and the man Clive drove off with a great burst of noise before the woman had even shut the door.

People were looking at Pearl's bloody, filthy clothes, her hair a thick mass over her face. She had to get home. Taking a step there was a tremble in her legs, as if she was still sitting in the motor car. It had got its roar inside her and she would never be able to stop shaking. If she could only get indoors and sit down, away from these all these people.

Pearl got to her front door but it was locked. That wasn't right. They never had to lock their door, her and Jack. And her little plants had gone.

'Mother?'

Nicholas was taking her arm and leading her away. Why was he calling her that, and didn't he see she couldn't go out in the boat now?

'No, I've got to get inside, Nicholas.'

'Mother, it's George.'

She passed her hand over the face before her and saw that it was. There was her nose and the shape of her eyes. He wasn't all Nicholas.

George looked her up and down. 'What on earth... come on home with me. You're all right. It's all right now.'

Sixteen

Their silence at the table is tart enough to pickle beets. When the chickens can be heard distantly prattling in the yard Jack seems grateful for the sound and bestows a shy smile on her mother. Guests aren't usually asked to dinner. This month there's been barely enough food for the three of them. No one has mentioned why Jack's come. They don't need to. Pearl can feel the looks darting from her parents, so knowing in their angles. The treat of a pasty, rare in recent weeks, isn't enough to banish the dread filling her stomach. She scrapes her knife across her plate, enjoying the shriek against the good china, saved from a long-forgotten wreck.

Her father can never bear awkwardness. He clears his throat. 'It's set fair, for the next week I should think.'

'We could do with a drop of rain,' Jack says. 'Might tempt the maids from their hiding.'

She won't meet his gaze. She won't make this easy for him. His cheek still holds the bloom of his fight that morning.

Her father taps out a tune on the table. 'I've never known pilchards so teasey,' he says. 'You know Jim Dingle, Ida's

259

eldest?' Jack nods. 'He sold his boat to a lad from Govenek, just yesterday,' her father says. 'For barely a third what it's worth. He's gone to the Tregurtha to carry bags and they say his sisters are looking to go to America when they have the fare.'

'The palace will be short of more hands then,' her mother says. 'Not that there's much for them to do.'

'There will be soon,' her father says. 'We must have faith.'

Jack doesn't stop lifting food to his mouth when he speaks. Crumbs of pastry cling to his chin. 'I heard the Wills boys are looking to sell their boat too, now their mother's so wisht. Timothy says he's no choice. And Peter Jenkins is to rent his loft out.'

''Tidn't right.' Her father shakes his head. Her mother puts her hand on his, capturing his tapping fingers.

'The Lord will provide,' she says, but her voice is brittle.

Pearl's father can't raise a smile, even for her. 'I don't blame these boys,' he says, 'none of them that have given up. I just can't understand what's the matter with the fish.'

Jack leans forward. 'One of the huers saw a shoal coming this way last week and a boat from Lowestoft cut right across its path, broke it up and saw it off.'

Her mother puts her hand to her throat. Her father nods. 'I heard that too. Shoal's sorely needed. A good season would set things right again, get us back on track.'

'An east coast boat taking food from our mouths, seen by one of our own,' Jack says. He stops chewing and stares hard at Pearl, challenging her.

Her pulse quickens and a slow burning anger creeps up her chest, threatening to clamp her breath.

'But what if there's something else making the pilchards leave?' she asks and hears Nicholas inside her head. 'What if it's us and not the east coast men?'

All three stare at Pearl but she doesn't give way, thinking of Nicholas facing up to Jack and the Pengelleys that morning. Heat floods her face but she doesn't look down.

Her father returns to his pasty, tearing it apart. 'That's ridiculous, girl. What are you thinking? Morlanow's fished for pilchards for hundreds of years, hundreds. There's always bad seasons. Not unheard of for them to run together like these last few.'

Her mother lays her hands in her lap and turns her face from her food, as if too disgusted to finish it. 'You'd be better keeping your half-formed notions to yourself, Pearl. Others know better than you.'

'East coast men have got to be stopped or this winter will be even worse than last,' Jack says. 'Master's trying to keep word about this last frightened shoal quiet, and those with him.' Jack doesn't miss a beat but he's conjured Nicholas into the room, nonetheless. 'And after what happened to my nets.' The trump card's played.

'What about them?' her father asks, as Jack must have known he would.

'I'm sorry, I didn't mean to bring such bad talk into your house.' Jack does a smart job of looking contrite but Pearl can feel his need to tell. Her palms sweat. Her head is light.

'Oh, don't mind that,' her mother says. 'Can't be helped in these wicked times. What happened to your nets?'

Jack licks his lips. 'Well, they were ripped. Deliberately. East coast men, I'm almost certain.'

Her father thumps his knife handle on the table. 'Of all the low tricks. They're keeping decent folk from eating.'

Jack nods sadly. Pearl opens her mouth to mention the likelihood of the hake ripping the nets but he cuts her off.

'Of course the Master, or rather Nicholas Polance, doesn't want to fire any tempers.' Master's making a profit by foreign boats putting in here. Tillotsons won't lose out through him.'

And the Tillotsons won't stand any nonsense from Morlanow, Pearl thinks. Beneath the table she presses her nails into the flesh of her thigh.

'We must stay united,' her mother says. Jack continues to gobble his pasty, the slyest hint of a smile playing on his lips. Pearl feels the toe of a boot nuzzle her ankle.

She shoots her chair back from the table, making it screech across the slate floor. 'I've got to help old Mrs Pendeen. With her shopping.'

'Now?' Her mother stands too. 'But you've not finished your dinner. Jack's come special.'

She tries to get a purchase on Pearl's wrist but Pearl pulls herself free and nips to the door. She forces her voice to be light while grappling for the catch.

'I promised. I'm sorry. Jack... sorry.' The wind bangs the door shut behind her.

Up the street towards the cliff, in the opposite direction to the seafront. If she sees Nicholas now she will more than likely bawl her eyes out in front of half Morlanow. Past the drapers with its taunting ribbons; past chapel and its bolted door; past a flock of pupils from the art school; past a young man on a bicycle, carrying his sketchbook to the front. On and on, climbing higher and higher up the rough track road. The houses thin and scrub grass rises on either side. A motor car bumps along towards her, heading into the village. Pearl doesn't stop. On the flat of the hill she joins the cliff path. She wants to walk free of Jack, and herself.

The lie came to her lips in an instant, as ready as breath. Will her mother ask old Mrs Pendeen about her shopping? The lie itself is out of her now, twisting through Morlanow. And with it twist Jack's words at dinner, and Nicholas's:

There's a packet expected, she'll take us. Pearl pictures their three voices as nets cast into the water, drifting with the tide.

She stops as Govenek appears. Houses stretch back from the water's edge rather than huddling against it as Morlanow does. Still, it's an ugly place, Govenek. Even in summer the sunlight is weaker here, as if seen through a dirty window. New, misshapen buildings fill the streets and a towering warehouse rises at the village's heart. There is work to be had even though the train doesn't pass through and no visitors come. There isn't a proper harbour or seafront, and there's no stretch of beach; the pilchards won't stray along its craggy shore. The mackerel fleet berths in a sheltered but shallow cove that often dries out, leaving the boats stranded on their keels. It's harder to live there than in Morlanow but Govenek's men have lightened their burden. They hold fast together. They fish on Sundays.

The horizon is a blue streak across the pale sea, giving the trick of land close enough to sail to. Pearl imagines a packet ship surging to another world with two passengers safe in the bows, their hands joined together.

Seventeen

She wakes just before the sand scatters against her window, anticipating the moment the grains leave his hand. Nicholas is waiting for her. She can feel his patience through the thick cottage walls, knowing it's him without having to look down to the street below. Jack wouldn't dare be so bold and Nicholas has nothing to lose.

With little thought and as easy as telling the lie about old Mrs Pendeen, Pearl gets dressed, pulling a black shawl over her head and shoulders. She carries her boots and keeps to the far right of each stair where the wood creaks less. The front door doesn't betray her, slipping soundlessly closed.

Since she went to bed the sky has clouded over, trapping the fug that clung to the day. The gas lamps are lit and dawn is far enough away that darkness is still heavy between the pools of light. She sees a flicker in the shadow by the pump. Nicholas slips into sight. Barely five feet of cobbles lie between them but Pearl is on the edge of a plunging drop. If she moves towards him now there will be no going back.

'You're out late,' she says. How easy to say these words.

'So are you.'

She's warm beneath her shawl but pulls it further over her face. She moves towards him and takes his hand.

She knows where they need to go and leads the way. Witch Cove is between Morlanow and Govenek but far enough from each that they can talk in safety. They walk into the deepest part of the night, side by side for as long as they can, and only letting go of each other's hands when they're on the narrowest stretch of the cliff path. Every so often Pearl turns round to see that he's still there. The dry air is full of the sweetness of wild thyme. She fills her lungs with it, for courage.

On the descent to the cove Nicholas breaks into a run behind her, propelling her down the last few yards so that their feet crash onto the pebbled beach and their bodies are wrapped together.

'Steady! You'll have us both over,' she says, then is suddenly aware of their closeness. She moves a few paces away, pulling off her shawl and smoothing her skirt.

Nicholas moves his hair from in front of his eyes and grins. 'Nothing can break you, Pearl. Your bones are granite.'

'That's a pretty thing to say! And what about you? I know. Your belly's a bag of pilchard tails.'

'Your blood is salt-water,' he says.

'And your head's all maps, no wits.'

'So I've no wits at all?' Nicholas says.

'None,' she informs him.

'Well, now that's a blow. I'll have to let the Master know as his figures will be backward.'

'I expect he already knows and he's keeping you on to be kind.'

'It's a good job I'll soon be ridding him of the chore then,' he says.

Pearl's skin goes cold. 'When?'

'Next week. That's when the *Isabella*'s due.'

'But that's so soon.'

He spreads his hands wide. 'I can't stay. Not with the way things are. And if I'm going to leave Morlanow I think I might as well cut my losses and go abroad.'

'What about your parents?'

Nicholas shrugs and sits down, his hands gripping his hair and his knees pulled up to his chest. 'They'll be glad to see the back of me.'

'No, surely they won't,' she says.

'Pearl, how can you not see?' He looks up at her and the frustration is laid bare on his face. 'The only reason I'm still here is you. My father turned me out last week.'

Pearl's breath comes quicker, rasping. Nicholas hears and comes to her side. He smoothes the stray hairs from her face.

'Shh, shh. It's all right, limpet-legs.'

But her chest doesn't ease. 'Why didn't you tell me?' she manages to croak.

'They didn't want a fuss, people knowing. Especially at chapel. They're hoping I'll leave off defending the east coast men. And besides...' He leans his face close so that she smells the seafront on his clothes, the mustiness of his hair. 'I didn't want you to fret. I've been sleeping in the Master's hut.' His breath is on her cheek. She feels her hands lifting to his arms. 'It's cramped but I've been all right,' Nicholas says, his lips hanging close to hers. 'I think of you.'

They sit together on her shawl and at every point her body is in contact with his her skin sparks.

'Where will we go?' As she says this she wonders if it even matters. Once they have left Morlanow everywhere will be the same to her: new, and not home.

'The packet's coming from Naples,' he says. 'But I'm not

sure where she's bound when she leaves here. She's due to unload timber onto the train but no pilchards are ready for her to take back.'

'Getting on a ship and leaving, it's not the only way,' she says. 'We could go to Plymouth. Get the train and go over the bridge. That's far enough, isn't it?' She waits for him to say something and when he doesn't she blunders on. 'Or to Bristol, London even.'

Each is far away but by following a trail of sleepers and puffing steam there's the means to get back. She sees her mother and father waiting at the station, forgiveness in their eyes. She will always be able to come home. She won't go as far away as Polly.

Nicholas takes her hands in his. 'That map, it's filled my head for too long.'

He looks into her eyes. The train and the station and the list of familiar names on the timetable all blur before her. There is only Nicholas.

Then they are kissing. She's not sure who began it because it has no beginning or end, only stretches on and on into the night. She feels the tip of his tongue flick against her teeth, her tongue. She bites his lip without meaning to but he only kisses her harder. She leans into him and feels the buttons on his shirt press into her chest. She holds his shoulders, his thin, delicate shoulders she has wanted to touch for so long, and then his hands are at her waist. She lies back on the shawl. There are no words between them. She has no words for what is going to happen.

He shifts his weight so that he is above her. She thinks of how it was in the boat, of her fear. She wasn't ready then but tonight is different. She is different. Nicholas puts his hand on her thigh. He squeezes her leg through her skirt but then his fingers rest in the folds of fabric when she wants him to do more, to do something she can't even explain. She has to show him; she rucks up her skirt. The night air is cold on her bare skin. Nicholas' hand slides up the inside of her thigh to the thin cotton of her drawers. She can feel his fingers through the material and wants him so badly to press through it, to touch her.

She pulls off her clothes, feeling the rough weave of the shawl against her, and then helps Nicholas with his. His legs are cold and pale and when he presses himself against her thighs she feels faint. She is frightened and happy at the same time but these feelings are too much for her body. Her hands are trembling. Her chest is hot and tight but she won't tell him to stop. She can't.

He uses his hand first. The pebbles beneath her seem to melt away. The shawl is warm and damp. Then there's pain, as she knew there would be. He wants to stop when she cries out but she won't let him, biting down on the sound until the first hurt has gone. He whispers to her, noises that aren't words but murmurs of care and she thinks that she's making them back to him. The pain ebbs and something takes its place, something stronger, deeper. A motion inside her that she hasn't felt before. Her chest swells with the force, her breath coming in deep pants. The night air is cold in her mouth. Now she doesn't recognise the sounds she's making. They have changed too, into something louder, animal-like. She's shouting and the sea is loud suddenly too. The tide is with them, in them, running its waves over their now hot bodies. They are in the water. They are swimming.

She wishes whole days away. All that matters are the nights. When she gets into bed her body forces her into a doze, worn out with lack of sleep, but it's poor rest. She's only waiting for the scattering of sand against her window.

Thoughts of Nicholas consume her. She's known of people for whom drink has become more holy than the Lord. Mr Tremain for one, his hands unsteady and a furtive, seeking look in his squinting eyes. And there's a worse sin than taking to drink. As she drifts on the edge of sleep a memory plays out before her. Alice was often to be found in the arch beneath the harbour wall, her body reeking of spirits and her skirts all pulled awry. Once, Nicholas nudged the sleeping woman with his boot and was rewarded with a curse. Pearl fled, terrified by Alice's grey lips drawn back across her face and the warm cloying stench of seaweed. She rushed to her mother in the palace, telling her of poor Alice's plight, wisht and alone under the arch. But instead of going to help Alice, her mother and old Mrs Pendeen and Aunt Lilly and all the other women made their hands dance faster through the gurries of pilchards, none lifting their heads to meet Pearl's eye.

*

The dry weather holds. At night she and Nicholas make the most of it, slipping through Morlanow to the hidden places it offers. The far end of the beach below the drying field, Witch Cove's stony shore, and the palace. There are many ways to disappear. The sea hides them too, shielding their nakedness, dampening their voices. They swim until they are out of their depth and can't see the shoreline.

Others will see sin in her meeting Nicholas but there should be no wickedness in loving someone. It's a gift to be able to do so and to be loved back in this way is the greatest blessing she has ever known. Of course God is meant to love her too but His love isn't the same as this. It hasn't been enough.

She knows that she and Nicholas should be married, not

for God's approval but in case of a child. She knows that that is what must happen. But Nicholas hasn't said the words and when Pearl hears the sand against her window she has only one thought. When daylight drags them apart once more and tiredness descends, Pearl tells herself that once they are away from Morlanow Nicholas will make it right between them. They can't marry here, that's all.

Nicholas loves her. She's certain. He hasn't said it, in those words, but the look he gives her when she stands before him, her clothes discarded on the ground, tells her that it's true.

The packet from Naples will be on her way. Every breaking wave brings her closer to Morlanow. The village ticks on around Pearl, keeping her locked within its cogs. Still there's washing to be done and the chicken run to be cleaned out. The palace calls her to its empty floors where she joins the other women waiting for the next shoal. There are trips to any patch of ground that might harbour an overlooked potato or turnip. Sluggishness and hunger dog her. Invisible pressing stones weigh on her shoulders. Day follows day, each bleeding into one great stretch of tired longing.

Morlanow fixes its eyes on the sea, desperate for a blush to appear beneath the surface. The season is drawing to a close and many bussa jars hold only dust. But all that can be seen from the huer's hut are the sails of east coast boats coming in to unload their varied summer trawl. No one notices where Pearl's gaze lingers.

Her mother and father fret at her lack of colour and the heavy shadows beneath her eyes. They are forever whispering when she leaves the room.

'Have you a pain, my sweet?' her mother asks as she and Pearl draw water from the pump.

There are grimed channels of sweat on Pearl's arms. The sun's brighter than her eyes can stand. She bats away a fly and doesn't answer. How can she explain the ache inside her? It's a kind of pain but one that carves her up so wonderfully.

Her mother stops working the pump handle and wipes her forehead with the back of her hand. 'It's the lack of good food on your plate, I shouldn't wonder. My poor girl. We have to think ahead, to have you settled in a home of your own.' She puts her hand on Pearl's check.

Pearl pulls her head away sharply. 'Love isn't the same as food,' she says. 'I can starve two ways.'

She can't bear to look at her mother holding her arms out, her mouth jibbering its confusion. Pearl drags the pump handle. Her mother picks up the bucket they have already filled and sways awkwardly back to the house. The heat resettles in her wake.

Jack is everywhere. Even when Pearl can't see him she feels he is close. His step is the gull suddenly taking to the air. His eyes are the lights in the huer's hut. Only when Nicholas wraps his arms around her does the sense of Jack's presence disappear.

At chapel there is no escape.

Her mother takes her arm. 'Why don't you sit here?' she says to Pearl. Pearl doesn't have the energy to protest. She lets herself be steered so that her parents are on the outside of the bench and she's closest to the middle of the building. What does it matter where her body rests? Her mind is far away from here, with Nicholas, in the closeness of the dark.

A stiff hat is placed on the bench next to her. Jack sits down. He nods to both her parents who beam back at him. He looks at Pearl for a long moment without speaking. His sunburnt skin is angrier than usual, from shaving, and a lick of hair sticks out behind his ear. He has cut it himself. Pearl imagines him struggling in front of the mirror, trying to do a good job and more than likely getting in a rage.

She tries to gauge what he's thinking but can read nothing in his pale blue eyes. He simply stares. She shivers against his look. Jack lowers his head as if in prayer. 'Feeling cold, Pearl? You need a decent hearth to sit by. My father's not long for this world. When he passes over, the house will be mine. It's not much but it could be yours, too.'

She matches his whisper but makes sure her voice is light, whimsical. He can't think she's taking any of this seriously. She can't let him entertain the idea. 'You shouldn't wish such a thing for you father,' she says. 'And what about Alice and Samuel? They're your family too.'

Jack presses his hands on the back of the pew in front of them, staring hard at his stretched fingers. 'They're not family. And they're not worth your care. Neither is Nicholas. He can't look after you right. Can't provide for you.'

'I don't know what you mean,' she says. Though she keeps her gaze on the preacher arranging his papers at the front of chapel she's aware of her mother's face angled towards her, trying to hear their conversation. Her father is pretending to study his hymn book. Pearl tries to move away from Jack but her mother stiffens next to her and elbows Pearl closer to him.

'There are things you don't know,' Jack hisses. 'I'm trying to protect you.' He glances at her mother and father. 'We all are.'

'I don't want any part of your stirring, this trying to cause a row,' she says.

As he tries to hold her hand the organ shrieks into life and the congregation gets to its feet. Pearl folds her arms across her chest. Jack's mouth pours forth the glory of God and Pearl struggles to steady her breathing. The singing packs together into one great wail, banging against the blood that throbs in her ears. She can't make out any words. This is the sound of the fallen, not the saved.

Despite the morning's promise of sun, little light has found its way into chapel. The Minister speaks but his words possess no truth for her. They are as bare as the palace floor. His voice is broken by shuffling as people rise to sing and then fold their knees to pray. Up and down, up and down goes the sea of bobbing heads. She will leave it all behind. She must. Nicholas is right. A prayer of wickedness tramples through her head. *Let the packet come. Let the packet come.*

Finally there's the creak of the rear doors opening. She climbs over Jack in her hurry to get out into the fresh air. As she stumbles past, his fingers trace her bare shin and she kicks out, half falling into the aisle but then she's outside and free of those reaching to grab her. Pearl spreads her arms wide and throws back her head. The sky expands above her. She rolls her eyes to take it in. To be a bird lost in that space, to disappear over the horizon – Pearl flexes her fingers. Her feathers lift.

But she can't leave the ground. Something is wrong. People leaving chapel stand in groups murmuring to each other. They aren't looking at Pearl. They've noticed the change too. She lowers her arms then rubs her hands against them. It's cold. It hasn't been cold in so long. The air pressing against her face is damp and drifts around the broken congregation on a breeze. On its tail lies the smell of rain.

More and more people pour from chapel and none leave its narrow courtyard. Each body hums excitement. Their hope lies so close to the surface of their skin that they glow. The promise of rain is a gift, of sorts. Pearl should have seen its arrival, should have kept a closer watch on the signs, but she has been looking away from the sea and her wits have grown dull. The pilchards may well come but if they come today it will be a sore test of faith. There will be prayers to slow their approach, to make them wait just a few more hours so that Monday can be breached.

She sleeps deeply, without dreaming. The keygrim has retreated. Knowing that nothing can be done brings some peace and she's rested by the time she hears the sand against the glass, though it's muffled by the rain.

The front door bangs shut behind her but it doesn't matter. What's the sense in caution now? She's soaked within a few moments of being outside. It feels as if months have passed, or years even, since she started meeting Nicholas like this. So much has changed. She has changed.

The rain smashes down, pummelling the top of her head, clipping her ears. The space immediately around her is more water than air and for an instant she knows that this is what it would feel like to drown. She stands and lets the rain take on her shape. All water finds its way to the sea eventually. Each drop is called home. Pearl will go to it too, one day, but not now. Not tonight.

Barely able to see, Pearl runs to where the blur of Nicholas is crouched beneath an overhanging gable. Without a word she kisses him, fiercely. Beads of water streak his face and drip from his hair, but he doesn't feel cold to her. Heat steams from his clothes. Nicholas holds her. He understands her urgency, that they are themselves like these droplets of rain, lost within a downpour. They stay pressed together as they run through the deserted, sluicing streets, the rain making the surrounding buildings melt clean away.

The palace isn't locked. No one from Morlanow would steal from such a precious, shared store. Not that there is anything to take tonight except the empty hogsheads standing against one wall. Their bellies curve, brooding in the streaming darkness. They are waiting for a shoal to grace their black insides. And the rain could grant their wish. The pilchards may come to Morlanow tonight.

She leads Nicholas inside. The water races down the courtyard's slope, between the cobbles and into the uncovered pit where it slaps in the pool collecting there. Dawn can't be far off. Through the rain the dark is softening. The sky is hinting a wan yellow, revealing the undersides of heavy clouds that drag their burdens towards Morlanow. The huers will be aching for daylight, straining to see what has so often disappointed.

Nicholas stops just inside the arch. 'We shouldn't have come here tonight,' he says. 'The palace will be needed.'

'Where else could we go in this weather? There's still time.'

If pilchards come, enclosing them in the seine net could take half a day if the shoal is spread wide. Everyone will be watching the crews edge their way around the fish, praying for the nets to hold. Her mother might wonder where she is but let her wonder.

They run under the roof that rings the palace courtyard. The rain is louder here, firing off the corrugated iron. Pearl's skirt is heavy and drags round her boots. Her worn old blouse, handed down from Polly, lies rigid against her as if stitched from ice. Pearl wants to take everything off and feel this amazing, terrifying rain on her skin. She and Nicholas stand and shiver together. He moves close to her and starts to unbutton her blouse. Pearl tries to do the same with his trousers but her fingers are jammed with cold. He kisses her neck. She wants him to hold her tighter, to press her into his skin. She wants him to never let her go. Wherever they are bound, they are bound together.

His lips move to her ear. 'The *Isabella*'s here. She leaves tomorrow.'

They have stayed too long. Not sleeping, but not awake, curled together on a torn piece of sailcloth. Pearl is roused first by the quiet – the rain has stopped – and then by its disruption. Shouting, feet pounding past on the other side of the wall. She jerks to a kneeling position, Nicholas with her. The only way out of the palace is through the door to the street.

They are rigid, waiting. The sky is washed clean of darkness but no sunlight takes its place. Fog curls through the air. They hear one more burst of running feet and then silence. Pearl flails for her clothes.

'What are we going to do?' she whispers.

'Go, now.' Nicholas helps her into her damp skirt, the weave dripping against her legs. 'Come on, quickly.'

They creep to the door. He puts his ear to the wood. She tidies herself, knotting her hair and covering her limp blouse with her shawl.

'Do you think the fish have come?' she says.

'Must have,' he says. 'All this fuss.' He puts his finger to his lips, opens the door a crack, peers up and down the street, and then turns back to Pearl. 'Go straight home. I'll wait and then go the other way. If your mother asks where you were, say you went straight out when you heard the huer's call.'

She nods then follows him into the milky street. She can't see more than a few paces in front of her. 'The packet – when will we go?'

'I'll come for you, over the yard wall. Be ready.'

He kisses her briefly, distracted. She will have to pass by the seafront and her heart beats faster as she nears it, anticipating the sight of seine boats spread before her, of her father taking the weight of the net in his hands and dropping it into the water on the huer's signal. If this catch is good it will be some comfort to her parents when she has left them.

The fog is thick as whitewash. She hears shouting again. It grows louder with every step. They aren't shouts of joy or relief. What she hears is closer to a cry and there are many crying voices. People and gulls, filling the air with noise. She turns and sees Nicholas coming back down the street towards her, drawn by the sound.

The keening rids Pearl of her fear of being caught with him. She takes his hand. They walk into the fog together. A sour taste nips the back of her throat then fills her mouth and nose. She knows this smell so well but not like this, not like this stench.

Pearl stops. The sea lies before her but it has no waves. It has appeared from nowhere, butted high against the seafront and frozen in its silver bed. People drift into her vision. They are pointing at this sea of stillness, they are crying. Nicholas lifts his hands to his mouth.

This sea isn't made of water, it's fish. More pilchards than she ever thought could exist, piled in banks against the front. Up and down the beach, as far as she can see through the fog, there are drifts of fish. Men and women clamber between them, falling over and disappearing behind peaks. Some rush about, trying to fill gurries and shouting to others to do the same, but most people can only stare, as Pearl does.

The Master is a few feet from her, looking down at the fish as if he can see them through his blindness. And perhaps he can. Even with the fog so low the pilchards gleam with some strange light. Their silver could pierce any darkness. But to see so many dead – in the palace, even when the largest shoals came in, the numbers were manageable. The fish were kept alive, and fresh, in the moored seine net until there were hands free to tend them on land. There was no waste. This morning that is all there is.

The sky is littered with gulls that drop to the pilchard tide, beaks open to gorge. Pearl's stomach pitches and the seafront skews sideways. She drops to her hands and knees and coughs up hot, yellow liquid. Her legs quiver then cramp. She grips the stone edge of the seafront and heaves nothing. Nicholas is at her side, his arms around her, but she can't let go of the ground. Too many accusing, glassy eyes stare up at her.

Eighteen

Heat dug its way through her knee. She flexed it and felt flares of pain, muffled. Lifting her skirt she saw the joint was wrapped in a clean strip of linen, hiding the cause of the discomfort. There was a stain on her skirt. When she tried to brush away what she took to be dirt, there was damp warmth. Pearl bent and breathed in: blood. That she couldn't remember where it came from didn't make it any less true, laid there in front of her.

The skirt needed a soak in cold water else it would be ruined. She could never bear waste. It was wicked to be careless the moment times were easier. Those who readily forgot what it was like to go without deserved the hardship that would no doubt follow. Lean months would always come.

She had known hunger too well, had been kept awake by it for many nights, but George hadn't starved. He was too precious to risk losing and he had thrived on her shared rations. Never one for coming down with anything was her George.

Look at him there, fetching a shawl to keep this tremble out of her. He was a good lad, taking care of her, and poor Elizabeth. The two of them had a cosy little place here in the loft. A low slung bed where nets had once been piled. Shelves planed to fit the unevenness of the walls.

Elizabeth stood in the doorway, twisting her hands. She was a frail thing and the way she wore her hair made her look all the worse. It was too thin to be clamped to her scalp with pins like that. And that loose dress bagging about her knees. Her daughter-in-law was like a shapeless piece of sacking. But George loved her, so Pearl must try. She watched her son bustle round the room. She settled back in her chair. It was good to come visiting like this. She should do it more often.

She gave Elizabeth what she hoped would be a warm smile. 'And how are you keeping, my dear?'

Elizabeth skirted Pearl's look. 'Well. I'm well, thank you. And... and you?' Elizabeth frowned and dipped her shoulders. 'How *are* you?'

'Oh, I can't complain,' Pearl told her. 'Bit of stiffness in my hip most mornings but I soon walk it off. There's others worse I shouldn't wonder.' George and Elizabeth looked at one another. 'What's the matter with you pair?' Pearl said. 'It's only a bit of an ache. If I was still swimming it wouldn't trouble me. Shall we go now, to swim?'

Yes, that was what she needed. She was filthy, dirt all up her legs, horrible stain on her skirt – she should get it in some cold water – and she could feel the early itch of sunburn.

Pearl stood and struggled with something laid over her shoulders. A shawl – why was she wearing that when it was so warm? Who had put that on her? Some foolishness on her mother's part, no doubt. Always cosseting, even when the sun was high. If Pearl crept out quietly she might get to the sea unnoticed. Nicholas would swim with her to where the seabed shelved, make her laugh and swallow water. When the cold finally got the better of them they would lie on the sand, drying one another. Except that there was something wrong with the beach. It was covered by a spread of silver and it stunk to high Heaven.

A girl was staring at her like Sarah Dray used to stare. Pearl shrank back under the shawl. There would be no swimming today.

The girl fumbled for the front door latch behind her. 'I'll leave you to it, I think.'

And she was gone. Not one to be relied on, poor Elizabeth. No backbone, and no effort with anything. She had given George no children. The precious life he carried in his blood would turn to dust with him.

George came and knelt on the floor in front of Pearl's chair. He took one of her hands into his own and held it firmly. 'Mother. I think... we think, Elizabeth and I, that it mightn't be a bad idea for Dr Adamson to call on you. Just for a chat. He's a good man. You'd like him, I know you would.'

'He doesn't need to go wasting his time with a tired old thing like me. He should be seeing to the little ones. They need him, wretched things without a bite to eat.'

'What are you talking about, Mother?'

'The babies! The babies need seeing.' She could hear her voice rising above her, sending her words to the ceiling where they shifted until she couldn't recognise them as her own.

He was shaking her hand, wrenching it. 'No one's starving. Listen to me, Mother. No one is starving.'

'But there's nothing to eat. The catches have stopped. It's too late. You were there. You saw the beach covered with fish. You saw it, Nicholas. Nicholas?'

He dropped her hand and stepped back. She saw that it was George, hunching himself in his arms.

'I don't like asking this of you when you're not yourself but

I can't bear it.' His voice was barely hiding its cry. 'Why can't you just tell me? I need to hear it from you.'

It was only ever for his own good but now George's face was red and his eyes screwed with tears. She had to give him something.

'They would have taken you away,' she whispered.

'Why? Why would they?'

But still she couldn't free what had long been hidden. 'You were such a bonny little scrap.' Her words came easily and her voice held. 'They wanted to get a look at you, that was all. I was forever handing you to someone else for a hold.'

He dropped his hands to his side and shook his head. Her chest began to tighten but her mind was clear.

'And you'll go out and play now, my sweet? You'll go and find me some pretty shells to brighten up the garden, won't you, Georgie?'

And he came back to her, falling to his knees and resting his head in her lap. Pearl stroked his dark hair, relieved he couldn't see her face.

'Oh, Mother. What will we do with you?' He lifted his head. 'You'll have to see Dr Adamson.'

'I don't need to see him, my love. It won't do any good.'

'Father can't care for you,' George said, 'not with his hands the way they are, and not with his temper. You're not well. You can see that, can't you?'

She could see so much, more than she could ever explain. Looking at George, she could see Nicholas. He had walked with her again on Skommow Bay. He was coming for her.

'Look at the state of you.' George toyed with the filthy hem of her blouse. 'When I found you trying to get into the old house... do you even know where you'd been?'

Pearl pushed him away and he toppled onto the floor. 'Don't you cheek me, my lad!' She got to her feet; they were unsteady though she wouldn't let George see. 'I don't have to explain myself to you,' she shouted. 'Where have *you* been, eh? Seeing you only some Sundays and then there's rows. That new house is eating me up. Being stuck on the hill, with Jack – and nothing staying where it should.' The shake in her legs rattled to her hips and up her back. 'There's some things I don't want to see again, George. Awful things. But they come over me and I can't look away because they're happening inside my head.' She banged her fist against her temple and the dull pain felt good. She would knock it all out of her.

Her little boy was on the floor, drawing his long legs under him. This was how he sat when he was reading, tucked into a corner so as to be safe from Jack's notice. But her boy was getting to his feet and as he shook his head, a man appeared. She had sent the boy away with her frightening tales. Telling truths did no good to anyone.

George didn't come back towards her. He was wary and skulked by the door. 'You must see the doctor, Mother. You must.'

He was the same as everyone else, always telling her what she must do, for she couldn't decide for herself. No swimming. No Nicholas.

'I don't need the doctor,' she said, trying to sound kind. 'I've got you, George.'

They stood and faced one another across the loft floor. George sighed and put his hands behind his head. 'That's just it. When I found you today I was on my way to *Wave Crest*. There's something I have to tell you.' He paused.

Pearl's heart quickened. 'Well, come on then. Out with it.' Perhaps it was a baby.

'I'm leaving, with Elizabeth. We're leaving Morlanow.'

Pearl didn't speak. Couldn't. George was leaving as Nicholas had left and as Polly had too. Pearl felt her head nodding and then there was salt on her lips. People, places, things – they all went on being lost. Pearl was the slate on which to chalk them up. She was only the keeper of their going and their staying gone.

George wrapped her in his arms. 'We can't get by on the fishing anymore. My boat's barely afloat and I can't afford to patch her up, let alone buy a new one. We've been putting off thinking about it. We don't want to leave.'

'I've a little bit of money put away. You can have it, for your boat. You can have it all, only don't go. Please, don't go.'

He stroked the hair from her face and it was another's hand as he did so. It was Nicholas, if she only closed her eyes.

'It's no good,' George said. 'I had a letter last night. Mr James has sold this loft, all this street, to the railway company. Pascoe's going to do them up, like the Carew Street houses, for visitors. We've got to be out by Christmas. There doesn't seem much use in hanging on until then.'

'Where will you go?'

'Matthew Tiddy said they're looking for men at Southampton. I'm good with my hands and can turn to. I'd be building boats instead of sailing them. Well, ships.'

'Southampton.' It didn't sound any more real when she said it aloud.

'Come with us.' George managed a smile, though she could see it was an effort. 'Elizabeth wants it too.'

'And what about Jack?' Pearl said.

George hesitated and looked at the floor. 'He's welcome.'

Pearl patted his hand. 'As welcome as all that?' George looked as if he were about to protest and she shook her head to stop him. 'I can't leave just yet,' she told him. 'But it's not Jack I'll stay for.'

'Then why?' George said. 'Morlanow's changed. I know you don't like the building work, the palace coming down. And that new house is bad for your chest.'

'I have to be here when he comes back.'

She felt George stiffen. 'Who?' he said. 'Who's coming back?'

But George was no good with secrets. He wanted to know everything, even when it caused hurt. It wasn't that he was tricksy like Jack, but he didn't understand why some things needed to be kept safe.

'Have you got a drop of water for a poor old fool like me, Georgie?'

He looked at her for a moment, as if weighing her up. 'Course I have,' he said. 'We'll have a good talk. You can tell me all about it, and then I'll walk you home and drop in on Dr Adamson on my way back.'

George stood and went to the little kitchen at the far end of the loft, tucked into an alcove. Pearl waited until he was hidden from view, clinking cups together, and then moved to the door.

A pebble lay in her palm, hard and cool. Where had it come from? She had been with Nicholas – no, she had run away from him, because he was going. It was a game. They were playing hide and seek and had both been looking for a place to disappear but she hadn't seen where he had gone and here she was still in the open.

She cast about for him and saw, on the ground nearby, a little tower of stones. The pebble she held was similar to those arranged in the tower but smaller. A white line wove across its back. *It had to go on top* – the thought came to her as if a voice had just whispered in her ear. She spun round. There was no one nearby. The beach was empty except for a few people in the distance, lounging on the sand.

She laid the pebble on the top of the tower. The action felt familiar, as if she was working pastry or pulling the pump handle. It felt right, as so little did any more.

An arm around her. A hand in hers. Gentle words as she was steered away from the cairn, back along the beach towards the harbour wall.

'Here we are, now. I'll get you home. Come along, Pearl.'

Pearl looked into Polly's kind eyes, her fair face creased with care. Her sister looked older.

'Is it time for supper?'

But Polly only sighed and patted Pearl's arm. She shook her head and said, so quietly that Pearl could barely hear her, 'George'll have to do something. This can't go on.'

'You mean Gerald?' Pearl said. 'It's Gerald you're stepping out with, Polly. He's a nice boy, even if he is from Govenek.'

And Polly smiled. 'Yes. Yes, Pearl.'

Nineteen

Pilchards flooded into the room. They swam from shadow-corners, lifting out of the skirting boards and breaking from the paintwork. A colossal shoal of strong, smooth bodies, too alive to wreck themselves on a beach.

Riding the room's warm air as if it were a tide, the fish coursed over the top of the wardrobe, under the bed and out the other side, then across the window. Their rushing threw coins of light that revealed, for a flickering moment, the whorls of damp and the blistered paint. Water gleamed on every surface.

The room had become the belly of a ship. It was heavily laden with a cargo that had escaped the confines of hogsheads, finding sparks of life to move pressed scales. This dripping, tilting ship was low in the sea. Waves pressed in on all sides, desperate to find a crack to breach. Walls creaked; taut planks instead of bricks. Pearl heard timber groan and drag, buffeted by an invisible tide. The sound clustered at her temples and pressed against her skull.

The moon had reached half its grace and sent choppy rays

through the curtains as clouds passed across it. More and more fish poured into view. Their dancing made the shape Pearl had seen so often in the moments before the great seine net was shot. The shoal woman rolled her hips and shook her hair of tails, constantly breaking and mending her glittering form so that she was many women. Her mother. Polly. Aunt Lilly. Clara. Alice. Pearl saw herself as a child and longed to plunge her hands into the twisting silver to get hold of the untucked little girl but the fish were too quick, darting out of her reach.

She had only ever touched pilchards when they were dead. How she had burned to go with the men in the dipper boats and drop a basket into the circle of seething water then tip the twitching flesh into her lap. She imagined feeling the pulse of the great shoal beat against hers. Or, even better, to swim into the enclosed net and be surrounded by the still thrashing fish. To be part of such a mass of living that was desperate to escape its end.

It had never been allowed. Tonight, as so many nights, Pearl was still waiting for what she wanted. Propped up in bed, more awake than she had felt in weeks, though her eyes were closing. That didn't matter. She could see in darkness and when sleep crept into her mind and fogged her it was all right, because that was how Nicholas came.

Waiting, waiting. The pilchards danced on, always just beyond her grasp. A passing ship brought news. A finger traced the coastline, winding in and out of coves. He was coming back. He was coming back for her.

From far below the bedroom of the new house a single wave broke louder than its fellows, and Pearl knew Nicholas had returned.

The room's creaking increased. There was the drag of ropes. A door banging. In bed next to her, Jack lay as stone. The pilchards surged in front of the window and circled there, weaving a live mesh between the bed and the glass. Pearl's chest began to tighten as she made out a familiar shape forming behind the fish. She gripped the blanket and pulled it towards her, tempted to bury her face and hide. Seeing Nicholas was all she had ever wanted but she couldn't be sure of him, even now. How could she trust the fleeting glimpses? How could she trust a person she didn't know anymore, and perhaps never had? The man she loved had left her, after they had lain together in Morlanow's hiding places.

This wasn't how it was supposed to be. Nicholas was supposed to come for her in the open, in unflinching daylight, so that all the world could see she was worth coming back for, that she was wanted, more than anything. This creeping, never showing himself, drifting away again – it was all wrong. Pearl needed to see him properly, to be sure. She wouldn't be taken for a fool any longer.

Behind the moving wall of fish his body was coming clear. She made out a shoulder. Then an arm. A hand. It was like watching Miss Charles painting at great speed. Nicholas was going to show himself to her. He was going to give her what she wanted. Fingers swelled from the hand. The jut of his hip. He was so close. If she reached out she could touch him through the shimmer of silver. But she couldn't find the strength.

There was the too familiar flutter in her chest. Her breath furred into rasps. She tried desperately to quieten it so as not to wake Jack because this visit was important; she could feel it in every crumb of air, every drop of damp. The whole room was charged.

Already this Nicholas was firmer than the shape that led her from Skommow Bay. Through the silver curtain Pearl saw the white of his face, the colour of his lips. He was moving, coming towards her. She pulled the blanket closer to her face.

Twenty

The fog doesn't lift. The night's rain-storm has moved on but as the morning passes, the white veil thickens. No sun comes to burn it off. Scarves of mist roll past, twisting to blankets heavy with damp. Whole houses disappear. The small harbour is crowded with masts and men. Somewhere amongst the tangled wood is the packet ship from Naples, the *Isabella*, but Pearl can't think of her now. She can't think beyond the fish.

The squalling joy of gulls drowns all other sound. The beach is a mess of feathers and scales; dirty white and silver. The catch was missed. And now, when it lies on the sand, huge and dead, there aren't enough women to build walls from the bodies before the fish perish. Too many have left. Catching and bulking pilchards is what this village is meant to do. It's why the first houses were built against the cliff. Yet Morlanow's people have forgotten their talents. The past, parcelled together by fish, by catches, by stories shared then shared again – is fading.

Her father, whose usual part in the catch keeps him on the water, is now land-bound, filling a gurry. His hands move slowly. Each time he lifts a pilchard from the sand he stares at it, as if he has never seen one before. And then, when he lays each one in the barrow, he gazes along the length of the silver beach, at the piles and piles of fish, before he bends to those lying near him again.

Others rush, their movements feverish. Aunt Lilly runs along the seafront, grabbing hold of every woman she meets. 'Come to the palace!' she shouts, though there's no need in the eerie quiet of the beach. 'We must get as many as we can before they drop scales. Come on!'

But the women turn away, some crying, some only shaking their heads. The rising stench tells that most of the fish have already turned and are good only for enriching soil, not pockets.

Pearl is curled on the seafront. Her stomach still twists into gurgling knots every time she breathes a lungful of the foul air. She knows she should leave the front, get far away from the beach's flotsam, but she can't will life into her legs.

Everyone has come to see the catch. Artists stroll, looking down at the fish. One young man has taken out a sketchbook and squats unevenly on the drifts, pencilling the rigid features of a single pilchard onto his page. Most are silent, respectful. They have stayed for enough seasons to understand the loss.

Visiting fishermen, trapped in port by the fog, goggle at the shoal. They gather on the harbour wall where they talk in groups, watching the local men with a kind of fear at their grief. Until the fog burns off they are as stranded as the fish and there are many, many fishermen Pearl doesn't recognise.

Nicholas. She remembers him then as she sees the east coast men. He has gone to get her some water. How long has he been gone? How long has it been since they sheltered from the rain's onslaught in the palace, her skin frozen and burning all at once?

The thud of running feet. A pack of young men streaks into view, skids to a halt, and looks to the harbour wall. Boys from school – the Pengelleys, three lads from her father's crew, Timothy Wills – and others she recognises from chapel. They dance like horses brought up in mid-flight. One spits, another curses. Murmurings and sharp movements of hands. Timothy points and the herd careers in the direction of the main street. Someone crouches beside her.

'You don't look well,' Jack says, marking a line in the dirt.

'I'm not,' she says. 'But I will be.'

'You need looking after. Have you thought about what I said in chapel? Your father's keen, and what with this,' he waves at the mass of fish, taking in their many deaths with a flick of his wrist, 'your house'll need more coming in.'

'Jack, I...'

He lays his hand on the ground, very close to hers but not touching. 'There mightn't be another shoal this year,' he says, sounding almost pleased at the thought. 'It makes sense to put our needs together. I'd do for your parents too. You've only to say.'

Pearl looks him in the eye and makes certain not to blink. Lies are coming easier. 'I have been thinking on it,' she says, 'but I can't say for certain yet.' Her tongue is washed with sourness but still it moves. 'Mother's been low since Polly left. I need more time.'

Jack smiles and his face is transformed. Pearl clenches her hands, rolls her toes – anything to stop him hoping like this. Yes, she needs time, but only for the packet to take her away. Only for an escape.

'Well, as long as you don't make me wait too long.' Jack's finger brushes her hand and she feels no chill, no revulsion at his touch. She feels nothing at all. His finger might as well be driftwood and her hand a stone.

'I care for you, Pearl,' he says. 'More than you know. That's why—'

He's interrupted by a shout. They turn to see Stephen Pengelley on the other side of the road, waving to Jack.

'I have to go.' Jack stands and peers down at her still seated. 'Pearl, you'd better get yourself home.'

'I'm all right, really. This smell—'

'No, listen to me. You need to go home.' He says these words slowly, as if she is soft. 'You need to be indoors with the door locked. Don't let anyone in. Stay upstairs.'

'Why? What are you talking about?'

Stephen Pengelley whistles. Jack makes a frantic sign to him with his hands. 'Just do as I say,' he says to Pearl. 'Please.'

She reaches to grab Jack's shirt, to wring his riddles from him, but he's gone, running up Pendennis Street with Stephen.

The blood flows back to her feet with sharp tingles. She stamps the discomfort away. There's the noise of pounding boots again but their owners are hidden by the village's tangled lanes and short-cut passageways.

The bell from the huer's hut clangs mournfully and its sound makes her heart kick. The bell should have rung when the catch washed in but the men on the cliff top wouldn't have been able to see the shoal. Why is it ringing now? Local people begin to leave the front, filing silently into the streets. The artists melt away amongst them. On the harbour wall, the visiting fishermen watch people go. A hand closes over her shoulder.

'What's wrong?' Nicholas asks. 'I brought you the water.'

'You've been gone so long. I waited. Why were you gone so long, Nicholas?'

He proffers the tin cup he has retrieved from somewhere. 'Have a drop. Go on, it'll make you feel better.'

She makes to speak but again he offers the cup. She takes it and drinks a long mouthful. The sourness is sluiced away, the air in her throat feels cleaner, though the fish stench still hangs overhead.

'There was trouble at the pump,' he says.

'Trouble?'

His arm steals round her hip to rub her back. 'Is that better? Do you feel better now?'

'Yes. But stop – people might see. What happened at the pump?'

'Oh, just a flare up,' Nicholas says. 'Some men were trying to get a drink and they were stopped.'

'What men? Who stopped them?'

'The women stopped them,' he says. 'Your mother, for one, and mine. She didn't look too pleased to see me with the men queuing, and would have seen me off with her rolling pin as well.'

'As well as who?' She pushes the cup into his chest. 'Just tell me.'

'East coast men. Trying to get a drink, that was all.' He shakes his head and looks up at the sunless sky.

'It's not long until the packet goes,' she says. 'Don't get into trouble now, please.'

'But the fog. The packet won't be able to leave, Pearl. And today...' The bell's last peal dies and with it his voice.

She puts her hand to his face and speaks gently, prompting, not wanting to sound afraid. 'What will happen today?'

'I can't tell for certain. But something must. Something must change. You feel it, don't you? If only the fog would lift.' Nicholas looks around him. 'I can't see to save my own back.'

'Then let's get to higher ground,' she says. 'It'll be clearer. We can wait for the weather to turn.'

He smiles sadly at her, but nods. It doesn't matter that he doesn't believe the fog will clear today. Pearl's hope is enough for both of them. She knows that the packet must leave because the net they have cast is drawing tighter with each moment passing. Jack is caught there, and her mother and father, and Pearl too, because she has stood unclothed before Nicholas and knows the fate she has chosen.

'You'll not be cold?' he says. 'We could call at your house, get something warmer?'

'No.'

He was lucky to leave the pump unscathed. She has to keep him close, safe. They have to be together when the packet is able to go.

'I'm all right,' she says, though her clothes still hold the night's damp and aren't getting any dryer in the wet mouth of the fog.

Nicholas takes her arm and steers her in the direction of the cliff path to the huer's hut. She pulls back. The bell's late ring has set a cloud of doubt over the place.

'Let's go to the drying field,' she suggests. 'Look, it's clearer over that way.'

Nicholas peers up at the sky. 'Is it? Well, your eyes are sharper than mine.'

They come to the harbour wall and the visiting fishermen eye them nervously from its other end, where the sea clings to their half-shrouded boats. One man raises his hand and Nicholas does the same in return.

'Do you know him?' Pearl says.

'Only to say good morning when they unload,' Nicholas says, nodding at several other men. 'Friendly enough and he's seen a fair bit of the world. Been on whaling ships most of his life. Where are you going?'

Pearl is descending the slipway, banked by fish on either

side. She points to the arch midway down the harbour wall. 'So we can get onto the other beach and up to the field.'

'But it's quicker to go through Skommow Bay,' he says.

The name is like a cold hand on her neck. She twitches against its grip and carries on, speaking to Nicholas over her shoulder.

'I'm not going through there,' she says. 'It's a rank old place.'

He follows her down the slipway, as she knew he would. 'It's not that bad,' he says. 'Just boats. They can't do you any harm. And would you really rather climb over these?'

Pearl's foot nudges a tail. Such a blue – the colour of the sea before rain; slate and heather blended with the hue of Polly's eyes. No artist can mix such a tone. And here it is, wasted, fading as Pearl stares.

'It'll only be for a few paces,' she tells him, stepping forward and trying to seem certain. 'The sand runs higher beyond the arch.'

The fish give under her weight, sliding away so that she sinks into their depth. She walks on, dragging her eyes from theirs, holding out her arms to steady herself.

She reaches the archway, Nicholas just behind. They pick their way through, the smell ripe in the low space. On the other side is a clear path between the top of the beach and the drying field, where the fish tide hasn't reached. She hurries, the fish sucking her feet deeper into their mass with every step. She tries to run but only ploughs in further, sinking to her knees, then her thighs. The fish pack against her skin, slippery and solid at the same time. They are granting her wish to swim with the trapped shoal – she is surrounded by them but they aren't moving. There is only the heavy weight of their death.

Nicholas is in front of her. 'I told you Skommow Bay would be easier.'

He takes her hand and pulls her clear, half carrying her the few remaining feet to the sand. Pearl is covered in pilchard scales. She brushes them from her skirt but they won't shift from her skin. She glitters in the thin light. Nicholas stares at her jewelled hands, turns them this way and that. He seems to have slipped through the fish without tearing any scales and is unmarked, as if he has glided over them.

They climb the hill, Pearl's boots slipping through the grass and finding mud. Her damp skirt weighs her down. Her head swims. She must keep going. Just a little further. Just a few more steps. The fog lessens, giving sweeter air. The washed up fish and the tension of the seafront seem mercifully far away.

Finally they reach the hill's brow and sit down. Pearl leans into Nicholas's chest. She is suddenly tired; tired of waiting, tired of lying, tired of not being certain of anything anymore. Not even of herself. When the *Isabella* turns her hull on land it will be better. Pearl will sleep and sleep as the ship courses across the sea. When she wakes there will be a new life waiting for her. Nicholas will marry her. He will do right by her and all will be well. If only she can sleep, all will be well.

Her shoulder is gently shaken. She struggles to open her eyes. Nicholas is smiling at her in the crook of his arm. 'You can't go to sleep here, limpet-legs.'

'Can't I?' she says. 'Just you watch.'

A short thunderclap – a loud, crisp bang. Then another. She feels Nicholas jolt. He scrambles to his feet and Pearl crumples to a heap. He looks down onto the tight pack of Morlanow below, his hands gripping his hair.

'What was that noise?' Even as she asks, she knows.

'Gunfire,' he says.

Pearl gets to her feet. Nicholas puts an arm round her. From the drying field she can just make out the shapes of people.

They look to be running through the whitened streets. The boats moored off the harbour wall lurch as if a storm tide has risen round them. Noise drifts to the drying field: shouts, cries, more gunfire. A twist of smoke is rising from the harbour wall. The Master's wooden office is on fire.

'Stay here,' Nicholas says, leaning into her hair. She feels the warmth of his breath against her scalp.

'You're not going down there? Nicholas, no! It's not safe. They'll go for you, if they're after the east coast men. You know they will.'

He's pulling away from her, trying to free himself from her panicked grip. 'The Master might be in his hut. They might not help him.'

'I'm coming with you, then,' she says. 'You're not leaving me here.'

'No, Pearl. It's safer up here. I'll come back when I know it's safe. Promise me that you'll wait.'

'But—'

'Please, limpet-legs. Please wait.'

She hesitates, then nods. 'You'll be careful?' she says.

He's nodding, moving away. 'I will. I'll go across Skommow Bay and round the back of the palace.'

'Nicholas—'

'Wait here, Pearl. Wait for me.'

She watches him run down the field until he enters Skommow Bay through the big wreck at the bottom of the hill, as they did as children. Then he's lost among the broken hulls and tilting masts.

A chill jitters through her as she turns back to look at the seafront below. People are massing there, but with the fog she can't see clearly. How long should she wait? Are her mother and father safe? Is her father chasing down east coast men?

She wrings her hands until the skin is raw and rips her

fingernails with her teeth. Minutes go by. The huer's bell rings again. There's the sound of many tramping feet. And whistles. Shrill, commanding whistles, different to those of the train. The fog looks to be getting thicker as she stares down at the harbour. She paces a patch of ground, wearing it bare.

And what of the packet? The packet might put to sea without her and Nicholas, the captain thinking it safer to try his luck in the fog than risk the wrath of Morlanow's men. She and Nicholas must leave today. The net is drawn too tight now.

She dithers only about which way to go. Following Nicholas through Skommow Bay is most likely the safest route but even though she is afraid of what might be happening on the seafront, she will not cross that ground.

Once she is moving down the hill she feels better, stronger. A course is set in place and she can only follow the pattern where it leads. At this moment, it leads to the seafront. The shouts grow louder as the beach rises to meet her: angry words, curses and cries of pain puncture the fog. Once under the arch she crouches amid the stinking fish, clutching her sleeve to her mouth and nose.

The seafront is crowded. The features of men she knows are twisted in anger. They run and bunch, grab strangers by the collar and hurl them down, slamming them with fists and anything else to hand. Broken oars. Lobster pots. Everywhere, people are running. Her eyes flick from each cluster of violence, searching for her father and Nicholas amongst the seething, reddened faces. But she can't see them from the arch.

On the slipway, two men tussle. One is James Pengelley. A beautiful voice in chapel, singing the wonder of salvation. His hands go to the throat of the other man, the former whaler Nicholas waved to. The men wheeze and grunt, wrestling each other before toppling on to the pilchards in a sprawling heap.

Onto the front proper and running its length, checking every face. Overturned carts block her way, their horses loose in the road. Flames still surge from the Master's hut, filling the street with smoke, but there's little left of it except ash and twisted spars. There can't be anyone still inside. She looks around but can't see Nicholas or the Master. As more shots burst overhead she runs across the road, huddling against the corner of the fishermen's stores. She has to know that her father and mother are safe. She won't leave Morlanow without knowing that, and she can't leave without Nicholas.

The whistles again – loud and close, so many of them and coming towards her. A wave of unknown men in dark blue pours from the street behind and launches itself into the fray. She sees some policemen go down before their truncheons are raised, felled by well-aimed punches. Others split fighting groups, dragging the Morlanow men from the east coasters and whoever else has fallen foul of their hands. She backs away, her hands scrabbling against the stores' wall.

She must wait out the danger, keep herself safe so that she can board the packet and leave when she finds Nicholas. If she can't find him, then he will find her, coming to her house when he sees she isn't at the drying field. Somehow, they will board the packet and go, as they have planned.

The streets she runs though are a blur of bloodied faces. Their pleas for help melt in the air as she rushes past. On her own street she hammers on Nicholas's front door until her fist goes numb. She tries the handle but it's locked. She thinks she catches the curtain settling, having been pulled aside, but can't be sure. She bangs on the door again.

'Pearl!'

She turns to see her mother peering round their own barely opened front door. Her mother waves to her, squeezing her arm through the gap. 'Where've you been?' her mother shouts.

Shots sound at the end of the street and Pearl darts in before she has time to think, to lie. Inside, her mother locks the door and shoves a chair under the handle, then pulls Pearl upstairs to her room where she huddles against her on the low-slung bed.

'Where's Father?' Pearl says. 'Is he out there? I couldn't see him.'

'I don't know. I don't know where he is. He didn't come back from the front. He was meant to come back when the bell rang.'

Pearl prises her arm from her mother's grip and gets to her feet. Her mother won't meet her eye. She rocks gently back and forth.

A tight band forms round Pearl's chest and begins to squeeze. She backs away, the fear that has followed her from the drying field shifting into something harder, sharper.

'What's happening?' Pearl says, her mouth drying over the words.

Slowly, her mother lifts her face to Pearl but only shakes her head. They stand and look at one another until Pearl hears her breath thicken into rasps. Her mother holds out her palms; they tremble.

'We couldn't risk you telling him,' her mother says. 'You see that, don't you, my sweet?'

The net is closing round Pearl but she knows now: her hands aren't the ones that are pulling it tight. Her mother is standing, coming towards her.

'The east coast men have brought sin here. Sin that corrupts decent flesh,' her mother says, her arms outstretched.

Pearl takes a step back, then another, then spins and bolts from the room. She takes the stairs three at a time and drags the chair out away from the front door. She can't breathe. The floor tilts beneath her. Her mother's tread is on the stair.

Pearl's fingers fumble on the lock. She is nearly gone, nearly free. *Nicholas. Nicholas, I'm coming.*

The grain of the door blurs, twisting into waves, waves that are lilting the sides of a great ship. Her sails are raised and she is turning from port. She is turning away.

'I have to… to go… I'm leaving… I'm leaving with Nicholas…'

But her voice is a whisper in her ears. Her body goes limp and a reddish haze covers her vision. The shade of a pilchard shoal racing to land. Her legs buckle and her face falls hard on the earth floor, dust filling her mouth. She must get to Nicholas. She must leave. But the darkness is coming for her.

Twenty-One

The resistance of tightly tucked sheets. Coolness on her forehead. A hand stroking hers. Pearl breathes deeply to rouse herself and a throb follows each breath, her chest shuddering between gasps. Her eyes flicker and she sees her father. His bottom lip is split and swollen and his nose looks crooked.

As she stares at him he brightens, leaning his head on her hand. 'Oh, my sweet. We thought you were lost, that the good Lord had seen fit to call you home.'

Pearl struggles to lift her head. The pain in her chest pins her to the bed. She hears a whistle through her lips and remembers the shriek of many others. She has to get to the packet – it's time to leave.

Her father holds down her arms. 'You mustn't move so fast. Doctor said.'

She tries to think back, to stop her thoughts whirling, but can't remember the doctor coming. 'What's the matter with me?' she says.

'Doctor thinks your heart took a flutter, serious one, so your mother says. You've to rest now, for a few days at least.'

Neither speaks for a time. The only sound is the roof creaking its beams awake. The stillness is sharp, exposing the memories of the fighting like the shore at low tide. All is tangled and salt-swollen as flotsam. So much to be teased open and understood. But not yet. Not today. First she must find strength to leave this room and then she must find Nicholas. There will be time for thinking on their journey across the sea.

She is in her own bed, the curtain open to let in the stark light of day. The fog has finally lifted. There's a corner of rich blue sea just visible. Pearl eases herself on to an elbow, all the while her father hovering at her side.

'Where's Mother?' she says.

Her father paws the hair from Pearl's face, his hands clumsy but gentle. 'Taken to her bed,' he says. 'Was too much, watching you fade like that. She's been in quite a state.'

'And you? Your face.'

He fingers his cheek, probing the hint of a bruise, and sucks in his tender lip. 'Came up behind me. Two held me down while one laid in. Lucky the constables had arrived by then or I'd have been for it.'

The whistles tinkle in her ear again. 'How did they know to come?' she says.

'The Master tipped them off. For the best really, far as I can see, despite what some are saying. He sent word to Pentreath and the policemen came on the train. We hadn't counted on the Govenek men fighting alongside the east coasters. We were outnumbered, by our own neighbours.'

Pearl swallows. Her throat is lined with coarse sand. She has to find the words, though. She has to know.

'It was bad, on the front,' she stutters out. 'Did anyone, was anyone...'

Her father cups his hands over his face. When he speaks

she can barely hear him. 'Five,' he says. 'Five souls were lost. Three of our own and two from Yarmouth. They're lying in the Council rooms now.'

She is as cold as the sea in winter, caught in an undertow of freeze. 'Who of ours?' she manages to ask.

'A Teague boy, from Fish Lane. Edward Richards. And Peter next door.'

So Jack's father launched himself in too, sober enough to get out of his chair for once. Wickedness heats her skin, fires her cheeks. Good riddance to him, and the others. They were taken and Nicholas wasn't. Their bodies lie stiffening in the dusty Council rooms while he breathes and thinks of her.

A tremor in her arm. Pearl sinks back on to the mattress and closes her eyes, the light suddenly too rich for them. Her pale lids glow red with the pressing sun. She buries her face in her pillow, drowning the red in black.

When she opens her eyes again the daylight has all but gone, replaced by a lamp. The smell of pilchards lifts from the oil, a faint memory of their rotting stench. Her father is still seated by the bed, asleep himself now, his head tilted back, mouth open. Spittle glimmers at the join of his lips. Deep, sun-baked lines criss-cross every inch of his skin, packed with dirt and dried blood.

Pearl tests her chest, breathing in hard and fast to gauge the pain. It is still there, clamped across her ribs, but she feels more able to bear it. She will take nothing with her, leave no note. Gone is the heavy drag of guilt. She has done all she can here.

So practised now at hidden leaving she doesn't disturb her father's rest and pads past her parents' bedroom. Her mother must still be sleeping. Pearl doesn't stop to look in. The front door seals her going.

Nicholas might only be a wall away. As she knocks, the Polances' door swings open, revealing an unlit kitchen. Shadows stretch the room to odd proportions. Pearl steps across the threshold and picks out two figures huddled together by the empty hearth. They don't stir at her entrance and Pearl's first thought is that Nicholas's parents are asleep. She hovers by the table where two bowls of settled liquid lie untouched, each topped with a skin. Flies collect on a loaf of bread and a butter dish. The breeze from a shattered pane in the back window stirs them.

Annie Polance breaks the spell, speaking without moving from her seat, her face hidden in darkness.

'What do you want, child?'

'Is Nicholas here?' Pearl asks. In the gloom, she makes out Annie's shaken head.

'He's lost to us,' Annie says.

'Did he come here, in the fighting?'

'No,' Annie says, finding some gentleness to ease the hurt of her words. 'He didn't. We didn't see Nicholas, and now he's gone.'

Something inside Pearl is stretching, pulling to break.

'Perhaps you missed him. I came and your door was locked. Perhaps—'

'I was here, upstairs. I saw you. Nicholas didn't come, and he won't now. He left, Pearl. We heard this morning.'

'No, he can't have done!'

Mr Polance gets to his feet then and comes towards Pearl. He's a big man, tall as well as broad, carrying his strength across his shoulders. The look in his eyes makes her back out of the house. He follows her to the doorstep.

'Go home to your own family and leave ours be,' he says, shutting the door in her face.

Pearl leans into the wood and lets her lips brush its surface.

Her tongue finds a knot and she thinks of Nicholas's mouth on hers.

A bank of cloud lies on the horizon, the sky pink behind it. The sun itself hangs ready to drop into the sea, a raw red. She keeps it in sight as she walks away from her street, resting every twenty yards or so, able to carry on if she pauses to catch her breath.

She has never felt this wisht before, not in all the years that her chest has troubled her, air suddenly petering out even as she gasped for it. Now, in the sag of her limbs, the weight on her back, she feels how much time is needed for her to mend. Nicholas will have to help her and she knows he will, in their new life beyond the sea.

But even as she thinks this, her chest gives a different, tighter twinge. Nicholas can't have spent the night on the drying field, surely, and his old place to sleep, the Master's hut, is a pile of ash and nails. Would he have come for her at her own home? Would her father have sent him on his way?

Coming to the seafront she smells the pilchards before she sees them. The stench is heavier today. The silver bodies have dulled overnight, their brightness leaching into the sand. They have seen all that has happened, lying still, waiting to be remembered. Not many have been taken for enriching the ground yet but the farmers will have their fill in the weeks ahead. Free to those who can carry them away and take the sight from Morlanow's eyes.

Signs of fighting litter the front. Smashed lobster pots. Stained, tattered pieces of clothing. Splintered wood – carts, hogsheads, and the remains of a familiar skiff, painted red. She stops briefly by the stoved hull lying in the road.

People mill about, gradually restoring order to the mess. Those she passes are themselves recovering, limping, leaning on roughly fashioned crutches, or just sitting, waiting for their wounds to heal. All are faces she recognises. The strangers have left, the artists and visitors keeping indoors.

The harbour wall comes clearer before her. Some masts still cluster on the returned tide but fewer than the day before. The visiting fleet has gone. And the packet too? There is still the chance. Always the chance.

Her breath runs short again so she stops and leans against a cart abandoned on its side. A man limps by her. Timothy Wills. His gaze is fixed on the ground and he's shivering.

Pearl touches his arm. Timothy jumps. There is blood across his shirt and his usually narrow eyes are staring.

'Timothy, do you know what visiting boats are left?' He gazes at her blankly. She gestures towards the harbour wall, wondering if he can hear her. 'Do you know which have gone?' she asks.

He shakes his head. 'Any with sense.'

'But which – which have gone? There was a packet from Naples, the *Isabella*.'

'Why do you want to know?' He curls his lip. 'Doubt many foreigners are still here and I wouldn't go hunting them out neither. Few constables are still abroad.'

Timothy lingers by her. She feels his gaze sweep across her body. The need to ask if he has seen Nicholas swells through her but before she can ask, Timothy is opening his mouth.

'It's funny,' he says, 'what men will fight over.' The pitch of his voice makes her shrink back and clamps her tongue. 'One man's prize is another's folly, eh?' he goes on, becoming more certain. 'Got nothing to say, Pearl? Quiet as when we were in the schoolroom. Always hard to know what you were thinking but you'll lead a merry dance. Oh yes, been dancing all over the place, haven't you?'

'Timothy—'

'Never look at anyone else though, would you? No one but that back-sliding Polance.' Timothy coughs then spits on the ground. When he speaks again his voice has lost its edge.

'The Frenchies and an Italian boat have gone, I know that much. Left without their cargo but in one piece, which is more than can be said for some.'

Again that strange new twinge in her chest. But she stands tall, her shoulders braced. It isn't done yet. There were many boats in port, waiting out the fog.

Pearl walks away from Timothy and keeps on towards the harbour wall, the thin forest of masts blurring as her eyes smart then stream.

He calls after her. 'You'd best go home, Pearl. There's nothing for you here.'

When she is at last out of earshot and certain he isn't following her, Pearl stops and rests again, wiping the tears from her face. Some part of her knows but she needs to be sure before she lets go and gives in. It's too important to have doubt.

The approaching harbour wall is a wet mess of wood and stone, boats and land. A familiar face is in front of her, a face with a smile, but not the one she wants.

'Come here, come here,' says Sarah Dray, wrapping Pearl into her thick hair. Polly's old friend holds her while she sobs, Sarah all the time murmuring into Pearl's cheek. 'Shh, shh. There now.'

When her eyes have cried themselves dry, Pearl pulls back and tries to straighten herself, catch her breath. Sarah kindly looks away, out to sea, for once her smugness gone.

'Sorry,' Pearl says. 'I'm not myself today.'

Sarah turns back and nods. 'I know. I'm the same. To be expected. All this.' She puts her hand on Pearl's arm, steadying, reassuring. 'You look proper wisht though, Pearl. Shouldn't you be in bed?'

Pearl shakes her head. 'I need to find a ship, from Naples.'

'The *Isabella*? She's gone. One of the first.'

The new twinge comes again but this time lengthens into a long note of pain. Pearl wraps her arms around her chest, holds her heart as her lips quiver words into the air, barely holding back their spasm of fresh sobs.

'And on it? Do you know who was on board?'

'Well, the crew I'm guessing they were, and…' Sarah takes a deep breath. 'And one other. It was a dash to get out to sea before they were boarded.'

'Who was it that left with them?'

Sarah hesitates then grips Pearl's elbow, looking her dead in the eye. 'It was Nicholas Polance that left with them. He's gone, thank the Lord. He was a sinner, Pearl, and you're best off without him.'

But the words are fading in Pearl's ears, replaced by a scream, sharp as a diving gull and pouring from her throat. It isn't true. Nicholas wouldn't go without her. He loves her, he loves her. Though he never said, she knows.

Sarah who has told such a wicked lie is trying to gather her up.

'Leave me be,' Pearl says as the coughing starts. She stands, somehow, and turns away. She walks back in the direction she has come, swerving, stumbling, just to get away from the lie. Nicholas is here, hiding. He doesn't know that it's safe now, that the fighting is over. She just has to find him and tell him. Sarah doesn't know him, how would she know where he is? No one knows him like Pearl does.

She doesn't cry – her lungs can't manage the effort. She crosses the road and feels along the wall of the buildings for support, looking only at her feet, thinking only of Nicholas. She will search every alley, every building. She will go to Witch Cove, to the palace, to the drying field. He can't have left her behind. He must be waiting for her.

Past the last doorway, about to turn the corner and strike away from the seafront she catches sight of a figure on the opposite side of the road. Her eyes are sore and scritched up. She trips over her own feet with a cry, trying to get to him. Then the figure raises an arm to her. Jack's light hair and stocky build bleed into the person she imagined, hoped, she could see.

Neither she nor Jack move. He is ten, fifteen yards away and his face, the way he stands – he doesn't bear any obvious signs of injury. In fact there is some grace in the way he holds himself, some pride stretched across his shoulders, up his straight spine. The east coast men have gone, Sunday fishing is over. Jack has had his way.

As the last curve of the red sun slips over the horizon, Jack turns and walks up the cliff path, towards the huer's hut. Pearl watches his retreating back until he is hidden by the gorse crop.

The seafront darkens. A single star pierces the deep blue of the sky. The dead fish gleam a strange light on the sand. Beyond them, the sea slaps the shore, black and cold. It disappears into the night, stretching further than she wants to understand.

Twenty-Two

'I'm not going anywhere,' Jack said, addressing the back of the chair. 'You can't be left on your own and I can't very well take you down to the front with me, can I? Right state you're in this morning.'

He took a step towards Pearl. She took one back, keeping the kitchen table between them. Outside, the wind was rising. The window rattled in its frame. A cool draught stroked her legs.

'No, no, no,' she said, striking the table with each word. 'You can't be in here with me. Not today. I've got too much to do.'

Nicholas was coming and she was meant to be getting ready. Had Jack guessed? He was pointing and looking cross.

'Oh yes,' he said. 'You've plenty to do, all right. House has gone to ruin in the last month.'

She looked around her. Jack was right. The house was in a mess, but it could only just have happened. Couldn't have been like this for a whole month. Someone had come in and roughed it about, dirtied it up. She would never have let such filthy dishes grow into tilting piles or left the milk bottles cloudy with un-rinsed milk. The sink was caked in grease and dirt lay scattered across the floor.

Pearl peered down. The dirt was white. She bent and ran her fingers across its roughness. Salt. The kitchen floor was laid with salt and a fair bit at that. It was ready for the shoal.

She looked hard at the kitchen, trying to see beyond the trickery of time; of days, weeks, years gone by and snuffed out like bedtime candles. Spreading from the corner of the room was a pile of stones. Each stone was roughly the same size – to fit in a palm – and each bore a distinctive mark. These stones were familiar but she was sure she hadn't had anything to do with bringing them inside. Nicholas's work again.

He had come to see her. The visit flared and swallowed the kitchen. Nicholas, dripping wet and walking towards her. The deep cut on his head.

How could it now be morning and Nicholas gone? She could feel him by her side but just out of sight. Each time she turned her head to see him, he slipped from her. Her skin was clammy and a shiver stole across her back, as if she had been out in mizzle. It was too dark for morning to have charged in. It was still night, surely. She went over to the window and saw that the darkness came from clouds as black as seine boat paint.

'Pearl, can you hear me?' Jack whined. He was always pleading for her to play games.

'No hide and seek today, Jack Tremain. I've got to be sorting everything. Getting ready. Outside now, go on. Go down to the front.'

He stood and gaped, his swollen hands rising then falling onto the table with a dull thump.

'Getting ready for what?' he shouted.

Someone knocked on the front door. Jack turned, his face pale, and she took the moment to go upstairs.

There was much to do. The packet was coming and they would board it together, as they were meant to. The wind was louder upstairs, clunking over the roof. Pearl wrenched open the wardrobe doors and began pulling out the contents, dumping them on the bed. Wool. Oilskin. A silky ribbon trailing. When every scrap of clothing was piled on the bed, she turned her full attention to the heap, making herself concentrate on the task in hand. She must keep focused. She mustn't forget.

She dug in the nest of fabric, pulling clumps out every so often and rubbing them on her face, smelling them to make herself remember the part of life they belonged to. She hadn't given anything away – George's first shoes were here, her mother and father's clothes – and she was going further back with each find. There was something she was looking for.

She heard Jack opening the door. When she turned back to the bed the reason for sorting through the clothes had slipped from her. She began from the beginning. Wool for her mother. Oilskin for her father. A ribbon for Polly. No, these weren't what she was looking for.

She had to be quick though, she knew that much. Jack would be coming to stare and make unhelpful suggestions. You shouldn't stare – her mother said. But Jack didn't have a mother so perhaps he didn't know.

Voices below. Words loud and angry enough to cut through the ceiling and find her. Nasty words they were. She didn't want to hear them so she sang to herself, which made sorting the clothes easier. Their owners came to mind more quickly. This was Polly's pinafore that she wore to the Sunday school treat. This was her father's belt, pitted by salt.

Ah, here they were. A navy skirt, its full length showing its age, and a blouse; worn-white, a high, scalloped neck and full shoulders tapering at the elbow. She remembered stuttering fingers pulling at the cold, wet buttons. Nicholas would know her in these clothes.

Rain began firing against the window and the glass was a melting square, the sea heaving greens and reds and blacks somewhere beyond. The clothes didn't fit. The blouse gaped across her chest and hung loosely from her arms. The skirt was tight at her waist, so she left it undone, pulled up as far as it would go. How could her body have changed so much?

It was better with these clothes on though. She was more certain. Despite their washing and long spell in the wardrobe, the clothes still held traces of that final night in the palace, the dead fish the next day, the gunfire. It wasn't a smell, or even marks – the past clung on deeper in the fabric.

The voices from downstairs were coming closer. A foot sounded on the bottom stair. George's voice called up to her, followed by Jack's retort: 'What do you think you're doing? Coming in like this. We're fine.'

They came to the doorway of the bedroom. Jack put his arm across the frame, barring George.

'I need to see Mother,' George said. 'She's not well. Why won't you let me help you?'

'We don't need any help,' Jack spat.

George pushed him out of the way. 'People have been telling me she's not coping. Margaret Pendeen caught me on the front this morning. And I know what it is. Mother doesn't like this house, the palace coming down.'

'How dare you tell me how to look after my own wife?'

'I'm not. I'm only worried.' George lowered his voice. 'The doctor needs to see her. I'm taking her to Adamson.'

'You've no right.'

'I've every right. She's my mother.'

317

'And she's my wife.'

It was almost time. She sent clothes flying in an arc of black, grey and brown. There was no proper case to pack her things in so she dropped what she wanted to take onto the floor, ready to be scooped into her arms. A shawl. Stockings. A nightshirt. There hadn't been need for a suitcase until now. She and Jack had never been away. They lived in the land of other people's holidays.

George was gaping at her. 'What are you wearing, Mother?' he said.

'My going away clothes,' she told him.

'Pearl, you're not going anywhere.' Jack held his hands out and open, like the pictures of Jesus at Sunday school. 'Don't fret. I won't let anyone take you away.'

'It's not up to you.' Her voice was shrill, gabbling out. 'I want to go.'

'You see!' George rounded on Jack. 'She knows she's not well.'

'She's better off here with me,' Jack said. 'I can look after her best. No one can take her away.'

'You mean she can look after you. That's what this is about, isn't it?'

Pearl went and stood by the window. The rain was falling. Nicholas would throw sand soon, to let her know it was time to come down. She put her ear to the glass. It was damp with condensation. The vibration of the wind soothed her. The storm was rising. On its tail would come Nicholas. Her chest pulled at the thought.

Jack pointed at George with a shaking finger. 'This is your fault, interfering, getting in between us like always.'

Pearl covered her ears. Her lips stumbled into song. *And my heart is dead with sorrow for the lad I love the best.* Quiet came into the room.

Jack and George stood over her, their brows furrowed. They almost looked alike. She laughed. George knelt by her. He put his hand on her shoulder and smiled. A smile of bad news. She kissed his cheek.

'You mustn't frown so, Georgie. You've nothing to be sad about.'

'I know, Mother, I know,' he said. 'But you'll come with me, won't you, to see Dr Adamson? He'll sort you out.'

Her chest was hurting. That was why she had to see the doctor. Maybe he would put the cold metal to her ribs and say she had to stay in bed. That wouldn't do. She would have to slip away, out into the street in the dark, where Nicholas would be waiting.

'No, my sweet,' she said. 'I can't, not today. I've too much to do.'

'Well how's about I get him to come here, then? You can get on with... what you need to be doing.'

She gave him her brightest smile and nodded. George sighed and looked relieved. There was such a mess of clothes on the bed. She would have to tidy it away before she left. Wouldn't do for her mother to see this.

The front door slammed shut. Rain beat on the roof. George had been here. That was him going. Pearl's breath was furred and loud. He would do all right without her. He had Elizabeth.

Jack slumped onto the bed, the clothes crumpling beneath him. He covered his face. Pearl went back to the window. She pressed her forehead against the glass. The rain was still streaming down. She could feel the wind less than an inch away.

Jack was speaking but she hardly heard him over the noise of the rain. 'I know that's what you want,' he was saying. 'No one else. Just me and you, Pearl.'

He came and stood by her, put his swollen hand on her

319

shoulder, and pulled her back into him. His jersey smelled of tobacco and earth. It scratched her neck. She screwed her eyes shut. The rain pounded the glass, desperate to let her out and carry her to the sea.

Twenty-Three

She sees so much from up here, her own lookout point; everything, except what she longs for.

The huers have abandoned the hut and returned to their wives for the winter. No one is certain there will be wages for them next year when pilchard season comes again. No one is certain of the fish now.

The hut isn't a comfortable place this time of year. There's no glass in the slit windows. The wind blows in a chill straight off the sea. Two narrow shelves serve as beds and a broken-backed chair clings to a table that has mossy legs. There's a hearth but any fire smokes and the heat soon vanishes.

Each morning, her mother brings her food. At first, she tried to convince Pearl to come home, with kindness, then threats, and finally Pearl's father dragging her down the cliff path. But Pearl returned to the hut the next day, and the day after that when her parents tried to force her home again. If they mention Jack she refuses to speak.

She sits outside the hut long before the sun rises and only retreats beneath the lintel if the rain comes. Some days she doesn't even notice it. She never closes the hut's broad, wreck-timber door. Though she hasn't found Nicholas in the waves yet she sits and stares at them until night falls and they are only noise below the cliff. There has to be an answer in their endless tumble. There has to be something for her.

He wasn't in the village, keeping his head down in a net loft or sheltering in the palace. At Witch Cove the sea mocked her as it raked the empty pebbles. The drying field held only the memory of goodbye. Maybe he had no choice but to board the *Isabella* without her. Sarah said the boat was nearly taken by those waving their fists, shouting their blood-foolishness. He had to save his own skin and then he would come back. He told her to wait.

Her chest troubles her, the hard, new pain lodged there since the day Nicholas left seems embedded. The effort of breathing, of moving around, tires her. She sleeps fitfully, in short bursts, and can't untangle her dreams from the days.

She doesn't know how long she has been sitting here, looking out to sea. She guesses that it has been many weeks, perhaps a month, or even two, because much has happened in the village below.

The bay was empty of boats at first. Word must have spread as no visiting ships came and of course the east coast men were gone. Morlanow's own dwindling fleet kept on shore, as if the men were afraid to re-join the usual pattern of days, as if too much had altered around them. But the draw of the harbour and the train has brought the foreign boats back. The hope of full nets and the cries of hungry children have reawakened the local men. The sea is clustered with craft again. Today two big ships are moored off the harbour wall and familiar boats pepper the waves. Jack's little boat is bobbing its way out. He will be setting his drift nets over the wreck of the *Mary Ann* where the ling gather. He will wait there all night, rocking on the swell.

The east coast boats returned a few days ago. The waters off this coast hold some riches, even if pilchards are scarce. With their bigger boats and their long, scooping nets, they can strip more from the sea. And they do. They work all hours of daylight, all days of the week, dropping and lifting the mesh. But they keep their distance from Morlanow's shore and her boats, staying clear of anger. When their nets are full they don't risk losing their catches. They head for Govenek. Even without a proper harbour or a train to take the fish to London's deeper pockets it gives a good welcome. There is no violence, no Sabbath fury. The east coast men are among friends.

Many nights Pearl has woken, certain Nicholas is with her. Tonight, in the last hour before light, the sea calls to her with every wave. She rises from her curled cramp on one of the beds and stands in the doorway. The sky wears a tender blue, hinting at dawn. Spread before her, the sea is a maze of colour; deeper water snaking navy amongst the shallower greys and greens. The purple line of the horizon is as absolute as ever. There is peace in the space it encloses and she finds herself walking towards the cliff edge, to see it better. She teeters there, her bare feet on the last of the ground.

It would be so easy to give in. In daylight's unforgiving stare she doesn't allow herself to consider the future. He will come back. This is a mistake. He has only gone to escape the trouble of that day and now it's over it's safe for him to return. But at night it's harder to stay so sure.

Autumn has well and truly settled on Morlanow, blessing it with showers and thin sunshine. There is frost some mornings. The waves squabble, foaming over the rock. Pearl huddles against the wall of the huer's hut, wrapping herself in the blanket her mother brought her and for which she is now grateful.

The sickness has stopped. In the last day or so she has felt more able to eat. When it began she blamed the lingering smell of the fish on the beach but the farmers soon took their spoils and the dead shoal has gone. Pearl is ill but not wholly because of her chest, as her mother endlessly suggests. If only that were true. She has been a fool. She sees that, up here with the dark sea spread before her. Not for loving Nicholas but for not waiting. Her trusted means of marking time, her regular clock, has stopped its tick. There is a separate warmth in her, far greater than that provided by the blanket. And it's getting warmer.

Her father's crown appears from the cliff path and he climbs into view. He stands by her though doesn't speak at first. He joins her looking out to sea. Eventually he squats beside her.

'You'll not come home today, Pearl?'

She shakes her head, never lifting her eyes from the sea in case she should miss the flash of a sail on the horizon. Every time he comes to the hut he asks the same question and she gives the same answer, and he accepts it today as he did yesterday and the day before. She knows it's hard for him and her mother, back in the heart of Morlanow. The questions. The sniggering pity for their soft and sinful daughter. Being ignored at chapel. She will end it soon and come down, making it right. But not yet. She has to wait just a while longer. To be certain. She will know when Nicholas's ship crosses the horizon. She will be able to feel him coming home.

Her father reaches inside his jacket and pulls out a crumpled piece of paper. He turns it over and looks at it, then hands it to Pearl.

'Letter came,' he says.

Pearl's heart knocks into a gallop and she fumbles trying to open the single folded page. Nicholas. It's from Nicholas. He has sent for her. But she is reading words that haven't come from his hand. *The Council has voted...*

Her father touches her arm. 'Read it aloud,' he says. 'It came this morning but we'd no one at hand to ask to read it, you being... Please, my sweet. I think it's important.'

She clears her throat and forces herself to concentrate. 'The Council has voted in favour of the construction of a green for the playing of miniature golf, which it is hoped will add to the draw of Morlanow for visitors.'

'I don't understand,' her father says.

Pearl scans the rest of the page. 'It's a game, Father. There's an explanation of it here. Says it's "gentle amusement".'

'What's that to do with us? Visitors get up to their own merriment. Don't usually ask us permission.'

Quickly, she reads the last few lines to herself. 'It's the ground,' she says. 'They want the ground the seine boats rest on during the season.'

He grabs the paper from her and holds it close to his face, as if that will force the strange twisting shapes into something he can read. 'What? That can't be right. We've kept the boats there for years. My grandfather tended a seine boat there.'

'Can they go back to their lofts?' she says.

Her father sighs and leans his head back against the hut. 'Some could, but since the boats came out many places have been rented, fitted with beds and the like. And anyway, where would they go next season, when we're waiting for the fish? We have to be close to the water.'

'It says the Tillotsons want the boats to be destroyed,' she says, watching his mouth open, his eyes widen.

'No, you must be reading it wrong.'

Pearl goes back to looking at the sea, drained of all strength and unable to console him. 'That's what it says,' she tells him. 'They want the ground cleared as soon as possible.'

Her father blows air through his nose and mutters darkly. 'I'm going to see that fool Trevisco right now. What does he think he's playing at?'

'But the boats. Do you really think they'd last another season? With no more money for repairs, and these bad years… there mightn't be many pilchards left.'

He doesn't lose his temper at this suggestion now; his anger has cooled. 'There have always been spells like this,' he says. 'My great uncle William told of a run of eight poor years. Not a pilchard to be seen on this coast, yet further up they were throwing themselves into the nets. They'd all but given up in Morlanow. Many gone hungry, many left, including his three brothers. And then the fish were back and kept coming. They're funny creatures. You should know that.' He playfully nips her cheek and she smiles, unable to remember the last time she did so. 'They never truly go,' he says. 'They're just playing, waiting until we've all but given up. It's a test of faith, of a kind, but don't you tell your mother I said so. Trevisco and the Council have forgotten that, too concerned with what the railway men have to say, and I think me and some others had better remind them.'

'No, Father, please. No more fighting.'

'Don't fret, my sweet. Been enough arguing here. We don't need more amongst ourselves. Govenek men are waiting for us to fall out again.'

'I've seen the east coast boats putting in there.'

Her father grunts and gets to his feet, stretching his tight joints. He looks along the cliff path towards the neighbouring village.

'Govenek's welcome to them, but I'm uneasy all the same.

I heard they're planning to build a new wharf over there, to make a proper harbour.'

'Who'll pay for that?' she says. 'Surely they've seen from Morlanow that the money's running dry.'

'That's the worst of it. The youngest Mr Tillotson was seen there. Got a new agent measuring up, ordering the stone.'

They are both silent then. Gulls swoop over them, hunting their nests on the cliff. Their cries sift down.

'What about us?' she says.

'Tillotsons have had enough, it seems. The Master's been shaken up by the rioting, though he was none too strong before it. And if we won't go out on Sundays, change to taking different fish with these bigger boats like the east coast crews, well – the Tillotsons think there's nothing for them here, don't want to mend their own boats. But the pilchards will come back, and we'll manage on our own somehow.'

'But the letter—'

'Misunderstanding, that's all. I'll get off now, straighten it out.'

The next day she sees the fire. Her father has failed. Men drag the seine boats from their summer home by the rock pools and pile them near the slipway. The letter said the Council wanted the boats removed quickly and with as little fuss as possible. Taking them to Skommow Bay and leaving them to be slowly claimed by the sea would only prolong the grief. It's more fitting that they are burnt.

It's the same when older people die. After their mortal remains are taken to chapel for proper burial and the minister has retired home to an understanding ignorance, friends and relations take the bed of the newly lost, and the sheets and blankets, their clothes, any special trinkets they were known to like, down to the beach. They build a pyre without a body and light it, staying and watching the flames until every last piece has burned away. But there are less who keep the old ways, and with the pilchards staying away many can't stretch to rid a house of its wares. This fire for the boats is the first she has seen in a long while.

The wind blows smoke up to the hut. It mixes with the salt water on Pearl's cheeks, smarting. What would Nicholas think of this, the end of the seine boats? He said change had to come, before it was forced. And he was right. Is anyone on the shore, those watching as the fire devours the boats, thinking the same? Does anyone think of him at all?

She turns so that she can't see the bonfire and instead looks out to sea in the direction of Govenek. It's a calm day, good for making land.

She wakes one morning and Alice is there.

Alice is so still, looking out to sea, that at first Pearl thinks that she's dreamt her. But then Alice turns and something about the look in her eyes tells Pearl that this isn't a dream. The softness that came to Alice when she married Jack's father has gone. She looks like she did when Pearl was a child: thin, worn ragged.

'Where's Samuel?' Pearl asks.

Alice bites her lip, shakes her head. 'He's making us leave,' she says.

'Who is?'

Alice puts her head in her hands. 'He says the house is his and he wants us out.'

Pearl's about to offer comfort, to say no, of course Jack won't. He wouldn't. But then she thinks yes, Jack would. Now his father's dead he can do as he pleases and no one in Morlanow will take Alice's part, not even for Samuel's sake.

'Can you talk to him?' Alice says. 'Ask him if we can stay?'

'Have you anywhere to go?'

'No,' Alice says. 'Only the workhouse. Will you speak to him? Tell him I'll do anything. I have to think of my child.'

'Yes,' Pearl says. 'The child.'

When Alice walks back down the cliff path Pearl looks the other way. Even with her stick Alice stumbles. It will be a hard walk for her and Pearl can't bring herself to watch.

Nicholas comes to her from across the sea but not by ship. He walks on the water, the waves lying down for him. Behind him comes a storm, dark clouds billowing as if they are a cloak. Nicholas smiles at her. She feels that smile when he is still only just visible on the horizon. It wraps her in comfort. She's back on the edge of the cliff, waiting for him, unable to move but not afraid. He comes slowly, achingly slowly, and finally he's in front of her, hovering there. She's unsteady. She will fall but doesn't know how to stop herself. The rocks are coming closer. The ground is rising up to meet her. The air is rushing past her face. She's falling and all the while Nicholas is kissing her.

A stinging pain at the back of her head. And another. Laughter. She opens her eyes and sees two boys, each no more than six years old, standing nearby. She doesn't recognise them. One, a little taller, holds a stone in his hand, weighing it up. His companion stands just behind him, staring shyly at Pearl. They whisper to one another. The taller boy pulls back his arm and flings the stone at Pearl. This one misses and bounces off the hut wall. She tries to stand and the boys turn tail and fly down the cliff path, towards Govenek.

She puts her hand to her head and there's blood. The ground rolls away and the pitching sickness returns. It's early evening, the first star hanging in a wash of orange-pink. Pearl steadies herself against the doorway of the hut. Local boats are coming into shore. Jack's is amongst them.

She doesn't want to leave the hut. At the huer's lookout she is halfway between Govenek and Morlanow and she lays claim to neither. If it weren't for the presence of another that she can no longer ignore she would stay here, living in the hut, walking the cliff path and being mercifully forgotten. But the village wouldn't let her forget. And the child is a gift, in a way. Part of Nicholas is left behind and she must care for it, not condemn it to a life of scandal. She has to do what's right by the child. Her child. Alice has shown her that. At the thought of Alice and Samuel, Pearl is washed with guilt. They lose out if she is to gain. But she stands up, dusts herself down. She knows what must be done. Alice will have to make her own way.

Pearl gathers the few items her mother has brought from home: the blanket, a plate and cup. In the last of the daylight she picks her way down the cliff path, keeping an eye on the progress of one returning boat.

Twenty-Four

Jack turned on the bottom stair. 'No, you've got to stay upstairs, Pearl.'

She clutched the banister. 'Why have I got to? I haven't been bad. Don't make me stay there. I need to go outside.'

'In this weather?'

The rain lashed the house then, to remind her of its presence and what she had to do. Straightening up, her chin out, she marched down the remaining stairs, pushed past Jack's astonished face and went into the kitchen.

He was at her side, trying to steer her back towards the stairs. 'Doctor's coming, remember. And he mustn't see you, Pearl.'

'Why mustn't he? If there's something the matter I should see the doctor, Jack. Is there something the matter with me? Am I ill?' She felt fine. Better than fine.

Jack put his hands to his head and stared at her. 'You've not been listening at all, have you?' He raised his voice, shouting each word slowly. 'He wants to take you away from me and I won't let him. You belong here.'

There was the truth of it. She hadn't been on her guard, had let her thoughts slip. With his sneaking and tricksy ways Jack knew that Nicholas was coming. Pearl found herself against the wall. He got his arms round her and began hauling her back towards the stairs.

She cried out. 'No, please. Let me go. Let me go to him.'

He held on tighter. He was going to keep her in the house and the packet would go without her. 'You don't know what you're saying, Pearl. This isn't what you want.'

They struggled together, Pearl squeezing Jack's swollen, hot hands, knowing that was where he felt the greatest pain. He sucked his breath over his teeth, baring them like a fox, but still he held on.

There was a sharp tap on the front door. When the second knock wasn't answered, a voice called through the rain.

'Mr Tremain? It's Dr Adamson. Your son asked me to call by.'

Pearl felt a tremble go through Jack's arm and slipped sideways out of his grip. She backed into the kitchen.

Jack pointed at her. 'Stay in there. Don't come out until I tell you.' He began to close the door.

'Is it hide and seek, Jack? Are we playing now?'

With only an inch of open doorway between them, he paused. 'Yes. That's it. You've got to hide in here. Stay very quiet.'

She didn't know why Jack sounded so sad; this was his favourite game. The door closed. In the corner of the room there was a heap of stones, some of which were scattered across the floor. She crouched and began stacking the stones in front of her. Jack was best at hiding and was never keen on doing the seeking but this time she was going to win.

She could hear Jack on the other side of the door. He was talking to someone, a voice she didn't recognise. They were getting closer. They would find her. She needed a better hiding place, further away. There was another door, by the window. She opened it and remembered.

Standing in the puddle that had collected on the doorstep, Pearl held out her arms to the water pouring from the sky. It was sweet on her lips. Her hair was a tangle of damp within seconds, her clothes heavy.

The sea was calling. She looked down and saw its efforts to reach her. The waves were high, higher than she could ever remember. And the noise – a thousand doors banging shut, a life's worth of thunderclaps beating the cliff. How the sea had hidden from her, pretending peace when this storm had been in the water all the time, waiting to bring Nicholas back.

The waves stretched up to the new house, heads of smashed china, backs black with rage. Yet within the darkness there was another colour. It was still a way off, where the seabed dropped into deeper water at the edge of the bay. Pearl stepped from the shelter of the house and the wind whipped her long, knotted hair, playing it across her face. The colour in the sea danced in and out of her vision, a spread of red and purple, moving closer to shore.

Pearl laughed and clapped her hands. Rain drops spun off her, shook from her hair. She hurried to the cliff path.

'Pearl?'

A sound picked up and thrown by the wind. Just audible, she heard her name again and turned round. Mrs Tiddy was huddled in her own doorway, her skirt blown by the wind, revealing her shift and thick brown stockings. She came towards Pearl.

'What in Heaven's name are you doing out here?' Mrs Tiddy's words were all but lost in the wind and she blinked hard against the rain. 'You'll be pulled off the cliff by this gale!'

'He's come back. I have to go.'

'Let's get inside, out of this rain. I'll fetch Jack. These clothes you've got on.'

'No! Nicholas is waiting.' Pearl pulled away and fell. The ground was more water than earth and she sank into mud.

Mrs Tiddy bent over Pearl. Her mouth hung in a circle of disbelief. The rain trickled down her cheeks.

'What did you say?' Mrs Tiddy shouted.

'Nicholas is here.'

Mrs Tiddy shook her head. 'Come on, up you get.'

Pearl scrabbled from her on hands and knees. Her chest was heaving, pushing her lungs as high as the strange waves, but the feeling was good and raw. The pressure was coming to her temples again. She couldn't keep her thoughts fixed when her body pulled towards the sea. Her head was hot with the effort of trying to stay here, in this moment. She closed her eyes against it.

When she opened them an old woman stood before her, shivering and clutching at her soaked clothes. Pearl wasn't sure who she was. She looked familiar but there wasn't time to talk now.

The woman looked as if she was going to speak. Something in her expression, her eyes drooping with pity, made Pearl remember: it was her fault that Nicholas had gone. This woman had said the words, had made it real.

'You should have stopped him,' Pearl screamed over the wind.

The woman swallowed and reached to grasp Pearl's hands. 'Come inside.'

The sky split and shot thunderclaps. Waves smashed against the cliff, spray filling Pearl's lungs with salt. They stood together. Pearl knew this memory and yet it was shifting as she tried to follow its course. She was on the cliff top in the rain but at the same time she was on the seafront, surrounded by broken wood. She was full of ache and cold, sinking into mud, but she was high above it all as well, watching two women holding hands. She was with a stranger and yet Sarah was going to tell her that Nicholas had gone. She braced herself for the pain she knew must come but Sarah was saying the wrong words. She was forgetting her part.

'I wasn't there when he left, Pearl. I didn't see Nicholas go. Jack told me.'

Pearl was running, running from the lies and the cough that couldn't be left behind. It gnashed her throat, drawing blood and chasing away air. There was a terrible booming and the ground swayed beneath her feet. The huer's hut clung to the cliff edge as the wind shrieked through its open windows. Below her, the sea boiled fury. The waves were racing into land, giants of dark, fierce water. She had never seen waves like them. This tide was too high, too strong. It would wash Morlanow away.

She stared out into the bay, searching for the packet ship, and there was the cloud of purple beneath the water. Even though the rain pelted her and the wind raked her eyes, she could see pinprick flashes of silver amongst the foam. The shoal woman had swum back. But there were no seine boats and no great nets to shoot, no maids to tend the fish and no palace to keep them safe and salted. There was nothing but forgetfulness in Morlanow.

As the shoal woman danced her way into shore, whirled along by this strange high tide, Pearl danced down the cliff path, slithering on the wet soil, ensnared by the prickle arms of gorse. The rain made everything turn back to front. The cliff fell away on her right and as she tumbled on a jutting ledge of rock the angle flipped, making the sea the sky. A gull whisked past, close to her face; the wind tossed its body as if it was no more than a scrap of paper. Down and down Pearl went, sometimes on her feet and often on her hip, her backside.

The sea had claimed the front. Waves reached over the road, breaking against the buildings lining it. Murky water, curdled grey and blue, flowed into town, still surging.

Rubbish floated past: newspapers, an umbrella twisted beyond use, a child's boot. Leaves were plastered to everything. Scum lay on the surface of the water where it slowed and she wrinkled her nose at a ripe smell.

There was no one else to be seen. The wind drove the rain into the mouths of the streets and each drop struck Pearl's skin with the sharpness of flint. Her breath came in shorter and shorter rasps. She had to be quick – if Nicholas couldn't find her, he might go without her. He had told her to wait at the drying field. She must go back there. Why had she left it? Snatches of thoughts wheeled and dropped away – whistles, a dark-haired woman telling lies – but she couldn't shape them into sense, into a reason for not being with Nicholas. That was all there was.

The bright light was in her eyes again, inside her head. She couldn't see. She was falling from the cliff. Pearl put out her hands to save herself and caught wood. The darkness eased to broken masts and hulls, rotten fingers reaching to catch her on their nails. Skommow Bay had lured her again. She tried to remember the steps that had brought her there but could only think of water. The sea had reached inside her thoughts and flooded them.

She was lying on the ledge of rock and could hear loud banging. She forced herself to sit up and a cry loosened from her lips. A ghost fleet sailed before her. The high tide had lifted the broken remains and set them on its back, floating pieces of shattered spars and planks. They knocked into one another, crowded into the new, narrow bay. Wood scraped against metal. Wrecks were wrecked again. Splintered timber covered the water.

The sea grabbed at her ankles. She went slowly so as not to slip. Every inch of her wanted to run across the ledge, to get to the field and to Nicholas. The broken boats loomed close as the waves battered them up and down. Once she had to crouch and nearly fell into the seething foam as a prow lurched towards her.

The grass appeared on her right, slick with rain. Nearly there. Only a few feet more to the foot of the hill. Just ahead was the upturned deck of a large wooden boat. It was so big and had been driven so hard onto the rocks that the sea hadn't yet managed to re-float it. The boat was half-raised, sucking water. In the swirling dirt around the wood there was movement.

The handkerchief sail that closed up like a jellyfish after Jack threw a stone. There it was, bobbing out from under the wreck, but it was so much bigger than she remembered. The rain forced her to keep shutting her eyes. As she blinked through the streaming, shifting curtain, the sail grew, climbing from the water. The handkerchief stretched to a shirt. A shirt domed with air, or something firmer. She was sure it was pulled over angles, some kind of frame. Her hair slipped across her face and all was broken again.

The cloth drifted closer.

It was a shirt. It was torn and yellowed, needing a good scrub. Washday tomorrow. She would take hold of its sandy seams, its salt-stiff sleeves, and rub it clean of its hidden years. And the chest beneath it would need care too. She would soap his collarbone, clear the mud from his ribs. She would make him better, hold a compress to his forehead, wipe away the blood.

He had been waiting for her and she had kept away. She had been too afraid to see what Skommow Bay was keeping safe. But it didn't matter anymore because at last she had found him.

Fins of bubbles crossed one another as currents fought for control. Nicholas rolled his shoulders and the shirt pulled in the water. He was waking up, ready to leave.

A wave crashed over her and she let it take her. Her vision dipped in and out. Each time she looked for Nicholas he seemed further away. But not gone.

She was in water up to her neck. She pushed out and kicked, needing to swim. Her breath was still short but she felt so well. Each muscle softened as she flexed her toes, curled her fingers in the water. Her feet couldn't find the ground.

The pain in her chest became warm and not unpleasant. She knew Nicholas was smiling at her from beneath the surface. His back rippled a laugh and she laughed too. Salt water slopped into her mouth and she swallowed its goodness, feeling it wash away her aches.

The stuck boat began to lift; there was groaning as it wrenched clear of the ground. Nicholas broke from its grip and skewed away, towards the open sea. Pearl held out her arms to catch him. The water pulled her back against the rocks, pinning her there as Nicholas disappeared from view.

Twenty-Five

A bird was trilling in her ear, pecking at her. It wouldn't leave her alone. All she wanted was to sleep. She tried to bat the bird away but it caught her hand.

'Thank the Lord!' the bird said.

Pearl opened her eyes. Jack was kneeling by her. She eased herself into a sitting position, her hands knocking over a little tower of stones. This memorial was in the right place.

Jack was speaking. She watched his lips move but heard nothing. He seemed to be waiting for an answer.

'What?' she said.

'Are you hurt?'

A wan light gleamed between the scraps of cloud left in the sky. The wind had dropped but Pearl shivered as it stirred her sodden clothes. She glanced over her shoulder; the tide had retreated, putting the broken boats back on the ground.

'Pearl?' Jack's face was blotched and ashen all at once. He tried to hold her hand and she pulled it away, letting it rest on one of the stones near her. She watched his features darken, the care drawn back inside him.

Pearl rolled the stone from palm to palm; the weight of a bag of sugar. She kept her voice flat. 'I was in the water. It nearly had me. The boats were floating, bits sailing round. You should have seen it.'

He was going to speak but hesitated. The wind lifted his thinning white hair. Gulls looped above. They were the only two people in the world, together on this ledge, the air between them thick with static.

She inclined her head to the muddy sand below, where the broken boats lay back at rest, and Jack's restraint broke. He grabbed her elbow and hauled her to her feet. 'Come on,' he said. 'We're going home.'

She wrenched herself free in one swift jerk. 'No more hiding, Jack. I've found you. You've got to come out now.'

His shoulders sagged. Pearl braced herself for anger, ready to hold off his rage, but the man who faced her was just the motherless boy who had sat in her yard, tearing at his hair.

'I can't reason with you, but we can't carry on like this,' he said. 'If you've got to go and stay somewhere to be looked after, then so be it.'

'Where can I go? The packet didn't come.' She pressed her hand across her mouth to keep the cry inside but sobs escaped and she was coughing. The stone banged against her thigh with the drum of a pulse.

'Shh now,' Jack said gently. 'Stop this. You'll make yourself ill.'

'What did you do to him?'

'Please, Pearl. I only want to help you. Stop.' He tried to catch her arms and hold her still but she stepped back, onto the edge of the rock. He raised a rigid hand. She closed her eyes but he merely brushed the hair from her face.

'Nicholas wouldn't have looked after you,' Jack said.

She shook her head and the sky jumped up and down and

wouldn't stop jumping. The stone in her hand felt bigger, or was her hand shrinking? There was a ringing sound and it was getting louder. She had to shout over it.

'You're a liar!'

'He left, Pearl. I thought if we married you'd forget him but he's always been here, hasn't he?'

'He loved me. And I loved him.'

The stone fell to the ground with a crack. Jack staggered then slowly dropped to his knees. He let go of her hand. She waited but he didn't move again.

What was this mess all up her sleeves, on her hands? It was everywhere, sticky and warm. She wanted to wash it off, wash her whole body clean. Swimming was the best bath in Morlanow. No need to lug pails of water from the pump.

The sea had been careful where it set down the scrapped boats, leaving Pearl a safe path between them to reach the water's edge. She took off her boots and hitched up her skirt as if she was working in the palace. She walked towards the sea but there was no sound other than the waves and the seagulls. There was no keygrim whispering her name.

Her chest was tight and everything was growing lighter. The sea had the polished sheen of the Tregurtha Hotel's best tea trays. A gleaming mist spread between the clouds, filling the sky a good, clean white. Even her skin was brightening as she looked at her hands. Soon she would be as pale and smooth as bone.

She was at the water's edge. A little way out she could see a foaming purple patch. She peeled off her clothes and stood before the sea. An offering. A request. The wind ran its fingers across her.

She waded in and the currents parted, admitting her. When the water passed her knees, Pearl pushed off. The shoal woman was waiting, buoying up a precious cargo; a white shape bobbed in her cloud. She beckoned with her many tails then disappeared as a wave covered Pearl. The currents took Pearl then, lines of cooler water hooking her knees so that she was pulled, legs-first, past the point where the ground disappeared. Her chest contracted and she could breathe underwater. She didn't need air any more. The sea was filling her body, thinning her blood with salt.

She surfaced. The purple cloud was glittering, flickering light. There were no keygrims here, she realised. There was only fear. Fear of drowning, of being washed up, far from home, swollen with seawater and carved bloody by the rocks. That fear had twisted into figures of shell and rank seaweed, made a hand reach out in darkness, made a dead voice call a name. Because worst of all was the fear of not being found, of having a cairn not a headstone. Of a lifetime of loneliness. She had been alone since the riot. Even George hadn't been enough. But she wouldn't be alone anymore, and there would be no more keygrims.

The shoal woman had slipped further away to where the seabed dropped into deeper water. The whiteness was everywhere. Pearl's eyes were full of the white sail, his shirt, the white of the waves breaking. She would stay in the white light now, in the hot pain that was spreading from her temples down her cheeks, across her mouth, making her stiff as a salted fish. He was here in the white, asking her to come with him. He was leaving but she was here. Pearl had found him. They would go together.

She was too far from the shore. She couldn't go back. There was nothing left on land. She closed her eyes and felt a hand take hers; a hand of water, not shell. His hand, the sea in his hand. He wrapped his cold arms round her, holding her close. He showed her how to sink, how to give in, finally. He kissed her and the white light turned to pressing darkness, pulling her down and down. He was the sea and he was the darkness and he was filling her veins. He was with her and she knew then that it was this she had been waiting for.

Acknowledgements

The Visitor was written as part of my PhD in Creative Writing at Aberystwyth University. Thanks are due to my supervisor and friend Jem Poster, and staff in the Department of English and Creative Writing. I am very grateful to the Arts and Humanities Research Council for a Doctoral Award which supported my PhD.

Thanks to my editors – Kathryn Gray who saw something in the novel in the first place and who helped shape it with a wise touch, and Caroline Oakley who was meticulous and sensitive. Thank you to everyone at Parthian.

Thanks to Luigi Bonomi for some early enthusiasm and ideas, and to all who have read the novel and been kind enough to give me their thoughts: Katy Birch, Kate Wright, Kendall Klym and Julia Roberts. Thanks, too, to Charlotte Goatman, who brilliantly organised and managed the research trip to St Ives and Falmouth which kick-started this project, and my sister, Liz Stansfield, who came too and was a fine research assistant and ice cream eater.

Special thanks to Dave, for more than I can ever say.

I am indebted to the work of Cyril Noall, in particular his definitive *Cornish Seines and Seiners: A History of the Pilchard Fishing Industry* (Truro: Bradford Barton, 1972), as well as John Corin's *Fishermen's Conflict: The Story of Newlyn* (Newton Abbot: Tops'l Books, 1988). In addition, the articles in *Cornish Studies*, published by the Institute of Cornish Studies at the University of Exeter, have been invaluable in my research, especially the work of Sharron P. Schwartz: 'In Defence of Customary Rights: Labouring Women's Experience of Industrialization in Cornwall c1750-1870', *Cornish Studies, Second Series, Volume Seven* (ed.) Philip Payton (Institute of Cornish Studies, University of Exeter Press, Exeter: 1999), pp.8-31. Wilkie Collins' wonderful *Rambles Beyond Railways: or, Notes in Cornwall Taken A-Foot* (London: Richard Bentley, 1861) was also very helpful in taking me inside the pilchard palaces.

Pearl's song is Katharine Lee Jenner's poem 'The Boats of Sennen (Cornish Fisher-Girl's Song)', first published in *Songs of the Stars and the Sea* (1926), and reprinted in *Voices from West Barbary: An Anthology of Anglo-Cornish Poetry 1549-1928*, (ed.) Alan M Kent (London: Francis Boutle, 2000).

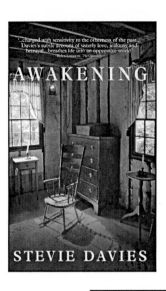

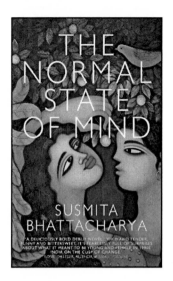

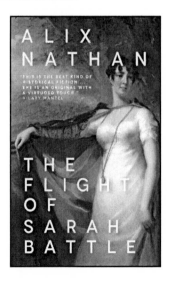

PARTHIAN

www.parthianbooks.com

Lightning Source UK Ltd.
Milton Keynes UK
UKOW04f0224250615

254096UK00002B/27/P